The Fo

MW01140388

By David Forsmark with Timothy Imholt

"*The Forest of Assassins* is a unique combination of startling fact and gripping fiction—which gives readers a new understanding of the war in Vietnam. It is must-read on every page."

-THOMAS FLEMING: Author of *A Disease in the Public Mind: A New Understanding of the Civil War*

"*The Forest of Assassins* is a great read, a novel as good as the best journalism, with vivid and accurate details driving a tale of danger and deception and betrayal during the Vietnam War. This book doesn't just feel researched, it feels *lived.*

Whether tightening the suspense – our protagonist, Navy Lieutenant Hank Dillon eyeball to eyeball with a VC soldier and watching for the skin to whiten on the man's finger curled around the trigger of his AK-47 – or describing the oppressive heat of an innocent afternoon on the Mekong Delta, David Forsmark and Timothy Imholt make you believe every word of it. I couldn't recommend it more highly."

-ROBERT FERRIGNO, NY Times best-selling novelist, *Prayers for the Assassin*

"As real as fiction gets. A non-stop ride into combat told with perfection."

- BOB HAMER, veteran FBI undercover agent and the author of *The Last Undercover*

This book is dedicated to Harry, who braved Charlie's night and lived to not tell about it

Chapter One

07:00 April 20, 1964
Republic of South Vietnam
Rung Sat Special Zone
"The Forest of Assassins"

Navy SEAL Lieutenant Hank Dillon was so tired he was having trouble seeing. Which was not a good thing considering his predicament. He was proud of himself for having found a spot with a tangle of underbrush and nipa palm fronds making him invisible to almost anyone, even if they were looking right at him.

That didn't stop him from having clear view of the Viet Cong motor sampan making its way across the muddy water coming directly toward his camouflaged position.

He instinctively knew the sound of the motor that woke him was not the deep growl of the American River Patrol Craft he was waiting for. Moments later, the VC sampan emerged from one of the streams that emptied into the Vam Co Dong River a mere hundred meters from his position. The loaded sampan was so heavy in the water that the guns sticking out the sides were sitting just above the river's surface.

As it passed in front of him, Hank read the words on the boxes stacked in the boat. It was a shipment of U.S. carbines and crate after crate of ammunition. He knew a boat so full of materiel had to be part of Hoa's operation.

Until the day before, his team had been hunting for the stolen American weapons and Hoa, the thieves' leader. But now, after running from the VC for the past twenty-seven hours, the hunter had become the hunted, and he was in real trouble.

Despite the sodden heat and buzzing insects, Dillon had nearly dozed off in the peaceful stillness of the jungle before the boat's sputtering engine caught his ear. He slowly pivoted his head, listening carefully for any signs of his pursuers. He was on the verge of being so exhausted he would no longer feel fear. Watching the AK47-wielding VC on the sampan scanning the shoreline for signs of an ambush brought a chill that let him know he was not yet at that point.

He froze in place, knowing he was invisible as long as he remained still. His instincts screamed at him to creep further from the water's edge, but his brain told him even the smallest move could spark a volley of automatic weapons fire that would cut him to pieces.

A mosquito landed on his face, followed by another on his neck. The damn bugs were everywhere in this country, and they had found him particularly delicious ever since he landed here from stateside. It took all of his willpower to let them drink their fill without so much as a twitch.

Something bigger than a skeeter buzzed around his head before alighting on his ear, and without provocation, it delivered an electric sting. The searing pain made his eyes tear up. He blinked fast and hard to clear his vision.

The bug bites he could deal with later; the bullets he needed to avoid now.

He prayed the boat would continue on its way. If he were forced to sit this still for too long, he knew he would be covered by hordes of crawling, flying, biting and stinging jungle pests. He didn't want to think about it.

If the VC found him, he knew the Department of Defense's official notification of his fate would not give his wife any information about his mission, let alone details of the nuisances he'd endured. His secrets would die with him. There was no chance they'd admit her husband had been killed deep in a miserable Commie-controlled jungle. No, whoever delivered the news would be like Farmer Alfalfa. They'd bury her in bullshit.

"Sorry, ma'am," they'd say, "the lieutenant was lost at sea." She'd be fed any tale but the truth; he had been killed in the Rung Sat Special Zone. In English, *Rung Sat* means "Forest of Assassins," a name it had earned decades ago when it served as a hiding place for pirates and outlaws. Criminals loved the place because it was so easy to disappear into the many streams and rivers twisting through the thick mangrove forest.

Dillon tried to think of ways to make himself appear smaller, but no amount of concentration could reduce his six-foot-tall, 180-pound bulk. His size had helped the commander of his SEAL team platoon in some hand-to-hand confrontations, but now it was a liability.

The sampan leisurely chugged along the narrow river, coming within ten meters of his position. Dillon even partially closed his eyes in hopes the enemy would not spot their whites, trusting that his brown eyes and black bandanna would become part of his camouflage.

As the men in the boat were scouring the riverbanks for their enemies, Hank's rifle was tracking them-- but he knew any exchange of gunfire would make his escape impossible. Other VC already were on his tail, so he would become the center of a 7.62mm round sandwich if the men in the boat spotted him. Even if he managed to kill everyone in the sampan, he would give away his position to those on his trail.

Adding to his worries, he had taken a bullet in his left forearm the previous night in a firefight with the VC. Now it was numb and useless. That would be yet another disadvantage in a firefight where he already was out-manned and out-gunned.

A scrawny little man in black pajamas crouched at the back of the boat, slowly swinging his AK-47 back and forth as his eyes tried to pierce the walls of jungle growth lining the river. He suddenly snapped his head up and stared right into Dillon's eyes. Almost hesitantly, he lifted the muzzle of his assault rifle until it was pointed directly at him.

Time stood still as Dillon studied the man's bony frame and picked the location he would put his shot. He tensed his body to roll away to avoid the return fire that was sure to come from the others on the boat the instant he pulled the trigger. He wondered just how many VC he could kill before the return fire became organized.

They were close enough that he could see the Viet Cong's trigger finger. He watched for it to whiten as the man applied pressure on the trigger. Once that happened, 10 rounds per second would pierce his body.

For the hundredth time, images of the previous 24 hours flooded back into his brain. As they mocked him, Dillon cursed in silence.

***

"We are very close, Lieutenant," Nguyen, a Vietnamese

Marine, whispered.

"How close is very?" Hank asked.

"One, two hundred meters at most," came the soft reply.

Hank peered into the black jungle night and could see nothing. The only clue to human habitation was the smell of cooking fires permeating the thick, humid air. The village was where the *hoi chanh*, the Viet Cong defector, had said Hoa was hiding out. No part of this operation was simple.

Hoa, a Vietnamese citizen suspected of dealing arms and other contraband to the Communist guerrillas, had a well-organized operation. Hank's mission was to put him out of business. Those up the chain of command wanted him to take Hoa alive so they could interrogate him and determine how he got the weapons and ammo he sold.

At his pre-mission briefing, however, Hank was told the commanders would settle for putting the man out of business forever if capture was not possible. His written orders had used the phrase "neutralize the target."

Hank had no idea how to spirit the man alive to an American base without the mission turning into a combat zone with him vastly outnumbered. But it was his job to try.

Hank checked his watch and saw it was 4:05. They were right on schedule. So far, things had gone as well as could be expected on a mission with this many possibilities for fucking up.

He signaled Gunner's Mate Brian Ayotte, who was on point, to move out with all possible caution. No words passed between the SEALs. The men in Hank's platoon had been together since their SEAL training and had an elaborate system of hand signals that were all their own. It was a lot safer than speaking this deep in enemy territory.

The normally cheery Ayotte, who had such keen eyes the men swore he could see in the dark, moved out quietly. He was a full head taller than Radioman 2nd Class Russ Bush, the man who followed him and Ayotte's swim partner. Hank had selected Bush, who had just barely passed the Navy's height requirement for a SEAL, for his team because he had acquired first-hand knowledge of the area from an earlier firefight. Bush needed to be near Hank and the point man to give directional guidance whenever possible.

Hank also wanted to be close to the Vietnamese Marine they

had brought in to assist them. He didn't fully trust Nguyen, but he knew he might need his language skills in a tight spot.

Following Hank were Chester Hack lugging the heavier M-60 machine gun, and his swim partner, Gunner's Mate 2nd Class Lanny Vispo, who was on rear guard. The lanky Vispo was a joker who kept his comrades loose and amused at the base, but he was all business in the field. He was the only man Hank could dream of protecting their backs.

The *hoi chanh* had said Hoa was easily recognizable because he always wore a safari jacket and hat and kept a pearl-handled Colt .45 strapped to his hip. Hoa had bragged the pistol had come off the body of a dead Green Beret. Hank, however, doubted that his quarry wore the jacket, hat and pistol in bed, which is where the platoon planned to nab him. He silently hoped the intelligence they had about Hoa's sleeping quarters was accurate. Intelligence in the past did not always live up to its name.

The silence of jungle was absolute, raising Hank's suspicions. Had something interrupted the calls of the night birds and driven off the insects? A chill went up Hank's spine, and he lifted his hand to signal a halt.

An explosion shattered the darkness and the quiet. Ngyen was flung screaming into the air as he tripped a land mine. His puny frame was silhouetted by the multicolored flash of high explosives.

The SEALs dove for cover a moment too late as flares lit the skies above them. Bush and Ayotte were riddled with bullets before they hit the ground, their bodies jerking in the macabre dance all SEALs feared. The chatter of AK-47s filled the night air as dozens of muzzle flashes erupted from the surrounding jungle.

Hank quickly crawled to where Vispo and Hack were scrambling for cover.

"It's a fucking trap! The bastards knew we were coming. Head for the primary extraction point — I'll cover you," he shouted over the noise.

"What about Ayotte and Bush?" Hack protested. "We can't leave them behind."

Hank shouted back, "Take off, God damn it. That's an order!"

The two men melted into the jungle as Hank returned fire.

He rolled to his left, firing a burst in the direction of a cluster of muzzle flashes, and worked his way over the downed SEALs. Even if they were still alive, he didn't know what he could do for them. He had to get to them; they were his men, his brothers. He would not just leave them without knowing for sure.

As he rolled again, his left arm was knocked out from under him. He fell on his face as more rounds streaked just over his head.

With adrenaline coursing through his veins, Hank was blissfully unaware he had been hit in the forearm until he saw it. He flexed his fist to see if the hand still worked. Luckily, his fingers still worked. The bone wasn't broken, and the bullet had passed through. His arm felt as if it were pierced by a hot poker, but he could function. Mostly.

The flares started to burn low, and he pushed his back against a large tree. He readied his M-16 and waited for the VC to charge.

There was no charge. The jungle again was quiet.

As he listened more closely, Hank realized it wasn't completely silent. He could hear the VC changing position in the dark, making their way between him and the direction his evacuating teammates had gone. "Fuck!" he screamed inside his skull. He should have gone with them. He'd known damn well from the way Ayotte and Bush had been torn apart by slugs that they were dead. That many hits would kill anyone.

Besides, with his wound, he was in no condition to help anyone.

The VC were making enough noise to cover his retreat, so Hank took advantage and headed in the opposite direction. He would make his way out by a different route.

***

As dusk fell, he checked for VC on his trail with as much focus as his exhausted brain could muster. He was drained after a full day on the run, but he still had a long way to go. At least now he was headed in the right direction. He hoped he at least had drawn the VC away from Vispo and Hack.

He was following the standard procedure that was ingrained in him during training at the Escape and Evasion School.

Everything he learned in that school was coming into play and serving him well. His biggest problem was there were just so damn many of the bastards on his trail. They were everywhere.

Every time he heard Charlie in pursuit, Hank headed the other way at top speed. He was sure he could outdistance anyone on his trail—he was in peak shape, better conditioned than most professional athletes. His months upon months of SEAL training had made sure of it.

During his training, he had seen young men who seemed to be in great condition—including a former linebacker for the Midshipmen—sink to the ground, unable to go on. Some just sat and sobbed because their bodies would no longer do what they were telling it to.

If he could outlast those men during training, he could certainly open up a lead between himself and some malnourished guerrillas. In their own propaganda, the VC claimed they subsisted on a handful of rice per day. All of this worked to his advantage.

To his disadvantage, though, was his left arm, which was seeping blood and throbbing with pain.

He stopped and listened for three or four minutes, waiting for normal jungle noises to return. For the first moment, there was dead silence before the chattering of a bird broke the quiet. It was quickly followed by the screeching of another bird and the wailing of some other animal. Yes, he had outdistanced the VC. None of the animals in the area were spooked by other humans. Eighteen months of living in the jungle had honed in him a sense of what a normal jungle sounded like. Gradually the forest returned to the buzzing, squawking commotion that was normal when no humans were around.

He knew it was a sure sign of pursuit if the jungle had stayed silent nearby. If the natural order was disturbed, his training and common sense told him to speed in the opposite direction. His only alternative if anyone was too close was to take cover and prepare to fire from an ambush point. As long as there was no evidence of pursuit, he would continue toward the secondary extraction point. For now, his main concern was putting distance between him and the VC. Getting his ass out of the jungle altogether was a close second.

With the beast and the bugs of the jungle acting normally, he decided to take the five-minute break he had been yearning for. The persistence of his pursuers was really starting to wear him out.

The VC were out in large numbers, probably thinking he was just part of a larger force. While hiding in the underbrush, a few guerrillas had come so close he could overhear them. His Vietnamese was less than shaky, but he understood enough to know they wanted him bad. But they also seemed to think more SEALs were on their way, which finally stoked a flicker of hope in his heart. Given they knew that much, hell, they might even know who he was.

In a raid on a VC-infested village not that long ago, his men came across wanted posters bearing their names, and he found himself staring at his own face in a photo among papers strewn upon a peasant's table. A SEAL officer would be the biggest prize the VC had bagged in a long time.

In an instant, the jungle fell silent, and four small pajama-clad guerrillas appeared a half-dozen feet from where he was crouching.

Either his fatigue had dulled his senses to a dangerous level, or these four were very good. Or both. He was good enough at his job that no one should have been able to surprise him like that.

Hank turned his flesh into stone, silent, still and solid. He wasn't sure if they had seen him or just suspected he was in the area. His grip on his M-16 tightened into a death hold as sweat made his palms slippery. He knew which guerrilla he had to take out first and who had to be next.

Adrenalin coursed through his veins, and his ragged breathing seemed unbelievingly loud. He was sure the VC could hear it. His jaw ached, his mouth was dry. Bad situation all around. He told himself not to blow his cool, then almost smiled at the irony... as if there were anything cool in this damned hellhole of a jungle.

He prayed his M-16 wouldn't jam if he had to use it. The damn rifles were notorious for jamming at the wrong time. Any bit of foreign matter screwed them up. Hank had come across the fallen bodies of Green Berets who had died trying to clear a weapon jam. After his overnight escapades in the jungle, his rifle wasn't exactly spotless.

All of his instincts screamed at Hank to kill them, but he

held his fire. Above all, he had no idea how many more guerrillas were around. The first burst of gunfire would bring every guerrilla within a mile down on him. Killing VC was a big part of his job description, and he was eager to avenge his friends' deaths. But in the bigger scheme, his duty was to evade the enemy and return to base.

Even so, as the tension continued to ratchet up, he envisioned the little men toppling one after the other as he raked them with a burst of slugs on full auto. Inside his body of stone, his blood lust was boiling over. The primitive part of his brain, the home of all rash emotions, looked forward to a fight. He could taste sweet vengeance in his mouth as he prepared to prove he was a better warrior than these men and their allies. He just had to pick the time to make his move.

As suddenly as they had popped up, the four VC vanished into the Forest of Assassins. It was as if they had never been there. A second later, after determining he again was alone, his body turned back into flesh, and he, too, disappeared into that jungle.

***

Hank's arm stopped bleeding, but it was swollen to twice its normal size. The numbness had been replaced by throbbing pain that nearly made him gasp with every heartbeat. Pushing through the vegetation was white-hot agony, but he had no choice. He was a SEAL who had to press on. Better to live with pain than not live.

The rest of the night passed without incident, and Hank was confident he had lost his pursuers. He was pleased with his escape and the possibility that a rescue could be on the way. Still, he fought off his fatigue and pain to stay alert. A moment of sloppiness could cancel out everything he'd achieved.

When he could go on no longer, he found a hiding spot a dozen meters off the trail. As he hunkered down, his thoughts drifted from his miseries to another world, a place as distant as the end of the universe. Home. He couldn't help but think this was a fucked-up job for a man with a red-hot wife and adoring three-year-old daughter who depended on him.

The real irony, he thought, was he had seen joining the SEALs as a shortcut to winning a sea command. Hah! He was in the

Navy, true, but he'd almost become a landlubber since coming to Nam. Join the Navy and see the jungle — great recruiting slogan! His career move had caused much more trouble than he had imagined. It could turn out to be more trouble than he could handle.

It was so different in the beginning. As a signalman first class, he had spent far too much time at sea, aching for his far-off young family. He didn't even know the term SEAL stood for SEa Air Land commandoes until after he was into UDT frogman training. Then, he thought becoming a SEAL meant shore duty in San Diego and more time at home.

Yeah, sure, that worked well, he thought, as he flicked a spider that had dropped down off his left shoulder.

Another perk was decent pay. Not only did a SEAL draw a bigger monthly check, but he also got diving duty pay. With a new baby in the picture, that mattered a lot. Besides, it was a chance to do something new and exciting, which always was a plus in the military. A true warrior always wanted to be somewhere else, doing something better, something ... else.

You bust your ass for the chance to be on a destroyer. Soon you notice, hey wait a minute, those guys on that cruiser are riding smoother than I am in this godforsaken little tub. Once you get on the cruiser, you see a carrier up close. It never ended. Whatever was new seemed so much better than the old. Right now, though, being somewhere else and doing almost anything else sounded fantastic.

But the SEALs posed an even bigger lure; scuttlebutt said they were the up-and-coming thing that offered fresh opportunities-- especially to a man who had worked his way up from the enlisted ranks. Competing against all of those guys with academy rings was hard. Far more men were angling for a sea command than there were ships in the fleet. If he managed to live up to his ambition — and not die — it would mean sea duty again. Sure, there'd be less time at home, but that was a sacrifice any real sailor would make if it meant a sea command.

He had been closed-mouthed about his ultimate goal, but his superiors had figured him out and dangled his ambitions in his face like some damn carrot. One tour of duty in country had been enough for him, but the brass had played him like a tin whistle.

Appealing to his pride, they used his ambition to destroy his resistance and come back to the jungles for an encore. He sighed, realizing that was true but not the full truth. A part of his core was drawn to the men he had trained with, and the notion he was part of the world's most elite fighting force was part of his DNA now. It was an identity he was not yet willing to walk away from, no matter what it was doing to his body.

His thoughts turned to Ayotte and Bush, with whom he'd shared a bottle of cheap Scotch just two days ago as they argued whether the Yankees were good enough to win a fifth straight pennant. Bush, who believed his Westchester County upbringing practically made him a native New Yorker, said even Yogi Berra could manage a winner if Mantle and Maris were healthy again; while Ayotte claimed the Bombers proved their day was over by flopping against the Dodgers in the World Series. Hank managed a smile as he remembered barely keeping the guys from coming to blows.

If he got out of this mess, Hank would have to write letters to their families, who would be devastated by the news. He dreaded having to write his first letters of condolence. What could he tell confused people wondering how being an "advisor" to a foreign military could get their son, brother, father or husband killed?

The families would not be the only ones who would have to get used to getting along without those two superb men. Hank missed them deeply and knew they always would be part of him.

As dawn was breaking, Hank rousted himself from cover, feeling as fresh as a daisy that had been pierced by a rifle round, run over by a Mack truck and dumped into a boiling pot. He could smell the Vam Co Dong River and knew he was making progress. Soon he bulled through a clump of bushes and set his eyes on the yellowish brown river. He eased forward for a better look at the situation.

He hadn't hit his destination on the money, of course, but that was par for this fucked-up mission. He was pretty sure he was upstream from the finger of land jutting into the water that marked the extraction point, so he spent the next hour working his way downriver until he found his personal Promised Land. He settled down under cover ten feet from the river to await rescue.

As he waited, Hank felt his scalp crawling under the black bandanna that kept the sweat out of his eyes. It was the first sign of dehydration he had developed. He suddenly recalled it had been forty-eight hours since he had last popped some salt tablets, a necessary daily ritual. He cursed himself for not bringing along the tablets because this was supposed to be a quick, in-and-out mission. Things weren't serious yet, but it wouldn't take long in this damn heat and humidity for the lack of salt intake to cause real trouble.

As the time passed, he managed to focus his mind, shake off his fatigue and analyze his situation. The VC had been waiting for them; that was clear. But how did they know his team was coming? The SEALs had made two mock insertions before going in, and they had done everything right. Up until when the shooting started, it had been textbook, tactically.

Hank thought about the VC patrol they saw on the way to the target. Three weeks ago, when this had been a free-fire zone, he and his men would have burned them down. Now, the rules of engagement were different. Did the VC double back and run across their trail? It didn't seem likely. First, it had been dark. Second, the VC had been without communications of any kind. It was inconceivable they could have been able to get back to the village ahead of his team and set up the ambush.

To hell with the rules, he thought, we should have killed those fuckers. Why take the chance? But, no, we were good soldiers and obeyed the damned rules. No shooting unless in self-defense, unless in specific performance of mission orders. What kind of bullshit is that? We still had our K-bar knives. No noise, in and out, and no risk.

He could still see Ayotte and Bush being torn to bits by the ambushers' rounds, dying before they hit the ground. The thought of what the VC would do to their bodies sent a shiver up his spine.

He wondered how Hack and Vispo turned out. Had they made it to the primary extraction point on schedule? Or was he the lone survivor?

Not that he was out of trouble yet, not at all.

As he reviewed the mission step by step, Hank convinced himself there had been a leak … maybe even an outright betrayal. If that happened, who was responsible?

The taxing of his brain was as tiring as last night's romp

through the jungle. All his good intentions couldn't stop his mind and body from drifting into sleep. It took him a second to remember where he was when the puttering of the VC motorized sampan shocked him awake.

***

The guerrilla in the sampan's bow stared in Hank's direction with blank, puzzled eyes. Hank maneuvered his M-16 around so slowly it was barely perceptible as the all-too-familiar rush of adrenaline pumped through his system.

Without warning, the river erupted in gunfire, and engine noise, and geysers of water erupted around the boat.

Stunned by the sudden noise, Hank fired a burst at the VC on the bow before realizing the man was already being shredded by a heavy machine gun. His pajamas turned into tatters as he disintegrated into a red mist of flesh, blood and bone.

Hank involuntarily cheered in approval as the Navy extraction boat roared out of its hiding place with every gun on board spraying bullets, but his shout was lost in the unbelievable racket.

The river rats had learned it was lot better to be the ambusher than the ambushed! He marveled that the extraction team was good enough to sneak in and set up their hiding place among the palms trees on the opposite riverbank right under his sleeping nose. He was so happy to see the boat he didn't feel stupid for not hearing it until later.

The other two VC in the sampan tried to return fire but were quickly chewed up by the river patrol boat's .30- and .50-caliber machine guns that also chopped the sampan to pieces. Wooden splinters flew everywhere as the water around the destroyed craft churned and bubbled from the impact of the American firepower. The smoke from the machine guns floated above the sampan's debris like a twisting blue cloud. Once the smoke cleared, Hank could see the guerrillas' mangled bodies bobbing in the water.

Hank sat perfectly still during the skirmish, knowing if he tried to get involved in any way he probably would have been blasted himself before the gunners noticed he was on their side. They were thorough in their deadliness, killing with the efficiency of someone mowing the lawn when he found a patch he had missed.

He knew the VC were on his heels and had to hear the gunfire, so he quickly grew impatient as the boat lingered in mid-river. He was damned if he was going to come this far just to have the guerrillas catch up with him from behind with rescue at hand.

Impulsively, he stood up, waved his arms in the air and shouted, "Hey, don't shoot, it's Lieutenant Dillon!"

The business end of every weapon on board immediately swiveled to his position. He was about to yell again until he realized the crew recognized him. Of course they did. They were looking for him. That's why they were at the extraction point, probably at the direction of Vispo and Hack. The thought cheered him.

"Swim out," called a swabbie, and Hank gave it his best try. He didn't get far with his bad arm, so a crewman jumped in and hauled him to the boat.

Trembling from pain and exhaustion, he gasped, "Charlie's right behind me," to the boat captain.

The tall, lanky blond with a buzz cut — a kid, really — didn't even crack a smile as he said, "Got it." All business, the captain told his crew to check the VCs' remains for documents and salvage whatever they could from the sampan before the debris sank beneath the surface of the river forever.

The boat swung around and headed downriver for Vung Tau.

Chapter Two

Anytime Lieutenant Commander Lawrence Beebe imagined what a United States Navy base should look like it was not what he saw here. This place was a far cry from the Coronado base at San Diego that was SEAL Team One's permanent residence. Technically this was a Vietnamese outpost, but in reality it was an American used and funded base of operations.

This SEAL outpost upriver from Vung Tau made even the worst place he had ever been stationed, his worst experience in the military, look like the Ritz Carlton Presidential Suite by comparison to this shit hole. Bravo Platoon, Commanded by Hank Dillon, had set up his little shop at a small Vietnamese Navy outpost a few kilometers, or klicks, west of the South China resort town of Vung Tau, where Beebe had his position.

When he first saw this place he thought it looked like the depression-era shantytowns he had seen in black and white movies when he was a kid. It looked like it was straight out of one called, "The Grapes of Wrath."

The outpost, if you could really call it that, was barely the size of a single city block. It had a few Quonset huts connected by wooden walkways. The only purpose to the walkways was so that the men could stay out of the mud during monsoon season. The various huts served as the mess hall, workshops, and the all-important sick bay.

The other "hootches" were the living quarters for the SEALs as well as the Vietnamese navy personnel (VNNs) who, in theory, ran the place. The Boat Support Unit that worked in support of the SEALs was here along with ten Vietnamese Marines (VNMC) who were here as support when they were necessary. There were also the Montagnard tribal scouts who chose to make this base their home. The Vietnamese were there for training and advised by the Americans, who, because of the recent formation of their type of unit were constantly being tested and evaluated by those up the command structure-- and received no end of advice from those with no operational experience in this country.

Outside of those charged with operating the base virtually no one knew what went on here. For that matter almost no one knew that Americans were operating in the Delta at all. Only a few officers in the Special Forces were in that particular loop. Beebe was the only officer in all of Vietnam who knew all of the specifics and those he reported back directly to his superior, who was safe and sound in Coronado.

The base was defended on its land side by trip wires that would set off a flare, as well as claymore mines in addition to the two rows of concertina wire. On top of that there were two guard towers equipped with floodlights and armed with thirty caliber machine guns. These elevated positions were deadly for anyone approaching from any of the landside routes.

The water side of the little base was protected by an old junk style boat anchored off the store. It was equipped with two fifty-caliber machine guns to handle something heavier from the water side.

Every hootch was surrounded with sandbags to offer protection to the inhabitants in the event of shrapnel or small arms fire. He had found in a long bitch session with Vispo and Hack they also served to cut off any possibility of breeze that might offer some kind of relief from the heat.

It was probably the most unusual 'base' he would ever serve at. Beebe was well aware that with his unusual career path he could be wrong in that assumption. Ever since he had served as part of the Underwater Demolition Team (UDT) in Korea as a frogman, he had thrived and survived in the world of the more elite units. Now he was an integral part of the Navy's most unconventional experiment in its history.

He walked into the sickbay and found Hank sitting up in bed. His left arm was now covered with bandages. He was the only patient in their six bed bay. He had been picked up by the RPC about twelve hours ago from his mission deep in the jungle. Beebe had debriefed Hack and Vispo first, opting to let his platoon commander get some desperately needed sleep.

"Commander!" Hank said as he sat up as straight as he was able.

"Hello, Hank. I talked to Doc Padget. It seems like you are in good hands. How do you feel?"

"I'll survive," Hank said wearily.

Beebe noticed the man was covered in sweat, despite the fan blowing directly on him. Hopefully his wounds weren't infected causing him to have a fever. That would be bad news for a SEAL they needed back in the field as fast as he could manage.

Sweat was just part of daily life in Vietnam – sweat and the mosquitoes that always came along with it. The moment Beebe got of the nice, cool, air conditioned C-130 transport plane when he landed it started and had yet to stop. The only way to imagine relief from it was to think of air conditioning. Beebe knew that would not be a part of his life until he left the country.

"It isn't as bad as it looks. It missed the bone and went straight through," Hank said. "The worst part is I gotta sit here on my ass for damn near a week. The medication Doc's got me on has my head all weird."

"Be sure to follow his orders," Beebe commanded. "Infections in this climate will kill you just like a bullet. Get your rest and don't push it until Padget gives the okay."

"Yes sir," Hank answered with reservation.

"Hank, I just talked with Vispo and Hack, and I heard some disturbing things."

"I know sir," Hank ran the hand on the good arm through his short hair and let out a sigh. "The three of us were up most of last night goin' over everything forward and backwards. To the best of our knowledge, we didn't screw up. This was as close to a textbook op as it comes, Commander, we did everything by the book."

He sat up as straight as he could. His eyes were showing only determination and anger, "They had us cold, sir. They knew we were coming. The only explanation that works is they knew we would be there."

Beebe pulled a folding chair over to the beside, "Walk me through it."

As Hank related the events of the past few days, Beebe studied the young Lieutenant. As this point, Hank's reactions and the body language were as important to his boss as the details of the mission. Besides, he had already extracted virtually every detail imaginable from Vispo and Hack.

He did have legitimate concerns over the situation. Despite that he had heard and seen nothing that changed his opinion of the young officer. Hank had come to his attention during his SEAL training while at the Coronado Amphibious Base at San Diego

California.

Dillon had been one of the best in his class. This was accomplished in a program that was designed to be the toughest military training on the planet. Even before someone could enter the SEALs they had to make it through the UDT program. That program had a washout rate that was so large many people didn't even try.

Once through this 'easier' school, for two months, the trainees were put through tortuous physical training, in addition to specialized weapons training. Every single graduate was an expert in the use of all light weapons, explosives, and in a form of Korean hand to hand combat known as Hwarang Do. These SEALs were parachute qualified, experts in combat first aid, could set and disarm booby traps, pilot small boats, repel from helicopters, and a few could probably even fly those same helicopters in a jam.

Most of all, these SEALs would have proven that they could make it through hellish situations when the body as well as the mind would be pushed further than most people believe possible.

Beebe knew he still saw that quality in the eyes of the young platoon commander. The mission, despite its challenges, had not destroyed his spirit.

"You're right, Dillon," he said when Hank had finished, "You've got a leak. We'll be an investigating on our end – I think we will start with that *hoi chanh* who gave us the info on Hoa. But...you're the one who's out here on a tightrope. Tighten up your security. From now on it is strictly need to know on all missions. Out here it is not that simple to tell the good guys from the bad guys."

Beebe leaned forward. "Hank, this is the kind of thing that could damage the entire program. There is a huge debate going on back in San Diego about if the SEALs are a good idea or not. There are people who ask what they hell the Navy's doing out here in the boonies."

"I might have asked that same question last night," Dillon grinned weakly.

Beebe allowed himself a short laugh before moving on, "They say if we need counter guerilla operations, continual raids into enemy territory, snatch and grabs of VC, well then we have the Army and the Marines. Why not just train those guys to go do it?

This is the biggest criticism that Captain Bucklew is dealing with. So far his argument is that we can deliver people anywhere on the planet better than any other branch of the service. He also said, and he is right, that UDT training is the best foundation for a commando force. He is still winning the argument.

"Of course, there are those in the officer corps who resent the type of fraternization with the enlisted that happens in Special Forces units. They think it's bad for order and discipline. They think we've really gone over the line with our small team concept.

"We do have supporters who think what we are doing is the appropriate role for the teams. Many of them are also afraid we are biting off more than we can chew down here. They are uncomfortable with all of the experimentation of mission types we are doing with you at this base. They think that failure could derail our plans for expanding the number and missions of the teams.

"Your people are basically, to use a Navy phrase, still on a sea trial, Hank. You are the prototype of a new weapon. We've gotta put you through your paces, and see if you can do what you're designed for, just like we would a new ship.

"If there's a traitor in the ranks, and he can neutralize your effectiveness, or worse yet, cause heavy casualties...well it could lead to the entire program being cut back, or the role being changed from what it has the potential to be. This guy could do a lot more damage to the long term interest of our country than in his wildest wet dreams.

"On the bright side, you're doing a hell of a job. We had a *hoi chanh* say that among the VC there is a saying, roughly translated, 'If the devils with the green faces come for you in the night, you will never be seen again.' There may be a damn few back in the States who know you even exist but the word is getting around here in the bush. The enemy certainly knows it."

"We'll try our best to keep 'em nervous, Commander," said Hank.

"I know you will. One more thing, take care of yourself. Keep your head in the game. Don't let the losses get to you. In Korea, I saw good men endanger the lives of the living, all because they became so overcautious and obsessed with the ones they had already lost. You can't bring back the dead. What's done is done. The best way to ensure it never happens again is to stick with your training. Just do your job in the same excellent manner in which you have done it so far. Do you copy?" Beebe asked.

For a moment, Hank let the mask down, and the Commander could see the pain the young officer had been hiding over the loss of Ayotte and Bush.

Hank swallowed hard, and then snapped instantly back to his professional bearing, "Yes sir. Thank you."

****

"Hey, Lieutenant."

Hank blinked the sleep out of his eyes to find Lanny Vispo and Chester Hack standing in the door to the sickbay.

"Hey, come in you two."

They obeyed, and sat on the edge of the bed next to Hank's. Hack was carrying an armload of paperback books. "How ya' doin', Lieutenant?"

"I could use a drink."

Vispo laughed, "Hasn't Doc gotcha pumped full of good dope already?"

"Yeah, but it's a pain goin' in, and it don't taste nothin' like a good Johnny Walker," Hank joked. "Whatcha' got there, Hack?"

"We made everybody pitch in. Only the best stuff. We got Louis L'Amour, Matt Helm - if you can believe the idea of a good spook - and a brand new John D. MacDonald. He's got a new detective, Travis McGee, who's a real badass. Make a good SEAL."

"We could use a detective around here," Hank said still half asleep.

The two enlisted men looked at each other, "Yeah, that's the way we see it too, Lieutenant," Vispo said. "Commander Beebe didn't say much about it to us, when we brought it up. I don't think he disagreed, but he didn't confirm or deny that."

"No, you're right there," Hank told him, but volunteered no further information on the matter. "We gotta tighten up around here. I don't think we've been slackin' by any means, but we gotta go to real extremes in security 'till we flush the bastard out."

The two men stood, "You get better, Lieutenant. Doc said we could only stay a minute," Hack said. "We'll come back for a bit tomorrow."

"It's real thirsty in here," Hank hinted jokingly.

Vispo laughed, "Doc would kill us slow. He said if you mix what he's got you full of with liquor, you'd have yourself a permanent pain killer."

"Shit. Well, when I get outta here I guess."

"You got it, Lieutenant."

As the two men left, Hank barely had time to think how lucky he was to have men like this on his team. That was his last thought before he slipped back into the haze of exhaustion and pain killers. ➤

****

The first thing Hank saw as he stepped out of the sick bay and blinked his eyes used to the merciless sunlight, was the smiling face of "Three Toes," his Montagnard bodyguard.

Whenever Hank thought he had reason to bitch and complain about his situation in Vietnam he thought about these Montagnards. These tribal people had been practically at war with the Vietnamese for as long as anyone he spoke to could remember. The American Special Forces had harnessed this traditional hatred and turned it to a weapon against the Viet Cong.

The 'Yards' were great and experienced jungle fighters as well as top notch trackers. They were also fiercely loyal to the Americans. The Americans, in turn, had mostly talked the South Vietnamese into leaving the Yards alone. Incidents of cruelty towards the tribesmen were still known, but had slowed to a virtual crawl by comparison. Before the American presence, a South Vietnamese officer could shoot a Montagnard in the street for any offense, even those that bordered on imaginary. The officer in question would be virtually guaranteed there wouldn't even be an investigation much less any action taken against him.

Friction between the Yards and the VNMCs still went on here on the outpost. It was something Hank had to deal with from time to time. The kind of hatred between these two groups was not changed by an agreement made from military necessity. It was also not eased by the fact that anyone who looked at duty assignments could quickly figure out that he preferred working with the Yards. They better suited his missions.

He mainly used the Montagnards for reconnaissance and other intelligence gathering missions. He also sometimes took them along on raids if they were familiar with the area.

Y Bli was from the southern part of the highlands, and had traveled south to fight the Communists. This was after the VC had gone from village to village terrorizing the poor proletarians they extolled in their propaganda, and in the process, killed his brother. When Y Bli had protested, he was relieved of two of his toes. It was supposed to teach him to be a good supporter of the Revolution.

As far as psy-ops, or psychological operations go, Hank thought, the VCs recruitment of Y Bli had been an abject failure. The Montagnard fought the VC with a fierce hatred that was nearly an obsession. A few toes would never change that. Accompanying the SEALs on missions had become life's greatest pleasure for the little man. He was first in line for every mission they would let a Yard go on.

The Viet Cong had placed a bounty (sizeable in some cases) for dead or captured American officers. The amounts ranged from a hundred bucks for an ensign, two hundred for a lieutenant junior grade, and three hundred for a lieutenant. Three Toes had been assigned to watch Hank while he was asleep to avoid someone from attempting to cash in on that reward.

"No one get rich hunting you, lieutenant," Y Bli had smiled when given the order.

The loyal Yard was more than good at his word. Around camp, everywhere he went, Hank would catch glimpses of Three Toes hanging out in the shadows, always with him in sight. Once while on R&R in Vung Tao, Hank just happened to bump into the little man in the middle of a crowded street and acting like it was just another routine part of his day. He made it seem like it was just an incredible coincidence they had run into each other that evening.

For a while it got on Hank's nerves. He was one of the most highly trained fighters on the planet, why did he need a bodyguard? He could take care of himself. At some point wouldn't the damn Yard need to sleep? Sooner or later he just learned to live with it. As he got to know the little man better he even grew to like the fact that Three Toes had his back wherever he went.

Even though Y Bli was smiling as was his normal habit, Hank could tell something was on his mind as he approached.

"Feel better?"

"Yes, Y Bli, thanks for asking."

The man nodded, still smiling. Then he blinked and made his request, "Please come to our village. We like you to have loyalty ritual with us in six days."

Hank knew this was the highest honor the Montagnards could give to a westerner. He knew some of the Green Berets who live in the bush near, if not in, the Montagnard villages had received this tribute. He had not heard of any SEALs being honored in this fashion.

He bowed his head slightly, "I would be honored. I will meet you in your village in six days."

Y Bli's eyes lit up, his smile, if it was possible, grew wider. He nodded slightly and hurried away.

Hank watched him go. He was going to have to find a way to show up in style at Three Toes' village. It would be a good thing for Hank. It would also help Y Bli gain status among his people. In addition it would allow Hank to demonstrate to the entire village that he considered the occasion to be of the utmost importance. The Oriental concept of honor was as important to the Vietnamese and the Montagnards as it was to any people in this part of the world.

He turned his mind back to the problem of the day. He had considered Commander Beebe's promise of a formal investigation. He thought that entire process would be lacking. He would have to begin his own, more local, investigation.

Hank was the guy on the ground. He was on location. As a result he was much closer to the problem than any official investigation team would ever be. That was not his only, or main, reason for wanting to handle things himself.

Ayotte and Bush had been his friends. They and Hank had trained together. The bond they had formed as comrades in arms was as close as that formed by twin brothers.

Someone was going to pay for what happened to them. He wanted to be the person to collect that debt. He wanted to do it in person, and soon.

***

Hank was in the operations hut when he heard the

helicopter approaching from the north. It soon powered down after it settled onto the LZ near the boat dock. He had just sealed the envelopes on the letters to the families of Ayotte and Bush and was in the process of completing the paperwork to send back their personal effects.

This duty had put him in a pissy mood. He hoped that the chopper, which had to have come from the SOG outfit of the 5th Special Forces Group, was here on some form of pleasure instead of business. He really was in the mood to toss more than one drink back.

The Studies and Observations Group, and they were so benignly called, were headquartered 150 klicks north of Vung Tau, at a place called Bien Hoa. The SEALs operated on a shoestring budget. Many times they were dependent on SOG for explosives, ammunition, and helicopters.

SOG consisted of the Green Berets from the 5th Special Forces Group. It was filled with specialists from other services such as the SEALs as well as some guys from the CIA. SOG was a top secret organization, and it reported directly into the Joint Chiefs of Staff. With the obvious exception of General Westmoreland, who was the Commander of all Forces in Vietnam, and probably a few of the officers on his senior staff, the rest of the military brass in Vietnam had little or no knowledge of SOG operations.

SOG was comprised of five units. The Maritime Unit and Northern Infiltrators made extensive use of the SEAL teams. The other missions, Air Support, Psy-Ops, propaganda and intimidation tactics – Airborne, 'over the fence' missions, were all mainly conducted by Army personnel. There was no public admission that these units even existed much less ran operations against the enemy. They had no specific uniforms, with the exception of their insignia. Their insignia was a skull that dripped blood from the teeth, and they had even designed that themselves. Like Hank, these guys fought a secret war in forbidden zones.

Gunners Mate 2nd Class Lanny Vispo stuck his head in the hootch and hollered, "Hey, Lieutenant, these two guys in green beanies want to communicate with ya. Are ya home?"

Vispo leaned his lanky body away from the door opening and Master Sergeant Ken Nanski, along with the chopper pilot, walked by him.

Nanski was well known in SOG as a guy who could get things done. He was a likeable, albeit very tough man. He had been awarded the Silver Star, Bronze Star, and three Purple Hearts. In the Special Forces, a Master Sergeant was next door neighbors with God. Nanski stood out even amongst those guys.

Nanski saluted and asked, "Hey Lieutenant, how ya doin'?"

The two men shook hands warmly; "I'm fine," Hank lied. "How the hell are you, Sarge?"

Nanski introduced his companion, "This is Warrant Officer Jack Warden. He flew me in."

As Hank shook the man's hand, he asked Nanski, "What can I do for you, Sarge?"

Nanski settled his linebacker's body into the nearest chair. He wiped sweat out of his close cropped hair that was turning prematurely gray around the temples, "I got a problem with a VC operation in the area near a hamlet I'm tryin' to pacify, and I need your help," he told Hank.

Hank knew a little about the program the Green Berets were running known as CIDGs, Civilian Irregular Defense Groups. They were operating in hundreds of hamlets throughout South Vietnam. The Green Berets would enlist the help of Vietnamese or Montagnards in the hamlets to fight the VC. They would train the villagers, give them the weapons they needed, and even help them turn their villages into fortified positions.

When they left, there would be a militia of sorts operating on their own. The main purpose of all this wasn't really to have these groups defeat the VC in combat operations. It was really to deny them new recruits and territory for expansion. That would keep the VC in limited area and then combat operations could be planned to handle those areas.

These army units even taught them better ways to tend their crops and increase their yields. They held classes on medical treatment including sterilization and the basics of disease control. Without all of the aid being provided by the Green Berets these hamlets were helpless, easy targets for the Viet Cong.

"I'm fresh out of agricultural experts," Hank said sarcastically.

"From what I hear…you plant more than your fair share of VC," Nanski shot back. "Which brings me to my point. There's a cadre in your happy hunting ground that is continually giving me grief.

"This Charlie's name is K Xung," Nanski's lips curled around the name like he had bitten into a sour apple and found half a worm sticking out. "He's got a force of about twenty guerillas, and he is a real son of a bitch. He paid a visit to a cooperative village in our province a couple a' weeks ago. They raped young girls, and then proceeded to mutilate them with tool handles. They drew and quartered two old women with water buffaloes while placing bets on which old lady would come apart first. They lined up everyone left alive in town and made them watch. They castrated a half a dozen young men, then shot a bunch of others. Finally they piled up the bodies, soaked them down with gasoline, and put a torch to 'em. Only problem was some of them were only wounded and died screaming. They left just enough people alive to spread the word, and that is exactly what happened.

"Two days ago, we went to Minh Rong, a good sized hamlet that was pretty receptive when we first approached them. The chief was scared to death that K Xung would find out we were there and proceed to do a sequel at his village. He wouldn't listen to a word we said about training and equipment. He told us not to come back as long as Xung was around."

It was an ancient story. The familiarity did not keep Hank from getting pissed as he listened. Taking this bastard out would be a real pleasure.

"Only problem is, we can't find the little fucker. Our last intelligence puts him here in the Phuoc Tuy Province, but there's a lot of little hamlets around here that are sympathetic to Charlie. Can you help us out?" the Green Beret asked.

"You bet," Hank responded. "If he's in the area, my Yards will sniff him out."

"I figured you could, the way you crazy bastards go slinking around at night in bad guy land."

"Sarge, first I gotta clear this with my boss in Vung Tau..."

"Already been there. Commander Beebe will confirm it with you when he comes in day after tomorrow. I'm just here to deliver the bird and Warden here to fly you around," he said jerking his thumb in the direction of the pilot. "He'll take me back to Bien Hoa, then he's all yours for the duration."

"Well," Hank said, repeating an often echoed saying in the military, "There's always ten percent out there that don't get the friggin' world."

"Right," Nanski laughed. "Listen, you gotta be careful with how you use that chopper. There are new ROEs on flight ops. On some of our missions they got us using Vietnamese crew members. They even had us paint ARVN insignia on all our birds."

"Why?" Hank asked. "What the hell is goin' on?" It was one thing that their outpost flew the South Vietnamese flag…this was another. It was the first time he had heard of putting the insignia of the Army of the Republic of Vietnam on American equipment that was actually being operated by Americans.

"They think we're too aggressive when we are on our own – you know, too many locals getting killed."

"God damn Rules of Engagement!" Hank fumed. "What the fuck do they want from us? Most of those little ARVN bastards can't wipe their own ass in the field without help from an 'advisor.'"

"Don't worry about it. There's no question of your taking VNs along. Just don't get caught, if you get my meaning."

"Got it. By the way, what do you want done with this asshole when we get him?" Hank asked.

"Use your imagination. Anything that helps the round-eye cause in the hamlets. We just want him gone so we can go on winning the hearts and minds of our brown brothers," Nanski grinned.

Master Sergeant Ken Nanski hadn't been in the air three minutes before Hank was speaking with Three Toes and planning out a way to find said asshole.

***

The Bell UH-1A helicopter with Jack Warden at the controls had Hank Dillon in the copilot's seat. They circled the Montagnard village twice before heading in. Hank knew this would impress the villagers, as well as serve to illustrate to them that he placed great importance on the ceremony about to take place.

The term 'Montagnard' came from the French word that meant 'highlander,' or, perhaps 'mountain dweller.' The

Montagnards had been in Vietnam before the people now known as the Vietnamese moved into the territory. In fact, some sources say it was as much as two thousand years earlier. The Montagnards eventually moved up to the highlands to get away from those now known as Vietnamese.

They were broken into two main language and racial groups. The first of those, the Mon-Khmer, came from Burma and the Coho were their main tribe. The second, the Rhade, were Malay and Polynesian, and numbered about one million in South Vietnam. Y Bli's tribe, the Chau Ma, came from the southernmost part of the mountain range that extended most of the length of the two Vietnams.

They were short, wiry people, and resembled the Indian tribes of some South Sea Islands. They were just a shade or two darker than the Vietnamese.

As they circled, Hank could see the sharp bamboo stakes that were pounded into the ground. They formed a distinctive pattern between the rows of barbed wire and ringed as well as protected the hamlet. Inside the wire were neatly placed rows of bamboo longhouses with thatched roofs. The houses were all on stilts putting them about two feet off the ground.

There was an overall makeshift feel to the place, and it always made Hank wonder how long the people had lived here. He knew Y Bli was from the highlands, and he also knew the CIA was paying the Yards to fight for the United States. Maybe they had paid to relocate part of the village. More likely the families had just moved to be closer to their men who were fighting with the Americans – and to escape the continual persecution of the VC in, what was historically, their territory.

The chopper settled into the dust of the small rutted road that led into the village. They landed in a clearing just outside the wire. It was far enough away to keep the downdraft of the helicopter from blowing the roofs off the houses.

Y Bli and about twenty of his fellow tribesmen stood stoically at the edge of the LZ. They did not flinch in any way, despite the whirling helicopter blades kicking up some rock filled dust. They were hard, stone faced men of great pride. They would never let discomfort show and would look exactly the same in conditions far more harsh than these.

Hank turned to Warden, "It's gonna be a while," he warned, shouting over the noise of the engines still winding down.

"Not to worry LT," Warden replied with a grin. He turned behind his seat and pulled out a full bottle of Jack Daniels and a Playboy magazine. "I'll be just fine. You have fun in there."

Hank shook his head as he jumped out of the chopper. Great, his driver would more than likely be drunk as he could be by nightfall. Hank thought to himself that he was as likely to die in an alcohol related accident as he was by a VC bullet.

Hank, Vispo, Hack and another member of the squad, Dan Slade, had gone to Vung Tau the night before to drink to the memory of Ayotte and Bush. At least that was what started it all. By the time Hack had bargained for a case of scotch they were drinking just to drink. Hank's head was still home to a small hammer pounding away this afternoon. Vietnam was certainly no place for someone who believed what his Sunday School teacher had called "strong drink" was a blight to society.

Y Bli came over to welcome him. The Montagnard was wearing a brightly colored shirt with beads around his neck and copper wrist bracelets. On his chest was a tattoo that read, 'Sat Cong,' framed in a rectangle. Translated to English this meant, 'Kill Communists.' Three Toes got the tattoo as a sign of loyalty to the SEALs. He knew that the VC would do ludicrously painful things to him if they ever captured him and saw it. Some of the people in the boat crews saw it, and took it upon themselves to get the same tattoo.

"Thank you for coming, Lieutenant."

"I am honored by your kind invitation, Y Bli. I am humbled to be honored by so great a brave fighter as you," Hank gave his compliment. He could almost see Y Bli grow in stature in the eyes of the village elders during the brief exchange.

Y Bli and two elders led Hank inside the wire and into a long house in the center of the village.

The buildings were elevated enough to keep small animals out. Right at the entrance to each building was a log about twelve inches high with a notch cut in the top. To enter the longhouse, one had to put his foot sideways in the notch and step into the doorway.

The Montganards were a very neat and orderly people. They did not stand for any animals in their houses. In their villages,

Hank saw none of the squalor and mess he saw in the Vietnamese cities.

Once inside the house Hank was taken to a partitioned off room. Once there he stripped down and was given a loincloth to cover his genitals. When he had it on, he was handed a black tribunal blouse, similar to a cut off short kimono, with multi-colored piping at the sleeves, shoulders and a V-neck. Once dressed, Y Bli placed a set of ritual beads around Hank's neck.

Outside a drum started banging. It was soon joined by a rhythmic wind instrument and the bonging of gongs.

Hank was led barefoot into the main room where the elders and a select group of young men sat with their backs to the walls. They were all in traditional tribal attire. Hank was seated facing the Rhade sorcerer, who wore a similar black blouse, with the exception of the piping on his was only red and white, as was the square design on his chest.

The men in the room began chanting their prayers to cleanse Hank. This also served to drive the evil spirits away from the tribe. Hank eyeballed what he could of the room without turning his head side to side. He also knew not to appear to be staring. Every eye was watching him to be sure he behaved according to tradition.

The chief looked on impassively. Two tribesmen placed Hank in the chief's chair, and with a pan of water washed Hank's feet. The chant continued on with no breaks.

At the doorway a water buffalo stood hobbled by roped and help still by four Montagnards. At a signal from the sorcerer the four men pulled the ropes and the animal fell to the ground with a bellow. A man darted forward, he cut the animal's throat in a manner which would make it bleed to death slowly, which would get the maximum amount of blood possible out of it.

As the animal lay on the ground trying vainly to yell a large bowl was brought forward to catch the free flowing blood.

Hank knew enough to be honored that a water buffalo had been chosen for the sacrifice. The size of the animal was selected according to the perceived importance of the visitor. The water buffalo was the biggest thing in the jungle around here.

The man who slit the buffalo's throat brought in the bowl. He used it to anoint Hank's feet with the blood.

The small of warm sticky blood jolted Hank's memory back

to a time when he had to dress a chest wound on a badly hurt friend while still taking enemy fire.

The chanting stopped for a moment, and then started up again.

The Chau Ma sorcerer brought out a slim copper bracelet. Hank put out his arm to receive it. He was now a member of the tribe. The bracelet was the ceremonial symbol of acceptance. It cemented the alliance between Hank and the tribe, and was also a sign of mutual loyalty.

Hank looked at Y Bli and saw not only an expression of pride but also genuine admiration and fondness. In that moment, Hank felt spiritually what the physical ceremony was meant to accomplish.

He recalled the Vietnamese called the Montagnards *"mois"* which meant savages. But from what he had seen of both peoples, the name calling should be reversed.

The chief pulled out a long bamboo tube. He placed it into a vat of wine in the center of the room. The wine was fermented from a mixture of leaves which Hank had been warned by Ken Nanski tasted like 'panther piss.'

The chief took the first sip to show that the wine had not been poisoned, as was the custom. He then offered the tube to Hank who drank the same amount of wine. Because he had been forewarned, he was able to sip the right amount of wine without a grimace.

For the next hour, the bamboo straw was passed around the room, along with the main food course. This food was a rice dish covered in a thick disgusting tasting gravy.

When the men descended from the longhouse the celebration began in earnest. They drank and did tribal dances long into the night. This was all to the accompaniment of an instrument known as a *Kamboat*, a six piped mouth organ.

Hank stayed for a suitable amount of time. He generally enjoyed his status as the guest of honor. When he began to drift away from the proceedings, Three Toes saw this and walked him back to the chopper.

They did not say a word about the ceremony. There was no need and any words would be inappropriate. "Thank you for your hospitality," Hank said.

Y Bli nodded, "I see you tomorrow. I think I have good news about the man you seek."

"Already?" Hank was mildly surprised. "Great work."

Hank put out his hand, and the two men shook warmly as was a western tradition. Afterwards Y Bli headed back to the village without another word.

Hank approached the chopper and called out, "Warden, you sober enough to drive this thing?"

"Lieutenant!" a slightly slurred and offended voice protested from the darkness, "I only brought one bottle!"

Hank settled into his seat, Warden mumbled, "Another badass with a copper bracelet." His tone was mocking, but there was also a hidden note of envy and possibly respect. Warden had been around SOG long enough to know this honor was not granted lightly.

The helicopter rose and barely cleared the trees as it slipped sideways into the night, but Hank didn't notice at all. He fingered his copper bracelet and realized, to his surprise, that he somehow felt differently about himself.

Chapter Three

"Dillon, you've got trouble. You've got Charlie in the ranks," Beebe said.

That was hardly news, but he didn't say anything and allowed the man to continue, "Our *hoi chanh* checked out in interrogation, and both the CIA and the Vietnamese are confident he was not the leak."

Hank decided he would rather not know the details of how the defector's bona fides had been established. He was sure of one thing; it was not the result of a nice friendly chat.

"We've got our people looking into it," Beebe went on, "But in the meantime, I want you to tighten security 'till it squeaks. Plug the leak now. You do whatever is necessary; take any action you see fit. I'll back you on this if there's trouble."

"Yes sir," Hank replied.

"I see you got your chopper. That's good. Give SOG all the help you can with this K Xung. Lord knows they've helped us enough in the past. Besides it's good PR, right?"

"By the way," the tall, muscular, Lieutenant Commander changed the subject abruptly as was his way, "Your two replacements are outside, just in from 'Dago [San Diego]. Sorry for the delay, but we're spread more thin that you think. How is Belvins working out?"

When you talked to Lawrence Beebe you had to pay attention. He would hit you with a question before you had time to collect your thoughts, "He's doin' great, Commander. He's got his squad working well together, and doing well with mine. He left last night for the Vam Co Dong. I've had reports of excessive river traffic up there. He's checkin' it out. He's a good man in the bush, and a good man in any other way I can think of as a matter of fact."

"Good. Hank," Beebe lowered his voice, "this is for your ears only. I don't know when, but we're going to be moving to the Bassac River further down in the Delta, and up to Danang. We may have to split your unit up with a squad at each location. I hope not, but we'll have a lot more men soon. We'll need to put experienced men with the new ones at the start. You think Blevins is up to that?"

"I'd sure miss having him," Hank admitted, "But Keith

could handle the job."

As if on cue, a commotion was raised down by the pier, and Blevins' voice could be heard above the noise, raising hell.

"He's not due back 'till this afternoon," Hank said to Beebe cautiously as they left the hootch to investigate, "Something's up."

Blevins' words were clearer now. Hank could make out that the usually reserved (except in combat) ensign was cursing up a storm.

"Keith! What's up?" Hank called as they approached. Blevins, his squad, and two VNMCs were disembarking from the PRC at the end of the pier.

Blevins looked up, saw Beebe was with Hank, and visibly forced himself to calm down. Ensign Keith Blevins was a muscular five feet eleven, one hundred and ninety-five pounds. He had been a defensive back on his college football team. His fierce competitive nature was offset by a quiet demeanor which disappeared as soon as bullets started flying. His philosophy was 'When in doubt, attack,' and had earned him the moniker of 'Crazy Keith' with his men.

"We had to abort, dammit – uh sir. There were just too many things wrong. There were VC all over the place. I should've known something was wrong, we didn't hear a single shot going upriver," he explained.

Hank knew well the sound of the occasional shot coming from the jungle as they passed VC observers and patrols. They were used to warn their comrades up the line that the men with green faces were out and on the prowl. It was the reason the SEALs would conduct practice or false insertions to keep the VC off balance. This also kept the locations where the SEALs disembarked a secret as well.

"There were signs of too many people where there hadn't been any before, and they weren't just passing through. There was no boat traffic at all, and there should've been. Hell, that's why we were there in the first place! Charlie was waiting for us. The further I got, the more signs I saw of trouble.

"I got us the hell out before they boxed us in. It was very spooky," he looked meaningfully at Hank, "You know what I mean?"

Hank sighed; there was no way to write off his squad's

ambush as accidental at this point. He had been sure before, but this was proof positive. Two missions out of two being burned were astronomical odds even if one wanted to think they were coincidental. "Yeah, Keith, I know what you mean."

Beebe turned to go, and then hesitated, his steely gray eyes narrowed, "Until it squeaks, Dillon, 'till it squeaks."

***

After debriefing Blevins' Squad, Hank went to his hootch to get a little rest during the hottest part of the day. The SEALs missions were so demanding that they were given few other duties, other than maintaining their weapons and planning the next operation.

"Lieutenant," the low voice came from the entrance to Hank's hut.

Hank had been expecting Three Toes since their conversation the night before. He knew this must be the news he was waiting for. The Montagnards never came close to the American living quarters unless it was absolutely necessary.

"Come in, Y Bli, come in," Hank said.

Y Bli appeared in the doorway, "My people find K Xung," he reported.

"Have a seat," Hank offered, "Tell me where the bastard is hiding."

Three Toes entered officer's country reluctantly, and stood shifting nervously from one foot to another. "Him not hiding. Him stay with brother. Brother Vee Cee too. They in village past Cat Lo."

"VC village?" Hank asked.

"No, but maybe," Y Bli answered. Not know. Change sometime you know. When Americans leave, Vee Cee come in, sometime stay."

"How'd you find him so fast?" Hank asked.

"People hear of him, him very bad man. Him come to some of their villages, they hate him. Him not hide, think safe. Think him too strong."

"Yeah, well we'll just have to relieve him of that notion. Do you know your way around the village, and what he looks like?"

asked Hank.

"No, but Ha Jah, he know. He has seen K Xung do very bad things, not forget," the small man said.

"Good, he goes with us," Hank decided.

Y Bli's grin widened as he realized 'us' meant he was going to be included with the Lieutenant on the mission as well.

"Tell no one," Hank instructed. "Only Ha Jah, no one else."

Three Toes nodded, and Hank noticed the man kept stealing looks at Hank's M-16 leaning against the hootch wall. The weapon was a prized possession among the Montagnards, and very hard to come by.

Hank picked up the rifle, patted the butt, and said, "Maybe soon, Y Bli, maybe soon."

Y Bli nodded his head affirmatively, and if possible grinned even wider. The only thing that pleased him more than the chance to kill VC was the potential that soon he would be able to kill them more effectively.

***

Hank was losing sleep over how Charlie was getting information on his unit's movements.

Mission briefings always included a very limited audience of Blevins and himself as squad leaders, the SEALs going out, and two backups. Montagnards or VNMC were included if they were being used. Nationals were included in the missions only if they had special knowledge of the target area, or if the target was a person known to them. In other words the attendance list for briefings was built on a strict need to know basis. Lt. Tran Van Ngo, was in command of all the VNMC, was not even included in the mission details, and he was technically responsible for assigning people to the mission.

After every briefing the hootch would be sanitized. All the maps, reconnaissance photos, intelligence reports, and hand written notes were locked in a safe in the personnel office. In addition to all of that, the chalk boards would be washed clean with soap and water if they had been used.

Hank's first suspicion was, of course, that the leak came from the Vietnamese. Then he realized the one VNMC member on his blown mission was one of the casualties. He supposed it was possible that it was a mistake on the part of the Viet Cong, blowing away their own man. On top of that the VNMC had done his job in such a way that it was hard for Hank to believe he knew anything about the ambush ahead of time. Then there was the fact that Blevins had come back from a blown mission well after the Vietnamese Marine on Hank's mission had died.

He was convinced that someone in the Vietnamese contingent was the source of the leak. Hank could not talk himself out of that much. He knew he had to closely monitor that those men did during and after the briefings, perhaps that would lead to the rat.

He put the word out to those involved – Mission briefing at 2100 hours in the Ops Hootch. Then he sought out Blevins who was in the Mess Hootch, "Keith, we got somethin' to take care of."

***

"Lieutenant, Ngo's here," Vispo reported sticking his head into the Ops Hootch.

"Send him in," Hank said.

Lieutenant Tran Van Ngo of the Vietnamese Marines looked curiously up at Vispo as he entered the room. Ngo was about five feet four inches, and there was no way he topped a hundred and thirty-five pounds.

Hank understood the confusion on the man's face. It was not unusual for him to meet Hank and Blevins in the Ops Hootch. The added security was a bit out of the ordinary.

Keith Blevins sat in a folding chair off to the side, while Hank was behind the beat up desk. He looked up as Ngo neared, "Hello Lieutenant, have a seat." He motioned to another folding chair in front of the desk. It looked like the man was being sent to the high school principal's office.

Ngo sat stiffly in his chair, his expression completely neutral. The SEALs had nicknamed him Stoneface behind his back. This was because of his lean physique and his continually stern face.

"How can I help you, Lieutenant Dillon?"

"Well," Hank paused, "I'm not sure if you can to be honest. As you know, we were ambushed on the last mission. This is the one where Sergeant Ngyen was killed."

"A regrettable loss," Ngo interjected. "A good man."

"Yes," Hank said. "Perhaps he was. That is what I wanted to talk to you about. As I said, we were suckered on that mission. The VC knew we would be there." He stopped and looked hard at Ngo.

As the silence lengthened, Ngo looked over at Blevins who sat impassively with his muscular arms crossed over his chest. He slowly turned his attention back to Hank.

"You insult the memory of a good soldier. Sergeant Ngyun was killed by the VC and you show his memory no respect by your accusations!" By the end of the second sentence, Ngo's voice had risen to the point that he was almost at a high pitched scream. "If he was a traitor, why was he killed? Why did I have to visit his wife and children with the bad news?"

Hank answered calmly. Keeping his temper in check gave him the advantage in this situation. Perhaps he was wrong, "He tripped a mine in the dark as he led us into the ambush. Perhaps he made a miscalculation," Hank shrugged as though Ngo's logic had not already occurred to him.

"It is not possible," Ngo objected. "Three months ago Sergeant Ngyen was given a medal by my government for bravery in combat – a medal you recommended him for."

Hank already knew these facts, and they were one of the reasons – other than the man's death – that he didn't suspect Ngyen at all.

He changed tactics, deciding to probe the real reason he had called Ngo in. "Did Ngyen discuss the details of the briefing with anyone before the mission?"

Ngo shrugged, "How would I know this? Why are you asking only about Vietnamese, Lieutenant, what about Americans?"

Hank ignored the implication and pressed on. "Did Ngyen have someone he was especially close to? Someone he might have confided in who was not as reliable as he was?"

He could easily write off Ngyen as a suspect. If he had been the leak, their problems were over. Perhaps the extra VC activity in the area Blevins had been patrolling the day before was just bad luck. If that were the case they could batten down the hatches and just go back to work.

"He had friends…" Ngo admitted.

"We should talk with them," Hank said. "Did he speak with you before the mission?"

The silence in the room was complete. Ngo stared at Hank, his fury was unmistakable in his body language and facial expressions. He looked over at Blevins, who merely stared back at him, then back at Hank.

"It is not my practice, Lieutenant Dillon, to attempt to find things that I have no need to know, as you phrase it. Even though the Marines on this base are under *my* command. I am content to find out what happened after the mission is over, as you ordered," Ngo had regained some of his composure. He was attempting to match Hank's demeanor so as to not lose face.

It was time to get things going, "This was not our first problem, Lieutenant Ngo. We have had to abort several missions. All of these missions had VNMCs along – and not always Sergeant Ngyen. Are you sure that you did not speak to the Sergeant about this particular mission?" Hank stood up, using his size as an interrogation tactic, "We have a witness who saw you two talking," he lied, "And everyone says you spend a lot of time uptown in Vung Tau."

Ngo was speechless. Then the look of astonishment was replaced by a look of pure fury. He stood abruptly to his feet. The chair clattered on the floor behind him, "You accuse me? You accuse me! No one has ever questioned my loyalty! No one. Ever. Your people investigated me for a long time before I was trusted with this command. I visit the families of the dead. I give to them my own pay!"

Hank had heard that this was true and it did impress him. It was above and beyond the call of duty that much was for certain. Ngo did not go out of his way to be in the line of fire, but he did seem to care about taking care of his men.

Ngo was waving his hand now and walking in a small circle. He pointed at Hank, "Who are you to talk to me of loyalty? This is my country. This is our war! Our people die!"

Ngo leaned over the desk and reached into his shirt pocket, and Hank tensed, but all Ngo came out with was a small leather fold over. He opened it and shook the picture of an attractive Vietnamese woman in Hank's face. "People like her die. You say I work for VC? VC kill her, kill my beautiful wife. Kill her because I am Marine. Now I kill them. And now I do not take shit from Americans who come over here and question me or my men."

Without another word spoken Ngo turned and stalked out of the hootch.

A moment later Lanny Vispo stick his head in, "You want him back, Lieutenant?"

"No," Hank waved his hand, "Let him go. You get outta here too. And Gunner?"

"Yeah, Lieutenant?"

"If you heard anything, keep it to yourself."

"Yes sir," Vispo said and disappeared.

Hank looked over at Blevins who grimaced jokingly, then said, "I think that went pretty well."

Hank sighed. There was enough tension in the camp over who was invading whose turf and what priorities really mattered. Now he had pissed off the commanding officer of the VNMCs. On top of that, if Ngo's story was true, Hank felt bad on a personal level for questioning a man who had sacrificed more in this war than he ever could. He had effectively rubbed salt on a wound of a man who was reduced to trying to drown his grief with booze and local hookers.

"What d'ya think?" he asked Keith.

"Pretty convincing," Blevins replied.

"Yeah. I'd say we don't have enough on him to start with the fingernails. He also had a point. I'm sure our people, be it the Navy, the CIA, or whoever, vetted this guy pretty good before letting him work with us."

"Maybe so," said Keith, who was usually suspicious of the intelligence groups. He often said that the Central Intelligence Agency's name was the world's worst case of false advertising. "I was more impressed by the picture than the intelligence vetting."

"Yeah," Hank said quietly, "Me too." Maybe he really should just tighten security and let Beebe and the cloak and dagger types take care of the investigation. That way he could both follow orders and be free of this hassle.

He decided, however, that he would keep his eyes open. If the opportunity arose, he would know what to do.

***

At 2100, Hank, Blevins, and three other SEALs, Gunners Mate 2nd Class Lanny Vispo, Radioman 3rd Class Sheldon "Shelly" Brookwater, and Bosun's Mate 1st Class Daniel "Clutter" Slade, along with Y Bli and his compatriot Ha Jah, assembled in the Operations Hootch. Two men from Blevins' squad sat in the back of the hootch as backups with two others guarding the door.

As the men had filed into the room, Lanny Vispo noticed the copper bracelet on Hank's wrist. He made a limp wrist, and pranced past, "I see you're wearing a bracelet, Lieutenant. It's simply to *die* for!" he teased.

Slade grinned and joined in, "Did they throw in a couple of wives with the deal, Lieutenant?"

Hank took the joking in the fashion it was intended. He was glad the men had enough sense to cut it out when Y Bli and Ha Jah entered the hootch.

Pinned to a bulletin board on the front wall of the hootch was a pictographic map. There were a dozen or so aerial reconnaissance photos of the target area put together as a collage with broad white circles drawn around the areas that would be of special interest.

"OK, here's what's goin' on," Hank stood to the side of the map.

"We're going to this village here," he indicated a spot on one of the long range photos with a wooden pointer.

"We will depart at 2300 hours using the RPC. We will proceed northeast past Cat Lo one half klick to the Cua Lom River. Then we will head north upriver, and conduct two false insertions on the west bank of the river south of the village. That will put us about 2 klicks from the mouth of the river. The boat will then make a one-eighty and proceed south. We will then insert on the east side of the river here," Hank indicated a spot across the river from the village.

"If we're detected, the river will act as a defensive front as well as offering a completely unrestricted field of fire," he said.

"Our mission is unofficial. We're after a clown with the handle of K Xung. They want us to grab this guy alive if possible, that will give the ARVN a chance to interrogate him, and then we get the hell out. If it's not possible our orders are to make sure the son of a bitch is dead, and I mean whacked. The main objective is to get this guy out of circulation permanently, one way, or the other," he said firmly.

Hank returned to the intelligence information, "We will have dense jungle cover on both sides of the river. Reports say it is four to five feet deep at best. The river current is about four knots, and the tide will be ebbing. The sky will be clear with a half moon, and the temp will be cool, they predict about eighty degrees.

"We don't know if the village is VC or not, but there will be no other friendlies in the area. That makes this a free fire zone if it needs to be. After we insert, the RPC will move a half klick downstream and wait. We'll set up a perimeter, and if all is clear, we will cross the river."

He turned back to the picto-map. "Ha Jah, our source on this target, puts the man in the second largest hut on the southern edge of the village." Hank pointed to the circled hut in a photo that isolated just the village.

"We'll grab the guy, and return to the extraction point here," he pointed to a spot about a kilometer south of the village.

"Simple as that," Vispo drawled cautiously.

"Order of march is as follows," Hank continued. "Vispo on point, Y Bli, myself, Ha Jah, Brookwater, with Slade on rear security."

"Team call sign is Hornet One, the RPC is Bravo Six. Final inspection is in one hour. Are there any questions?"

No one spoke up, but after the last two SNAFUs, Hank knew the question that was on everyone's mind.

Would Charlie be waiting for them?

***

As Hank inspected the men, he knew they were ready. He checked anyway. This was anything but a traditional unit with the exception of the camouflage uniforms. Everything about these men spoke of a special unit. Here, individuality was allowed and, in many cases, highly encouraged.

Each man had specific tasks he was to perform. He was not told what weapon to carry but was given a choice. In the end, the weapons variance would give the small unit maximum firepower, depending on the circumstances. Some were better for offensive and others superior in defensive capacities. In these types of units, generally speaking, no two men in the squad carried the same weapon.

As he performed the inspection, Hank mentally ticked off the equipment the men carried. He was satisfied that they had the variety he wanted for this situation.

Hank carried the M-16 with three hundred rounds in banana clips, a .38 revolver, and a starlight scope.

Cutter Slade was so nicknamed because he had a particular genius for the M-60 machine gun. At five feet nine, one hundred and eighty five pounds, the moody bosun's mate was the strongest man in the squad. He fired the heavy weapon from the hip, his strong body absorbing the recoil as if he was firing a squirrel gun. The M-60 was traditionally fired from a bipod, but Slade had removed it and the sights, and had cut down the butt to save weight. He was strong enough to keep moving with the heavy weapon while actively laying down an accurate barrage of covering fire. Somehow the man was strong enough to carry four hundred rounds of the 7.62mm linked ammunition across his shoulders.

Shelly Brookwater was packing the PRC-77 radio. All of the SEALs were trained in its use, but he preferred to carry it. His weapon of choice was a Remington twelve gauge pump shotgun with a belt of double aught buck steel ball magnum shells. He carried brass cartridges whenever possible as the salt air was not good for the standard cardboard cartridges, nor was crossing rivers.

At twenty years old, Brookwater was the youngest on the team. He had been a college basketball player. A not so small gambling habit had led to some unfounded rumors, and those rumors that turned out to be true landed him in the Navy. He was an exercise maniac. He took to SEAL training like it was what he was born to do. His body was lean. He was five foot ten, one sixty five, and his wiry muscles rippled with every move. Even after formal training was over he was constantly working out in his spare time. He did this even at those times the rest of the SEALs were resting up for the next mission. Hank thought that just watching the young man made him tired.

Laid back Lanny Vispo carried the M-79 grenade launcher.

Vispo was very good with his 'Thumper' invariable landing his grenades within inches of the target. The M-79 was a terrific weapon. It was much better than the combination rifle/grenade launcher. The tall, lanky, blonde California-born surfer rarely ventured into the bush without it.

Vispo also carried ordinance tape for gagging and blindfolding the prisoner should they grab him. He also had the plastic flexible handcuffs and extra ammunition for Slade's M-60.

"You didn't tell anybody about this lovely little trip, did ya' Lieutenant?" Vispo cracked as Hank inspected his own equipment.

"Belay that shit," Hank snapped. Sometimes Vispo could go too far. Hank knew it was just a manifestation of what was on all of their minds.

Each man would be dealing with that question in his own way. Vispo had his way; the rest would never say anything vocally. It was as if saying it would help turn it into reality.

Out of the entire team only Lanny would find a way to deal with his fear and make a joke of it. Hank had to keep this under control around the other men.

Professional combat soldiers become superstitious just like professional athletes. In this case, instead of a lucky bat, or pair of sweat socks, these men might have a lucky K-Bar knife, a favorite pistol, or some other instrument of the craft. He noted Shelly Brookwater still wore a pair of cammo pants that had a hole in them from a close shot fired from a Viet Cong AK-47. The bullet passed through without touching his leg. As a result Brookwater figured that this pair had already taken a round and would not take another.

Like the other men Hank wore a standard H-harness with various items clipped to it. This night it was an M-26 fragmentation grenade, a K-Bar knife, a canteen, rations, and flares for emergency rapid extractions. Anything that did tend to dangle was, of course, taped to the uniform to keep it from making noise in the dark.

Vispo, Slade and Brookwater wore sweatbands. Hank ware the black scarf that covered his head like a gypsy, and also kept the sweat out of his face. Everyone had their faces and necks covered in green cammo makeup. Each man had also used black ordinance tape to wrap the cuffs of their pants tightly against their legs. They were going to cross a river, and doing this to their pants kept leaches from crawling into their pants.

Three Toes and Ha Jah carried thirty caliber carbines along with a machete-like knife in the belt of their uniforms.

A final check was made to ensure that all equipment was taped down to avoid noise. With that complete the men boarded the thirty-five foot River Patrol Craft tied at the end of the pier.

The RPC left the pier at 2330 without any fanfare and went off into the sweltering night.

As was his tradition, Hank stood in the stern and watched the camp lights fade into darkness. Those lights represented his last link to security and civilization. He hoped it would not be his last time to see them.

***

The RPC moved up the coast for an hour before they passed Cat Lo. That put them at the mouth of the Cua Lom River. The cox'n swung the boat north into the opening that cut a gash for miles in the dense jungle. The throttle was cut back, reducing speed to a few knots. This would also serve to drop the engine noise to a low rumble.

The SEALs locked and loaded their weaponry. Weapons were never loaded before they were in a position to be used for their intended purpose. There was a far greater chance of an accident on the ride up the river than not being able to quickly return fire from a pitching a rolling boat due to any incoming.

The boat crew manned the fifty and thirty caliber machine guns. All on board began to scan the dark banks of the river.

The river banks were solid black from the perspective of those on the boat. The moonlight was not sufficient to penetrate the jungle canopy. On the other side of the equation, however, it would be no problem for someone on the bank to spot the RPC cruising up the river in the moon's silver glow.

Apprehension gripped Hank. It always did at this stage. He scanned the river banks with his Starlight scope which magnified any light fifty thousand times. This made the details of the river bank visible to him in an eerie green glow.

There were no other boats on the river. Hank signaled the cox'n to make the first false insertion. The boat eased over to the west bank, stopped, then continued on up the river.

Mere seconds later, a single shot echoed through the night. The SEALs tensed despite the shot being some distance away. Was it Charlie's telegraph, or was it a VC mistake?

In a way Hank was ok with the notion that it was a warning shot. Blevins had heard no such activity on his blown recon. Perhaps Charlie was not expecting them? On the other hand, the VC could have decided to simulate a warning shot so the SEALs would think everything was normal.

Circular thinking could go on forever. There was nothing they could do but push ahead and see what happened.

They repeated the false insertion maneuvers just before coming upon the village. As the river began to narrow the lights of the village became visible in the distance.

The RPC crept past the village. They kept close to the east bank for two hundred meters. Hank gave the signal. The cox'n executed a U-turn and eased into the river bank.

The squad left the boat and set up a perimeter a few feet into the jungle. The boat continued on downriver to await their call. The SEALs listened to the engine fade and waited for the jungle noises to come back.

The noises arrived right on schedule. It was accompanied by fireflies, mosquitoes, and other pests.

Hank scanned the village with the Starlight. He saw only one person, who appeared to be an old man, entering a hut. There was no other visible movement. It was quiet, but was that a good thing or bad? On the other hand, it might not even be a VC village. Perhaps this was just the home of some normal peasants resting before another day of hard labor.

He looked at the riverbank near the village. There was nothing there but a few sampans resting at the river's edge. There was no movement near the boats.

Hank moved to Vispo, the point man, and whispered, "We'll cross here then move south as planned."

Vispo entered the chest high water of the river. The others moved silently behind him in the order assigned.

Hank could feel his adrenalin start to flow as his feet hit the water. He took each step carefully. His boots were sinking into the silt on the bottom with each step. Every step forward meant pulling himself free of the suction from the river bottom.

His calloused feet felt naked despite the protection of his boots. He knew his next step might step onto a pungi stick. If the village had gone over to the Viet Cong, they might have sown chunks of hardened clay with sharpened sticks protruding up from the river bottom.

The SEALs crossed the river without being detected. They made their way stealthily along the river bank past the sampans. This brought them to a point just south of the village. The entire way they were feeling for trip wires and pungi traps as well as looking for any signs of movement in the village.

They patrolled fifty meters into the jungle. This was the south end of the village. Hank signaled to stop.

Hank moved to an opening in the bush for a better look. Bingo, they were right on target. The hut they wanted was forty meters from where they had taken up position.

He wiped the sweat from his eye before looking through the scope. The Starlight showed no activity.

On signal Vispo took up position between the larger hut and the target. Slade moved past Hank and positioned himself at the corner of the smaller structure.

Slade and Vispo stopped and were perfectly still. They waited for some sign they had been detected. In the distance they could hear a baby cry. From the larger hut came a low murmur and a dry cough. The village was quiet, and more importantly, the jungle noises slowly returned. Vispo gave the all clear.

Hank led Brookwater, Y Bli and Ha Jah as they crept from the jungle and carefully entered K Xung's hut.

Vispo and Three Toes kept on going towards, and into, the room at the rear of the hut. Hank put his red beam flashlight onto the face of the man sleeping on the bed near the window.

Ha Jah grabbed Hank's arm and nodded vigorously. It was K Xung.

Suddenly he sat up in bed. His eyes were wide with fright. Before Hank could react Ha Jah had based him in the head with the butt of his carbine.

The man let out a sigh and sank back into his cot. Hank was impressed. The Montagnard's reflexes had been so quick and his aim solid Hank didn't think the move could have been executed any better. It was textbook. If Xung had cried out he would have been in a world of hurt.

"Surprise, you murdering bastard," Hank whispered.

There was a sound behind them and Hank turned quickly. In the red light he saw Vispo holding a young woman in black pajamas in front of him with his hand over her mouth. Vispo's other arm was around her waist. Her feet were off the ground and kicking wildly.

"What do we do with this one, Lieutenant?" Vispo hissed.

Before Hank could answer the woman's hand moved and she pulled a knife out of her blouse. She stabbed at Vispo with a vicious motion.

Lanny grunted in pain as she stuck him twice in the side and hip before he could release her waist. He caught her by the wrist.

Vispo drew her arm up. She fought with all her might to stop it, but she was no match for the SEAL.

She never gave up. The look of horror in her eyes said she knew what was going to happen. When the knife reached her neck, Vispo put everything he had into a short movement pulling it across her throat.

Blood exploded from the gaping wound. Her body went limp. Vispo let her slide to the floor where she lay in a dark and growing pool of blood.

"Is there anyone else there?" Hank whispered.

Y Bli stepped forward grinning, "Yes Lieutenant, but no bother no more."

Hank took the tape from Vispo who was checking his wounds and taped Xung's mouth and eyes. He rolled him over and fastened the handcuffs on his wrists. He was careful to stop just short of cutting off the circulation. Even with all of the stress of the moment Hank could not help but notice the man's body odor.

"Can you travel?" he asked Vispo.

"I'm okay Lieutenant, the bitch just nicked me," came the reply.

Hank knew it was more than a scratch, but he trusted Vispo's statement on his capabilities.

Hank threw the unconscious Xung over his shoulder in a fireman's carry. He was surprised by the man's overall weight. He was heavier than the average VC. He had been getting far more than his one handful of rice per day.

As he held the weight on his shoulder Hank felt a sharp pain in his forearm. It was a reminder of the screw up of his last mission. He forced the pain from his mind and headed out the doorway.

As they stepped back into the jungle Hank was sure no one was still alive who had seen them.

The SEALs patrolled south to the extraction point. Hank gave the word, and Brookwater operated the radio. "Bravo Six, Hornet One."

"Go Hornet One," came the immediate reply.

"Bravo Six, we're ready."

"Roger, Hornet One, enroute."

In about a minute they could hear but not see the boat. After a few tense moments Hank picked it up in the Starlight and talked them to shore.

"Turn port ten degrees, Bravo Six," he saw the boat correct its course. "Steady, you're on us now, Six."

As the boat nosed up to the shore Hank hoisted Xung to his shoulder. He waded out into the river and threw the man into the stern. With everyone on board and accounted for they RPC headed for home.

Hank looked at his squad. They were not out of danger yet. But at this point security was not as tight, "Good work men. Bravo Zulu," he said. This was the traditional signal in the US Navy dating back to the days of signal flags that meant 'well done.'

"That's the way to do a mission," he said.

"Yeah," Vispo drawled as he applied a field dressing, "with our own fucking rules of engagement."

Hank went forward to speak with the cox'n. When he came back Three Toes and Ha Jah were kneeling over the body of K Xung.

"What the hell's goin' on?" Hank demanded.

"Him dead, sir," Y Bli replied. "Hit too hard."

Hank looked closer. He saw the Yards had carved 'Sat Cong' on the man's chest with their knives. Ha Jah was holding the bloody right ear of the dead VC enforcer in his hand.

"Shit!" Hank exploded and kicked the body. "You got off too easy, you sorry fucker!" he turned to Three Toes. "The ARVN would have killed him anyway, after they were done with him.

Now we won't get a damn bit of information out of him. You didn't get revenge on the bastard, you did him a goddam favor!"

"Him dead already, Lieutenant," Y Bli said. He rolled the corpse's head back and forth with his foot. "Him hit deck wrong, break neck."

Hank wondered if the man had really been dead before the two men had done their cutting. It didn't matter now and he didn't really care.

"Him good Vee Cee now," Three Toes laughed. His genuine smile of pleasure lit up the night.

***

At daybreak an American helicopter slowly circled the village of Minh Rong to get the villagers' attention.

People came out of their huts rubbing their eyes and wondering what was going on. The Chopper made a pass down the center of the village then hovered high enough they would avoid damage to the huts on the ground.

With the villagers watching a bundle fell from the open door of the helicopter. It thudded to the ground in front of the amazed chief's hut. It bounced once then was perfectly still.

The chief approached the bundle. It was enclosed in a black American body bag.

He slowly pulled the zipper low enough to reveal the face and 'tattoo' of K Xung.

Ken Nanski's Green Berets had no more trouble setting up shop in the hamlet of Minh Rong.

Chapter Four

A shadow passing by the half open shutter to Hank's room caught his eye. At first he thought it was just a cloud passing in front of the bright moon. He even flirted with the idea of it being a tree branch blowing in the breeze.

He focused on that window. It began to slowly open.

His heart pounded, seeming to want to find a way out of his chest. His body tensed as he realized someone was specifically targeting him for an easy kill at a time when he should have been asleep.

Where the hell was that damn Yard that was supposed to be protecting him? No one should be this close. If they were that meant Y Bli may already be dead. Either way he had a problem.

He felt naked lying in his bed in his underwear. The only weapon within reach was his .45 automatic pistol, an arm's length away on his nightstand with a round already chambered.

His eyes could not leave the window even if he'd asked them to. A figure quickly detached itself from the darkness and stood framed in the moonlight coming from the window.

Hank tried to reach for the weapon. His arm would not obey for some reason. Damn! He was a Navy SEAL, not some old woman huddled frightened and alone. It was not possible that he was paralyzed with fear.

The dark figure paused, then slid silently through the window and into the room. Hank was frozen in the bed...an observer to his own death.

What was going on? His arms felt as if they were caught in a huge spider's web. He was entangled in the sticky patterned net.

The hair on his neck was standing up and tingling like mad. Another figure appeared in the window and seemed to glide easily into the room. These two were good, whoever they were. He could not help but admire them as a professional. So far, he had not heard any noise at all.

He could see the two shadowy figures moving toward him. Again, he tried and failed to reach for his weapon. He managed to turn his body but his arms would not obey.

The dark figures were very close. Hank could make out the features of two Vietnamese wearing black pajamas in the dim light.

The closer of the two figures raised his arm. Hank caught the reflection of the moonlight off of the blade of his machete.

As the VC assassin started to bring the machete down toward the SEAL's face Hank let out a scream. He was suddenly free from whatever it was that had kept him still and lunged at the man.

***

Keith Blevins woke instantly. He quickly determined that there was a commotion near Hank's bunk.

He grabbed his shotgun with one hand and threw on the light with the other.

"What the hell's goin' on?" he shouted.

He squinted from the sudden increase in light. He saw Hank tangled up in his sheet. His hands were twisting a narrow, bunched up portion of the sheet. The lieutenant's eyes were clamped closed, and he was screaming something, but none of the noises appeared to form actual words.

"Hank, wake up, dammit!" he shouted.

There was no response, just more of the same unintelligible screaming. "HANK!" he shouted at the top of his lungs.

The SEAL lieutenant suddenly was still. After a moment, he opened his eyes, which blinked repeatedly as he looked around the room. "Ahh, shit," was all he said.

"You okay?" Keith asked. The reading lamp next to Hank's bed had broken when the crate serving as a nightstand was knocked over. Keith was worried that his boss might have hurt himself.

"Just another damn dream," Hank mumbled, "I'll be okay," he said as he reached over for his pistol. It had also hit the floor in the confusion.

He looked so embarrassed that Blevins tried to make light of the situation. "Hank, you remember that time we came back here so drunk that I was loading a round in the chamber before hitting the sack and I blew the overhead light right out through the roof?"

A hint of a smile appeared at the corners of Hank's mouth, "Yeah, Keith, I remember."

"So," Keith waved his hand at the mess, "no big deal."

"Yeah, right," Hank said as he crawled back into bed, "No

big deal."

***

After Blevins turned out the light Hank searched along the wall with his hands. It took him just a moment to find the bottle of Johnny Walker kept tucked up against the side of the hootch.

As he tilted it up for a deep drink, he prayed that this time he would be able to drink enough to get him to sleep. He also hoped this time he could stay dreamless.

***

Hank heard the commotion by the dock a minute before Y Bli came running up, "Lieutenant, Lieutenant, Nungs coming!"

He quickly followed the Montagnard who was already heading back to the river. "What the hell are...Nungs? Is that what you said?"

The Montagnard nodded with no sign of his normal smile, "Yes, Nungs. Very bad men. Have no honor, not like my people. Sometimes Army use them anyway."

Hank made his was to the front of the crowd consisting of Vietnamese, Marines, Montagnards, and Americans that had gathered by the dock. He found Lanny Vispo, Chester Hack and Keith Blevins point an assortment of small arms at three Chinese-looking tribesmen in a sampan. Off to the side Dan Slade and his M-60 were ready. The additional weapons were not necessary as two fifty caliber machine guns covered the waterfront at all times. Hank understood that his men carried them as a matter of daily habit. They all felt more comfortable with them than they ever would without them.

The ludicrous amount of firepower did not seem to faze these men in the small boat. They stared defiantly at the shore and the men pointing all the hardware at them. The men were stocky and heavily muscled for Vietnamese. Their features were more Chinese in nature, only with darker skin. These were hard men, whoever they were. There did not appear to be any intention on their part to back down.

"What do you want?" Hank called out as he stepped onto

the dock and the sampan crept forward.

"Are you the commanding officer?" the Nung in the bow insisted. He spoke with precision. He was bare chested and wore a dark green knee length wrap around skirt that came went down to his knees. On his head was a green hat, of sorts, resembling a turban. The man directly behind him was similarly dressed but without the headwear. The man in the stern of the sampan with a pole to steer the boat wore a khaki safari jacket and a loincloth made of the same green material the other men wore.

"Yes I am," Hank answered. "What do you want?"

Instead of an answer the man grabbed a pole protruding from a bamboo basket in the bottom of the sampan. The SEALs who were holding the weapons had them in firing position at light speed. If this turned out to be a suicide attack, their lieutenant was in serious trouble.

Instead of an attack, he found himself face to face with a severed head of a Vietnamese male. It had been crudely hacked from the owner's body. The neck was hung in tatters where the pole had been inserted. The left eye had been gouged out. There was a large amount of blood caked on the cheek that Hank guessed must have been done while the man was still alive. Corpses did not bleed. The contorted facial muscles were frozen in an expression of pain and horror.

. It made for a gruesome sight. Though his first instinct was to recoil, Hank did not react outwardly in any fashion; and as a result he could sense the man's disappointment.

"It is Hoa," Y Bli whispered from Hank's elbow.

"I know," Hank answered. He finally realized why the safari jacket stuck out in his mind. For the first time he saw the pearl handled .45 stuck in the waistband of the Nung leader. It had been Hoa's prized possession, as well as his trademark.

"The men with green faces can not find him, no one can find him, but Tuk-Ba find him," the Nung boasted point his thumb at his chest. "We find him, we kill him." His speech was followed by a staccato, nervous sounding laugh, although the man appeared to be anything but nervous.

The Nung leader grabbed the head by the hair and pulled it off the pole. It made a sucking sound as he held it aloft and shook it. "You fail, so government men, they send us. Now we go and kill rest of his men. You stay out of our way, we do job for you." He pointed toward Y Bli at Hank's elbow, "You should hire real men, not these little mice."

"The Montagnards are number one around here," Hank answered. He was determined not to let this arrogant loudmouth get a rise out of him and gain face at his cost. "They do their fighting like men, and do not feel the need to run around chattering about it like women. How was to be captured for questioning. He is no good to us like that. You keep him."

Tuk-Ba's face darkened momentarily at the implied insult as well as the open rebuke at his manhood. He chose not to reply in kind. "Mah!" he spat. He carelessly tossed Hoa's head back into the basket. He gestured with his right hand as the man in the stern guided them away from the dock.

"You stay out of our way," Tuk-Ba called back when the sampan had reached a safe hundred-meter distance, then he laughed his odd nervous laugh.

Hank turned his back and made a point to ignore him.

"Well," Keith Blevins commented, "That was certainly over dramatic."

Hank turned to Y Bli, "Who and what the hell are they?"

"They are very bad," Y Bli repeated, "They…" he struggled for the right word in English, "Mercenaries. No honor. Fight for who pay them most. They take eye out of enemy to show those who pay them how…fierce they are."

"Good way to get paid on time," Hank said dryly

"Yeah, but who hired em?" Blevins asked.

"That's the big question," Hank replied. That was a question that was hurting his professional pride. Someone hadn't wasted any time in deciding the SEALs were not going to get Hoa anytime soon. Whoever it was had sent these arrogant sons of bitches to spread havoc in their sector. That could only be described as bullshit.

"And it is a question I am damn well going to get an answer to," Hank promised.

As he turned to walk back to the ops hootch he caught some glares from the VNMCs. He realized that he had let Tuk-Ba goad him into saying something unwise after all. He should never have called the Montagnards "number one" in front of the Vietnamese.

Fuck. He would have to find a way to repair the damage, and soon. There was enough resentment in the camp without him adding to it.

*****

There was one nice thing. The SEALs would not have to chase down a bastard with a well-organized set of guerrillas. It was also an organization that knew the SEALs were coming for him, deep in their own territory.

"The Army Special Forces use the Nungs a lot in their CIDGs," Beebe explained. "When the Green Beanies go in and organize a village there are always still sympathizers in the place. They use the Nungs as bodyguards, just like we use the Montagnards. They've done it with some reasonable success. These guys appear to be loyal, although there is a lot of static with the AVRNs and the Yards. They also use the Nungs if there's something that's just too bloody to risk our people on – like this thing with Hoa. No way was I sending you back after him, at least not anytime soon. It would have been far too risky. These guys will do anything – and I mean anything – as long as the price is right. The CIA plumbers up at the Consulate in Danang hired the Nungs to get Hoa, and you know how that group works. In their opinion we didn't have a need to know, so we didn't know."

"Well we know now. I guess our need changed when they came sailing into camp and raising a ruckus," Hank pointed out.

"Well, they shouldn't have done that. This Tuk-Ba is an especially arrogant bastard. Arrogant, but very good," Beebe said.

"Where do these guys come from?" Hank asked, "They look Chinese."

"I'm no anthropologist," Beebe said, "But it's pretty obvious the Nungs have some Chinese blood. There are a few tribes of them around here and some more in Laos – that is another reason the plumbers prefer them. I'll call Danang and tell them to keep their Tuk-Ba out of your hair-- that is unless he has something constructive to offer."

"Thanks, Commander."

"So, off to Saigon?"

"Yes sir. Shirl's comin' over in a few weeks. I gotta go up to the Naval Support Facility and get the paperwork all squared away," Hank said. "I'm just there overnight, flyin' up now, and I'll be back here tomorrow."

"Good. Try to relax a little while you're there. Listen, I've got a restaurant you should check out. It's called La Parisian. It's a bit off the beaten track, but you can't beat the food."

"Great."

At the Vung Tau airfield, Dan Slade was waiting for him as his wife was coming over the same time as Shirl.

"You get everything straightened out about those damn mercenaries showin' up at our camp?" Slade asked.

"Yeah," Hank answered. "Forget them; let's go take care of our women."

"Roger that!"

Chapter Five

As soon as he stepped out of the old but reliable World War II C-47 "Goonie Bird" at the Vung Tau airport, Hank was greeted by an excited Keith Blevins, "Hank, we gotta big problem."

"What's going on, Keith?"

"An Engineman 3rd Class named Sidney Sasser from the boat crews was found dead in his hootch last night. They found heroin, and all the necessary gear to shoot up with," Blevins explained.

"The guy who just transferred in?" Hank asked.

"The very same," Keith confirmed.

"You sure it was heroin?" Hank demanded not wanting to believe it.

"Doc Padget says it is," Blevins replied.

"Damn," Hank mumbled.

"That's not all," Blevins continued, "I immediately notified Beebe about Sasser's death, and now we got two NIS [Naval Investigative Service] guys nosin' around. They wanna talk to you."

"Great, just great," Hank said disgustedly. He was mad at two things, the least of which was the annoyance this would cause him. "What a waste," he said aloud as he wondered if he shouldn't have noticed something was wrong with the man. He should have noticed, despite the fact that welfare of the boat crews was not his immediate responsibility. The security leak was still distracting him from other important aspects of his job.

***

Joseph Olah had a cop's deep suspicion of things he couldn't explain. There was a lot of that in this bizarre outpost as far as he was concerned. These men were not normal GIs and all acted like criminals with something to hide.

"There's something goin' on here," he said and saw his partner, Waller, roll his eyes. Olah realized his partner had probably heard him say that a hundred times that afternoon alone.

"Well," said Waller timidly, "Lieutenant Dillon will be here shortly. Let's just be patient and see what he has to say."

Olah looked at him with scorn. To him Waller was just a paper pusher. He was the kind of guy who only cared about putting in his minimum time and moving on to collect his government pension.

"I'm tired of hearing about this Dillon character. Blevins was in charge while he was gone. He should be able to handle something simple like this. This stonewalling pisses me off. Since when can we be told enlisted quarters are off limits to us in the investigation of a non-combat death? That's bullshit."

Olah looked over his shoulder and saw the four men Blevins had talked to before boarding the boat. They were still hovering around watching their every move. Just for fun he took a few steps toward the enlisted men's hootch. These watchers nonchalantly positioned themselves in his path. He grinned knowingly at them, and then went right back to being annoyed.

***

During the ride in the RPC back to base camp, Blevins filled Hank in on the routine things that had happened in his absence. With the briefing complete, the subject returned to that of the men from the Naval Investigative Service, "These guys are gonna cause some trouble, Hank. They don't know what we do, and that pisses them off."

"Don't worry about that," Hank assured him. "If they try to interfere, or we get in a pissing match, those civilians'll find out real quick who's got the most pull out in the boonies. It ain't them."

The NIS was not staffed with active duty military personnel. They were civilian government employees with a GS number instead of a rank. Most had some sort of intelligence background. The best ones Hank had met usually came from the FBI or the Secret Service.

As they came around the bend and approached the camp the first thing that caught Hank's eye was the South Vietnamese Flag. It was yellow with three horizontal red stripes. The SEALs had a saying inspired by the color scheme: 'What isn't yellow is red,' which pretty much summed up how they felt about the Vietnamese.

"I'd give a month's pay to cut that thing in half and replace it with Old Glory," Hank grumbled.

"I know what you mean," Keith agreed, "but it is their base, and we're really not supposed to be here in the first place."

"I'm starting to think that is an understatement," Hank shot back.

The RPC had no sooner tied up against the tires used as fenders on the rickety pier the Boat Support Unit had fashioned from fifty-five gallon drums and wood planks, when Hank saw the two NIS men coming toward him.

He quickly sized them up. The taller of the two had that look about him that said, 'I'm in charge here.' He was a good sized, well-built man of over six feet, and an economical way of moving that told Hank he had some physical prowess, at least.

The shorter man was somewhat older and about forty pounds overweight. He was having some trouble keeping up with his partner's quick pace.

"Lieutenant Dillon?" the athlete demanded.

"That's me," Hank said.

"I'm Joseph Olah, with the Naval Instigative Service," he introduced himself and pushed his hand forward with his ID open. "This is Ted Waller, also with NIS," he said indicating the other man.

"I heard you were here," Hank told him. "I just got in from Saigon."

"Yes, well while you were on R&R, one of the men on your base here overdosed on heroin," Olah stated flatly. "I've been cooling my heels while your men have been obstructing my investigation."

Hank was instantly annoyed, he held his temper for the moment, "Not quite," he said shortly. "If you want to talk to me, let's go to the Operations Hootch where it's a little more secure. You people in the NIS do understand security from what I have been told."

Without looking to see if they were following Hank turned and set a quick pace for the Operations Hootch.

When he entered the building Hank went to the desk and sat behind it. He let the two investigators arrange their own seating from the chairs scattered around the room.

Waller was still puffing and sweating from the effort of the walk to the hootch when Hank started the interview. "I understand that Sasser, a repair man from the boat crews, was found dead. Do I have that right?"

"That's right. That's why we are here. You understand this is the routine in such cases as this," Olah answered. "Commander Beebe told me to work directly with you while we are here," he said asserting his position of authority.

Hank was not unfamiliar with, or impressed by the tactic. He knew exactly what his position was with Beebe, "Good," he said tersely. "I hope you will. You will have to do so because some places in this camp are restricted areas."

"Restricted?" Olah parroted, "What for? We're so far out in the boonies, who gives a fuck?"

Hank stared at him a moment, the said calmly, "I don't know exactly what you'll be doing, but if you need anything, you let me know, okay?"

"We'll need to talk to some of your men," Olah said soberly. He had no idea how this interview suddenly had turned tables and became a referendum on him.

"That's fine," Hank said. "Just let me know who as well as when, and I'll set it up for you."

"You'll have that list shortly," Olah told him.

Hank stood up and extended his hand. It was the least unfriendly way he could think of to signify that he was done with this meeting. He could afford to be cordial now that he had let Olah know exactly what the pecking order was around here.

The three men shook hands, and the two NIS agents headed for the door. Just as they were about to exit, Hank stopped them short for just an instant.

"Just stay out of the restricted areas," he reminded them. His tone was mild, but Hank knew just how mad this would make the cop. It was unnecessary, but fun all the same. After his trip to Saigon he had developed an intolerance to some REMFs [Rear Echelon Mother Fuckers] like this guy.

Olah went through the screen door mad enough to attack the next person he saw.

***

"He'd been using for some time. He was hiding it by shooting up between his toes." Hospitalman 1st Class Byron 'Doc' Padget reported to Hank.

Doc was thirty-three years old and looked every day of it, plus a few extras. Doc was the 'old man' of the SEALs. He was six feet one, made of solid bone and muscle. Most of the time he kept to himself; with reading and drinking as his two favorite pastimes. He did not speak often, but when he did, the men all listened. They respected his years of experience. Doc had been in for fourteen years. He had been awarded the Bronze Star and two Purple Hearts in his time with the 1st Marine Division in Korea. Hank had assigned him to Blevins' squad to help the young ensign, the hope being that he would be a stabilizing influence.

"My guess is that he picked up the habit in the States. He probably brought enough shit with him to last until just recently," Padget explained. "The challenge is that by the time dope gets to a junkie in the States it's pretty much diluted. It takes a bigger hit to get high. The stuff we found in his gear is light brown, and my guess is it's close to a hundred percent dope. The poor kid got himself a much bigger rush than he bargained for."

"Chief, how the hell does a guy do this right under your nose?" Hank demanded of Chief Bosun's mate Bill Pfaff.

The Chief was in charge of the fourteen men of the Boat Support Unit assigned to the outpost. He had been in the Navy for eighteen years. He knew everything that could be known about river craft and how to keep them moving. For once, the short, burly man was without a cigar hanging from the corner of his mouth. He did have his typical cap perched pretty far back on his head.

"I dunno, Lieutenant," he said nervously fingering the knife he always wore in a sheath on his belt. His usual gruff, brash manner had been replaced with a more subdued demeanor on this occasion. "We needed a mechanic on account of Donoghue's malaria, and Sasser had just come in from 'Dago. I was told he was a hot-shit mechanic. I don't know if somebody was just looking to transfer their problems to somebody else. I can't complain about any work he ever did. He was a moody guy, but so what?" Pfaff shrugged. "I ain't runnin' a charm school. None a' the other guys'll admit to noting anything either."

"Whatever," Hank said shortly. "This is bullshit and attention we just don't need. Now we got civilians running around the camp. Most military guys don't even know we exist. You've been to Vung Tau; they sell this shit on the street corner like the Good Humor Man sells ice cream. If this is gonna be a problem, I gotta know about it. I need you to keep an eye out on your crews for this kinda crap, got it?"

"Yes sir," the Chief answered plainly.

"Doc, I don't think we got a lot to worry about with our men. Despite that, I'm depending on you to keep an eye out."

"Right, sir."

"Okay, dismissed. I've had it up to here with this topic."

***

Hank spent the next few hours getting a handle on what had been going in the camp. He read all the readiness reports, intelligence data, and then he filled out reports on the effectiveness of their weapons and tactics. The experimental nature of their mission meant there was a constant evaluation and assessment of their performance. As he made his way through the endless pile of paperwork he could not shake the feeling that something was wrong. There was something missing. What was it?

Then it hit him. He had not seen Three Toes since he got back. This was odd, but not alarming…yet. Y Bli was really only obligated to watch over Hank during the night. The US Government had spent a lot of money to ensure Lieutenant Dillon could take care of himself during his waking hours.

Nevertheless, Hank felt naked without Y Bli on his heels. He had gotten used to the comfort of knowing the tough little Montagnard was around and always watching.

Hank saw Vispo walking by and called him over. The lanky SEAL casually came into the hootch. "What's up, Lieutenant?"

"Same shit different day," Hank replied. "How's the side healing up?"

"Doc Padget says the dressing can come off in a couple of days," Vispo drawled. "I'll be as good as new so Victor can try to take another piece outta me."

Hank grinned. Vispo was a nonconformist. As a result he always called the Viet Cong 'Victor.' The typical nickname of Charlie came from the military jargon for VC or Victor Charlie. Vispo told everybody that as close as he had been to Charlie, he had earned the right to call him by his first name.

"That's why they pay you the big bucks Gunner. By the way, you seen Three Toes hangin' around?" Hank asked casually.

Lanny thought about it. "No, I guess I haven't seen him since right after Mr. Blevins' mission briefing," then he grinned, "Am I your blood brother's keeper?" he asked dramatically.

"Go on, get outa here," Hank said laughing.

"Okay boss, if you say so. But if you need somebody to watch your back, you let me know."

Hank glared as Vispo retreated quickly.

***

That evening after chow as dusk settled on the camp Hank lay resting in his bunk. He was enjoying the relative cool of the rare dip in the temperature below ninety-five degrees. Hardison banged on his screen door, "Lieutenant, we got trouble brewing with those civilians."

Hank had just rounded the corner of the enlisted SEALs hootch when Olah came sailing through the screen door. He was accompanied by a loud crash as he knocked the door off its hinges. He fell into a heap at Hank's feet. Blood was oozing from the corners of his mouth.

Lanny Vispo, who had picked him up and thrown him from the hootch after punching him in the mouth, appeared in the doorway. He was waiting to see if the investigator was going to press the issue.

Olah scrambled to his feet, wiped the blood from his chin, and mumbled something about all the weapons he had seen in the hootch. In the regular Navy enlisted quarters did not look like an arsenal.

Hank grabbed a handful of the NIS man's shirt and brought him closer. He put his face in Olah's like a drill instructor and shouted at the man as loud as he could, "Forget what you saw asshole! What are you doin' here anyhow? That's a restricted area. If you keep it up, this whole damn camp is gonna be a restricted area as far as your civilian ass is concerned. You get your business taken care of ASAP, and get the fuck out of here. You got off to a bad start with me the minute I met you, and you have done nothing to make it better since. Now get back to your quarters!"

With that, Hank pushed the man away from him, turned his back, and strode off.

Olah just stood shaking with anger, fists clenched at his sides.

***

At 2300, Hank inspected the men of the Second Squad who were about the head out on a mission. Blevins and three others were conducting a reconnaissance in the area just east of the mouth of the Cua Lom River. It had been reported by the local friendlies that a large sea-going junk was lying at anchor with small boats shuttling cargo to the beach.

Satisfied with the readiness of the troops, Hank turned again to the mission leader. "Find out what's goin' on, Keith. Take a good look-see but don't start anything," Hank cautioned him. "Get in and out as fast as you can. If there's anything to the rumors, we'll go in later and do it up right," Hank knew Blevins would want to mix it up if he saw the chance, and thought it was their only chance to interdict the supply route.

"Remember the rules of engagement," he said, "No shootin' unless they shoot at you."

"I got it Hank. No problem," the young man said confidently.

"Okay, just watch your ass. We know there's been a lot of activity in that area."

Blevins was finally boarding the RPC when Hardison and Bostic appeared, hustling Joseph Olah between them. "Look what we found spyin' on ya' from the brush, Lieutenant," Bostic called.

"What the fuck are you doing down here?" Hank bellowed.

Olah seemed determine to bluff his way out of this. "What kind of setup you got here Dillon?" His tone was one of victory. He apparently thought he had caught Hank with his hand in the cookie jar. "You look ready to storm the palace in Saigon with all these weapons. Green faces, my, my. Who the hell are you guys?"

His questioning was met by silence. It was obvious that Olah had no idea who the SEALs were, or what their mission was. These facts appeared to bother him to no end.

Hank decided to bait him further, "I could tell you, Mr. Olah, but then I would have to kill you." It was the standard SEAL brush off when anyone asked too many questions. Commander Beebe had not told Olah anymore than he had to. He relied on Hank to handle it the same way.

Olah did not see the humor in Hank's statement, "I know a lot of drugs go up and down these rivers at night. Is that what you guys are up to? A little moonlighting?" he growled.

That was about all Hank was going to take, "Get him outta here," he said.

Bostic put Olah in an arm lock that the SEALs knew to be far from comfortable. Hardison reached through from behind and grabbed him in the balls. They marched him off into the darkness with the NIS man walking gingerly on his toes.

"You just flushed your career, Lieutenant!" Olah shouted before Jasper applied a little more pressure to an area of his body that doesn't appreciate pressure and he stopped yelling.

Hank smiled. At the moment it didn't seem like he had just been threatened. He was out here in the boonies with Charlie increasing the supply levels of their people in the field. If a better supplied enemy wasn't bad enough that same enemy seemed to know the SEALs every move long before they made it.

Hank looked at Keith and said, "Gosh, I sure hope the mean man doesn't get me transferred away from this soft duty."

Blevins snorted in reply, then said, "There's something to this guy we are missing."

Hank thought about it for a moment, "You might be right. Sasser could buy dope on any street corner in Vung Tau. Why be so persistent investigating the rest of us? Some people call the NIS the 'Admirals' Gestapo.'"

Every officer in the Navy understood that at flag level careers were very politicized. NIS would sometimes be used as weapons to see who gets the next star. Maybe someone somewhere was upset that they don't know what is happening at this camp.

Then he shifted gears quickly, "Keith, forget about that. He's out of our hair tomorrow, and you have other things to focus on, like not getting your ass shot off."

"Roger that, Hank, roger that."

Chapter Six

"If you ever do something like this again you will need a promotion to be authorized to write traffic tickets in Washington. Is that understood?" Commander Beebe said as calmly as if he had been giving his dinner order to a waiter.

"Yes, sir," Olah answered. His face was bright red. He was determined to save some of his dignity from this situation. He figured out that most of it was about slipping away fast.

"Right. Now get your ass out of my office. I have real things to take care of, things that are much too important to be interrupted by a G-7 whose head is too big for his shoulders," Beebe picked up the phone and dialed a number. He looked up as he finished dialing, "Are you still here?"

Olah left as quickly as was practical. He felt as though his face was on fire. He knew he had just received the ass chewing of a lifetime, and it was delivered by a real professional.

Before he could get off of the SEAL base camp Olah had figured out that he had screwed up pretty badly. He started this investigation with his eyes and ears closed, and yet somehow his mouth had stayed wide open. He treated people the same way a small town thug cop treats kids who are late for school. It was as though he learned nothing all those years working in Washington DC, and there he had worked on one for the most politicized police forces in the country. He would be lucky if he only got one more ass chewing from his boss in Saigon. He guessed it would probably go higher than that.

Olah had checked in with Beebe, as protocol dictated, and had run, sprinting, into a chainsaw. But something told him that Beebe would let the matter die where it now lay. Whatever Dillon was up to, it must be important enough to the Navy that they wanted to actively avoid scrutiny. If there was any criminal activity going on, they must think the mission was more important than whatever crimes, if any, were being committed.

That really bothered him. There was something very wrong going on at that camp. The people that ran it were just not what you would normally find. He had been told that Dillon's job was to protect the South Vietnamese camp while assisting the local villagers in defending themselves against the Viet Cong operating in the area. The men he saw at the camp were not men on defense. They were well trained killers. The Navy just didn't have units like that.

There was a flood of drugs pouring into the cities. The demand had soared due to the influx of foreigners – both military and civilians – into the area. Much of it was transported by river traffic. Lieutenant Dillon was not only perfectly placed to take advantage of lots of that, but he was also certainly up to something that just wasn't in the Navy's mission. Something was wrong.

Joseph Olah had been, until six months ago, a detective third grade in the Washington DC Police Department. He was the son of a West Virginia coal miner who had gone to the big city to make fame and fortune, or lacking fame certainly fortune. Mostly, he was happy to not be a miner. He had done some of what he set out to do. He completed a Bachelor's Degree while working as a cop, and he had married a beautiful girl he had met in college. Promotions had come rapidly for the young policeman. He even seemed to be on the fast track for an eventual command position.

That was until a drunk driver had crossed the centerline of traffic. Cathy Olah's little red Corvair was turned into scrap metal in an accident that killed her instantly.

Joe's life had been destroyed. When he did return to work, he had not been able to work up any enthusiasm for figuring out which junkie had killed the other to get a quick fix. He also could have cared less about tracking down boyfriends who expressed jealousy by murdering their girlfriends. He had lost passion for many things in his life.

Captain McBain, Joe's police force mentor, knew that the military investigative services were looking for men with investigative backgrounds. Being a good mentor he eventually convinced Olah to apply.

So, like many of the Foreign Legionnaires who died in French Indochina in the decade prior, he decided to try to leave his troubles behind. This decision had landed him in Vietnam.

For some months now Olah was tracking a criminal only known as 'the Fixer.' He was the man to see if you needed to get ahold of some contraband items, including weapons, information, or drugs, especially heroin.

Some rumors had the Fixer as a high ranking Vietnamese

official who played both sides of the fence. Still other rumors said he was a well-placed member of the American military. Perhaps he was a man with access to both the supply lines of the drug trade and also with some control over the distribution of American supplies.

In Olah's mind, Hank Dillon fit that description perfectly.

To be fair he wasn't the only American military member that fit the description. However, none of the others had interfered in the investigation of the NIS into a drug overdose. These others had also not run a maverick operation deep in the bush with little or no apparent oversight from their superiors.

Olah really disliked loose ends. He had a hunch the solution to his problems was somewhere in Dillon's base camp. He had to figure out how to ensure that today's ass chewing was not the last word in this investigation.

***

Hank was writing reports when he heard the RPC returning with Blevins' squad.

He stepped out of the hootch and found himself face to face with Three Toes, "Where have you been Y Bli?" Hank snapped.

The Montagnard was taken by surprise by the abruptness of the question. He hesitated, and then answered, "My mother very sick. I go home, take medicine for her I get from pecker checker...I mean Doc Padget."

Hank grinned at the slip. He still found it funny how those locals who truly liked the Americans had a tendency to pick up their slang. It was a paradox. This was an intensely proud culture in which respect and tradition meant everything. However, many of them, sometimes influential ones, tried very hard to emulate Americans.

Hank was going to yell at Y Bli for his absence but decided against it. He would not complain to Lieutenant Ngo either. There was enough strain in the camp between the Yards and the VNMCs without adding more to it by complaining. Besides, between those two choices, he considered Y Bli the better man. It would be better to just let the whole thing drop.

He would do one thing, he would check out Y Bli's story

with Doc Padget.

"I hope she's okay," Hank said to him. Y Bli said no more as Hank headed to the dock.

Keith Blevins was grinning from ear to ear as he climbed out of the boat, "Hank! I think we hit the jackpot!" he blurted as Hank asked how it went.

Hank looked around to see who was listening, then motioned over his shoulder towards the camp, "Ops hootch, now," he ordered.

Maybe something was finally going right.

***

"The junk was gone when we arrived," Blevins reported. "So we inserted into the area and patrolled parallel to the beach. We found a path already beaten down leading into the bush. We worked out way inland for about a half a klick, and bingo there it was.

"Hank, we were on top of it before we knew it. The camouflage was THAT good. The jungle was thick, and the liana vines ran from tree to tree almost like someone planned it that way as a camouflage net. There is no way anyone could ever spot this place from the air. They did an amazing job of hiding the stuff. We almost walked right past it without seeing it."

Keith shook his head as he continued, "This place is loaded. It has weapons, ammunition, and even a few rockets. They got bags of rice and boxes with Russian and Chinese writing on 'em. They even got American C-rats; now how do you figure that?"

"I tell ya', this place has got everything. They must have been stashing it for a long time. Right under our damn noses! There's enough food and firepower to sustain a large force for a reasonable amount of time. Hank, they could do an amazing amount of damage without the need for a resupply."

Hank interrupted Blevins rambling, "What about security? What've they got?"

Blevins shook his head, "I couldn't believe it. The damn place is lightly guarded. I think they depend on the camouflage instead of manpower. There couldn't been more than six men walking the perimeter, and they were careless as hell. There are three hootches on the north side of the area. One looks to be guards' quarters. The other two are probably there for the coolies who move the shit around. Those two were empty last night."

"They don't seem to be expecting company. Why should they be?" Blevins continued. "The way that place is hidden, and it is in their back yard. I bet the got setups like this all over the Delta. Look's like Charlie's getting ready to stir things up. But this place, this place is just askin' to be plucked."

"Well then," Hank answered, "Let's pluck it."

Keith grinned, "I was hoping you'd say that."

***

That very afternoon Hank went to go see Warrant Officer Warden to make sure his bird was ready to fly. "Our ass is going to be out in the shit soon, and we're gonna need it."

Then he made the trip to Vung Tau to brief Command Beebe. He needed to hear Blevins' report first hand as well as review what he intended to do about the discovery. This was not necessary, Hank had the authority to act on his own, but with politics being what they were in Vietnam, he felt CYA from time to time to be prudent. It made sense for his career to make sure the ROEs were not going to change in between when he left on this mission and when he returned.

That night Hank and Keith worked late into the night. They drew up a plan to do a rapid and complete demolition job on Charlie's jungle warehouse.

The following day Hank was very busy around the camp. He wanted to make sure all preparations were going well. He also wanted to triple check the RPC and chopper to ensure they were as close to 100% as possible.

Y Bli made himself more visible than usual. He must have sensed Hank's displeasure at his previous absence. It may also have been because he knew something was up. He wanted to be sure Lieutenant Dillon did not forget about him while planning a mission that must include killing 'Vee Cee.'

As Hank made his rounds, he saw Lieutenant Ngo coming toward him, "Lieutenant Dillon, I need a word with you."

"What's up?" Hank asked.

"Why have you not been using me and my men? That is why we are here," Ngo demanded. "You have no reason to suspect our loyalty."

His directness was confusing, and then just pissed Hank off, "I haven't needed you Lieutenant," he snapped. "You know we use as few men as possible in the field. We will not include men on a mission just for political reasons. That just gets people killed, and I don't do that anymore. Now, if you have no other questions, I have work to do."

Ngo had nothing else to say. The young SEAL officer could tell the VN commanding officer was still not satisfied. Tough shit.

Both Y Bli and Ngo knew a mission was in the works. It was no mystery. Even though neither had a role to play it was obvious the SEALs were planning something. Before a mission, the tempo of the camp changed dramatically. Men moved faster, there was more conversation. Activity increased as everyone got their own assignments ready to go.

Nothing was said directly. Anyone familiar with the camp had to be blind to not see that the men with the green faces were getting ready to go out on the prowl.

***

Hank held the mission briefing at 1600 hours in the Ops hootch. It was a simple plan. Hank and his squad, along with Blevins and four of the men from his squad would insert and patrol the way to the target area. If everything went according to plan they would set explosive charges, then get out the same way they went in. The four men of Blevins' squad would each set a Claymore ambush site along the route. They would man it until the last man of Hank's squad passed them on the way out to the extraction point. At that point they would set trip wires and follow behind, taking up position as rear guard. If Charlie was in pursuit, he would have a hellish surprise once they reached the Claymores.

The M-18A1 Claymore was a directional mine containing somewhere between seven and eight hundred steel ball bearings in a plastic shell. Once detonated, the ball bearings were propelled in the direction desired by a charge of over a pound of C-4 military explosive. Anyone caught in its field of fire was cut down like grass.

If things really fell apart that would mean that the SEALs were unable to extract along the planned route. If that was the case, Warden's chopper, still on loan from SOG, would be airborne one hour after the SEALs left the camp and orbit an area five miles west of Cat Lo. That would put their helicopter rescue just three miles south of the target area. The other two men of Blevins' squad, Hardison and Bostic, would be riding along to assist in the chopper in case of a hot extraction.

Hank decided it was a good plan. He hoped he would still think so in the morning.

***

Dockside at 2300, Dillon and Blevins inspected the men one last time. Each had his preferred weapons, grenades, extra ammunition, K-Bar knife, flares in case of emergency extraction, and all of the other usual mission paraphernalia.

Each man in the squad also carried two MK-26 HBX sack charges. The MK-26 was made up of eight 2.5 pound case blocks of HBX explosive which were fitted with a timing device.

One sack charge was enough to level a good sized warehouse. A dozen placed next to ammunition and explosives would be enough to create quite the show.

Nate Bowman, Machinist Mate 2nd Class, and Fred 'Tuck' Shantuck, Quartermaster 3rd Class, were the replacements for Ayotte and Bush. They were given a few extra instructions as this was their first mission against the enemy, rather than just a 'mock' enemy for training.

"You'll do fine," Hank assured them. "If I didn't think so, you wouldn't be in the boat."

Also along for the ride was Doc Padget. The sixth man was a morale booster just by his mere presence. All of the SEALs knew battlefield first aid, but it was reassuring to have him along for the ride.

Doc always carried two pistols, a .38 revolver in a shoulder holster, and a .45 automatic on his hip. He also had several hand grenades, a favorite of most SEALs.

After a final equipment check, the team boarded the RPC

and moved off into the night.

***

Slightly over one hour later the RPC passed the mouth of the Cua Lom River. No sooner had they done so than Keith Blevins began scanning the shore with the Starlight scope.

"There it is," he whispered to Hank, "There's the spot."

"Good," The boat moved further west and down the shoreline. They also took the time to make two false insertions. Suddenly, according to plan, the RPC headed back east to the spot Blevins had pointed out.

Hank wanted one more communications check before insertion, "Buzz Saw High, this is Reaper. Do you copy?"

Warden answered immediately, "That's a roger, Reaper, copy you five by five. How me?"

"Same same, Buzz Saw, out."

Once they were on land the coms checks would come every fifteen minutes, and always be initiated by the men on the ground. Two clicks on the radio would be answered by two clicks from the boat. The boat would radio check with the chopper using three clicks.

The RPC closed in on the jungle, and on signal all the men went over the side in the proper patrol order like the links of a chain. In a moment, they had disappeared in the darkness. They waited, their weapons off safe. The RPC moved off and soon, hopefully, the jungle noise would return.

The same old feeling came over Hank as he waited in the darkness. It was made up of equal parts fear and excitement. Hank decided he didn't care which one was dominant.

The mosquitoes were on them instantly. It seemed like they must have been drawn to cammo paint. The insects had to be brushed off or they would crawl up the men's noses and ears. It was easy to spot which of the men had been on a mission the next morning. They always had red welts that the oversized Vietnamese mosquitoes left as their calling card.

Blevins took point. He was followed by Hank, Slade with his M-60, and the rest of the squad in patrol order. The practiced routine was to move a few yards, stop, hold breath, listen, patrol again. All the time the mosquitoes were busily sucking the life blood out of them. Good discipline meant no noise. They moved slowly and cautiously watching for booby traps with every step. It was slow, tedious work. They all knew that the first time they let up on procedures that a hundred pound VC cadre was liable to ruin their whole night with his AK-47 assault rifle.

They monotonously checked every inch of the trail for booby traps and found none. Hank wondered if Charlie was that confident or if the men at the storage area had been derelict in their duty. After all, the route had been used just the day before. A lazy squad leader might have decided that there was no hurry in securing the trail.

Nevertheless, Hank, Blevins and Vispo, all of whom had a special skill for finding traps, felt their way forward with caution. All it took was one screw up. One screw up and a man could get himself killed or maimed for life. It would also put the rest of the squad under fire.

As he worked Hank ran over the plan in his head. The best, most successful missions often had the simplest plans. Was this one simple?

They had been patrolling for a half hour when Blevins signaled to stop as he raised the Starlight to his eye. Hank could see they were almost to what appeared to be a slight thinning in the jungle. There was a three-quarter moon. It provided some light, even with the thick jungle canopy.

Hank saw nothing in the direction Blevins was pointing the scope. After a moment, Keith handed him the Starlight and pointed. Hank began a slow sweep. Then he moved the scope back to where he had started. Damn, he had missed it. Covering the mounds of supplies was the best camouflage job he had ever seen.

Hank and Blevins moved closer and watched in silence for ten minutes. In those minutes they observed four armed guards. They ambled back and forth in their line of sight at no specific intervals. They were smoking and talking with one another.

Hank guessed that there were probably a similar number he could not see patrolling on the other side of the supply area. It didn't matter. They were not there to kill guards, just blow up supplies.

Hank and Keith returned to the platoon. They set in motion

the plan they had detailed at the mission brief. Checking their watches, Hank's squad went right, Blevins moved left. In precisely four minutes the men would move into the supply depot. They would attach their sack charges in positions allowing them to do the most damage. Ideally in a spot that would setup a sympathetic detonation.

The fuses were set at thirty minutes. That would allow enough time for the SEALs to get safely away from the blast area, while leaving a short enough time that the chance of their discovery was minimal.

"Kill the guards only if it is necessary to get to the target area," Hank reminded them in a whisper. Speed was of the essence with this many men moving through the target area. The odds of detection were high, and rose every minute the SEALs were on target.

After his squad deployed, Hank checked his watch and moved forward. There was a three to four meter space of light vegetation between his position and the target. He waited and looking to the faint moonlight. Seeing no one, he moved forward as fast as was practical.

In a moment he was surrounded by crates stacked taller than his head. He moved into a corridor of sorts and stopped between a large crate and a stack of smaller ones. The large crate had Russian lettering stenciled on the side. The smaller boxes were labeled in Chinese letters with the numerals 7.62. The boxes had rope handles on their sides. Hank assumed they were filled with ammunition for the AK-47 assault rifles used all over this area.

Hank wedged one of the sacks between the boxes, set the time, checked his watch and moved on. He stopped after moving another twenty meters, and lifted a tarp when he heard a faint rustle to his rear.

Hank froze in place to listen. He heard nothing, but his instincts told him something was there.

He strained his ears. He only heard things he should hear. He couldn't sit here and wait, time was ticking away.

Hank knelt down and was placing the second charge when he heard the noise again, only this time right behind him.

He spun to find a VC guard trying to unsling his weapon which was poorly placed over his head and shoulder.

In one swift motion, Hank dropped the sack, leapt at the man, grabbed him by the throat and threw him to the ground.

As Hank pulled his K-Bar from the sheath on his harness he could see the man's mouth flapping as he tried to scream. He made no noise as Hank was crushing his windpipe.

Hank plunged the knife into the guard's chest. He worked the handle back and forth to inflict maximum damage. He stopped the attack only when he felt the body quiver, then stiffen, and then go limp.

Hank moved his face closer. He wanted to check for signs of life. Then he saw the man's jaw gaping open, his mouth filled with blood from the broken membranes in his neck. The warm blood was running down the man's chin onto Hank's hands which still had a grip on the guard's throat. Hank realized his fingertips had actually pierced the skin on the guard's neck.

He tore his hands away, scrambled quickly to his feet. At the same moment he was knocked sideways into a pile of hard wooden boxes in a hit that drove the breath from his body.

The VC guard was on him before he knew it. It didn't matter; Hank was bigger, stronger and much better trained. He used the man's momentum to roll him over face down, then punch him with all his strength behind the ear.

It was a blow intended to stun. At the same time Hank drove his knee into the guard's back. His right hand was under the man's chin, and his left was pushing the side of his head down. Hank jerked the man's chin up sharply and snapped his neck.

He felt the whole damned world must have heard the neck crack in the night air. Hank moved off the man and waited on all fours, panting like a dog. His heart was pounding like a jackhammer. It felt like his heart was going to burst out of his chest as he gasped for more air.

His adrenalin was racing, making him feel almost high waiting for the next attack to hit him from some unknown direction. At the moment he was ready to take on the whole damn camp alone.

His only challenger was darkness.

He was quickly running out of time and those charges were going to explode one way or the other. Hank quickly set the second charge and made his way at best possible speed back to the jungle rendezvous point. Most of the SEALs were already there. Blevins had taken a headcount.

"All here?" he whispered.

"All but Shantuck," Blevins hissed.

"Shit," Hank cursed. Shantuck was one of the new guys.

Slade and Brookwater were in a position to act as a blocking force at rear security as soon as the group could move.

Damn, Hank realized, there was very little time left before this part of the jungle was going to become a crater.

"Come on Doc," Hank whispered. Then he felt someone tug at his arm. It was Bowman, the other new guy.

"Let me go, Lieutenant," the young man hissed.

"Shut the fuck up," Hank snarled. He admired the young man's courage and loyalty but this was a time for experience.

Hank and Doc headed back into the area. They knew from the patrol orders where Shantuck would have headed in. They stopped for a moment to listen. Then they moved toward the supply boxes leaving about three feet between them.

They had a need for speed. Hank used the red flashlight but as little as possible. Doc touched his arm and pointed. Hank aimed the light in the direction of the dark form on the ground. Kneeling they discovered it was the missing SEAL.

Shantuck was covered in blood. Gore covered the K-Bar still clutched in his fist. As Padget knelt to examine him Hank noticed another crumpled form at the edge of the flashlight's glow. Carefully Hank nudged the sentry's body. He held his K-Bar at the ready. There was no reaction from the still form. Looking closer, he saw that the throat had been torn open. There was no need to worry about this one. He turned his attention back to Doc and Shantuck. Something bothered him and made him turn his attention again to the body of the dead VC.

"Doc," Hank hissed. "Take a look here!"

Padget knelt close to the face of the dead guard, "What the hell? That's one of those Nungs," he said.

"You done with him?" Hank pointed to the fallen SEAL. They could discuss what this all meant at a later time.

"As done as we got time for," Doc said.

They dragged Shantuck quickly into the bush. Once there Hank hoisted him onto his shoulders.

They were running out of time. They had been forced to kill far too many guards. It was only a matter of time before someone noticed they were missing. There was also that small matter of some ticking bombs that were entirely too close given what their capabilities were.

"Move out!" Hank hissed as he and Doc rejoined the others. The SEALs moved quickly. They were less worried about noise now than distance. They still had to be careful, however, so Hank kept up easily, despite the weight of the man on his back.

They were halfway to the extraction when it happened. For several seconds the jungle was as bright as the brightest of white interrogation lamps. The light was quickly followed by a deafening rumble and crash that sounded as though the SEALs had been transported to the middle of a gigantic thunderstorm.

Hank could feel and just hear the rush of movement as the jungle rustled around them being pushed by the shockwave from the explosion.

The SEALs hit the deck as the heat and pressure of the massive explosion went past them. They could hear the secondary explosions as what was left of the VC supplies began joining the chorus.

***

Three miles away in the chopper, Bostic was standing in the doorway. He was jumping up and down beating on Hardison, "Lookit that sonofabitch!" he screamed and laughed. "The whole fuckin' jungle's goin' up! It's like the Fourth of July!"

The men in the chopper had known the approximate timetable of the mission. They had been staring anxiously into the darkness, when suddenly; two acres of jungle had erupted into a ball of light into the night sky. This had been followed by a huge multicolored inferno in the form of a mushroom cloud moving skyward. The stored rockets started streaking in random directions which caused Warden to ease away just a little bit further, just in case.

A few minutes later, Warden got the signal that the SEALs were safely aboard the RPC, and they were free to return to base. "Roger, Reaper," he replied, "Good show."

***

Some of the men began hoo-yahing it up as the RPC headed along the coast. Doc was working on Shantuck who had regained consciousness. Hank heard him tell the young man he was going to be fine. Hank knew he meant it. By now he knew the Doc's tone of voice when he was comforting a man who he knew would die.

"You did good," Hank told the wounded man. "You all did. Bravo Zulu."

"Thanks, Lieutenant," Shantuck croaked.

Hank motioned Blevins off to the side. He told him what he and Doc had found next to Shantuck.

"Holy shit," Keith grinned, "If he got surprised by one of those tough bastards in the dark and lived to tell about it, he's gonna do just fine."

"Yeah," Hank agreed, "But what the hell does it mean?"

"I dunno, Boss. Maybe your Yard was right about those guys," Keith said. "Even if he was, our proof just got scattered for miles."

"We've got to find out if this Nung was part of Tuk-Ba's bunch. If so, we got big trouble. Let's get our Yards and Vietnamese working on it as soon as we get back."

Hank moved to the stern and sat down. He did not speak as he watched the occasional rocket streak off into the night. His hands began to shake as he came down off of the adrenalin high. He hoped the other men didn't notice.

It was a common reaction, but it had never been this strong before. Hank sat in silence as the jungle crept by. He did not want to talk, or join in the celebrating.

Something was happening to him. He was changing. He was afraid it was not for the better.

Chapter Seven

Beebe was not as surprised about the Nung's presence at the ammo dump as Hank thought he would be.

The VC tried to overrun one of the CIDG camps last week," he explained to Hank. "They were not successful in their attempt, and the Fifth took a couple of prisoners. Under interrogation they claimed they got their arms from someone they called, 'the Chinaman.'"

"More likely a Nung," Hank postulated.

"Exactly," Beebe agreed. "Have you seen or heard anything about this Tuk-Ba character since his entrance at your place a while ago?"

"No, but I think maybe we should find out what he's been doing with his time."

"Good idea," Beebe said.

***

Joseph Olah listened carefully to the briefing at the Vietnamese police station. It was being held in a large conference room on the second floor of the three story building on Tran Hung Dao Street.

The police station was the newest building in Vung Tau. It had been built by the French near the end of their time in Indochina. The regular prison cells were on the top floor, but it was the basement of the structure that provoked fear in the citizens of Vung Tau. Knowing about it was enough to make Joe Olah more than a little uncomfortable.

That was the location of the interrogation rooms. There were also some 'special' cells for trouble makers or political types. It was said that at night the Black Mariah would visit. It was an old black American panel truck with the back windows covered in black paint. It would pull into the alley at the back of the building and the bodies of those who had not survived their interrogation would be loaded in the back for disposal.

Olah had received a call from Lt. Nguyen Hu Khoa of the Vung Tau Security Police inviting him to the briefing. He had worked with Khoa before. The man was a bulldog on a case. He actually felt some measure of pity for anyone of whom the man became suspicious.

Joe had often complained about the restrictions they had to conduct police work back in the States. More than once he had fantasized about having the kind of power Khoa routinely exercised. The Vietnamese Lieutenant did not have to worry about the ACLU or other civilian pressure groups that existed to protect criminals and second guess every move a cop made.

Once he had seen the Vietnamese system in action Olah had become disillusioned with excessive police power. It did not mean he wasn't worried about the direction American law enforcement was headed. It merely made him more grateful for the checks and balances back in the USA.

Khoa was barely five feet tall with a heavy lower body. His shape had earned him the nickname of 'The Pear' among the Americans involved with criminal investigations in the area. He was wearing dark trousers and a white shirt. He stood in front of a diagram of a large dwelling with a long point as he gave instructions to the dozen men seated in the room.

Olah was asked to go along on a police raid. They were breaking up the operations at a villa located on a beach east of Vung Tau. The information indicated drugs were being distributed from the house. From there they would head out to various dealers to be sold, primarily, to American troops. That was why at least one member of the American Navy was involved. It was standard procedure to have someone from either NIS or the CID involved if the arrest of an American military member, or members, was a possibility.

With the instructions for the raid complete, Khoa led the men quickly to the back lot. There they piled into unmarked compact cars. On the team were ten uniformed policemen, Khoa and a sergeant in civilian clothes as well as Olah.

Olah rode in the back seat of Khoa's vehicle with the Lieutenant. Khoa showed the NIS man the proper respect. He did not offer anything more that what was required and as a result there was no small talk among the group.

The cars moved quickly east on Cong Ly Street, which was parallel to the ocean. They passed a variety of upscale, expensive residences along with way. Joe knew that lately, people of questionable character had bought many because they had direct access to the ocean. Still others had been purchased by the high class hookers as well as various underworld types whose activities should not be discussed during daylight hours.

Khoa barked a command as he pointed at a beige villa with a red tile roof. Large shrubs and elaborate flower gardens surrounded the house. The driver nodded affirmatively. The car made a sharp turn to the right.

The four car convoy kicked up a large dust cloud as they made their way up the long drive leading to the villa. Khoa's car was the first in the line. The last two cars peeled off and bounced their way across the grass in opposite directions heading for the back of the villa. It was their job to cut off escape for anyone who might be scrambling for the back door.

The policemen piled out of the cars and took up their positions quickly and professionally. Two of the larger cops came forward carrying a five-foot long battering ram. Khoa checked the front door to be sure and found it locked.

There was no question of serving a warrant. They didn't even need legal or probable cause to enter the premises. Law enforcement was certainly different here. It took two huge swings from the battering ram before the oak door sprang open. The wood in the area of the lock splintered with a large cracking noise.

The uniformed police swarmed through the door first. Their job was, apparently, to run through the house shouting and kicking doors open. Olah stayed with Khoa and they walked along the marble floors of the hallway at the end of the foyer until they found a huge central room.

The room was stacked high with crates. The majority of them had English labels. Moments later, they were joined by the sergeant who had been in command of the men who had started in the back of the house. He and Khoa spoke in Vietnamese that was so fast Olah could not understand anything. Olah started examining the boxes.

Joe shook his head as he saw many of these crates still had the US emplaced metal bands strapping them to wooden pallets. It was obvious that the black marketeers had enough connections to be able to have the forklifts at the airbase take these shipments directly from the aircraft and onto the non-US Government truck.

The realization made Olah's pulse quicken. This was a major operation, not some rinky-dink shed full of picked pocket level goods. Despite the size of the operation it didn't seem like they were going to get any important prisoners. Despite that he thought that perhaps, maybe, he could find a clue leading to the 'big fish' still out there somewhere.

Many of the boxes still on pallets also had the shipping document envelopes still taped to the sides. Most of the individual crates had stenciled black lading numbers sprayed on them. Olah started ripping envelopes off the crates and tucking them en masse under his arm. He did this while going crate-to-crate writing down the lading numbers off those without documentation into a notebook.

Khoa walked up, "Good catch, eh?" he gestured to the piles of recovered equipment.

Olah always found it interesting that the Vietnamese officials tended to label everything a wild success. What the actual results were did not really matter it was how they labeled it that mattered. They should work for Congressional candidates, he thought contemptuously.

"I don't see the Fixer," he grunted.

"Ah, well, that, we were never sure if he would be here at this time of day," Khoa said dismissively. "Perhaps we will find something that will lead us to him."

"Perhaps," Olah kept writing.

There was a commotion down the hall. A half a dozen uniformed police were dragging an American serviceman wearing only his boxer shorts and dog tags and two scantily clad Vietnamese women toward them. The American was protesting loudly, as were the obviously stoned women.

"SILENCE!" Khoa barked. Amazingly it worked. Even through the drug-induced haze, the women could see that he was not a man to be questioned.

Olah studied the American. He was struggling to maintain some sense of modesty while standing in his underwear. The man was not heavy, but for a military member was slightly flabby. He could not have been a combat soldier. He was in his early twenties and had blonde hair and a furiously blushing red face.

"What's your name, son?" Olah asked in a surprisingly

civilized manner. Despite the calm nature in which it was asked it was clear that avoiding the question was not an option.

"Sergeant Henry Beckwith, US Air Force, sir," came the timid reply.

"What is your job, Sergeant Beckwith?" Olah asked.

"Assistant service club manager," Beckwith answered.

"That figures," Olah mused. "Lieutenant, I would like a private word with young Mr. Beckwith."

"I do not know if that would be a good idea, Mr. Olah," Khoa objected.

"I'll be fine, thanks," Olah assured him. He knew that his safety was not Khoa's real objection. "Sergeant Beckwith knows he can't outrun a .45 slug while in his underwear, don't you, Sergeant?"

Beckwith nodded furiously.

Olah stepped forward and grabbed him by the arm, "See, he's perfectly willing to cooperate with the authorities. We'll just step right behind these crates, here."

Olah lead a trembling Beckwith between the boxes for about ten yards. He stopped only when he was certain he was out of sight of the Vietnamese.

"Thanks for getting' me away from the gooks, sir," Beckwith was trying to play this cool, thinking that Olah was looking for a payoff.

"That's okay Sergeant, we can't have Vietnamese manhandling Americans. Besides I don't want him to hear what you are going to tell me."

"What's that sir?" Beckwith was gaining confidence.

"Who is the fixer?"

The prisoner turned white instantly, "I don't know. If I did, I don't think it would be worth my life to tell you sir!"

Without warning, Olah sunk his fist into Beckwith's soft belly. He knew, done properly, that it would not leave a mark.

The prisoner sank to his knees and started groveling. Olah grabbed his hair and forced the man's head back.

"Listen, you worthless little piece of shit," he hissed. "You have really stepped in it this time. If you want a free ride back to the States, you tell me who the Fixer is. If you choose not to I will make sure that you won't see your home for a long long long time.

Do you understand?"

Beckwith began crying, "I don't know, sir, I don't know. I'll tell you everything I know...I promise."

"Oh shut up," Olah snapped. "Get to your feet and compose yourself. You don't want to be like this in front of the 'gooks.'"

A sudden thought struck him, "Give me Dillon, or you get some more," he snarled in the man's face.

Beckwith's face was blank, "Who?"

"Never mind," Olah said with disgust. "Let's get the hell out of here. Being alone with you is starting to make me want to vomit."

Beckwith stood up, Olah snapped on the cuffs before leading him back to the others. A Vietnamese male prisoner had been added to the group, "You can be glad you're not that sorry bastard," Olah said seeing the other man's bruised and swollen face.

"Sergeant Beckwith has assured me of his full cooperation," Olah announced.

Khoa looked at him clearly, wondering just how much the big American had found out on his little fishing expedition. "Mr. Dong has promised the same," he smiled ironically. Khoa help up two plastic bags of light brown powder, which Olah recognized as heroin. He had discovered a suitcase that appeared to be full of them, "He is going to help us find out where this came from."

"It's always good to find public minded citizens," Olah said dryly.

***

Olah and the two investigators from the Air Force Criminal Investigation Division spent long sessions with Sergeant Beckwith over the next three days.

Beckwith was left with in an empty room with only a hard folding chair to sit on. From time to time the three interrogators would surround him and fire questions off quickly. They took turns performing good cop/bad cop, then of course there was bad cop/bad cop, and of course the bad cop/nightmare cop.

By the end of the third day Beckwith sat slumped and defeated in the chair. Olah was convinced they had drained every useful bit of information out of him. He did not even look up as Olah entered the room.

"I think that about wraps it up," Olah said cheerfully.

Beckwith looked up in surprise. An expression of gratitude briefly flashed across his face. Olah was almost sorry he would have to dash the man's hope so suddenly.

Almost, but not quite.

"Lieutenant Khoa from the Vung Tau Police will be here to pick you up shortly," he informed Beckwith with malice aforethought, "He has some questions of his own."

A look of horror crossed Beckwith's face, "You can't fucking do that!" he cried. "I'm an American citizen. You can't turn me over to those bastards!" He started forward arms outstretched, thinking of ways to kill Olah.

Olah pushed him back in his chair, "Don't worry, you miserable piece of shit. You won't be seeing the special cells. I don't think I would lose any sleep if you did. What you go through over there won't be any worse than what we just completed – well, not much worse, anyway," he said nastily.

"H-h-h-how long do I have to stay there?" Beckwith croaked.

"'Till they're done with you, Henry m'boy, only, 'till they're done with you."

Olah strode out and closed the door behind him.

***

"You are looking for an arms trader who goes by the name of 'the Chinaman.'" Hank told the three Montagnards as Y Bli translated.

He had instructed Y Bli to pick three good men who were resourceful. His only other requirement was that they were lighter skinned than most of his tribesmen. He knew it would help them attract far less attention as they traveled. It would have been logical to use the VNMCs, but he was still wary of security issues.

Tuk Ba had taken over Hoa's operation. This made sense as Tuk Ba had killed him. He might have even inherited Hoa's spy here in the base camp, whoever that spy was.

Hank still considered the Vietnamese Marine contingent to

be the most likely source of the leak. It was a continued basis of contention with the VNMC lieutenant, Ngo. Hank had the SEALs step up their training exercises with the Vietnamese to help hide the fact that they were not taking them out on real missions.

"I will provide you with carbines, canteens, C-rations, and American dollars. You should be able to fight your way out of any situation that you can't buy your way out of," Hank instructed.

That was met with a chuckle from the three men after Y Bli translated the instructions. The guns Hank was providing the scouts with were older and obsolete but they were in good working order. This was not without purpose. Nothing would attract more attention that a native carrying a new AR-15. He did not give them the name Tuk-Ba. There was still a chance they were wrong about the identity of the new guy, and he wanted these men to operate with information untainted by assumptions.

"Once you locate the Chinaman watch him until you know his habits. Find out where he lives, and how many men are around him. Once you learn this you should return here as quickly as possible. The first man to return will get to keep the money he did not spend. I will add to that money as much again as he started with. Are there any questions?"

The men spoke excitedly after Y Bli translated.

"They understand well, Lieutenant, and thank you for your trust," Y Bli said.

"Just find me the Chinaman," Hank replied, "That's all the thanks I need."

***

Much of the information they had extracted from Beckwith was not entirely new. But, Olah reflected, it was useful nonetheless. What had before now been rumors about the black market operations was now testimony. Not only that but now they had names and dates to go along with those rumors turned fact.

Beckwith had told them how the Vietnamese black marketeers would bribe American guards at supply warehouses. This would allow them to back their trucks right up to the loading docks and fill them just as if they were any legitimate delivery driver.

Some of the more entrepreneurial Americans involved, like Beckwith, asked for drugs instead of cash. This allowed them to turn around and sell the drugs for far more money than they would have ever gotten in a bribe.

Drugs were routinely sold for a huge profit in South Vietnam. The real money wasn't in local sales. That was only for those willing to ship the stuff back to the United States to an ever increasing market in the US.

The most common method of shipping them was to send the drugs back on one of the constantly coming and going C-130 cargo planes. These planes were on constant movement back and forth between Vietnam and the States. Every one of these planes was loaded with things such as men's duffle bags. These were for men going on leave, transferring out, or some finishing their tours. No one had ever noticed an extra duffle bag. One full bag would contain a fortune in heroin. Any Aircrewman who got into the business quickly had all the traffic they could handle, and the money that went along with it.

Security was loose on both ends as far as smuggling was concerned. American servicemen had always purchased bargains with American currency while stationed abroad. No one really cared. It was considered one of the benefits of a low paying and difficult job. American money was the desire of the world. The problem was that American servicemen were now stationed in ever increasing numbers in Vietnam. In this case the most attractive product, were not stereos or jade carvings, but drugs. Rather than taking back a cheap stereo for a small markup, drugs were being taken back for an enormous markup.

Beckwith had eagerly given up the name of the sergeant he contacted back in the States whenever he had a shipment on the way. It was easy for that man to grab the spare duffel and just walk off the base with it. Anyone with a base pass would routinely and automatically be waved through the busy gates.

There had been one bit of information Beckwith had passed along that really made Olah's ears perk up. It was more of a rumor he had heard than his own firsthand knowledge.

Beckwith said that he heard that some of the marijuana had come from two Americans who had pirated it from the river traffic out on the Delta. It was said these were very heavily armed men and as often as not, they just killed the drug runners on the boats they looted.

Olah's one and only thought was of the men with green faces on the dock of the Navy unit down the coastline. They had been armed as much as anyone he had seen and looked ready for just about anything.

He had thrown Dillon's name at Beckwith several times. Each time he only received a blank look in return. That look meant nothing. Olah knew that names would be changed. These drug suppliers were not going to advertise their names like brand name laundry soap.

There was something going on with Dillon's unit. So far, they fit the profile he was looking for. To a cop, that meant these men were suspects until further notice.

***

The invoices from the villa led to the supply offices of the United States Air Force facility located near the Vung Tau airport. Olah had contacted the Commanding Officer and was told to rendezvous with a Major named Lyon at the gate at precisely 0800 the next morning.

The CO was true to his word. Olah met a very officious Major Lyon as promised. "I am here to offer you any assistance you might need, Mr. Olah," Lyon said by way of greeting.

Olah mentally translated that to mean, 'How can I kiss your ass to keep you off my back?'

"First I need to go to the supply office," Joe answered. "I have a load of records to go through."

"Right this way." Lyons led him to the Quartermaster's Department, and turned him over to the lieutenant in charge.

"Mr. Olah is to be given every cooperation. He has access to all records. I think you should assign one of your best people to give him a hand," the Major instructed the younger officer.

"Yes sir," the lieutenant answered. "I know just the person, Monique Demarteau. She's very good, speaks Vietnamese, French and English. She also knows the system front, back and sideways."

"All right then," Lyon said heartily, "It sounds as if you are in great hands. I'm sure Lieutenant Taylor can take care of anything else you need. If not, don't hesitate to have someone come find me."

"I won't," Olah said seriously, looking him in the eye.

As Lyons left, the lieutenant turned and called out, "Monique, honey, come over here, I gotta job for you."

Olah saw a tall mulatto woman rise to her feet and walk toward them. Actually, she seemed to glide this way. The more he looked, the more he realized she had a very graceful manner, and that was not her only asset.

Monique Demarteau was simply one of the most beautiful women Joe Olah had even seen. She had long slender legs that seemed to make up half her height. They were remarkably well suited to the hemline of her short skirt. Her honey colored skin eliminated the need for nylons. Her hair was jet black, and coifed in a bouffant. It formed an oval when combined with her face. For a moment, Joe felt like applauding the choice of assistant they had made for him.

The lieutenants voice snapped Olah back to consciousness, "Monique, this is Joseph Olah of the Naval Investigative Service."

Monique extended her well manicured hand, and surprised Olah again with the strength of her grip, "Glad to meet you," Joe managed to say.

The lieutenant continued speaking as though there had been no one else speaking, "He needs to do some research in the records department. He may need your help in questioning some people who don't speak English. You are assigned to him for as long as his investigation takes. During this time he has no restriction to the data he is allowed to access. Do you understand?"

"I think I understand, Lieutenant," there was an almost sarcastic tone in her voice.

Olah saw a spark of contempt in her large brown eyes. They were the kind of eyes that a cheap romance novel would call bedroom eyes. Olah sensed she had a quick wit. She also seemed to have the essence that she knew she was the smartest person in the room.

"Well, I'll leave you to it," Taylor said as he turned and walked away.

"Follow me..." Monique smiled, "Is it detective, inspector, or something else?"

"It's Joe," Olah tried to sound casual, "Just Joe."

"Don't be so modest. Joseph is a perfectly nice name, not to mention it has historical significance," she smiled again.

Olah could not tell if she was joking, but she did not seem to be mocking him.

"Okay, just Joe, let me see what you need," she paused at the door of the records room.

Olah handed her his sheaf of invoices and bills of lading. Monique rustled through them quickly. "Let me understand this. You want to follow each of these back to their source and know everyone who handled them in an official capacity?"

"That's right."

"Well, Joseph, it looks like you and I are going to be spending a lot of time together."

That was the first really good news Joseph Olah had heard since arriving in Vietnam.

Chapter Eight

"Lieutenant," Y Bli banged on the door of the ops hootch as Hank sat filling out paperwork, "Muna find the Chinaman."

"YES!" Hank yelled, gesturing with a fist he said, "Bring Muna to me, now!"

Y Bli hurried off. He returned in just moments with one of the Montagnards Hank remembered sending out into the bush. They were accompanied by Keith Blevins.

"They got him?" Blevins asked as he entered the hootch.

"Looks that way," Hank answered. He turned to Y Bli, "Let's hear it."

Y Bli translated as Muna reported. The man was four inches taller than Y Bli. Although he was short by European standards he was lanky compared to most of the other Montagnards. He had a much lighter Muna definitely looked more like a Vietnamese peasant than a Montagnard.

Muna began speaking, and then paused. "He live on big junk boat," Y Bli said, "By village of Can Gio..."

"That's not far," Keith interrupted excitedly, "The SOB's in our damn backyard!"

Hank quickly checked the map on the wall, "It's only about twelve kilometers," he confirmed. "Cocky bastard."

He turned back to Muna, "Let's make sure. Can you show me on the chart where you saw the Chinaman's boat?"

Muna nodded in the affirmative. Hank was sure the man could at least understand English. He was too proud to try to give his report directly because the speaking errors might cause misunderstanding and he wanted to be sure.

Muna stepped forward and studied the chart on the wall. Y Bli said something sharply in Chau Ma, and then pointed to the location of the SEAL camp on the map.

"Y Bli, what are you saying to him?" Hank asked.

"I tell him to be very sure about what he tells you, Lieutenant," Y Bli answered.

"Good, very good," Hank said.

Muna stood in front of the chart for another long moment. He pointed deliberately to a spot just northwest of the village of Can Gio.

"This place," he said.

"Are you sure?" Hank asked.

Muna spoke to Y Bli in Chau Ma, then Y Bli answered, "He is sure, Lieutenant. He will take you there."

Hank debriefed Muna through Y Bli for the next two hours. The Chinaman lived in a large junk he had anchored just off shore from a camp he had set up to handle the traffic of weapons and supplies. The junk was easily distinguished as the living quarters on the stern were painted green. It was a larger craft than most of this type with two masts and was around thirty meters long.

Muna had observed the junk for two days. He saw smaller sampans and fishing boats constantly deployed back and forth from the large boat to unload crates. He learned from the locals that the larger boat made trips to sea about every ten to fourteen days. It always returned from these trips heavy with cargo. Muna had even talked with a fisherman who claimed to have seen the green junk rendezvous with a steel hulled trawler at sea.

Villagers complained that the Chinaman was worse than Hoa ever was. He took what food he wanted with no thought of paying. He did similar things to the local young women. Two fishermen protested the Chinaman's claim to their daughters and were beheaded. That action, and their memory of Hoa's fate, kept the locals in line.

The mention of Hoa confirmed in Hank's mind that the Chinaman was indeed Tuk-Ba. He kept that thought to himself and let the story continue uninterrupted.

The Chinaman had about fifteen men in the camp. That made him very well guarded. Most of them were Vietnamese with only a few of them being Chinese like their leader. Despite all of the security he still did not feel safe living in the camp and chose to reside on the junk.

"Perhaps he is as afraid of his own men as he is of the villagers," Muna said through Y Bli.

Hank had Muna repeat the story over and over. He asked probing questions. He tried to pull out more detail with each repetition. Finally, he was satisfied, and told the two Montagnards they could go.

Muna said something in Chau Ma to Y Bli, who rebuked him sharply.

"What is it, Y Bli?" Hank asked.

"It nothing, Lieutenant. It...." Y Bli searched for the word, "Stupid," he finished.

"Tell me," Hank ordered. There was nothing about this he did not want to hear.

"He ask about his money," Y Bli spread his hands apologetically.

Hank grinned. In this country, it was almost refreshing to meet someone with transparent motives, "No problem, Y Bli. We'll take care of him right away."

***

Hank stretched and yawned. It was almost midnight. Shit, he had been at this for nearly eleven hours, and he still wasn't sure what he had done could be called a plan.

Keith Blevins stuck his head in the door, "Still at it?"

"It's not gonna be easy to nail this bastard, Keith," Hank admitted wearily.

"Yeah," Blevins agreed, "How're we gonna get in there without the whole world knowing?"

Hank was quiet for a moment, "You know about the junk force operating out of Vung Tau?"

"Not much."

"Like us, that is the way they prefer it. Anyway, they've officially been here since '60. In reality it is probably in reality a few years before that. It's a paramilitary force made up of Vietnamese civilians. They are officially trained and led by the South Vietnamese Navy. The American naval personnel attached to them are merely 'advisors,' of course," Hank explained.

"Of course," Keith echoed ironically.

"Anyway, these guys in the black pajama navy are a real wild bunch. They cruise up and down these waterways in various types of junk boats. It allows them to blend in with the local traffic while doing their damnedest to stop the flow of VC supplies to the south," Hank said.

Hank got to his feet, "I've got a buddy, Dick Sutherland, who's operating with them in the 3rd Coastal District out of Vung Tau. I'm gonna go see him first thing in the morning. Maybe we can just sail up to Tuk-Ba and blow his ass right out of the water. I'll be back as quickly as I can. We gotta move on this before we lost track of the bastard. Let's go, I gotta get some sleep."

Hank picked up the bottle of Johnny Walker that had been sitting by his desk and headed for the officer's hootch.

***

Keith Blevins was working in the small machine shop with Nate Bowman on a modification he wanted to try on his M-16 when he heard the shouting.

"Hey, Lieutenant, goin' for a cruise?" Vispo hollered.

Hank was back, "Come on," Keith said to the young machinist's mate, "Let's see what's cookin'."

They reached the pier just as Hank threw the lines to Vispo to tie up a forty foot junk. It had come in under diesel power even though it had two sail masts, one forward and one amidships. The Vietnamese captain, who was dressed as a peasant, steered the boat from the stern, just aft of the twelve foot deck house. Another Vietnamese crewman was aft and was preparing to throw a line to the pier. There were several fish barrels on the deck along with a pile of fishing nets. With the exception of the SEAL lieutenant in the bow this could have been any other Vietnamese fishing junk.

Once Vispo grabbed the line, Hank leapt to the pier, grinning from ear to ear. "What d'ya think?" he asked Keith.

"Well, I guess the Missouri wasn't available, so...."

"So this is just what we need," Hank said abruptly. He was all business, "Let's go, we got work to do."

***

"Hank, you sure you want to take Muna on this mission?" Blevins asked him later in their hootch. They had spent the day planning the mission, and the evening was spent briefing the men who had been chosen for the mission. "He's a civilian. If something happens to him, it's gonna hit the fan."

"You bet I do," Hank who was already in bed, took a long pull from his bottle. "I want all the good cards on my side of the table for once. Anyway, he's the only one who's seen the junk and knows for sure where it's at."

"What about the rules of engagement concerning civilians?"

"What rules are those?" Hank asked sarcastically, "This is the SEALs. We aren't big Navy, Army or whatever. We have to do things a little differently here and if he is willing to take the risk, I am willing to let him."

***

Hank was low and out of sight as he watched the town of Can Gio slide past. It was what he would have once considered, unimaginably hot and stuffy in the deck house of the junk. He was hunkered here with Blevins, Vispo, Slade, Padgett, Hack and Nate Bowman. They had been confined for hours through the hottest part of the day.

He checked his watch. They were right on schedule. The Vietnamese crewing the junk boat along with Y Bli and Muna were on deck and doing a great job. They had come across the shipping lanes leading to Saigon. Hank had been amazed at the amount of traffic. It was more along the lines of the shipping lanes of San Francisco or New York than what he would have expected to be a minor shipping lane.

There were heavily laden commercial junks of all sizes moving in seemingly random directions. They were swarming around the big freighters who were laying on heavy steam and heading out to the open sea. The fact that the sea was not littered with the wreckage of these things was testimony to the good seamanship of the various captains. He included his own in this admiration who was threading his way skillfully and smoothly through the traffic.

It was almost 1800 hours now. Soon the fishing junks and sampans the SEALs had just made their way through would be making their way home with the day's catch.

Y Bli came to the door of the deck house as they left Can Gio behind them, "Muna say we are getting close, Lieutenant."

"Thank you, Y Bli."

Half an hour later the shoreline opened up to a wide inlet. Muna pointed up into it, "Stay on course," Hank said as he brought up his binoculars.

The village was about six hundred meters up the inlet. Hank began scanning along the shore, further up from the village. There it was, in perfect focus. He called Muna into the cabin and asked the man to take a look, "Is that the Chinaman's junk?"

Muna searched for a moment, then became excited, "Yes, Lieutenant, that Chainman!"

"Keep heading up the coast," Hank ordered the Vietnamese captain. When the village was finally obscured from his view by the tree line north of the inlet he called out, "Anchor here."

While they waited, the SEALs dug into their C-rations and checked their weapons. It was still hot and miserable, but not as bad as it had been during the mid-afternoon. The American's were even more careful not to be seen than they had been up to this point. One white face glimpsed by a passing sampan, or by unseen eyes watching from the jungle, and it was all over.

An hour passed. Hank was starting to get impatient when Y Bli called, "They come," and pointed toward the horizon.

Sure enough, the fishing boats that make their home in this village were making their way to the mouth of the inlet. Within half an hour, the procession had grown to a steady stream of junks and sampans of all shapes and sizes heading to the villages along the inlet, as well as up into the river that fed into it.

"Let's go," Hank told the captain.

The river rats' boat eased in amongst the fishermen as though it was just another boat at the end of the day. No one noticed the new junk, or if they did they were too tired to care.

Their sampan approached the large junk. Hank kept his binoculars trained on it the whole way. He was searching for some sign to confirm that this was indeed the right target. He could see figured moving on deck atop the living quarters. As they came abreast of the target he could make out their features.

"There's the bastard," he said aloud to the other SEALs, "Lookin' fat and happy."

Tuk-Ba was sitting at a table with two other men. Hank recognized one of them from the unexpected visit to their base camp; the other man was a Vietnamese man he did not recognize. The sun glinted on the pearl handled chrome revolver Tuk-Ba had taken from Hoa.

Tuk-Ba's attention was riveted on his other companion, a

Vietnamese woman in a tight fitting dress cut very high up her leg. She was laughing at whatever her host had just said. Whoever she was, Hank decided, she was not someone the Nung had forced to endure his company.

"Keep on for about another hundred meters," Hank called to the captain once they had passed Tuk-Ba's junk. "Then drop anchor."

They captain obeyed. A few minutes later they were at anchor. They were barely a hundred and twenty-five meters away from their target. As soon as it was dark, they would attack.

***

"We can't ask for a better set-up," Hank said to Blevins, "Let's do it now."

For two hours they had watched the goings on with Tuk-Ba's junk. They did this more in cynical amusement than amazement at the openness in which the Nung conducted his black market dealings. Everything, from the unloading of weapons from the boat, to the distribution of them in the makeshift camp, was in plain view of the village. It was obvious that Tuk-Ba did not give a damn who saw what went on.

The villagers were no doubt cowed by the "Chinaman;" but Hank figured it was equal parts fear and indifference. Saigon could have been the far side of the moon as far as these ordinary people were concerned. The Capital City and its temper tantrums didn't change their poverty stricken world. Politics meant little to them. Many had never even heard the term 'Communism.' Village officials might be more informed, but they would either be afraid of Tuk-Ba, paid to look the other way – or had been killed.

Hank, Vispo, Slade and Bowman stripped to their swim trunks in the darkened cabin, and cammoed their entire bodies. Hank checked Vispo to make sure there were no white spots on his back, and then Vispo returned the favor.

"The Lieutenant from twenty thousand fathoms," he joked.

"Yeah, but I'm more of a sonofabitch than him, and don't forget it," Hank shot back.

On deck, in the evening darkness, he made a final check of the MK-26HB haversack charges. The men who were staying on the boat checked their weapons, "Are we ready?"

"Ready, sir," came the reassuring reply from six pair of lips.

"Mr. Blevins, what does it look like out there?" Hank asked Keith who was continually surveying the area with binoculars.

"There's movement on the beach, but Tuk-Ba's party has gone below, there's no traffic on the water, and even the village is pretty quiet."

While Blevins was talking, Hank drew near, then he said quietly, "Keep an eye on the Vietnamese sailors, Keith. When things start poppin' you take over the boat if you need to."

"Roger, Hank," Keith whispered.

"Ok, let's go," Hank said to the others. They eased themselves over the side into the warm water. The four men slipped their swim fins on as Blevins handed each swim team their haversack. Hank and Vispo were together, Slade and Bowman made up the other team.

Hank signaled, and they started the slow breaststroke toward Tuk-Ba's junk.

They were a hundred feet from their junk, when suddenly; the night was lit up by a bright light from shore. Hank felt his ass pucker. He was sure that they had been betrayed. All that was missing was a hailstorm of bullets to come their way.

Then the light receded. Then he realized it was a large bonfire being lit at the Nung's camp. They must have poured some sort of accelerant on the wood, and there had been an initial flash of flame.

Shit, what was the matter with these people? It goes down below ninety degrees for a minute and they feel the need to huddle around a bonfire.

He changed course slightly. He was headed directly for the shadow now cast over the water by Tuk-Ba's junk. From what they could see, Muna had been right in his estimate of Tuk-Ba's defensive force. Unfortunately, it looked like every single one of them was awake. Hopefully they were already drunk or high. Their reaction time would be slower than normal. From the noise that drifted across the water, they seemed to be having a good time.

It was not going to last for long.

The SEALs reached the shadow from the large junk. They turned at a right angle to the left. Soon, they were within a few meters of the dark boat which loomed above them. Hank could hear men talking and working on the deck.

Separating from Slade and Bowman, Hank and Vispo headed toward the stern of the junk. They were very careful not to make hard contact with the hull.

Just as they came on the huge wooden rudder, a motorized sampan chugged around the stern of the boat.

The two SEALs immediately submerged. They clung to the slippery rudder and stayed under. Hank could hear his heart pounding in his ears. It was loud even as compared to the sound of the sampan's engine. As the sound of the engine faded they slowly, silently resurfaced. Hank took a deep breath, and listened for the sound of any disturbance. Apparently Slade and Bowman had also heard the sampan coming and reacted in time.

The sounds of laughter reached them from the shore. In the shadow of the rudder hank took a moment to check out Tuk-Ba's strength in numbers on the shore. The party was in full swing with dozens of men milling around with whores and cooking fires. Many of them were noticeably drunk, even from this distance. It was obvious they were arrogantly sure of their safe position.

Pretty soon they were going to be sobered up.

Vispo was lashing the charge to the rudder when Hank heard a familiar high pitched nervous laugh. Hank strained to listen, and then heard it again. The same voice talking in Vietnamese, he had a clipped, very precise manner of speaking.

"That's him!" Hank hissed. There was no doubt in his mind. His first and only meeting with Tuk-Ba was burned in his memory, "That sonofabitch is only ten feet above us!"

Hank quickly began to unleash the charge, a plan half formed in his mind. Vispo looked at him questioningly.

"Why take a chance?" Hank whispered. "I'm gonna put it right under his ass," he gestured up toward the open window.

Vispo held the rudder for support. Hank climbed onto his shoulders. He could hear Tuk-Ba clearly now. He was trying to coax a woman to do something she was hesitant to do. For a moment, he felt a twinge about what was going to happen to her, but realized it couldn't be helped. She had literally made her bed.

He could now reach to within a few feet of the window to the living quarters. He found to his dismay that there was nothing to lash the charge to. Frustration gave way to a wry grin as he took the K-Bar from the sheath at his waist. He quickly worked the knife into the calk between the planks right under the window. Then he hung the charge from the hilt, wrapping the strap around the hilt a few times for good measure. When he was sure the charge wouldn't fall he pulled the ignition fuse.

Slade and Bowman appeared out of the dark. They were curious what was taking so long. Hank gestured toward the charge hanging under the port hole, and the two SEALs grinned and gave him thumbs up.

As quickly as they dared, the four SEALs made their way away from the junk back to their own boat. They remained in the shadow for a hundred meters, then turned toward their own junk positioned to the west.

Hank was dripping wet by the deck house. He had just given the order to fire up the engine and get out of there when the first charge went off.

The blast lit up the sky. It formed an orange and white pillar of flame. The sound was deafening. A cloud of splinters and debris came roaring across the water. It pelted the SEALs' junk. The SEALs and their crewmen huddled beneath the gunwale for protection from the flying wreckage.

Hank took a look in the direction of Tuk-Ba's junk. He saw the stern section was completely gone above the water line. The second charge exploded as he was looking. He dropped to the deck as another wave of debris swept over them.

"Put full power on, and get the hell out of here!" Hank hollered to Blevins once the blast passed over them.

After the second charge had done its work, there were burning timbers scattered all over the surface of the water. Most of Tuk-Ba's junk was gone. There were a few secondary explosions coming from the shattered hulk.

Chaos reigned on the beach. Most of the hootches had been destroyed in the explosion. The fired had been scattered and bodies were everywhere. The survivors staggered around and tried to collect their senses.

As their junk sped toward the mouth of the inlet, it drew even with the burning hulk. Hank could feel the heat from the intense flames.

That was when he heard the sound of automatic weapons fire. Some of the noises were the sounds of rounds hitting their boat. He fell to the deck, hollering for everyone else to do the same.

Nate Bowman hit the deck beside him. There was something wrong with the way he went down. It had been more of a crumpling than a dive to the deck for the young SEAL.

Hank crawled over to him, and turned him over. Blood was pouring from a wound in the man's shoulder, "DOC!" Hank cried out.

Padget rushed over. Hank took his place at the fifty caliber machine gun that until now had been hidden under the fishing nets.

He cut loose with the heavy weapon. He loved the feel of its power and exulted at the destruction it caused as he walked the tracers up and down the beach. On either side of him, Slade and Hack sprayed the area with their M-60s.

It did not take long to suppress the fire from the camp. Those who had been visible on the beach had either taken cover or died. As they pulled away from the area Hank saw no one attempt to follow them.

He went over to where Doc Padget was still working on the fallen SEAL. "How is he?"

"Not good," Padget snapped, then sighed, "But he'll live."

Damn. Both of his replacements for Ayotte and Bush had been severely wounded and lost to him. Ironically, they had been hurt while in combat with the Nungs who had taken over the operation of the man responsible for the death of the two SEALs. In this part of the world they called this kind of thing Karma. He called it bullshit.

He checked out the rest of the junk. The Vietnamese captain was still at the wheel, and had done an amazing job. The other sailor was sitting quietly, along with Muna, in the deckhouse. Y Bli stood over them, grinning ear to ear. Hank thought that the two sailors had gotten a little more than they had bargained for. But they would have a great story to tell the Junk Force people when they got back. It was a story that they would no doubt embellish their own roles in the results.

He cared only one thing and one thing only. He had gotten Tuk-Ba out of his hair; closed down his operation, and he had done it before Shirl's visit.

Chapter Nine

As Shirl came down the ramp of the MATS DC-9, Hank could feel a little bit of sanity returning.

It was easy to tell she was tired from a long flight with layovers in Hawaii and the Philippines. To Hank's eyes, it didn't matter. She looked more beautiful than he had ever seen her.

Shirley Dillon was a brunette of medium height and slender build with a quick smile and a bright disposition enlivened by a quick wit. Overall, most people considered her a pretty woman, but not what you would call flashy. She had the type of beauty that registered more strongly to a man on his second look-- that was, if he had the good sense to take that second look.

Hank had a good wife. He considered himself lucky. He had no worries about other men. He had no worries about their daughter. Shirl was the ideal Navy wife. She took amazing care of her man when he was around and competent care of the family when he was not.

She was night and day different from the woman that led her down the stairs. Nancy Slade was a bleach-blonde whose flashy clothes and thick makeup were designed to take attention away from her prematurely lined face, and thickening figure. Unlike Shirl, she gave her Navy husband much to worry about when he was gone.

Those worries may serve to endanger Slade's life. In fact, they could also hurt those in the bush with him when he screwed up if he was distracted with worry. This thought really bothered Hank.

Thoughts of Slade's problems vanished from his mind for the moment. Shirl was in his arms, her cheek still cool from the air conditioning of the airplane. The scent of her Shalimar perfume filled his nostrils with a familiar and welcomed fragrance.

Their long, deep kiss brought Hank the rest of the way out of the cesspool he had been living in of late. She stirred in him the natural desires that had been dormant, forced to the back of his mind by necessity. No human could deal with the horror he had been facing without some measure of compartmentalization.

They broke the kiss, and gazed at each other. They were mere inches apart.

"Hey there sailor," Shirl whispered.

"Hello yourself," Hank responded. "Let's get outta here."

"Good idea, sailor. There's not much privacy on the tarmac."

"It's kind of hard on your back, also," Hank agreed.

"Not to mention your knees," she answered.

"That's my girl, always thinking about me."

In the taxi on the way to the Continental Palace Hotel, Hank broke a kiss long enough to ask, "How was the trip, besides long and tiring?"

"That about covers it. Nancy Slade just about drove me nuts."

"What d'you mean?" he asked.

"Her mood swings cover the spectrum. She was bitchy, hyper, whiney, and then she'd just mellow right out. It seemed like she spent about half the trip in the bathroom," she explained.

"So?" Hank asked leadingly.

"So what?"

"So what do you think it means?" He asked.

"Well, the first thing that crossed my mind is she might be pregnant!!"

"Oh, shit," Hank groaned.

"What?"

"Those two haven't seen each other in four or five months. If she's knocked up and not showing through that outfit she had on, it's not Dan's," Hank's brow wrinkled as he wondered what this all meant for Slade. He had been distracted and worried enough before he really knew anything was wrong.

"Well, I'll tell you," Shirl was saying as Hank turned his attention back to her, "She hasn't been hanging around with the other Navy wives back in San Diego. In fact, she's been running around with kind of a rough crowd."

"Rough in what way?" he asked.

Shirl waved her hand vaguely, "You know, kind of scruffy, beatnik types. Speaking of a rough crowd, Saigon sure has grown since I was here last," she commented purposefully changing the subject.

"Bigger is not always better," Hank said sourly. "The whole country's turning into the wrong side of the tracks in a military town."

Shirl shot him a worried look at his tone, but the taxi was pulling up to the Palace.

Hank had already checked them into their room. The air conditioner was whirring steadily as he opened the door. It had almost gotten the room to a comfortable temperature.

Shirl quickly headed to the bathroom to freshen up after the sticky taxi ride. Hank opened the curtain and looked out over the city. The streets seemed to have gotten even more crowded in the short time he had been away. The growing roughness of what was once one of his favorite places seemed even more oppressive.

Ten minutes later, when the bathroom door opened, he was still so engrossed in his gloomy thoughts he did not turn around until he heard her voice.

"Aren't you a bit over dressed for this occasion, Lieutenant?"

He turned, and saw her body shadowed in the light of the doorway. The sight took his breath away.

"I'll take care of it right away," he promised.

And he did…

***

Sometime later, after Shirl had dozed off in his arms, worn out from the trip coupled with the sex, Hank stood at the window. He was pondering the situation.

He was not sure how long he had been standing there. There was a faint rustle of sheets as Shirl slipped up and wrapped her arms around him.

"Hank, what's wrong?"

"I don't know what you mean," he avoided the subject.

"Well, for starters, I've never had to remind you why we checked into a hotel before. In fact, I usually had to remind you to wait until we got to the hotel."

He was not sure he wanted to burden her with his doubts. It would only give her more to worry about once she went home. Having her husband fighting in a war wasn't enough to worry about.

"Just getting old I guess," he said.

She snorted, "Don't give me that crap, I've got a feeling you won't need that kind of reminder twenty-seven years from now, much less at age twenty-seven," she squeezed his strong, muscled arm again, then asked, "What's it like out there?"

Hank laughed then tried to answer her, "It's not like the real world. You wouldn't believe it if I told you all of it – the things that go on out there, or the things I do. It's like a bad dream. It just doesn't seem real while you are doing it. You can be sitting down to dinner at a plush restaurant one day, and then humping the boonies hiding from Charlie – or trying to blow him up – the next."

"There is no real front line, or single place in which we battle. Things are happening everywhere all at once. The VC are everywhere, even here," he waved his hand at the city lights.

"There are times when they know what the Vietnamese or Uncle Sam is up to even before we do. Things are building up, and it's really getting poppin'. It will take a long time to dig these bastards out. Right now, it's a no-win situation. They won't let us do what it really takes to beat 'em. We're not even sure if we want to commit that far. This 'bear any burden, pay any price' is pure bullshit. There's always a point where the price is too high for what you get, and I think that may be the case here. What I'm really afraid of is that if we screw this up now we will pay an even larger price in the long run if we really want to win this. Victory may have a very high cost. Kind of like the difference between a slow internal hemorrhage and a quick clean flesh wound. One hurts more and is messier, but the other's more prone to kill you."

"What's going to happen here if we can't do what we need to?" she asked the question more out of concern for her husband and to keep him talking than due to any interest in national security policy.

"I thought I knew, but now I have doubts. Half of the Vietnamese don't want anything to change. The other half is so busy taking money they don't give a damn what happens, as long as the Americans stay and they keep getting paid. I'm sorry; I didn't mean to complain like this. This situation is making me so goddam mad, it keeps my insides all churned up," he said.

"If I didn't want to hear you complain, I wouldn't have

asked," she said matter of factly. She did not want to betray her feelings of unease at Hank's description of the situation.

She put her arm around him, pressed her body to his, breathed into his ear and said, "Why don't you concentrate on keeping my insides churned up for a while?"

***

During the next three days, Shirl observed a huge change in her husband's character. He really enjoyed her company, as a husband should. But now, unlike before his deployment, he was noticeably more distant, he internalized things more. Not only was he preoccupied, but he could not sit still. While he waited for her to get ready he would pace the floor in their room, if he was waiting for her to shop for something he would walk laps around the shop or block.

At evening meals he drank like alcohol was about the leave the planet forever. No matter how much he drank it seemed to have no effect on him. When he slept it was anything but restful. He trashed around, mumbling and dreaming about something. His breathing while those dreams took place was rapid, he would sweat profusely, and yet when she touched him, he was cold and clammy to her touch.

On their fourth night together, she had just gotten to sleep when Shirl was shocked awake by a sharp blow to the back of her neck.

Before she could move Hank's hands closed around her neck. They tightened like a vice, squeezing and shaking her back and forth like a rag doll.

She opened her mouth to scream, no sound could escape his grip. "Hank!" she croaked. But there was no answer. She knew he had to be asleep. He did not mean to hurt her, but that knowledge was no good to her right now.

She kicked him, but due to the angle she could get no force behind the blows. She was starting to see spots in her eyes. She knew she had to do something or die.

Her fear gave her strength. Gradually, inch by inch, she was able to pull and drag herself to the edge of the bed. She struggled to stand. She pulled at his fingers one by one, but his grip was like iron. She could feel herself starting to lose consciousness. She wanted to scream but couldn't which made her want to scream more. She was too young to die; she had a daughter and a husband who needed her.

He was just too strong for her. She was not going to be able to stop him from choking the life out of her. Then, for a moment, his grip relaxed. She flung herself away from the bed.

Slowly, never taking her eyes off the figure thrashing in the bed, she backed into the corner of the room. She slid down the wall until she was sitting in the corner. Once on the floor she put her face in her hands and began sobbing and shaking uncontrollably.

***

When Hank awoke he realized he was alone. Then he heard the sounds coming from the corner. He slid over to her. As he approached, he saw fear on her face. She flinched as he reached out to her.

"Honey, what's the matter?" he asked.

When she saw he was back to normal the fear changed to anger, "You damned near broke my neck, that's what's the matter!" she snapped.

Hank pulled back. He rubbed his hand over his eyes, "Oh god, dammit, dammit, I'm sorry honey, I'm so sorry."

"How long have you been having these nightmares?" Shirl pressed.

"I dunno, a coupla' months, I guess," he admitted.

"Have you seen a doctor?" she snapped.

"No, not yet," he answered timidly.

Hank pinched the bridge of his nose with his thumb and forefinger as he tried to come to grips with what had just happened. He was ashamed, angry, and afraid of what was happening to him.

"I'm sorry, so sorry," he repeated and began to weep.

Shirl was speechless for a minute. She had never seen her husband in this state. He was a man who kept strict control of his emotions, except for his tenderness with her and their daughter. She went to him. She put her arms around his shaking shoulders. They stayed in this position for a long time without saying a word.

Eventually, she began to stroke his hair, and she could

finally feel him calm down, "I love you," she whispered in his ear.

He wrapped his arms around her. He held her so tight she, once again, had trouble breathing. This time she made no protest. "I could never hurt you," he said hoarsely, his face buried in her shoulder. "Not on purpose, not in a million years."

"Baby, I know that. It was just a nightmare. It wasn't you, it wasn't me. It was a dream," she said in soothing tones.

"Yes," he said despairingly, "But my fear is that the dream is starting to be me."

They sat in silence for a while. They sat until Shirl thought he would be ready and capable of a reasonable conversation.

"Hank, you have to get out of this line of work. Whatever it is you're doing, you've been at it too long. You need a transfer," she said.

"I know that, but I am afraid that isn't the way it works. In this outfit you have to complete your tour. If I try to leave on this basis it *will* destroy my career. I've worked too hard, and we've sacrificed too much to ruin it now." A pleading tone came into his voice. Hank didn't care if it made him seem weak. "I don't want to have spent all this time away from the two of you for nothing. I want to be able to give you the things you deserve. We are getting close."

"Hank, I want to spend the rest of my life with you," Shirl told him. "I want you to be worth spending it with, not a burned out wreck. They picked you for this because they know you don't have an ounce of quit in your system. Once they figured that out they spent the next eight months beating that tiny amount that was there out of your system with that damn training. Persistence isn't a bad trait in a husband, but you have got to learn your limits. I sure as hell don't want to have one of those damned ceremonial funerals at Arlington! If all of Southeast Asia goes Communist, so be it. As long as I don't have to wear those damn widow's weeds," she said.

"Listen. I can't leave now, but this is my last tour. Besides, there is one thing I have to do before I go," he explained.

"Hank, the war effort can go on without you," she protested.

"I know that," he grinned regretting what he had said. He knew she had hit his weak point, "But we've got a serious security problem. These guys are like my brothers. I don't want to leave them with Charlie in the ranks."

"But you said Charlie was all over this country," she pointed out.

"Yeah, but this guy is special. He's very good, and he's gonna get more of my men killed if I don't find out who the sonofabitch is. There's no way I can let my relief inherit this guy. It's my problem, and I'm gonna solve it."

There was a steely sound in his voice that Shirl recognized. She knew there was no changing his mind. Running away was not in his skillset. He liked being a part of this elite unit. He liked it more than he would admit. This unit had become an end in itself, not just a means to an end. She did have one minor victory. He promised to leave at the end of this tour. She decided to accept her small victory and changed the subject.

The Dillons sat in their room and talked through the night. They talked about their hopes and dreams, about their daughter, Susan, and about the time when Hank hoped he would be able to be a father to her. Sometime during the night, they drifted off to sleep.

When they awoke, it was late in the morning. They were still on the floor, leaning against the wall in each other's arms. The events of the night, both good and bad, seemed like a dream.

But if it was, it was a dream that would change their lives in ways they had not yet realized. It had forged an even closer bond between them. At the same time, Shirl could not forget the feel of Hank's hands on her throat – hands from which she, previous to that night, had only known love. It was unsettling in a strange way. She put it aside and determined that she would use the knowledge she had gained to help the man she loved.

***

The next day Hank took Shirl on a tour of Saigon. They did the tour in one of the ever present blue and white taxis. She was amazed at the boom town atmosphere.

"Are you sure there's a war going on here?" she asked Hank. "It's more like somebody struck gold in that there delta."

Hank replied morosely that he was pretty sure a war was going on.

The influx of wealth was not just among the business class.

The peasants who had moved into town had been met with a flurry of new employment opportunities and were living beyond their wildest dreams. On the other hand, so many people had moved into the city so fast there was no housing for them. People lived in cardboard shacks, many of which were merely discarded crating material from the numerous US bases. Some of which clearly had various product labels on the side.

Sanitation and sewer facilities were nonexistent in the shanty towns encircling the city. As they rode past one in the taxi, Shirl saw a man washing his face using water from the gutter. The garbage was piled everywhere. What garbage trucks were in the area only serviced the tax-paying sections of Saigon.

It was like two different worlds. There was a booming town, bristling with activity and new found wealth. Surrounding it was the most destitute of slums imaginable. As far as Hank could see the local government had made no attempt to extend civilization to the shanty towns. Hank knew what those political types filled their time with.

Shirl remarked on how drugs were being dealt on street corners. The vendors were behaving as though they were selling hot dogs or pretzels back in the US.

"I thought drugs were illegal here," she said to Hank.

"Technically they are. There is some effort to go after the big operations," he answered. "But it's so plentiful here. Besides, I'm not so sure the Vietnamese authorities, such as they are, don't just put pressure on the bigger dealers to pay them off."

Suddenly Hank turned to Shirl and put his arm around her, "Enough of this crap. We're here to have a good time. I know a place that's got our kind of music. I'll dance your bones around," he suggested.

"Take me to it, lover, take me to it," she said.

***

That night, Hank waited until Shirl's breathing became deep and regular, "I love you," he whispered to her sleeping form. When he received no reply, he knew she was asleep. He slipped out of the bed, and moved silently to the easy chair.

He marveled that she had been willing to let him sleep in the same bed with her at all. He loved her for that and so many other things. There was no way he was going to risk a repeat performance of the previous night. No way.

***

He awoke just before dawn. Shirl appeared to still be asleep. Hank slid back into the bed. He lay with his hands behind his head waiting for her to wake. It struck him that this week had been the first time in a long time he had not had to carry a bottle of liquor to bed to be able to fall asleep. He pushed that thought aside. This comfort wasn't going to last forever, but that was a problem for later.

Shirl smiled to herself. She was completely aware of her husband's attempt at being sneaky. Her recollection of the night before last had turned her into a very light sleeper. She pretended not to know he had crept out of bed to sleep on the chair. She snuggled in close to him and fell back to sleep. It was the most comfortable she had felt since before he deployed to this hell hole.

***

Two nights later Hank received a telephone call from Doc Padget. "This better not be what I think it is," Hank said sourly when he recognized the voice.

"Don't sweat it, boss. I just need to talk to you in the lobby for a minute," Doc said.

"Make it the bar," Hank decided. He saw Shirl shoot him a look only a wife could give, "Don't worry babe. It's no problem," he promised.

Five minutes later, the two men were shaking hands. "Lieutenant, you look good. R&R agrees with you." Padget had been a little worried about Hank. He had not felt it was his place to say anything about the officer's mental state.

"Just so you aren't here to end it," he said.

"Nothing so drastic. Commander Beebe sent me over to let you know we're moving north. They're setting us up near Danang. We're moving in three days. You don't have to report until your leave is over. That way, by time you get back, we slobs will have done all the grunt work," Padget grinned. "Mr. Blevins said he would pack all your gear, and we will get it to Danang for you."

"Any idea on why we're moving?" Hank asked.

"Not a word. You are to report to the White Elephant in Danang, and that may give us some clue," Doc said.

"Oh, shit. Not those CIA bastards." Hank had heard of the building known as the White Elephant from Ken Nanski. He knew of some of the weird happenings generated by that place.

"You guessed it. I guess we have just about cleared Charlie out of our sector," Padget said. "So, we gotta go rid Danang of the Red Menace."

"I bet the villagers around our old camp would have a different opinion on that one," Hank said with some sympathy for what would likely happen to them.

"Well, it's not our problem anymore. Don't worry about it. You have a good time, and I'll see you in a week," Doc said.

"Check," Hank answered and raised his glass to Padget's. He could not help but wonder what the future held for him and his platoon.

***

The next week passed in the blink of an eye. Hank and Shirl danced, ate, shopped, and concentrated on just enjoying each other's company. Shirl knew Hank missed seeing their daughter, but they both realized this time was important for the two of them.

Hank still dreamed. Thankfully it was nothing like the night he had frightened her so badly. That night had also mortified him. She was concerned about his heavy drinking. She did not know that it was actually a reduction from what his normal week was like.

It was a nearly perfect week. It was like they were a honeymooning couple, only with the advantage of a comfort level only married couples know. Shirl treasured every single moment.

When it finally ended there was no long lingering scene at the airport. They were used to being apart. They established years before that the real goodbyes were to be said the night before.

They arrived at the airport with mere minutes to spare. They were so close that all the time they had to spare was spent on the necessary paperwork to get her on the flight.

She turned to him for the goodbye kiss. Shirl took Hank's face in her hands and spoke seriously. "I haven't seen anything here worth dying for. You just get out of here alive and come back to me in one piece. You understand me sailor?"

"You're the boss," Hank grinned. She knew her message was received. She turned and quickly went up the stairs to board the plane.

***

Hank stood at the edge of the tarmac watching until the DC-9 carrying her disappeared into the cloud cover. As he turned away he felt alone. The jungle that had seemed so far away only hours before was once again closing in on him.

Chapter Ten

At the same time Shirl was enroute to Manila somewhere over the South China Sea in the DC-9 her husband was headed north in a C-130 toward Danang.

During the length of the four hundred mile trip Hank could not tear his mind away from the two weeks with his wife. He was preoccupied with the few minutes in the middle of the night when he tried to choke her.

He stared at his hands in disgust. How could they be used in that fashion, even unconsciously? His self-loathing crowded out all other emotions. What the hell kind of person was he? The butchery was starting to get to him. It got worse every time he went into the field.

The only time he felt somewhat normal was when he was with Shirl. That was just not going to be possible for a while. The bottle would have to do until he got back to her. He knew he was becoming dependent on that particular escape – which really was not an escape. It was just a method of numbing the senses.

He felt guilty being gone so much. He was missing out on an important part of his daughter's life. When he had sea duty he often had long stretches in a home port. The life he had in the SEALs only had room for glimpses of a child growing up fast. Every time he saw her it seemed she had undergone astounding changes.

Hank had told Shirl about some of his dreams. He also told her about some of the troubling thoughts he was having. He had not come completely clean with her. That would not have been fair. He knew that. It would have frightened her in ways that she didn't deserve, and for no good reason.

He could not tell her the real nature of his work anyway. This was a miserable place, she had no real point of reference and wouldn't really understand anyway was how he justified it. He would not tell her of the brutal things that they did on their missions. He wouldn't complain to her about the restrictions they operated under that their enemy did not. Besides, there was always the possibility she would think they were doing too much instead of not enough.

The plane's engine power changed abruptly and the pilot

made a sharp turn snapping Hank back to the present. He quit brooding and turned his thoughts to the immediate future. The internal complaining was a ritual of his that *must* be completed before he returned to the field. Once in harm's way, the focus had to be on the job in front of him.

Hank looked out the window at the city located at the south end of a large bay. The old French maps he had been given, because they were the only ones available, referred to the bay as Tourane Bay. It got that name because its shape resembled a large soup tureen.

The Han River bordered the east side of the city running north to south. A peninsula ran north from the city about five kilometers out past the east side of the bay. At its end the peninsula widened to about ten kilometers across. It served to enclose the eastern part of the bay.

On the peninsula was Monkey Mountain. It rose sharply for several hundred feet from the surface of the bay. The bay side of the slope had been defoliated. The bare reddish brown surface presented a startling contrast to the lush green of the other side. It was like the mountain had been shaved clean.

The cargo plane literally dove straight for the runway. It pushed Hank back in his seat in the process. It seemed to him that the pilot aimed to crash them straight into the ground.

"What the hell's goin' on?" Hank demanded of the nearest crewman.

"We gotta land this way because of the VC snipers and small arms fire, Lieutenant. This gets us down fast, no glidepath. Sometimes the little bastards even fire rockets at us. We use JATO [Jet Assist Take Off] when we leave. That gets us the fuck outta here in a hurry," the young man said.

"I thought this place was pretty secure," Hank said ironically.

"Not bad, just don't get caught in the wrong places after dark without your weapon – you'll lose your ass. I carry a pistol everywhere I go. You better do the same. Officers are the best targets, Lieutenant," the crewman warned.

"So I've heard," Hank said, thinking of Y Bli. It sounded like he was going to need an extra pair of eyes in this place.

***

Blevins was there to meet him, sitting at the edge of the airfield in a vintage World War Two German command car with an open top and cut away sides. He waved as Hank approached.

"What is this relic?" Hank laughed.

"This is our jeep while we're here," Blevins grinned. "Jump in; I got lots to tell you. This is the least of it. You're not gonna believe where we're living."

"Surprise me," Hank drawled as the huge car lurched forward.

"It's a French villa, no less," Blevins said enthusiastically.

"You're shittin' me," Hank laughed.

"Nope. We got it made for now, livin' high on the hog," Blevins said.

"What about the rest of the platoon?" Hank asked.

"Don't worry they got it nice, too," Blevins assured him. "They got a classy French-style two story over on Ly Thuong Trong that they share with the new MST guys and the boat crews."

"Who's payin' for all this? Don't tell me the Vietnamese are gonna start pullin' their share of the load?" Hank asked.

"Not a chance," Blevins confirmed his suspicion, "We're working for MAC SOG for a while."

"These crazy border jumpers? Damn, now I know who's paying the bills." It was just has Hank feared. The CIA was their new sponsor.

As they drove Hank was impressed by Danang. The neighborhoods they passed through were clean and quiet. There were nice stucco houses with tile roofs. It was like Saigon before the influx of Americans. He wondered how long the relative tranquility would last. How long would it be before people seeking Yankee dollars ruined everything?

As Blevins wheeled the ungainly vehicle onto Le Loi Street, he pointed, "Be it ever so humble, there it is."

Hank could not believe his eyes. Their billet was a cream colored three story villa with a red tile roof. A six-foot tall wall surrounded the compound, broken only by a single iron gate.

Blevins parked the vehicle; Hank grabbed his B-4 bag and followed him inside. He was met by the sight of polished wood floors, nice furnishings, and large rooms. Keith took him on a quick tour of the house. There was a large kitchen with several refrigerators, a large lounge area, overhead fans were everywhere, and there was a large patio surrounded by a well-tended flower garden.

When they reached the rear of the villa, Keith pointed to a small house in back where the servants lived.

"Servants?" Hank exclaimed.

"Yeah, there's an old man who runs the house, and a couple of laundry and cleaning women," Keith explained.

Hank just shook his head. Upstairs, Blevins showed him to a large bedroom. A ceiling fan turned lazily, and there were louvered shutters on every window.

"This is yours," he waved his hand.

"Just like home," Hank grinned.

"Yeah, but don't drink the water, or even make ice cubes with it. That is unless it comes out of those two plastic bottles in the 'fridge. We get the drinking water from the Army. They got a purification plant set up over by the airfield," Blevins explained.

"The local water's really that bad?" Hank asked.

"Just like Tijuana. Okay, enough chit chat. Drop your gear and let's go. Beebe wants to see you ASAP. I just wanted to let you get a handle on the situation first," Blevins said.

As they came down the stairs an ancient, slim, balding Vietnamese man waited for them. Keith made introductions, "Lieutenant Dillon, this is Giai Vu, he is in charge of the servants. Lieutenant Dillon is my commanding officer. Hank, Giai Vu used to be a pharmacist in Hanoi."

"Oh really?" Hank said politely.

"Communists take business," the old man explained, "Very bad people. No education," he scowled. It looked to Hank as though that expression came very naturally to him.

"We have to go now," Blevins said. "We'll be back soon, and the Lieutenant will want something to eat."

The old man nodded in acknowledgement and stalked into the kitchen.

Blevins drove along the Han River waterfront on Bach Dang Street. They come to a stop in front of a large white impressive colonial building on the corner of Tran Quy Cap Street.

Hank read the large plaque near the double doors that identified the building as the United States Consulate.

"Oh boy, hellzapoppin'," he murmured.

It was the first time he had seen the infamous White Elephant. It was home of the CIA operatives the SEALs called 'plumbers.'

Blevins lead the way inside. They turned down a long corridor past several unmarked doors to Commander Beebe's office.

When he saw them at the door, Beebe got to his feet and shook Hank's hand, "Glad you're back, Hank. We got a whole new ball game up here. You're lookin' good. The R&R must have agreed with you."

Hank glanced sharply at Beebe to see if there was any deeper meaning to the words. He could see nothing beyond the friendly comment. Of course, not having an easy to read face was a prerequisite for a man in Beebe's position.

For the next hour, Beebe briefed Hank on the situation, "You will be working with MAC SOG and CIA case officers under the operational name White Elephant. The operation will include SEALs, a UDT detachment, Army Special Forces," some of Ken Nanski's people Hank thought cheerfully, "as well as an element of US Marine recons. You'll be known as the Naval Advisory Detachments.

"The group will also involve Vietnamese Marines, and boat crews who will be trained by the MSTs. They'll be operating four PT boats. All the operations will be under the cover of the South Vietnamese Coastal Survey Service."

Hank grinned at the handle. The survey service would answer such burning geographical questions like how many VC prisoners can fit into a PT boat. How quickly can the North Vietnamese Navy react to penetration of their territorial waters?

"Your missions," Beebe continued, "will include prisoner snatches, recon raiding teams, aiding the escape of downed pilots, direct action missions, insertion and extraction of agents, and the assassination of high ranking targets. All the same as before, just a little more sensitive," he grinned.

"Hank, you'll be living where you are for now. We've no place else to billet you, but we're working on that. That's not too hard to take is it?" Beebe waited for the obligatory laugh before continuing. "You've probably heard some old China hands brag about how good they had it out there, back in the good old days of gunboat diplomacy. Well, let me tell you, this is even better – except you can't brag about it."

Beebe went on, "Just have your men keep a low profile, these people aren't used to us yet. Also, there's plenty of VC running around this town, so act accordingly. We've set up operations on Phoenix, a small island off the coast. The PT boat base is operational at the foot of Monkey Mountain. I've moved myself and my staff up here to be closer to these operations. Some of these missions will be very sensitive, as you may have already guessed. We will, at times, be working very closely with other outfits. Situations can get sticky. So if you have any beefs, bring them to me. I'll do your hatchet work. After all," Beebe smiled, "We don't want any misunderstandings with our brothers in the fight against Communism, do we? Any questions? No? Good. Get settled, enjoy yourself. We got work in two days."

***

"Lieutenant! Welcome to the Alamo!" Lanny Vispo hollered out the window as Blevins turned off the engine.

"What?" Hank said to Keith, he wasn't sure he had heard correctly. Vispo's speech had been somewhat slurred.

"The Alamo," Blevins enunciated. "It's what the guys named this place."

Besides the obvious symbolism of the name, the house did have a literal resemblance to the historic landmark. It was a large, white, square, two story stucco building. The trim was rose colored, as was the tile roof.

"The guy at the gate didn't seem too interested in us," Hank commented.

"We can't quite figure that out," Blevins confessed. "Sometimes he's there, sometimes not. I guess he's some kind of half-assed security for us. He just sits there and never comes inside."

The front door was open, and the two men walked inside. Hank looked around and saw cases of liquor and food stacked everywhere. The Alamo looked like the storage facility for a PX on a military base.

Blevins opened a refrigerator, it was crammed full of beer. He tossed one to Hank.

"Where did all this come from?" Hank asked as he opened his beer.

"We sold the stuff we took off some dead VC," Vispo answered. "These REMFs are crazy for the stuff. The Danang commandos want to go home and look like heroes. They eat this shit up, and give us top dollar for it. Hell, we got enough booze to stay drunk for the rest of our tour."

As he took a long pull of the beer, Hank noticed there were loaded weapons of every variety lying around the room. His eyes narrowed a bit. It was lousy security and very dangerous.

Blevins caught his look, and said, "Come on, let's go up to the roof."

Hank followed him up two flights of stairs, not saying a word. "Some of the guys sleep up here at night," Blevins explained. "It's cooler – and safer."

On the roof, a few men were dancing with Vietnamese women to the sound of a blaring radio. Brookwater was as drunk as anyone could be and still stand. He greeted Hank after letting the slim Vietnamese girl he was dancing with slip out of his wiry arms, and then remarked that with the weapons and the field of fire they had, they could, with ease, "Hold this place for six months."

"Let's hope we don't have to," Hank replied. "Speaking of which," Hank turned to Blevins as Brookwater went back to his dance partner, "You need to establish better control of the weapons in this place. We don't need an accident with the locals. A stolen M-16 will get someone's ass in a sling. Plus, let's not give any free toys to Charlie."

"You're right," Blevins conceded. "Everybody's basically been letting off steam since we got here. Tomorrow we'll get back to standard operating procedures."

"I haven't seen Cutter since I got here," Hank commented. "He get back okay?"

"Yeah, he's back. I don't know about okay. He's been moody and drunk ever since he got here two days ago," Blevins said.

"Great," Hank sighed. "There's something goin' on with

him and the missus. We're gonna have to keep an eye on him. Let's make sure he keeps it together. Well, enough of this, let's join the party."

Hank found a bottle of Johnny Walker Scotch and a clean glass. He settled into a big couch in the main room. Blevins told him about the hangout they discovered in town.

"It's at the end of Quant Trung Street by the waterfront. It's run by the US Military Advisory Detachment. They got good food and topside movies. You pick your own steak, and they cook it right up for you. It got grenaded once by Charlie, but it's guarded now. You even gotta check your weapon at the door like the Wild West, but we always keep a sidearm under our shirts. An Air Force guy got shot on a side street a couple of days ago. You gotta watch your flanks around here," Blevins was rambling a bit.

The drinking continued, Bostic staggered over and flopped on the couch next to Hank, "Lieutenant, you know what? I think I got a VC parrot here. She's pissed about how we're treating her comrades."

"How's that, Bostic?" Hank played along.

"She won't talk to me anymore unless I give her some booze," Bostic slurred.

"Who can blame her?" Vispo called out. "I find you a lot easier to take after I'm smashed myself."

Bostic ignored Vispo, and kept talking to Hank in a serious tone, "After she dips her bill in the hard stuff, she blabs like a magpie."

Bostic staggered to his feet, and took the bird out of its cage, "If you don't start shaping up, my fine feathered friend. I'm gonna wring your fuckin' neck. Hear that, Penelope? I'm gonna wring your fuckin' neck!"

Penelope was noticeably unperturbed by her owner's outburst. She blinked twice, and then squawked, "Fuckin' jerk."

That brought the house down, even Hank had to laugh. He knew the humor was forced and, in any other circumstance, Bostic's antics with the parrot would barely get a grin from most people. However, it had been a long time since any of them had known anything remotely resembling normal circumstances.

Coming off of the time he had spent with Shirl, and the pleasant surprise of the new situation, Hank felt some of the tension leaving his system. Maybe sticking it out with this unit wouldn't be so bad.

Maybe…

Chapter Eleven

Monique Demarteau could not figure Joseph Olah out.

Most of the American men she knew flirted with her openly. It made no difference if they were married, single, or any of the various relationship points in between. Sometimes it was serious; sometimes it was just for fun. But there was no overt word from Joseph to show he was interested in her, yet his eyes revealed that he certainly had an interest.

She was sure it wasn't a racist thing, though she had detected an accent in his voice that suggested he was from an area where this sort of thing had not yet disappeared.

She also felt that Joseph Olah had treated her with nothing but respect. In fact, he seemed to enjoy working with her. His manner was friendly, professional, and he even treated her as an equal. He deferred to her judgment in certain matters. That was very unusual for an American.

The often laughed together. She even considered them to be on the way to becoming friends. Monique would have just written it off as a case of non-attraction, but she knew better. Women always know when a man is attracted to them.

When he didn't think she was looking, she felt him staring at her. She noticed him looking almost every time, but didn't let on that she knew.

She decided she would take action on her own. She knew this was the last day they would be working closely together and she did not want to lose the opportunity. She wanted a bit more information on the situation, and the man.

Why had he not asked her out on his own? Perhaps, just perhaps, he didn't want to put pressure on their professional relationship. If that were the case, after today it would be over.

She knew he wasn't shy. They were comfortable together. She had seen throughout the investigation that Joe was indeed, a take-charge kind of guy. If anything he was the kind of bold American the rest of the world saw only in movies.

Monique wanted to know what he was like outside of work; surely not the same thing she saw during the day. There must be more to the man. She wanted to hear his opinions of this crazy war torn world they were living in. She wanted to know what he did for fun. What did he care about besides work?

Most of all, she wanted to know what had put the spirit of sadness in his eyes. It seemed to creep into his face in those brief unguarded moments.

Ultimately, passionately, she wanted to see if she might be the one who could drive that sadness out.

***

Joe Olah had a lot to feel good about. He had almost wrapped up this investigation into the black market ring being run out of the airbase. He had successfully netted four American non-coms who were now under arrest and waiting for their court martial. He also had nabbed three Vietnamese military personnel who were in the custody of Lieutenant Khoa.

These arrests were good, but they were the small people involved in this criminal enterprise. He knew he did have some decent leads developing that should help him find the Fixer. Unfortunately, none of his current prisoners seemed to have specific knowledge of the man.

He did get his share of attaboys throughout the week. It seemed his new career was moving along well, if not a little bit ahead of schedule. If all that was true why did he still have that empty feeling in the pit of his stomach?

Even the usually reserved Khoa had expressed appreciation of Olah's police work during the week. Joe remembered the shudder that Monique had shown when he told her about that one. She knew what kind of man Khoa was. She had seen too many men like him back in her native home of Haiti.

Now he had to face the real problem. This would be his last day of working with Monique. If he wanted to spend any more time with her, and he did, it would have to be outside of work. He would have to arrange such a meeting in a manner that certain intentions would be inferred. There would be no more risk free excuses to see her, like work.

He had not thought seriously about seeing another woman, not once, since Cathy's death. The thought of dating someone, much less sleeping with someone, had just struck him as ludicrous for some reason. Mostly when he met other women he compared them to his late wife and they just could not measure up. Maybe it was that he just hadn't bothered to work up enough interest for whatever reason.

The concept of a relationship with another woman made him feel disloyal in some way. He knew intellectually that he was just being silly with such feelings.

All of that had held uniformly true, until now. Now he had more than a passing interest in a woman. He was consumed by her. When he was not thinking about work – and even occasionally when he was thinking about work – he was thinking about Monique.

Why was it that he had not just come out with it and asked her on a date? Despite his brash behavior in other facets of his life, he had never been too bold with women. It had cost him in the past. Women who had known him had told themselves he must not be interested. They thought that if Joe Olah felt a certain way, everyone would know about it. He was that kind of guy. Subtlety was not something they thought he was capable of.

Even though he had justified his reluctance with women he knew it wasn't the complete answer. He was from a place where a guy could get the hell beat out of him for trying to date a black girl. He remembered his mother's tones when they had once seen a white man with a black woman walking together in the city. 'A man only goes out with a woman like that for one reason,' she had said.

Joe did have one problem in his own mind that he could not shake. He was not sure what he was more afraid of, that Monique would think she was only after one thing, or that maybe, deep down, he really was after only one thing.

"Well," Olah said as they entered the records room, "I guess this is what you call full circle."

"What do you mean?" Monique asked.

"This is where we started working together, and this is where we finish," he said clumsily. Dammit! This was not at all what he had meant to say to her.

"Oh," was all she said, her eyes cast to the floor.

"It's been great working with you, Monique. I'm sure the next partner I get won't be nearly as good as you are. I'm going to miss it – I mean you... I mean we won't be working together anymore, but we're still in the same town..." he was floundering and knew it.

"Joseph, are you trying to ask me out for a date?"

"No!" he blurted out, and then he cringed visibly. He realized the idea was not one she objected to at all. "I guess, yes I am," he said timidly.

"Then ask me."

"Monique, would you accompany me to the Officers' Club tonight?"

"No, I don't think that would be a good idea," she said seriously.

His heart sank, and then he became annoyed. Why had she just put him through this? He opened his mouth to snap at her, and then saw the smile on her face.

"That's for making me wait so long!" she laughed.

He decided she had a sexy laugh.

"What time shall I pick ya up?" he grinned.

***

The Officer's Club at Vung Tao airbase was housed in a large rectangular one-story frame building at the edge of the airfield. Along one wall was a very long bar. The rest of the room, which took up most of the rest of the building, was a large dining room.

The restaurant was pretty nice; it had an open-air terrace, plenty of tables, and reasonable decor. The terrace, which made up the open-air grill, was decorated nicely with concrete blocks. They served as protection in case of an attack, but were disguised well.

As they walked in, Olah felt a rush of pride that every man feels when he enters a room with a beautiful woman on his arm. There was something more to it this time. He was not sure if it was because he was there with someone everyone recognized, and many had tried to date, or if he was just wondering if they shared his mother's old-fashioned, out of date, and incorrect feelings about interracial dating.

He wondered if there will still those rare places, even in Washington DC, where she would not be allowed to accompany him as a matter of policy.

They made their way over to the bar. Major Lyons stopped and congratulated them on the week's work. "You did a great job, Mr. Olah," he grinned, his eyes running over Monique.

Something in his mannerisms irritated Joe. He was not sure if the condescension in Lyons's tone had to do with his present company, or not. "Thank you Major," he said stiffly. He offered no further interaction with the man.

Lyons moved on after giving Olah a wink, Joe turned to Monique and sarcastically said, "That was really sincere."

"Don't worry about him," she said dismissively, "He just feels that anything that goes wrong on the base in the supplies area is his fault. He wanted you to find nothing and no one," she shrugged.

Olah ordered a bourbon and water. Monique had a gin and tonic.

"Do you want to eat outside, or in?" he asked.

"Outside is more private," she answered, "more background noise."

"Outside it is."

They made their way to the patio. Several officers offered Monique a greeting. She introduced Olah as her date every time. She was obviously a very popular person around the base.

They found a table and ordered their dinner. As they waited, for the first time since they had met, the conversation was awkward and stilted.

Suddenly, she just popped the question, "Joseph, why did you ask me out?"

Olah had not expected the question and was at a loss for an answer, "Why does any guy ask a girl out?" he asked defensively. He wasn't sure what kind of response she was looking for. "Why did you say yes?" he threw it back at her, like a good investigator would.

"Maybe I just have a sexual curiosity about white men," she said looking him square in the eye.

Olah blushed deep red. Even though he was embarrassed and somewhat ashamed, he could not look away from her gaze.

"You have been on pins and needles ever since we arrived. Does it make you that uncomfortable to be here with a black girl?" she asked.

Olah thought for a moment, then spoke from the heart, "I'm sorry, that's all I can say. I asked you out because I want to get to know you better. I like you a lot. For the first time in about a year I looked forward to going to work in the morning. I have you to thank for that. I guess I was kind of uncomfortable about this because we weren't talking about it. The way I was raised – I don't know, that's not really an excuse. It isn't right to fill a kid's head with that stuff. Can we start our night again?"

Monique smiled, "That's the first genuine thing you have said tonight. Of course we can start again. You mentioned your upbringing. Where are you from?"

"Coal country back in the states," he drawled.

"Is that in the southern part of your country?" she asked quickly. Olah understood what she was getting at. Worldwide people knew about the long since past US Civil War, and the reason it was fought.

"Actually," he said with mock defensiveness, "West Virginia, and we fought with the Union in the Civil War. In fact, they had to separate from Virginia, which was a slave state, to do it."

"I didn't mean..." she started, but Olah didn't let her finish.

"Yes you did, now who's being disingenuous?" Then he let her off the hook, "Actually, to be honest. West Virginia didn't really stay with the union out of any new change in attitude towards blacks. Hill folk can be just as prejudiced as any other. I'd like to change that, and it is changing. At the time they just wanted to be part of the Union, and stick it to those high falutin' Virginians who were rich enough to actually own slaves. We've always been one, and remain today, one of the poorest states in the Union."

"What would your family say about the two of us being here together?" she asked.

Olah grinned, "They never even completely accepted my wife. She was too 'citified,'" he drew out the word, and exaggerated his accent, "for their taste, and her skin was as white as milk."

Monique felt her stomach sink, "Your wife?" she asked quietly.

Joe's grin faded and was replaced by a far away look. "I should have said my late wife. You know, that was the first time I have ever mentioned her in casual conversation without having to compose myself first."

"How long has it been?" she asked.

"Eleven months and five days," he answered without having to stop and think at all. "She was hit by a drunk driver. I was a DC cop, and my friends thought this job would provide me a needed change of scenery. I guess I was a pretty sorry case."

"You were very much in love with her, weren't you?" she asked sympathetically.

"Yes. Yes I was," he ran his hand through his hair and sighed.

"Now I know what you were thinking while we were working when you would get that look in your eye in slow moments," she smiled.

"Am I that obvious?"

"Let me say this, you had better never, ever, join the CIA."

He snorted, "Not likely," then smiled at her. "Thank you."

She shook her head, "You know, I think your wife was one lucky lady. I hope someday someone is in love with me that way. I will let you in on a secret. That is almost every woman's hope."

"Don't worry," Olah told her. "It's going to happen. You are one special lady."

He met her gaze, and for a second, the moment almost seemed too intense.

"Hey," he cut in, lightening the mood, "I'm doing all the talking here, what are your deep, dark, hidden secrets?"

***

It was a pleasant night, so they took a pedicab on their way off the base. They sat together, comfortably silent and still enjoyed each other's company, despite the silence. Their mere presence together was just comfortable. Olah had learned that Monique was the illegitimate daughter of a rich French planter and a Haitian maid. Her father, though she was not officially acknowledged, had treated her as the apple of his eye. He sent her to private schools, hired tutors, bought her the best clothes, and used his connections for her whenever she asked.

The job in Vietnam was of her own choosing. She wanted to

be used to working with Americans. She figured they were the world's movers and shakers. She had grown up speaking Creole, French and English. She had an affinity for languages. Learning Vietnamese had come easily for her and taken mere weeks. She viewed her job at the base as a good experience, not as the start of a civil service career. She considered it a stepping-stone to better things.

About half way back to her apartment, Monique slipped her hand into Joe's. He covered it with his other hand, clasping it. In response she laid her head comfortably on his shoulder. They stayed that way until the pedicab stopped at their destination.

They both climbed out. They stood facing one another. "I take it I can call you again?" Joe asked rhetorically.

She smiled, "If you don't I will be very angry. Goodnight, Joseph." She quickly stood tiptoe and kissed him on the mouth, then turned and walked away. At the door to her building, she turned to him and smiled. With a little wave she was gone.

When the pedicab driver deposited Olah at his quarters, Joe gave him double the tip anyone else would.

For once, he never thought about the money.

Chapter Twelve

On Hank's first morning in Danang, Blevins drove him out to show him in the PT boat base at the foot of Monkey Mountain.

As they drove through the clean, quiet streets of Danang, which were absent of vehicle traffic, Hank was impressed with the serenity of the city.

It was a bright day. Hank was wearing the darkest sunglasses he could find to counter the effects of the morning's hangover. A few people turned to look at the Americans as they made their way to the Han River Bridge in the southern portion of the city.

Hank noticed there were some South Vietnamese soldiers around the steel bridge as they crossed it, "This is the only way to cross the river," Blevins explained. "Whenever Charlie blows it, it's a serious pain in the ass."

Once they reached the other riverbank the pavement ended and they turned onto a bumpy road that ran around an eventually onto the sandy peninsula. Each bump or pothole rattled Hank's teeth and reminded him of his headache in dramatic fashion.

"Damn, this Kraut truck is a hard ride," Hank gritted. Blevins chuckled unsympathetically.

The side of the road was littered with cemeteries or makeshift burial sites. He swore you couldn't go a kilometer without seeing one. When Hank asked Blevins about it all he got was a terse reply, "Frenchmen. The last guys who tried to fight a war here."

They followed the road for fifteen kilometers. They had to slow several times for water buffalo that insisted on having the right of way. Eventually they swung west along the bay. Hank saw people working crops in the fields. They generally paused in what they were doing to stare curiously at the white faces with round eyes.

All of this represented a side of Vietnamese life that Hank had not seen before. He felt like an intruder. For the first time he realized he had been too busy fighting to really learn anything about the culture of this country. He knew about the Vietnamese military, as well their corrupt bureaucrats and politicians, but there had to be more to this country than that.

Three times they passed guard posts set up by the VNMCs. They knew Blevins and he did not even slow down for them. He merely went by with a polite little wave.

"Nobody, but nobody's getting out here without us knowin' about it," Keith commented.

"What's that?" Hank asked pointing to several barracks-like buildings surrounded by high walls of barbed wire.

"Camp Tien Sha. That's where the VNMC and Army guys are billeted," Keith answered. "Lieutenant Ngo and his men came up here with us."

"What about our Yards?" Hank asked.

"Yeah, they're here too."

"Three Toes?"

"Yep, him too," Blevins said.

"Good, we're gonna need 'em. Let's move our Yards up to our place if we can. They're probably not all that welcome where they're at," Hank instructed.

Blevins grimaced, "We're gonna get static on that."

"Probably, but let's do it anyway. If you get static from anyone, tell 'em to see me. Let's find out how far this authority from Beebe goes. We can put 'em in that empty house out back. It should be big enough to handle them. Check into it for me?" Hank said.

Blevins chuckled, "It'll be the best damn accommodations any of them have ever had. It'll be nice for you to have your family close," he laughed, gesturing toward the copper bracelet on Hank's wrist.

"It'll be nice," Hank corrected him, "to have the extra security."

The road ended in a clearing near the end of the bay, "Well, this is it," Keith said. "We got this side of the bay all to ourselves. Like I said, nobody's getting out here."

Blevins showed Hank around the camp. There really wasn't much to the place. It had several small buildings: a power house, a parts and machine shop, an air conditioned Army trailer for storing weapons, and a small, floating dry dock.

There were two guard towers overlooking the camp. They were on the side of the defoliated mountain. They had a clear field of fire and could see for a great distance.

Hank stared at the Vietnamese red and yellow flag flittering above the power house. Same old shit, he thought, different place. "When the hell are we going to be able to fight under our own flag?" he mumbled.

"Come on," Blevins urged him, "this...you have to see."

Hank was a little surprised to hear a measure of excitement in his voice.

A small pier jutted out from the reddish dirt into the bay. Moored to it were four PT boats, loaded down with heavy firepower.

Hank whistled in appreciation as he looked at the hardware. Two of the boats were American designs; the others were Norwegian in heritage and were the type NATO had dubbed 'Nasty Class' boats.

They were covered with olive drab paint and lethal in their options packages. The boats looked wickedly sinister as they bobbed on the surface. Each eighty-foot boat was equipped with four mounted fifty-caliber machine guns, a forty millimeter cannon fore and aft, and twin twenty millimeter amidships. They were floating death. Each boat had the rough equivalent firepower of a flight of fighter aircraft.

"They can do forty knots," Keith said proudly, as if he had given birth to them personally, "As far as the real world is concerned these babies aren't even here right now. Our guys brought 'em over on a civilian ship. They went right through the Panama Canal. Can you believe that? The SEAL that ramrodded the mission told me that the captain of the ship figured they were heading for the Philippines to fight the pirates running around in that part of the world." There was an enthusiastic, almost childlike excitement in Blevins' voice that Hank had not ever heard before.

"You're really getting' into the cloak and dagger shit, aren't you?" Hank joked with him.

Blevins grinned, "It's just like Terry and the Pirates, boss. The plumbers from the White Elephant had us strip off anything that could identify them as US equipment. We removed builder's labels, name and nomenclature plates, and serial numbers, anything of US origin. They don't want the UN up our asses if anything goes wrong."

"I don't care what they identify just so long as you testify on my behalf at the War Crimes trials in Stockholm when this is all over," Hank said.

"I don't think that they'll consider an imperialist, capitalist, murderer like me a credible witness. That one could back fire on ya," Keith said laughing.

For about an hour Hank examined every inch of the boats. He was looking into everything and firing away with questions as they came to him. You could tell at a distance these boats were hauling a lot of power. Some part of him envied the PT boat skippers. His mind wandered to his sea duty before his assignment to the SEALs. He joined the Navy to work on boats, not this cloak and dagger – which was turning out to be mostly dagger – bullshit out in the jungle with the bugs.

A PT boat command in a combat zone was great for an officer's service record. That was assuming one survived the assignment. These were essentially floating loads of gas and ammunition without much in the way of armor. The American boats were made from aluminum while the Norwegians were primarily mahogany. One well placed round, and BOOM…Arlington National Cemetery funerals coming up with all the normal trimmings.

Hank and Blevins bounced down the road back to Danang and their ultimate destination, the White Elephant. Hank commented, "Keith, you can bet we aren't going to go up river in those hard charging gas-eaters. They're loaded for bear with that much firepower and they are not stealthy in any way."

"That's fine with me," Blevins commented. "I've seen enough of those muddy little tributaries and that stinking jungle to last me a lifetime."

Hank could not argue the reasoning.

Once at the Consulate, Commander Beebe continued filling in the blanks for Hank on the nature of their new mission. "SOG will be taking over the activities of Project Delta," he explained. "The Project will be run by us and the Special Forces. Your operations will include long range recon, intelligence gathering operations, rescue ops, and combat patrols deep into enemy territory in South Vietnam."

"SOG has been inserting South Vietnamese agents above the DMZ for sabotage, espionage, and psychological operations radio broadcasts being pushed into North Vietnam, and they had been doing these things for a while. Our intelligence from these missions indicates a large buildup for enemy forces in many areas in both the North and the South. The North Vietnamese are building radar sites all along the coast with the help of their Russian comrades, you know, those benevolent benefactors of self determination movements around the globe..."

"Except, of course, the Baltics and Eastern Europe," Hank cracked.

"Right. Anyway, these sites are capable of tracking our ships operating on Yankee Station in the South China Sea."

"Something tells me we're going to change all that," Hank said as Beebe paused.

"Exactly. Now tell me...what do you think of your new transportation devices you inspected this afternoon?" Beebe asked.

"First class all the way, Commander," Hank said speaking honestly.

Beebe grinned at the enthusiasm in his young platoon commander's voice. "I thought you'd like 'em. You're gonna be training out on Phoenix Island for a PT boat raid on one of those radar sites I mentioned. Sound like a nice change of pace for you?"

"Sounds like we are going to be busy, Commander," Hank said.

"That's affirmative, Dillon," Beebe looked at his watch. "Let's knock off for now. Get a good meal and some real rest. There is a CIA case officer who wants to brief you at 1300 tomorrow. You're on your own 'till then."

Hank and Blevins started out the door, enroute Beebe held Hank up, "Hank, by the way your friend Olah is in town. I don't know why, but I'm sure you'll be seeing him at some point. Don't take any shit from him. I managed to set him straight last time. This time if he gets in your way, I'll make sure it's the last time he does it."

Keith and Hank headed outside. There was a Nung headed toward them, dressed in American cammos. Hank eyed the man uneasily. He wandered if the Nungs around here had already heard about what had happened in the Rung Sat. He knew their reputation for disloyalty to employers. He was unsure about how devoted they were to the tribe.

The man saw Hank look, and returned the look with a scowl. The Nung opened a door and disappeared from view.

"Great, just great," Hank mumbled.

"Well," Blevins said, "I never said this place was perfect."

***

After a change of clothes, Hank and Blevins headed down to the club at the end of Quang Trung Street. It was contained in a two story wooden framed building that was painted beige and sported a few very fresh grenade attack marks. Now there were grenade screens added to each window to insure the results of future attacks would not completely ruin their patrons' evening.

It was just like Keith had said. It was the Old West come alive in Asia. Inside the lobby, just at the entrance, there was a large hand painted sign that read, "All weapons must be checked before going any further."

Just inside the door was a desk. Behind that desk was a peg board and shelves stacked with any kind of weapon a man could carry.

For the sake of show Hank and Blevins surrendered their M-16s at the door. Of course, they still had pistols tucked in their waistbands under the loose fitting, untucked civilian shirts.

After picking out their steaks, Hank spotted Ken Nanski at the bar. He told Blevins that he would catch him later. He wanted to talk to Ken.

He sided up next to him, "How're they hangin' Ken?"

"Lieutenant Dillon!" Nanski clapped him on the shoulder, "I heard that we will be workin' together. Welcome to the circus!"

"Hey, you've been here a while, right?" Hank inquired and received an affirmative grunt from Nanski. "Just how much is the CIA involved in our ops? What kind of mission d'you have going?"

Nanski held his hand horizontally at eyebrow level. "The plumbers are, at least, in it with us up to here. They're basically running the show. That is really why we have it so good in many ways. They've been providing arms and money for counter-terror teams."

"What's that?"

"Four to six man teams have been put together. They

basically do to Charlie what Charlie does to uncooperative villagers. It's a pretty good idea, except for the fact that the CTTs are made up of deserters, convicts and whatever kind of shit they can corral. These guys are recruited by the Vietnamese version of Special Forces. They are told they are going to get a chance to redeem themselves and get a decent paycheck in the process"

"Redemption and good pay. Best of both worlds," Hank said dryly.

"True enough. Anyhow, they'd slip these CTTs into VC villages at night. Their job is to kill the VC cadres who are pointed out in advance by CIA informants. They are dressed in black pajamas. This confuses and scares the hell out of Charlie for a while. It *was* pretty effective. For a while a lot of important VC were dying in their beds, only not peacefully.

"It turned out that it was too good to last. After just a short time it fell to pieces. Instead of finding redemption, too many of the little fuckers went back to their old habits. Some began acting like gangsters in the few friendly villages. Others hired themselves out to province chiefs as enforcers and bodyguards. Then the press got wind of the whole thing. Rather than allowing it to become common knowledge they had to shut the program down. They decided to fall back and reorganize.

"In a couple'a cases, we had to go in and physically shut it down. It wasn't pretty; it was wet work at its most extreme. You know what that's like.

"I heard about your Nung problems. The plumbers still got their hand in a lotta shit goin' down around here. Then, of course, there are all of their activities in Laos and Cambodia."

Nanski paused and jerked his thumb toward the back corner of the room, "Speaking of press, you see those guys at that table?"

Hank looked and saw a group of men easily identified by their demeanor and hairstyles as civilians rather than military. "You be careful about what you say when those guys are anywhere within earshot," Nanski warned, "or you might end up in print, or have Walter Crock-kite throwing a fit about your warmongering on the evening news. There is a big press center they all hang out at near the riverfront on Trung Nu Vuong Street. We found out the hard way that it is a good place to steer clear of."

"Speaking of Nungs," Hank said after his steak had arrived

and the two moved to a table so Hank could eat. "I saw one in American cammos comin' out of the Elephant today. What's that all about?"

"We used them a lot for a while in missions here, and especially when we cross the borders. The plumbers still use 'em a lot. They use them whenever they want some village chief bumped off or a high-ranking VC. Usually this is when they want to make it look like Charlie is cleaning up their own house. They can be amazingly brutal, and they can be scary when you are out in the boonies.

"For lack of a better term, they have ended up becoming arm twisters for the plumbers, and they are really good at it. Hell, the Vietnamese even still hire 'em occasionally, and they hate the bastards. The plumbers mostly use 'em in cases where they can't afford any whiff of US involvement. You know how that goes, plausible deniability. The other time they use 'em is if it looks like something so suicidal that they can't even convince you crazy green faced guys to try it. There's a group of them working out on Phoenix, out where you guys will be training. They keep 'em out there so they're out of the line of sight of the press. You'll probably see them hanging around while they are waiting for the plumbers to come up with their next gig.

"As for the plumbers themselves, we do some pretty hairy work for them. One thing I gotta say, you'll never want for anything equipment-wise that you'll need for a mission. Just say the word and they'll get anything short of a tactical nuke for you. The missions have direct Washington approval and authority. Money is absolutely no object for these dudes.

"Speaking of which, that Nung you saw today? It's payday. He was in getting his and his henchmen's share of the almighty pile of dollars from the plumbers. In cash, it goes without saying. No pay chits for these little bastards. No paper trail either."

***

The next afternoon following a late breakfast due to sleeping in, Hank and Keith hopped in the German command car and headed for the White Elephant.

As they turned onto Ly-Thuong-Kiet Street and headed for

the waterfront, Hank saw a crowd forming. As they approached, people closed in behind their vehicle. It made it all but impossible to do anything but go with the flow of traffic.

Blevins stopped when the mass of bodies became too thick for them to navigate. "As long as we're here," he commented, "we might as well see what's goin' on."

They wormed their way through the crowd. They came upon a large circle of Buddhist monks. They could not be missed in their bright orange robes and mostly shaved heads. There were also Buddhist nuns and other followers along with them. They were carrying unfolded banners with Vietnamese writings on them. Hank was surprised to see television cameras and reporters all along the edge of the circle.

"Must be a slow news day," he commented to Blevins.

Before Keith could fashion a wisecrack of some kind, the monks and nuns started chanting, "Na Mo A Di Da Phat. Na Mo A Di Da Phat." Soon, those in the crowd followed suit, until it was all the two SEALs could hear, "Na Mo A Di Da Phat," the traditional Buddhist prayer.

There was a very old monk sitting upon a cushion in the lotus position. He was not chanting. He was sitting absolutely motionless, just holding his holy oak beads. He was so still he did not even appear to breathe. The only way Hank could tell he was alive was because he steadily maintained a sitting position.

Hank looked at Keith. Keith shrugged in response to Hank's unanswered question.

After a few moments, the chanting stopped. The crowd was amazingly quiet. It was as the crowd was holding its collective breath. Hank could feel the tension running through it like and electrical current.

A young man darted quickly from the inner circle. He poured a clear liquid over the old monk. For the first time, the old man spoke. He was chanting the sacred words in a low and reserved voice, "Nam Mo Amita Buddha." Or 'Return to Eternal Buddha.'

The smell of gasoline permeated the air. For the first time Hank realized what was about to happen. He felt his scalp crawl. The old man took a matchbox from his robe.

"Holy shit," he breathed in disbelief.

The old monk struck the match, and with a loud *Ashwoosh* he was engulfed in swirling, roaring, hot flames.

Many in the crowd began to cry and moan. Some lay down in the street, howling in anguish. Hank was unable to move or look away from the spectacle. He stood motionless, his mouth hanging open.

A man with a megaphone was repeating commands in English and Vietnamese, "A Buddhist priest burns himself to death. A Buddhist priest becomes a Martyr," he shouted as the old man burned.

The old monk did not as much as flinch as his flesh was burned from his bone. He made no sound. He did not cry out in pain. Hank was unable to tell at what point he actually died. It was all over in about two minutes. At that point the blackened mass that had once been a human being toppled over and lay smoldering in the street. The body had strangely unburned lower legs. They had been protected form the flame by the position of the body. The dead body began to convulse uncontrollably. It added a grotesque touch to the proceedings.

Finally, the sickeningly sweet smell of burning flesh drove the two shaken SEALs back into their vehicle.

The street around the Jeep was now cleared of people. Blevins started the vehicle wordlessly, and headed slowly down the street.

Neither of the two men said a word all the way back to the Consulate. Each was pondering the grisly spectacle they had just witnessed. Hank had seen death in many forms. It had never once been in such a casual and deliberately self-inflicted fashion. Death to him was a common occurrence. It was something to be resisted. It was not something to bring upon oneself with pomp and ceremony.

For the first time, Hank was truly amazed with just how alien they were to this country. He wondered if it were possible for them to have any kind of impact in a place where such things happened. No war would ever change a culture that could encourage this kind of ceremony.

Chapter Thirteen

"What we have just seen and discussed is currently happening all over the country," the CIA briefing officer told Hank and Keith. The two officers had just described the self-destruction of the old monk.

John Ludwig was a bookish young man of average height and build. This bookishness was emphasized by his horn rimmed glasses and his businesslike manner. He delivered briefings like he was lecturing a college class or reporting the day's commodities prices. Physically, his most distinguishing feature was a very dark beard that darkened his face no matter how closely shaven he might be.

"It's the Buddhist form of protest," Ludwig explained.

"Buddhists not allowed to form picket lines?" Blevins asked weakly. His was so disgusted by the situation he needed to express his frustration and confusion about this situation. He could not fathom what would drive a person to do this type of thing to himself.

Ludwig ignored the comment. Small talk and jokes were not his way. "The Buddhists are complaining that Catholics are getting the best of everything in South Vietnam. They get the choice of land being redistributed by the government. They get preference for promotions in their military. They even get the best civil service jobs. They are charging that there is corruption in the government," Ludwig's ironic smile was testimony to what an open 'secret' the claim was, "They are also claiming harassment, false arrest and even murder by the Security Police.

"Things really flared up when they were forbidden to fly their religious flags. Some resisted and were taken down by force. Some young monks actually took their story to the Western press. The government retaliated by raiding their pagodas and making some mass arrests. That resulted in something like one hundred dead as a result.

"As you know, Khanh took over from Big Minh around the first of the year. The people here are already getting fed up with him. Our President has been trying to stabilize the situation by referring to General Khanh as 'the American Boy,' and starting a campaign of support. We have to support the government and stop the desertions being seen in South Vietnamese Army.

"In the field, some South Vietnamese troops have been committing, well atrocities may be the right word. We have seen stealing, raping and looting. The situation is shaky on a good day. With all of this turbulence, the VC have stepped up actions in the South.

"We have actual reliable intelligence that multiple regiments of the 325th People's Army of North Vietnam have moved into Laos and are using the Ho Chi Minh Trail to reinforce the VC fighting in the South. The Vietnamese fishermen are reporting increased boat traffic is bringing supplies and manpower to the VC on junks and trawlers. On more than one occasion we have recovered heavy weapons of Chinese manufacture. We have people currently working to track their way back to the dealers of these weapons. The last thing that Vietnam needs is another Korean War type situation with thousands of Chinese pouring over the border.

"Then, of course, there is that nutty speech our 'boy' just gave. He tried to incite the South Vietnamese people by calling on them to march north with him to conquer the NVA in one blow. He did this to stir things up and pull us deeper into the war to come bail his ass out of a slaughter. We are the only ally he has. He has zero experience at running a government. His ministers are, to a person, jealous and suspicious of one another. Support is low among the general population. There are constant rumors coming from everywhere about another coup about to take place at any moment.

"By now you have at least heard about, if not seen the students in the streets protesting the war. There is a built up frustration with the poor economic conditions in the country, and, of course, the draft. There have been some anti-American incidents, but the police and the army have controlled the troublemakers so far. A few Americans have been beaten by dissident mobs in Danang, so if you see a mob forming, get your head down and get out. The next time, they may be looking to burn something other than themselves. You will get catcalls and objects thrown at you on a regular basis, so I reiterate, keep your head down and your eyes open. In general, most people are indifferent toward us, so just try not to stir things up.

"As you are in civilian billets in the city you can get to the

Consulate quickly should trouble with civilian crowds get out of control. Try to avoid confrontation of any kind with Vietnamese people."

"What if we are attacked while in our billets by some individuals?" Hank asked. He already knew than answer – and what he would do no matter what the answer was – he was merely engaging in what the military officer corps called a CYA operation...Cover Your Ass at all times.

"Defend yourselves with any means on hand," came the official sounding reply. "Any other questions?" Hank and Blevins had none.

"Then that does it, gentlemen. It isn't a pretty picture, but it is what we have to work with."

***

The next morning Hank and Keith made their first trip over to Phoenix Island. The seas were slightly more choppy than normal. They hoped it wasn't an omen of things to come. Hank always liked pure clean sea air. It helped clean the memories of the jungle from his mind. He was enjoying his first ride on the PT boat with its massive V-16 engines that put out ten thousand horsepower. It pushed the craft quickly through the water. It moved effortlessly through the spray and choppy seas.

The island was approximately ten miles off the coast of Danang. In these fast boats the trip only took about fifteen minutes. As they approached, the boat's skipper circled the island. It was hard to access the sheer terrain which, in places, seemed to come right out of the water's edge. In other spots, heavy jungle started only a few feet from the shoreline. There were only a few spots where there was any kind of a beach for a landing. At the southern tip of the island was a small harbor with two piers.

As they approached, Hank could see the base camp coming into view. There were loads of hootches, a few Quonset huts, and curiously, a barbed wire enclosure with two guard towers.

The boat skipper led Hank and Blevins to the Ops Hootch. Beebe was already there waiting for them. He wasted no time getting started and skipped all small talk.

"What we're about to do is of a very sensitive nature," he

began.

"Sensitive," Hank reflected, knowing that meant, mostly likely, bloody or illegal. In some cases it meant both.

"We are going to execute a raid into North Vietnam in a body of water the Vietnamese call Bac Bo. To us it is known as the Gulf of Tonkin. This is part of the Joint Chief's plan for expanding covert actions against the coast of North Vietnam.

Commander Beebe pulled the green felt cloth off the table between them, revealing a large picto-map. "This is the radar site our reconnaissance has been taking pictures of for the last month. It is near the village of Xom Bang. It is on the coast thirty miles north of the DMZ into North Vietnam. That's about one hundred and twenty-five miles from here. Your mission will be to destroy the site and kill as many defenders as you can in the process. Of course it goes without saying, we would like a prisoner -- if possible.

Hank and Keith came forward. The three men gathered around the picto-map. It was as clear and detailed as any Hank had ever seen. "Some of these sites have new Soviet air-search capabilities. They are monitoring our ships in the area as well as our flights north and south of the DMZ."

Beebe pointed to the map, "When you are finished there we don't want anyone left who can point a finger at the US. Every trace of your presence must be erased from the surface of the earth. No witnesses at all. Period. Is my point getting through, Hank?"

"What if there are Russians at the site?" Hank asked.

"Under no circumstances are you to take Russians prisoner," Beebe instructed.

Hank nodded. It was the answer he had anticipated. Even though there would be propaganda value in proving Russian presence in North Vietnam. The US government would not be prepared to admit how the prisoners were taken. As far as interrogation went, it would not help the cause to have the Soviets know that the Americans had kidnapped one of their people. If that were to occur the propaganda advantage would shift to the other side. Even though no one had spoken the word Hank knew that the "no witnesses" rule applied in the unlikely event that there were still Soviet personnel at the site.

"The raid," Beebe continued, "will be conducted using Vietnamese Marines, as well as people from your platoon."

"Can we just use our people?" Hank asked quickly.

"No," Beebe answered immediately. "We will use the Vietnamese because as soon as they are familiar with the operations, and demonstrate the capability to do so, they will be taking over PT boat operations north of the DMZ. We will still have 'observers' ride along once that happens."

Hank did not say it, but he figured it would be a snowy day in Vietnam before the Vietnamese would have the ability to conduct the operations on their own. The SEALs would have to help for the length of their time in Viet Nam.

He decided to try to take a different route to a better answer, "How about taking along some of our Yards? I'd feel better if we had them for interpreters and for the extra security." Hank preferred to have the Montagnards along to keep tabs on the Vietnamese conversations. There was no question which group he trusted most, and who he considered more likely to be the source of the security leak continuing to cause them problems.

"Fine," Beebe agreed, then went on. "We have a plan of attack on the site drawn up, and we'll go over it later today. Naturally, we want your input as to its feasibility and any recommendations you might have. You will have everything you need for this op. For logistics you will work with Mr. Eli Kasman at the Elephant. He will handle all your needs. Remember, this place and everything about it are classified Top Secret. Now, let's get some chow."

Before lunch, Hank and Blevins made a head call then took a quick look around the camp. Some Nungs were sitting around outside the hootches. Hank had told Blevins what Nanski had said about them. "Keith, they look like real bad-asses, don't they?"

"Almost as bad as us," Blevins quipped.

"Nobody's that bad," Hank agreed cheerfully.

The prison compound was approximately one hundred meters square. It was surrounded by a fifteen foot barbed wire fence topped with the even more treacherous concertina wire. The concertina wire was hung in two rows, one inside the fence and the other outside. There was no going over it from the either direction. You couldn't break in and you couldn't break out without having to deal with that wire.

There was one longhouse in the enclosure. Several Viet

Cong prisoners sat outside silently. A few appeared to have been beaten badly.

"I would hate to be one of them," Keith quipped.

Hank agreed. There was no way any of the men inside that wire would leave the island alive.

***

After lunch, Hank, Keith and Commander Beebe spent several hours going over and finalizing their operational plan. "Start training the moment you are ready," Beebe told them. "It will be a few days before we have all of the equipment you will need."

Hank thought it would be longer than that, but said nothing.

"You will use part of the island for training. We have a mock-up of the site in an area not far from here. Again, no one outside of this room is to know about the location of the target until you are enroute. The training mock-ups themselves reveal nothing about the location of the target, just its nature. One last thing, all your enlisted personnel, and the VNMCs going on the raid, will stay here on Phoenix during the training period."

***

The following morning, John Ludwig introduced Hank to Eli Kasman at the White Elephant. Kasman was around thirty years old; he was of medium height and build, with unremarkable features. He even had generally light colored and balding hair. He was what all the handbooks called for in an intelligence agent-someone whose face and body did not warrant a second glance.

"Glad to meet you, Lieutenant," Kasman greeted him brightly. "I've been expecting you. I've got some of the things you need already here."

"How do you know what I need?" Hank asked suspiciously.

"Trust me, I know. Now let me see your shopping list," he said, holding out his hand.

Hank did not know whether to dislike the cocky sonofabitch, or admire his confidence. "I don't write things like that down, Mr. Kasman. You should know better than that."

"Of course," Kasman answered smoothly, "But you'd be surprised, sometimes. Now what do you need?"

As Hank told him what he wanted, Kasman made no comment, and took no notes. When Hank finished he merely said, "I'll have it all in three days. Check with me then."

"Three days?" Hank echoed. "You can get Inflatable Boats in three days? How the hell are you going to manage that?"

Kasman grinned, "It will be here, Lieutenant, all of it. Even your IBs. Three days, trust me."

"Yeah, sure…see you then," Hank answered unconvinced. Who the hell was this civilian to say he could get things in three days that a military request through normal channels, even with highest priority, would need a month or longer to procure?

As he walked down the hall, a Vietnamese officer and a Vietnamese civilian left one of the unmarked offices. They carelessly left the door open behind them. As Hank passed the open door he saw a table stacked ludicrously high with American currency.

An American civilian on the other side of the door saw him looking and quickly closed the door without saying a word.

Hank shook his head. He left the building wondering what the hell else was going on at this spooky place.

***

Hank notified Lieutenant Ngo he needed six of his best men who must also be good swimmers for an upcoming mission. The Vietnamese officer brightened noticeably at this as the SEALs had not used the VNMCs for a combat mission since the ambush that had killed Ayotte, Bush, and Ngyen.

Hank, Blevins, and the men Hank had selected from his platoon, Vispo, Hack, Slade, Brookwater, Bostic, and Padget, spent the next few days going over the operational plan while out on Phoenix Island. They made the determination that the best way to use the VNMCs (other than Brookwater's suggestion of dumping them halfway to the target) and drilled mercilessly on the mock-ups until Hank was satisfied they had it right.

When Hank brought his men back to Danang, arriving just after midnight Saturday night, word was waiting for him that some of his equipment had been delivered to the PT boat base at Monkey Mountain.

That morning Hank remarked to Blevins, "I didn't think that smug bastard could do it, but I guess he did."

"We haven't seen the stuff yet," Blevins pointed out.

"Yeah, but something tells me it is there and is top notch shit."

And it was. The two SEALs tore through their deadly packages with the delight of kids on Christmas morning. Hank looked over the containers holding the Inflatable Boats he saw the French nomenclature stenciled on the sides.

"This is just as good as our stuff," he told Keith. "The Frogs have been running these kinds of missions since before World War Two."

"That ain't all," Blevins hollered, "Look at this, we got Russian Ah Kahs."

The Russian-made AK-47 (or as the Vietnamese pronounced it, Ah Kah) was a rugged automatic rifle. It was legendary amongst combat soldiers for its reliability. It was easy to field strip for cleaning under the most adverse of conditions. It also fired a hefty 7.62-millimeter bullet. It was a very popular weapon among the Viet Cong and the North Vietnamese Army, though the NVA greedily kept most of them for their soldiers.

"That's not all we've received courtesy of the Worker's Paradise," Hank commented, holding up a Russian Makarov nine-millimeter semi-automatic pistol, complete with silencer. "This will replace our Hush Puppies nicely."

The SEALs usually carried silenced High Standard twenty-two caliber pistols on raids. From time to time it became necessary to silence village dogs before they could raise a warning – hence the nickname.

"Now I know why that bastard was toying with me," Hank remarked, "He's probably got a whole warehouse full of this foreign made stuff for covert operations."

"Yeah," Blevins agreed dryly, "He's got people doin' shit every single day that Uncle Sam doesn't want a bit of credit for."

***

Monday morning over at the PT boat base, the SEALs going on the mission attended their official briefing. Commander Beebe introduced a Mr. Somolie, a plumber who was all business.

"As you know, this operation is very sensitive. We have not yet officially acknowledged any overt or covert missions above the DMZ. We are not going to start acknowledging any at this time. In the highly unlikely event that any of you should be captured – it's unlikely, as our agents in the North tell us the target is very lightly defended – you *will* stick with this cover story.

"You are ex-servicemen in the employ of the South Vietnamese and French agents working out of Saigon. This will be easy for them to believe. After all, it's only been a few years since this whole area was known as French Indochina. They still have huge business holdings in the South and have been known to pay well for ex-servicemen. You are mercenaries, soldiers of fortune, in it just for the bucks. You don't care who wins, just so long as you stay alive and get paid regularly.

"They'll ask specifically where you work out of. These places are already set up to support your story. We know VC agents here and in Saigon, and have already started making them suspicious about the places. It's not enough to compromise you, but it will be enough to validate your story, if need be. It's the same cover most of SOG operations use. We haven't had to use it yet, so it should hold.

"This isn't widely known, even in our community, but there are prisoner exchanges going on all the time. These are handled by the South Vietnamese Security Police and their North Vietnamese counterparts. Both sides figure these things are better handled away from the military so that neither the press, nor any official source gets wind of it. The South is holding prisoners that the North wants back in the worst possible way, so there will be no problem if an exchange is necessary.

"The important thing is that you stick to your cover. You will be given more details, which you must memorize. Do it, and then destroy the paper it is written on. Remember, the price for a mercenary is a lot lower than that of a US Navy SEAL. Stick to the story, and there will be no problems. Deviate from it and we will have larger problems than how much money they will want for you."

Sure, Hank thought cynically. It is no problem for you, Mr. Somolie. No matter what happens to us you'll be sitting back in your air-conditioned office in the White Elephant. We'll be the guys missing fingernails, or standing on our tiptoes with a piece of bamboo shoved up our asses, all the while trying to remember your cover story.

***

The next day at noon, the SEALs, the six Vietnamese Marines, and the two Montagnards boarded the two PT boats, which were to be used in the raid. Once on board they headed out to Phoenix Island. As they streaked out through the relative shelter provided by the harbor and into the open sea very few words were spoken by those on board.

Hank was thinking about the kind of mission they were going to be training for. He was trying to get his head wrapped around the type of circumstances they would be operating under. There was a little bit of ridiculousness to the whole idea. They were going to commit acts, which their government would vigorously deny involvement with if they were caught. Yet, at the same time they were still bound by the rules of engagement. But if those rules were truly observed, this operation would not be taking place at all.

One thing Hank was pleased about was the individual VNMCs he had on the mission this time out. The five non-coms and one officer had been painstakingly chosen. Most had lost family members to the VC and had lost them in some brutal atrocity. Additionally, all of them had combat experience. Ngo had sent reasonably senior men who could pass any experience gained on to others. Hank made a mental note to personally commend Ngo on his good judgment.

When Hank and the others arrived at the camp, they were eyeballed by the Nungs. It's the same at every camp, Hank thought. Those not involved might not know the details, but they always know when a mission is coming up.

When Y Bli first saw the Nungs, he because apprehensive. "They are working with us, Lieutenant?" he asked.

"No, Y Bli, just those in the boats are going along."

"That is good, they are very bad people. Bounty men, they

kill everybody. Very bad to everybody, they have no belief," Y Bli said.

Hank noticed his own men were eyeing the Nungs warily. Their recent experience with Nungs was still fresh in their minds. Hank reflected that his attitude toward this war had certainly changed since he left San Diego. He was not so young anymore. While the Yards were just as dangerous as the Nungs, they were not savages. The Yards, to a man, despite their experience, were still idealistic in many ways. They had witnessed, even participated in, a fair amount of brutality. But it was all justified in their minds. But there were still things they would not do, there were several lines they would not cross.

Hank still believed-- hell he *had* to believe-- they would not be asked to cross those lines.

***

The following morning, all personnel involved – the SEALs, VNMCs, the Montagnards, and the PT boat crews, were given a briefing by Hank in the Ops Hootch.

Using the picto-map, he would take them through the mission step by step. He detailed the insertion, who would be on the ground and do what as well as how. He also explained what equipment would be used, then the all important extraction order, and contingency plans.

For the next five days, the SEALs trained the VNMCs in ways they had never been trained before. They were merciless in the pursuit of perfection. They stretched the Vietnamese to the point of exhaustion. They continued to drill them until even their lieutenant was vocally wondering if it was really necessary.

Hank merely smiled and pointed out his men were doing every task they were asking the VNMCs to do. As the lieutenant walked away, mostly content, Hank remembered his own tortuous training. What he and his men were putting the VNMCs through was nothing by comparison. This was really a walk in the park for the SEALs.

SEAL training started with four weeks of physical conditioning that was designed to push the limits of the men both physically and mentally. Every day started with two hours of calisthenics, including hundreds of sit-ups, push-ups, and pull-ups. For what seemed like endless hours they duck walked, sometimes for so long it seemed that they would never be able to stand up straight again. Running on the wet sandy beach in combat boots for hours became second nature. It was like brushing their teeth, just another part of a long day.

They rowed IBs in and out of the surf, up and down the coast, and then carried large IBs with them everywhere they went. They carried water-soaked telephone pole-sized logs over their heads in teams; they even did sit-ups with them on their chests. They were required to sprint everywhere they went. It didn't matter if they were going to chow or to the head, they ran.

As men dropped out, the evolutions became more difficult, and the harassment offered up by the instructors increased. It was capped off by the aptly named Hell Week, a continuous triathlon with no sleep. Hank had managed three hours of sleep that entire week. As soon as an instructor spotted a sleeping trainee, a bucket of cold water would soon appear. The purpose of Hell Week was to push men beyond what they thought their physical and psychological limits to be. If a man could make it through that, he would most likely make it through the remainder of SEAL training.

Of course, they could not put the VNMCs through anything resembling even the first week of SEAL training. Especially if they wanted them to be in any kind of condition they would need to be in order to go on this mission. They did, however, keep a fairly rigorous schedule.

They practiced breaching the surf with the IBs. They repeated capsize and recovery methods until the men were feeling waterlogged. The SEALs gave exhaustive weapons and explosives training late into the night. They simulated assaults on the mock-ups until each man could find his way around them blindfolded. It was obvious to Hank that the VNMCs had been given good training prior to this. They adapted well to what they were being taught. Hank was actually beginning to view them as an asset to the mission.

On Sunday, the training was complete. The men drank beer, wrote letters, cleaned and checked their weapons. They inspected the Inflatable Boats and their satchel charges. It was a busy day, but restful compared to what their days had been like.

The mission was set for 1800 hours Monday evening. The men spent that entire day checking and re-checking the equipment their lives would be depending on throughout the night.

Commander Beebe was present for Hank's final briefing. It was highly unusual for him to be present. It lent a lot of weight to the importance of this mission.

After the briefing, Beebe pulled Hank aside. "If everything does not go precisely our way up there and you have KIAs, do NOT leave our people behind unless you have no other choice."

Hank knew Beebe was concerned with more than just the deniability for this mission. "Understood, sir. We all come back together or not at all."

"Right, good luck."

***

The boats were warmed up when the raiding party arrived at the dock. The PTs were loaded down so heavy they sat low in the water. They were topped off with a full load of fuel and ammunition with the engines purring loudly. The skippers were waiting for their throttles to jump them to high speeds in the pounding seas.

Beebe watched as Hank, Y Bli, Brookwater, Vispo, Hack, and three of the VNMCs, boarded one PT boat, and Blevins, Padget, Bostic, Slade, the other Montagnard, a tough young man by the name of Phat, and the other three VNMCs boarded the other. The boats moved slowly from the dock into the calm harbor of the island. In unison, the engines began to roar. The rooster tail of water at the stern of the boats shot higher as their speed increased to thirty knots, and suddenly they were out to sea.

The SEALs were taking the war to North Vietnam.

Chapter Fourteen

Hank had been in the boat for three hours. That was three hours of a hard ride in choppy water. These PT boats inflicted pain on the body, especially on the kidneys. The PT boat skippers did what they could by altering speed based on sea conditions, but it was a hard ride no matter what attempts were made. That was just the price of doing business, as they say.

They traveled almost due north. That meant they would go out to sea away from the Vietnamese coastline which curved off to the northwest. There was constant heavy boat traffic close in along the North Vietnamese coast. With all those boats someone would have been bound to notice a couple of heavily armed PT boats and they would not have been able to escape detection had they stayed close to land.

After reaching a point eighty miles north of Danang, and seventy-five miles east of Xom Bang, the boats turned west to a heading of 265 degrees. They slowed their speed to twenty knots in the process.

They had just crossed into an area designated by the US Navy as Yankee Station. As there were many American warships patrolling the coast, the Navy had developed quick to understand and communicate designations for different sectors. The destroyers *USS Maddox* and *USS Turner Joy*, a tanker, and the aircraft carrier *USS Ticonderoga* were known to the SEALs to be in the general area this night. Hank had been briefed that the Seventh Fleet had destroyers patrolling the North Vietnamese coastline.

They were currently operating under the code name Desoto. They had large transportable communications vans bolted down on the decks. The vans were full of highly sophisticated electronic equipment that was under the control of the hush-hush National Security Agency, and gathered intelligence information that would, in the end, be used by MAC SOG.

Hank knew the warships had a 'Scant' briefing on the PT boat mission – the fact that they would be operating in the area, and almost no other information about their little foray into the North – only to be enough information to preclude any overt action against the PTs as they came streaking down the North Vietnamese coast in a giant hurry later that night.

At 2400, Hank began to see lights from the heavy traffic of the North Vietnamese shipping routes that clogged up the coast. The PT boat skippers reduced their speed even further as they continued to close in on the enemy coast.

Below deck in the messing area of the boat, Hank and his raiders went over the plan of attack one last time. They exchanged any last minute thoughts and instructions. He knew that in the other boat, Keith Blevins would be doing the exact same thing.

At 0100, a quick radar fix was obtained. "We're five miles off the coast, and one mile south of the target," the captain reported to Hank.

"Excellent," Hank replied, "We're right on schedule."

The radar was immediately placed back into the standby mode so the North Vietnamese could not detect-- or worse track-- the location of the electronic signal it generated.

The boats continued on their journey to the target on one engine to limit the noise level generated by the massive power plants. With quick, periodic radar fixes, they maneuvered clear of the fishing boats in order to work their way onto the beach in the pitch black of the moonless night. The PT boats snaked their way back and forth in the same manner as the fishing boats still coming in with their catch. It would not serve them well to head directly, and perhaps alarmingly, straight for their target.

Suddenly, the fathometer indicated the ocean bottom was shelving rapidly. Another hundred yards, and they were at a mere five meters in depth. They were now in the midst of the Vietnamese fishing grounds. These fishing grounds were one of Vietnam's major food sources. The Vietnamese coast was covered with hundreds of miles of fishing nets connected to long poles stuck in the soft bottom. Fishing boats would move from net to net around the clock collecting their catch.

Both PT boats hove to the gentle sea. It was high tide, just as they had planned. "This is as far as we go," the skipper told Hank.

Hank radioed Blevins to launch the IBs. After everyone and the equipment were aboard, the boat captain gave Hank the course to the insertion point.

At 0145 the IBs pushed off into the night. Almost immediately, they lost sight of the PTs in the darkness of night. There was no moon and the sky was overcast, meaning no stars this night. There was no better condition for a covert attack.

The Inflatable Boats moved slowly toward the coast in tandem. Hank was monitoring the small boat compass, when suddenly a voice shouted something in Vietnamese.

"Who the hell is that?" Hank hissed. "Where did it come from?"

In both boats, everyone froze and listened. Hank's thoughts shifted into high gear as his eyes strained to make out what might be in front of them.

The voice rang out again, and at that moment, Hank could make out a small junk no more than fifteen feet in front of the IBs. He whispered to Three Toes, "What did he say?"

"Wants to know who are we and what are we doing," Y Bli replied.

Hank gave the order to pull hard for the junk, "Tell him we're fishing."

As Y Bli repeated the alibi, the IBs came quickly alongside the junk. From both boats came the muffled clicking of racking sounds of weapons being locked and loaded.

The voice was just sounding again, as the SEALs vaulted over the gunwale of the junk, weapons at the ready. Hank put his red-lensed flashlight on the figure of a man being held by Brookwater and Hack at the bow of the junk. His eyes were wide, he practically snarled into the light.

Another man was being dragged from the small compartment below deck at the stern by Vispo. The man at the bow began talking again.

"Y Bli?" Hank inquired.

"He say they fisherman, have done nothing wrong. He asks who we are."

"Tie them up," Hank barked.

"Lieutenant, I don't think they fishermen," Y Bli said.

"What? How do you know?" Hank demanded.

"No fishing barrels," Y Bli said.

Hank was torn on what to do. He did not have time to interrogate them to find out who they really were. He could not just leave them behind. They just might be VC trying to get loose. Even if they weren't VC, they might raise an alarm, which could be worse. He had to do something, and right now. He was not about to risk compromising the mission. He checked to see if all the VNMCs were in the IBs. He did not want them to witness anything. He'd had enough bad feelings with them without killing unarmed Vietnamese civilians in front of them.

He knew he would have to make a decision that would haunt him the rest of his life. He also knew that there was no way around it. He had no recourse. This war was the worst thing he could imagine. Being left in a situation where you could not tell warrior from civilian. People get caught in the crossfire. Perhaps it was humanity that was doomed, but this was his unfortunate duty.

Hank signaled to Vispo. Vispo snapped the neck of the man in his grasp. Hank hoped that the crack sound could not be heard by the VNMCs. He turned toward the bow of the boat and saw Brookwater lowering the body of the man whose throat he had just cut to the deck.

Suddenly the door to a small compartment opened, and a girl of around twenty years of age stepped out. Hank could see the fright in her face. It took everyone by surprise. Vispo must have missed her when he dragged the man out of the cabin.

Hank didn't quite hesitate long enough. The Makarov jumped twice in his hand, the flame from the barrel momentarily lit the cabin. Thanks to the silencer it made no sound other than at the level of a man spitting on the ground.

The woman was knocked back by the impact of the two nine-millimeter slugs. She was dead by the time she slumped to the filthy deck. Time seemed to stand still for a moment as Hank stood rooted to the spot. There was a roaring in his ears like the pounding of surf. The woman's features relaxed then became strangely peaceful. He knew it was an illusion. She had died quickly, in terror and pain.

Damn any military outfit that dressed their members up as civilians. Sooner or later civilians would get caught in the crossfire. Vietnam had already become that war. This prostitute had just gotten caught in the crossfire. She was in the wrong place at the wrong time. Nothing could change that now. Were these men VC? Had they been right or wrong? He was 99% certain they were. Why else would they attempt to interrogate fellow fishermen?

Hank shook himself out of it and checked his watch. They were still on schedule. It had been only six minutes since they had boarded the junk now ID'd as enemy boat number 1. "Let's get the hell out of here," he commanded. He was surprised at the strength in his voice. Who the hell was this cold bastard who killed women then calmly issued orders?

"Cut the anchor line. The junk will drift out to sea with the tide. If someone misses this bunch, maybe they'll just figure they ran to the South."

The two men and especially the girl preyed on his mind as they pushed away from the junk. He banished them from his thoughts; there was no time for it now. He knew that there would be too much time to wonder what kind of monster he was becoming once the mission was over. Was this war really necessary? Was this what man was coming to?

The IBs started for the beach again. As they neared, Hank used the Starlight scope to guide them clear of the remaining fishing boats. He was thankful for whatever engineer it was that figured out how to build that fantastic little scope. They literally had to pick their way through the nets, bumping into them in the dark and pulling their way around by hand.

Once through the netted area their pathway to the beach was free of obstruction. Hank's adrenalin was pumping, and he knew the rest of the raiders would be feeling exactly the same way.

When the boats hit the beach they were less than one hundred meters to the south of the target. In seconds, the boats were carried up and off the beach and into the bush. If some sentry found them it would be problematic for the remainder of their plan. The pounding of the surf easily covered any noises they made while hiding their landing craft.

The men waited inside the bush. They were listening for any signs of human activity. There was only the roar of the surf.

Hank sent a man in both directions up and down the beach to check for any signs of a patrol. A few minutes later they both returned. They had no sign of tracks or any other indication of this area being patrolled recently.

Hank radio checked with the PTs, and then with Brookwater on point. The team moved deeper into the forest, leaving Phat to guard the IBs. After about twenty meters, they turned to the north. They had to traverse a steep hill toward the site. The dense forest was thick with underbrush that looked as though it had never been disturbed. Despite that appearance the SEALs were diligent in their search for booby traps with every step.

Half way up, they crossed a path, but stayed off it, and continued straight up the hill. They followed their familiar pattern of movement. It was second nature to these men: patrol, stop, listen; patrol, stop, listen.

As they neared the plateau, Hank heard the noise of generators used to run the radar and feed electricity to the rest of the camp. There were no trees now. The undergrowth had even thinned out. The raiders now moved in a crouch. They worked to avoid the clear areas.

Hank halted the patrol. He moved forward with Hack and Vispo. There was no indication they had been detected. Despite the ludicrously tight security Hank was on the lookout for any signs of ambush. As the three SEALs moved slowly forward the noise level of the generators became louder. Hank motioned, the two men stopped with him at the crest of the plateau.

Hank sent Vispo to the left, and Hack to the right. He checked his watch. It was 0320. They were right on schedule. As planned, Hack and Vispo scouted the perimeter of the site to locate any sentries. They would determine if the buildings they believed to be sleeping quarters were, in fact, used for that purpose. They would also determine, hopefully, the functions of the other buildings, as well as which, if any, were occupied.

As they moved off into the dark, Hank took out the Starlight and scanned the area. He had a startling déjà vu. They had been over the picto-map, and practiced this raid so often with the mock-ups, he felt as though he had been here before.

They had thought the site was lightly guarded because of the lack of guard towers in the picto. They surmised it would likely be protected by a few walking sentries at night. With a location this far north of the DMZ, the North Vietnamese had every reason to be complacent about safety.

Hank could see in the Starlight the dirt road leading to the west end of the camp from Xom Bang. The site consisted of seven buildings, all of which were wooden frame structures, except for the radar foundation building, and the powerhouse, which were made of cement. The radar dish was facing east toward the sea near the edge of an eighty-meter cliff. Seventy-five meters due west of the radar was the powerhouse. Power lines ran between the radar control building and the powerhouse, which were encased in plastic tubing and banded together. The lines were resting on evenly spaced wooden supports.

The one large building just north of the power lines was probably a mess area where everyone would gather for chow time. Another large structure just south of the power lines was probably the sleeping quarters. This, the largest of the buildings, had windows on all sides with a small porch.

Flanking the radar sight were two small buildings. One had to be a radar control room, and the other was likely a repair shop. Together, the buildings formed a rectangle around the compound.

Hank noted a small Russian-made truck that was parked next to the control room. There were dim lights burning in the mess and in the powerhouse as well as the radar room. The site compound was clear of any vegetation, and, at the moment, free of human activity.

At 0346 Hack returned, "There's one man on watch in the powerhouse, and there's one guard in there talking to him. He's got his damn weapon leaning against the door outside. They appear to be very lax in their security. There's two other guards in the mess hall, eating something that smells like shit. Probably that Nuoc-Mam they like so much. It looks like they're getting ready to relieve the watch," he whispered.

Just then, Vispo slid in beside them, "Lieutenant, the small building just south of the radar has two people in it. I could hear them talking in there. I listened for a couple'a minutes and there's at least two. The antenna on the roof is radio, so they got good coms with somebody. It's gotta be the radar control room. They got one guard sitting outside on his ass near the door. The door is on the north side, just like the mock-up. The door on the other building was open, so I looked in. Had tools, spare parts, and no people. The long house is where they're sleeping. It's big enough to hold a lot of 'em. Lieutenant, we don't want let 'em get outside."

Hank swept the site again with his Starlight, and in the eerie green glow saw the two guards leave the mess area with their weapons slung over their shoulders. He watched them separate as one went to the power plant, and the other headed to the radar control room.

"That's what they're doin' all right," he breathed, "Relieving the watch. Vispo, pass the word along, everybody up."

Everyone silently joined the rally point, Hank gave a quick briefing. "Things are pretty much as we thought. We go as planned," he finished.

Blevins, Hack, Slade, and the three VNMCs moved left into the woods toward the compound. Hank, Vispo, Bostic, Brookwater, the other VNMCs, and Y Bli started towards the radar watch control building. There was no need for further instructions. Each man knew his job, and how to do it well.

Padget remained behind with the radio, and an M-18A1 Claymore mine. After the others had departed, Padget crept toward the road from Xom Bang, set a trip wire across the road, and armed the mine. It would not do to have unexpected company that night. The eight hundred steel balls in the Claymore would discourage visitors.

The SEALs' first priority was to kill as many of the site personnel as they could before their presence was detected. This would eliminate as much of the potential opposition as possible. If they were detected before the assault started they would be greatly outnumbered. Surprise was key to their success.

Soaking wet from the climb and the tension, Hank shivered from a chill in the breeze coming off the ocean. He took point. He moved the team forward in a hunched walk.

The camp was extremely quiet. They had picked the right time to hit it. Almost everyone seemed to be sound asleep.

They stopped again. Hank looked through the Starlight scope. The two guards who had been relieved were in the chow area grabbing some food. At the north end of the building he could see two of his men. He knew the others must be at the south side door. Their job was to kill everyone in the mess.

He checked the powerhouse. He saw Cutter Slade kneeling over the guard. He knew the powerhouse would be secure now. If Slade was taking time to check the body, the man inside must also be dead.

He checked the radar control building and watched the guard move to the other side. Hank signaled. Brookwater, Bostic, and the VNMCs started out into the compound. They were headed directly to the sleeping quarters.

Their job was for the two of them to put into position two MK-26 HBX Haversack charges with ignition fuses on the sleeping quarters. Others would take position to kill anyone who might emerge from the building.

Hank, Vispo, and Y Bli headed for the radar room. Hank felt naked and hopelessly exposed out in the open compound. It was the only way to get to where they were going in a reasonable amount of time, and a risk he knew was necessary. The cover of darkness would have to suffice. But as sniper instructors say, concealment is not cover. Darkness would not stop the bullet coming from anyone who exited that building with an AK-47.

Hank pressed his ear to the door of the radar control building and heard faint voices inside. He motioned to Vispo. The two of them headed in opposite directions around the building.

Hank peered around the corner. There was no one in sight. He moved silently and quickly to the next corner, his heart pounding. After a moment, he looked around the corner and found himself eyeball to eyeball with a sentry taking a piss.

The surprised man was unable to react as Hank raised his silenced pistol and pointed it at him. At that moment, Vispo appeared on the other side of the man. Hank could not fire for fear a bullet going through him would hit his fellow SEAL.

He did not have to fire. Vispo was instantly on the guard. His knee was in the sentry's back and his left hand over his mouth. Vispo's right hand flashed across the man's throat. Black-looking blood erupted from the severed jugular. The sentry was still pissing as his body slumped to the ground.

The two SEALs quickly moved to the door. Hank looked at Vispo, only a few inches away, who nodded and drew his silenced Makarov. He knew what Hank wanted.

Hank pushed slowly down on the door latch until it stopped. Then he took a deep breath, pushed the door open, and burst into the room. He moved to the right as Vispo covered the left.

A man was sitting monitoring the green radar scope. He turned and started to stand. Flame jumped from the muzzle of Hank's pistol. He was so close to the man that the spurt of flame almost followed the slug into the man's brain.

Another man wearing earphones started to turn in his

swivel chair. He was knocked to the floor by a blow to the head from the butt of Vispo's Makarov. He fell to the ground, unconscious and bleeding badly.

A third man who had been asleep on a cot on the other side of the room was getting to his feet as Vispo shot him twice in the chest. He hit the floor with a loud sigh. The man began twitching uncontrollably in a rapidly spreading pool of his own blood. Vispo stepped forward and calmly delivered the insurance, a shot behind the ear.

If there had been an alarm in the room, no one had set it off. Hank felt certain of that.

Hank confirmed the radar was indeed of Russian origin. He motioned for Vispo to examine a stack of documents, "Grab them when we leave here."

Two of the dead men were in the light green uniform of the North Vietnamese Army. Their pith helmets were hanging on the wall on pegs.

Vispo put plastic handcuffs on the unconscious man, and then taped his mouth and eyes with black ordinance tape. The man was regaining consciousness. Vispo straitened him to a sitting position.

Y Bli came to the door. "Take the prisoner back to Doc Padget," Hank ordered.

Three Toes jerked the man to his feed and carried him out the door. For a fleeting moment, Hank wondered if he made the right decision. He remembered the last time Y Bli had been in charge of a Communist prisoner.

Hank checked his watch. Time seemed to be moving quickly. All of the action had taken a few quiet minutes. They did not seem like minutes. The clock seemed to be moving faster than physics should allow.

Hank and Vispo moved to the edge of the woods. Padget had already conducted the muster count, "All here, Lieutenant."

"Thanks Doc. Keith, everything ready?"

"It is ready to go, sir. They're sleeping like a bunch of drunks in there," Blevins answered.

"Ok. Brookwater, Bostic, do it to 'em. Blow it," Hank commanded.

Each man silently moved to where the haversack charges

were secured. Brookwater signaled Bostic with his red flashlight. The two men pulled the fuses on the charges at the same time.

They had one minute to find cover. Hank moved everyone back down the hill several hundred meters below the crest. Brookwater and Bostic moved quickly to join them.

They waited a few seconds. The charges went off almost simultaneously. It lit up the entire area. Even from their position of cover, hundreds of meters away, they could feel the heat and pressure of the blast. Hank looked up and could see the tops of the trees lit up with the light of the blaze. Despite their height and massive weight the trees swayed against the black sky from the force of the explosion. No tree ever swayed that much in a storm. Burning debris had been blown into the air and was falling in the trees and all over the compound.

Hank hollered, "Let's get up there and finish it."

They reached the top and saw that the sleeping quarters were simply gone from the surface of the earth. Only a portion of the burning foundation with a few jagged timbers protruding remained. Naked bodies and dismembered body parts littered the compound. Some were on fire, others merely smoldered. Torn pieces of bedding and uniforms were blowing around in the breeze. Weapons and pieces of weapons were scattered everywhere. He knew there would be no survivors from the blast.

The compound was brighter than it had been thanks to the burning debris. It provided more than sufficient light for the raiders to work in. Two of the VNMCs ran to the generators and placed ANM-13 thermal grenades on them. The thermal grenades would become white hot in short order. They would then burn through the generators and turn them into junk piles. For good measure, they also placed one on the engine of the Russian truck.

The mess building and the repair shop were set ablaze using burning debris from the former sleeping quarters.

In the light from the fires, Hank could see men darting all over the compound. They were his men and were efficiently going about their business. They appeared as shadows at times.

After grabbing the documents, and anything else that might be of interest to the plumbers, out of the radar room, Vispo placed a haversack charge under the radar and radio equipment. He set the timer for five minutes to give them time to evacuate the area.

Outside, Brookwater did exactly the same thing under the radar antenna structure.

When this was done, Hank fired three shots into the air with his AK-47. The well-known popping sound of the weapon brought everyone back to the rendezvous point.

After a quick head count, Hank told Padget, "Get on the horn and tell the boats we're on our way down, if they haven't guessed that already."

He knew that explosion would have been visible far out to sea.

Hank took point as they started down the hill. Cutter Slade and his M-60 were on rear security.

On the way down to the IBs, the night was again disrupted by the sound of the two charges destroying the radar equipment. Hank grinned. If the Reds wanted to use this place again, they were going to have to build it up again from the ground up.

When they reached the IBs, he was relieved to see the two Montagnards with the prisoner. The prisoner in question was alive, uncomfortable, and terrified.

As they loaded the inflatables, Hank saw his men were carrying armloads of souvenirs, AK-47s, pistols, pith helmets, and officer's epaulets. They would buy a lot of goodies and booze for the Alamo was the argument.

They had just made their way back out into the surf when the heard it...the Claymore mine Doc had set on the Xom Bang road being triggered.

"Here comes the cavalry!" Vispo laughed.

"That'll slow 'em down," Hack called.

"Well, now we know they know," Hank said. "Get those boats in here, Doc."

Padget worked the radio, and talked the PT boats into their location. They had been laying close off shore ready to give fire support if needed. The sound of their rumbling engines gave Hank an immediate sense of security and relief.

Once they were aboard, Hank gave the order. He had been instructed to leave behind one of the IBs. He wondered what the North Vietnamese would think when they found French equipment at the site.

They PT boat crew told Hank they had seen the explosion

and fires. "It lit up the whole sky when it blew," one of the gunners said enthusiastically. "They must've heard that all the way to Hanoi."

"One way or another you bet they will hear about it," Hank told him.

The PT boats turned south. In a few minutes they were roaring along at forty knots.

Twenty minutes later, the skipper called to Hank, "We got a large radar contact off the port bow closing fast!"

"Don't worry about it," Hank said.

All US ships in the vicinity had been warned about their presence. The contact radioed the Identification Friend or Foe signal, the boat answered, as did the contact. The IFF revealed it was the destroyer *Maddox* on patrol, which immediately moved off.

It had been a successful mission. Hank congratulated his men on a job well done. Then he sat, isolated, on the port side of the boat near the aft forty-millimeter mount. He could feel the all-too familiar shakes returning. He did not want the men to see.

As the boats raced back south toward Phoenix Island, he analyzed the mission. No casualties and the target was now destroyed. It had not been just dumb luck. This was how things were supposed to happen if each man did his job. Hank was satisfied each man had done perfectly. He felt good about it. He knew the next mission would be different. It would no longer be this easy. Charlie would be warned by what happened this night. They would not be that lax on security ever again.

He sat thinking as the dark outline of the Vietnamese coast raced past. It had been more than a good mission. It had been a perfect mission. The bastards literally had no idea what hit them. They had destroyed the site. They had also found all kinds of good stuff for the plumbers to pore over. The best part, the absolute best part, there had been no friendly casualties. The body count had been seventeen, and probably enough body parts for five more. The fact that they had to waste time on those statistics was fucked up but tonight he would not focus on what was fucked up.

Hank thought about how the training had bonded him and his men together. During training, when a man could take no more, could not push or squeeze one last bit of strength from his body to keep on going, when his body would no longer do what his mind commanded, he would ring the bell in the middle of the training area. This signaled he was quitting the SEAL training program. He would then be immediately returned to his previous duty station...no questions asked.

Then there were the others. They were the ones who had pushed beyond their normal endurance. The ones who willed themselves to continue after their strength was gone. They were the ones who were dog tired and still kept pushing, ran another meter, and who would rather drop dead on the spot before ringing that damn bell. Those were the men of his platoon, and he was damned proud of them.

Dawn was breaking. Hank watched the familiar sight. It was a sight all seagoing sailors knew. It was a crescent of the sun pushing over the horizon and the glistening black of water. It seemed to immediately give him warmth. He closed his eyes and let the feeling wash over him.

But even as he reflected upon the success of the mission, he knew the delicate features of the Vietnamese girl on the fishing boat would be added to the fire of his nightmares.

Chapter Fifteen

That evening after the mission, Hank and Blevins headed for the Alamo in order to, as Vispo put it in the invitation, "Open a keg of nails, and have us a drinkin' contest." Hank was beat, but an invitation to the enlisted quarters could not be turned down lightly. Besides, after a mission like the one they had just completed, it was impossible to sleep without indulging in some strong libations. They would settle his nerves and allow him to sleep for a while before the dreams came back.

Their debriefing upon their return had not taken long. It was debriefings after a botched job that took days. Beebe had been more than pleased with the results, the performance of his men, the PT boats, the VNMCs and the Yards. The prisoner was singing like a canary after a ten minute visit from a Vietnamese intelligence officer and two Nungs.

"Take your men back to Danang and stand down for a few days," the smiling Commander ordered Hank.

After they got back, Hank picked up the stack of mail waiting for him and headed back to their billet with Keith. It seemed odd doing something as normal as picking up mail given what they had been doing less than twenty four hours prior. He read the letters as Keith drove. Sometimes he just stared blankly into space as he attempted to digest the content. He eagerly awaited word from home. He was hoping for assurances that his wife loved him, as well as the news of his daughter. What he found was that each letter was accompanied by a strong feeling of guilt that he, by his absence, was neither the husband nor the father he should be.

Shirl's letter contained a nugget of disturbing news, which made the situation worse.

'I can't be positive Hank. I think Nancy Slade was on something on the flight back. She didn't act drunk, it was something else.'

"Great," Hank murmured. As if he didn't have enough to worry about. As if Dan Slade didn't have enough to worry about.

He wondered if Slade had a clue about his wife's problem. Something like that would be hard to hide. He knew most men were more than willing to remain delusional over a woman. He had once known a seaman who had convinced himself that his wife had gone through an eleven month pregnancy rather than face the reality of the situation.

There was also a package for him. Hank waited until he and Keith were back at the villa to open it. The return address was his brother Jim in Flint Michigan, Hank's home town. From the size and weight of the package, he was almost certain he knew what was in it.

"Check this out," he told Blevins who had already started for his room to clean up. He tore the box open like a kid at Christmas, and pulled out a model MAG-10 Ithaca ten gauge semi-automatic shotgun. The barrel had been sawed off at the magazine tube. The stock had been reduced to a pistol grip. A special shoulder strap had been fashioned just as Hank had requested.

Blevins whistled, "That's a beaut, Hank. But why didn't you just have Kasman get you one instead of puttin' out the bucks?"

Hank grinned, "I ordered it before I ever heard of Eli Kasman."

Inside the box were also a half dozen boxes of 00 buckshot, Magnum load shells. The Ithaca was idea for close in work in the jungle at night when you might not have the time to aim properly.

"Well, John Wayne," Blevins said, still enviously eyeing the gun. "What say we get cleaned up and get some grub?"

Hank set the water temperature as hot as he could tolerate, and then stood in the shower for almost half an hour. He let the hot water do some work on his aching muscles, and wash away the blood, grime and sweat from the previous night.

Then he wandered down to the refrigerator and made a couple of cold sandwiches. Hank did not really feel like eating, but his body said he must. He took them to the living room and sprawled out on the comfortable couch and nibbled at the first sandwich. After about half was gone he began wolfing them down as he realized just how hungry he was.

After finishing, he leaned back and closed his eyes. He was in no danger of falling asleep. He might be tired to his bones but sleep was not going to happen. His nerves were still on edge. His body had not yet recovered from the adrenalin rush brought on by combat.

Soon Blevins wandered in, "Ready?" he asked.

"Yeah," Hank grabbed the Ithaca on the way out. He knew the other men would enjoy seeing it. In their profession, men displayed new weapons the way civilians paraded a new car.

During the ride to the Alamo, the car seemed to ride rougher than ever. Their bodies had taken six hours of bone pounding hard ride in the PT boats. That was on top of the stress of the mission. Hank felt like he had carried the football forty plays in a row against the Army defensive line. Every bump in the road reminded him of a different ache on his body.

To make matters worse, the engine was sputtering every time Keith slowed to make a turn. It made a strange rattle that sounded like a bad bearing coming from the engine.

"That was a tough scene with the girl and all," Blevins said hesitantly.

"Forget it," Hank told him tersely. It was the last thing in the world he wanted to discuss right now. "Listen, leave this sorry sonofabitch for Hack to look at," Hank told Keith as they pulled up to the Alamo. "We'll find another way back."

When he had first arrived Hank had enjoyed the unique vehicle. Now he longed for a good old, perhaps boring, American Jeep. It had been fun for a while, and he had sent pictures of home of himself in the antique. Right now he was tired of pretending to be Rommel.

"Glad you said that, I got the papers in to junk it," Blevins replied as if reading his mind.

When they walked into the Alamo, everyone immediately wanted to examine the Ithaca.

"That ain't a gun, that's a fuckin' cannon," Bostic, who was already half drunk called out. "Look out Charlie!! Your ass is in a sling now."

Hank noticed food and medical supplies stacked in a corner. "You guys have already done some trading, I see."

"Affirmative, sir," Vispo told him, "Somehow those Air Force jockeys got word we were back."

"Yeah, somehow," Hack said sarcastically.

Hank motioned Doc over to the side, "Make sure you get the medical supplies over to the orphanage ASAP. Those are hot items on the black market, you know. Having them in our possession could lead to a whole heap of trouble."

Under Doc Padget's encouragement, the SEALs had all but adopted an orphanage located about a kilometer away on Trieu Nu Vyong Street, near the Pha Da Pagoda in Danang. Doc treated the children's cuts, bruises, burns, and the occasional broken bone. That was in addition to all of the typical childhood ailments. The American nun who ran the place, Sister Annabelle, had even grabbed him to help deliver a few babies in the nearby villages.

The orphanage was very poor. It housed some forty children of all ages all living and schooling together. Some of the other SEALs had starting going with Doc when he visited. They would help repair the buildings, and act like big brothers to the kids. Bostic, who was an orphan and been down a similar road as a child, spent essentially all of his spare time there. Every so often, some of the other SEALs would bring down some hamburgers and hot dogs along with the normal delivery of penicillin and food. They would then stage a cookout for the kids.

It was something Hank encouraged for the men. He let them do it right up to the point where it took them away from duties. He hoped it would allow the men some needed restoration of their sense of humanity. The bloody combat missions could cause someone to lose that.

Hank downed a few drinks. He was finally starting to feel some of the tension leaving his body. That was when he noticed Dan Slade was nowhere to be seen. "Where's Cutter?" he asked.

"He didn't get any mail from his old lady," Brookwater answered, "And he's really down. I mean literally. He's passed out in his room, drunk. It's best we leave him be, sir. He was really getting mean before he passed out."

"That's fine," Hank agreed. He thought he knew more of the story than the others. Maybe Dan Slade wasn't fooling himself the way he feared.

Hank spent another hour drinking at the Alamo, until some Army REMFs came in to do some trading. All of a sudden, everything caught up with him. The PT boat ride. The suspense of the approach. The raid. Then there was the fact that he had been awake for almost thirty-six hours.

He got to his feet, "I'm outta here," he said and waved.

As soon as he got back to Le Loi Street, Hank hit the sheets. As he faded to sleep he could hear Y Bli outside his window. He was trying to sweet talk one of the maids. He smiled. The woman had taken a liking to Y Bli. She had even taken some food out of the villa's refrigerator. Y Bli had refused it, and told her to return it. He would not steal from the Lieutenant and Mr. Blevins. Giai Vu had heard about it. He disciplined the girls harshly to the point that Hank was tempted to step in and pound the bastard.

Oh well, he thought, it sounded like Y Bli was making up nicely for Giai Vu's sternness. Y Bli just had to be happy after the mission. He had helped to kill a lot of communists. Now, to top off his night, he had found a willing woman.

At least someone was enjoying this damn war.

***

There was little activity at the Alamo late into the next morning. Bostic and Hardison were sitting out of the front in their swimming trunks and drinking beer. Vispo and Hack were up on the roof sunbathing in the nude. They were all dozing and still recovering from their loss of sleep and high level of tension the night before. The rest of the SEALs were still inside sleeping off their hangovers.

Bostic had Penelope with him. Her leg was tethered to a long piece of string. This enabled the bird to walk to get her exercise and fly for very short distances. Bostic was letting her feast on a variety of nuts and flowers. These were her favorite foods. He was paying a Montagnard for the flowers. He didn't care that the man was stealing them from a local cemetery.

Two Jeeps skidded to a halt at the gate. Their suspension system squeaked as they raised a cloud of dust. Four MPs with sidearms and billy clubs jumped out. They walked with purpose, as only the police do, as they strode through the gate and walked directly toward the front door.

"Hey, hold it Sarge," Bostic challenged the ranking man in the lead, "Where you goin'?"

"We're gonna search your billet, swab jockey, that's where," the man answered in what he had probably practiced as his best 'in command' cop tone.

"You better think on that, Sarge," Bostic answered. "'Cause ain't nobody goin' anywhere 'til we know what the hell is goin' on."

"You got nothin' to say about it," the large MP replied. "Now move out of my way."

"You try goin' in there," Bostic said, "And we'll tear your heads off and shit in the hole. Right, Jasper?"

"Henry, if they make it as far as the front door, I'll personally kiss their ass on Main Street in Danang, and give them thirty minutes beforehand to draw a crowd with cameras," Hardison drawled. He was backing up Bostic confidently even though the smallest of the MPs outweighed either of them by at least thirty pounds.

"Enough bullshit. You sailor boys don't get to tell us what we will and will not do," the sergeant barked. "Move out of the way and I'll forget about it." He drew his billy club.

"Better not do that," Bostic warned. "There's two of us, and only four of you."

That was all the MP could take. He gave the order, and his men drew their billy clubs and started toward the door.

***

Hank was sitting out on the patio drinking coffee and writing a letter to Shirl. He was annoyed at the disturbance of the Army ambulance speeding past. He winced at the noise flaring the headache caused by his hangover. He watched as two MP Jeeps tried to keep up with the Ambulances. Lights were flashing and sirens were blaring on all the vehicles.

He remembered seeing two other MP Jeeps speed by earlier, just as he rolled out of bed.

Moments later, he heard the German command car sputtered up the road. He looked up just in time to see Brookwater skid the vehicle to a halt in the villa's driveway.

He spotted Hank on the patio and shouted, "Lieutenant, there's been some trouble at the Alamo. There have been some injuries!"

Hank jumped in the vehicle. They took off down the street as rapidly as the vehicle was capable. As they neared the Alamo, Hank could see there was a crowd of Vietnamese civilians continuing to gather. Old men, little kids, and even women carrying their *don ganhs* – two baskets hung at the ends of a pole carried across both shoulders – and even some old women with their mouths blackened from chewing betel nut. They all stood with their mouths open watching the spectacle the Americans were providing.

Brookwater eased the vehicle through the crowd. He brought it to a stop near an ambulance as two medics were loading a stretcher. On it laid an MP with, at minimum, a broken nose and marks all over the left side of his face. His shirt was torn off, and his hat was nowhere in sight. He was holding himself carefully, obviously in pain, and making a little moaning noise that indicated he was far from comfortable.

Two of the other MPs were on the ground in the compound. One was unconscious, the other's arm was at an angle to his body that it really shouldn't be.

The sergeant who had argued with Bostic had lost all of his command voice. He stood dazed, shaken, and bleeding from the mouth. He was clutching the side of his Jeep with one hand for support while still clutching the radio mike he had used to call, begging, for help.

Hank approached the young Army Lieutenant who had just arrived, identified himself, and asked what had happened, although he was almost certain he knew.

"It seems my men were on a search, and your men resisted," the man, Harris, began.

"That's right Lieutenant," Bostic interrupted. He and Hardison were still standing in the doorway of the Alamo. They were spattered with blood, but they did not seem to be bleeding in any fashion. "They wouldn't tell us what was goin' on and tried to muscle their way in. It didn't go so well for them."

"Honest," Hardison pleaded, "That's the Gospel, sir."

A few of the SEALs wandered out in the skivvies, wondering what was going on. Hack and Vispo, still in the nude, started hurling taunts down at the Army from the roof.

Hank had reached the point where he'd had enough. Regardless of what his men had been through and whether or not the MPs had the authority to be there, the conduct of his men in front of the Army Lieutenant was starting to embarrass him.

"Knock it off," he shouted. "You people keep your mouths shut until we straighten this out." Immediately the SEALs fell silent. They knew what line they could not cross with Hank.

"Is it just the two of you involved in this?" Hank demanded of Bostic and Hardison, gesturing toward the MPs who still lay on the ground with medical personnel administering first aid.

"Yessir, just Jasper and me," Bostic answered.

"Who ordered the search?" Hank asked Lieutenant Harris, who was clearly annoyed that two men from the Navy had handled four of his men so easily.

"They're my men," Harris answered slowly, "But I did not authorize the search." He turned to the sergeant leaning on the Jeep, "What about it, Sergeant Willis?"

"We did it on our own, sir," Willis confessed. "We heard a lot of government stuff was finding its way to this place. I thought we should check it out."

"Well you thought wrong," Harris barked. "This place is off limits without my say so."

He turned to Hank, "I have to make a report because of the injuries to my men. Unless somebody's permanently disabled, it will go no farther than my captain."

"Good," Hank answered, "Now I think we better clear this area. These people," he said, indicating the Vietnamese civilians, "have seen too much as it is."

"I think," Harris grinned conceding defeat with style, "that they have certainly seen too much of those two." He pointed to the two nude men on the roof.

"Hack, Vispo," Hank hollered, "Get your ass inside! And get some clothes on, now!"

He turned to Brookwater, "Where's Doc?"

"He went to the orphanage first thing this morning, sir. He took the stuff to the Sister."

"When he gets back, have him check in with me."

Just then the crowd erupted with laughter, and Hank turned to see what could possibly be happening now to hurt his head further. He saw the people pointing up into the massive elm tree in front of the compound. Bostic was crawling out onto a limb, trying to coax Penelope back to him. All the time the bird was screeching, "Knuckleheads, fuck-ups, knuckleheads, fuck-ups!"

Hank stood shaking his head. He wondered if anyone had aspirin nearby. Harris tapped him on the shoulder.

"Uh, Lieutenant Dillon?"

"Yeah?"

"Could you please ask your men to return the weapons they took from my men?" he asked, obviously embarrassed.

Hank was happy to comply, and get the Army the hell out of the area. He had been holding his temper so far. He prayed nothing else would happen this day to try his patience further. This kind of thing in front of the Vietnamese was the one thing he knew they must avoid. He watched the embarrassed Lieutenant collect his men's weapons, and sighed to himself as they drove away.

Before today he thought the jungle was the worst thing for his nerves.

Chapter Sixteen

Hank was devouring a steak at the club when Ken Nanski saw him and sauntered over, as only Ken could, "That was a nice package your people did this morning on the MPs, Lieutenant."

"Siddown, Ken, and have a drink," Hank greeted him.

Nanski agreed, and ordered a Scotch, "What your men did is the talk of the town."

"My guys didn't start it, Sarge," he retorted a little bitterly. He was sick and tired of the subject.

"I know, but there's a lotta bad feelings over it, sir," Nanski said warningly.

Hank stopped eating for a moment, "What're you tryin' to say?"

"Nothin really. Except, uh, maybe your guys should back off for a few days? At least until the Gestapo finishes licking its wounded pride. A couple of those guys are real hot dogs, you know, loonies. You know how it can go sometimes," Nanski explained.

As an Army man, Hank could see he felt a little guilty about helping the Navy in an inter-service squabble. But as a member of the Special Forces, he had more in common with Navy SEALs than with the Army's Military Police.

"Point well taken, Sarge," Hank replied. "Now drink up," he said by way of thanks.

"By the way," Nanski changed the subject, "Our new place down on the beach is almost operational. It's only a half a klick from where you park those water hot-rods of yours. The Plumbers are picking up the whole tab. They put the place off limits-- except for us privileged few who are doing their odd jobs for them. We're gonna have a little bit of everything out there. If you're so inclined, Lieutenant," he said as he stood to depart, "come on by, and take a look."

Hank laughed, "I think you can count on us to check it out, Ken."

***

The next morning, Hank was out relaxing on the patio,

enjoying the quiet. He was trying, once again, to finish the letter to Shirl when he saw the man coming.

"Shit," he muttered and set the letter aside. If it wasn't one thing, it was another. So far, standing down had been more of a hassle than being operational.

"Good morning, Lieutenant Dillon," Joseph Olah greeted him pleasantly, extending his hand.

Hank took it cautiously, and then motioned him into a chair. "What brings you to Danang? We aren't being investigated again, are we?"

Olah raised his hands, "No, no nothing like that, Lieutenant," apparently deciding the bull in the China shop approach was not going to work. He also knew that would probably land him in trouble, once again. "Your Commander Beebe set me straight about that," he smiled.

Hank still did not understand why this man was in front of him, "Then what, exactly, do you want, Mr. Olah?"

"Joe," Olah insisted. "My friends call me Joe."

"Then this is a social call?" Hank said sarcastically.

"Well...I was in the area on another matter and I decided to stop by."

"That was real nice of you, Mr. Olah," Hank grinned.

"Heard your boys got in a tough spot yesterday," Olah began.

Hank interrupted him, "They did not start anything."

"Oh, I know that," Olah said. "There's no problem here."

"Good," Hank said shortly.

"By the way, just what were those MPs after?" Olah asked easily.

Hank shook his head, "Why me, Lord?" he asked rhetorically. He looked hard at Olah who started to shift around in his seat.

"Well, after all, Lieutenant, the report said they were after drugs."

"Pharmaceuticals, Mister Olah, not heroin." Hank abruptly changed the subject. "You got wheels?"

Olah was caught off guard. "Yeah, my Jeep's out in the road."

Hank stood up, "If you really want to know, let's you and

me take a ride."

***

As they drove down Trien Nu Vuong Street, Olah wondered nervously if he was just being stupid. All he knew for certain about the seemingly hard bitten man beside him was he had good connections. There was a lot of bizarre activity in this town, and it was possible his suspicions were totally correct. It was also possible that the more senior officers simply didn't give a damn so long as Dillon was doing whatever it was they needed him to do.

Jumping into a car with a suspected drug dealer, then going God knows where with him, with no witnesses, and no backup was hardly accepted police procedure.

There was something about the way that Dillon had challenged him to go along that had compelled him to accept the invite. It was more than just some male pride. There had been a tone in his voice that had convinced Olah that he was going to find out, one way or the other, what he wanted to know.

"Pull over here," Hank instructed, and Olah stopped the Jeep by the side of the road.

Olah looked around, puzzled. All he could see what a complex that appeared to be a school. It was well tended, and surrounded by a four foot wall. The wall was lined with trees and flower gardens. A wooden sign that arched its way across the iron gate was no help as it was written in Vietnamese.

Hank strode through the gate. Joe had to hurry to keep up. Hank pointed, "The cream colored building there, is the administration building and doubles as a school. Over there is the mess hall, those are workshops, and that two-story is the boy's dorm, that one is the girls'." He was pointing to buildings that surrounded a playground in the center of the compound. In the middle was a large swing set. It had huge airplane tires for swings. Joe was starting to have a funny feeling about who might have built this place.

Hank gestured toward a small two story house in the corner of the compound, "The people that run the place live there and here comes the boss now."

Olah had been suspecting he was about to feel foolish since

they arrived. Seeing the woman in the nun's habit hurrying toward them was the final straw.

***

"Hello, Hank, I see you brought a friend," the woman smiled. Sister Annabelle was of average height and had a slim wiry build from years of hard work. Even the hardship that had taken its toll on her face could not disguise the fact that she had been pretty in her youth. She had been a missionary in China in the thirties, and had been in Vietnam since the end of World War Two.

"Hi, Sister Annie," Hank grinned, enjoying Olah's discomfort immensely, "This is Joe Olah. I wanted him to see what a nice place you run here."

"I do run a nice place here. And it is in a large part thanks to some certain young men in the United States Navy. Come on, Joe Olah, and I'll give you the tour," she said cheerfully. Olah, of course, could not refuse.

Some of the children recognized Hank and gathered around, and he passed out candy, just as they expected. Hank always marveled at just how young and pure they looked. They were, as yet, untouched by the world outside the walls. In that world, kids the age of some of these kids were selling themselves on street corners. Others were being trained by the Viet Cong to be killers before they even reached puberty. Thanks to the Sisters, that world hadn't dirtied these kids. But Hank was afraid it eventually would. Whenever he wondered why he was wasting his life defending the crooked bureaucrats in Saigon, he thought of these kids. It didn't completely stop his questions, but it helped.

Hank lagged behind, playing with the kids. He grinned as Sister Annabelle bragged about the SEALs' good work to the NIS investigator. She showed him the dispensary, with the American medical supplies in the glass cabinets, Hank caught Olah's eye, and gave him a huge wink.

As they neared the gate after the tour, Hank was stooping down to let the two children he had been carrying off his shoulders. He saw Olah slip the Sister a wad of money as she shook his hand.

Hank said goodbye to the Sister. He was quiet as they walked back to the Jeep. Olah fired it up, and started the drive back to Hank's billet.

After a minute, Olah spoke, "That was a well stocked dispensary back there for a poor orphanage."

"Uh huh," Hank answered noncommittally.

"They even have a popcorn machine," Olah marveled.

"Yeah, I saw that," Hank grinned.

"You know, there's a popcorn machine missing from the Officer's Club that disappeared before it was even set up. It got a lot of people really pissed off. Important people. They had really been looking forward to having it."

"Do tell," Hank said, then he could not hold back any longer and started to laugh.

"They even," Olah whooped, "got three fifty pound bags of popcorn seed, just like the officers were supposed to have!"

"What a coincidence!" Hank howled.

Olah was laughing so hard he had to pull over. He leaned back in his seat and roared. Hank was also laughing uncontrollably. The tension of the past few days was finally leaving him like an exorcism had been successful. He had a hard time remembering the last time he laughed at all. He didn't think it was recent, even when he was partying and horsing around with the men.

After a few minutes, Olah wiped his eyes and stuck out his meaty hand, "Lieutenant, I don't know who you guys are, or what you are doing; and I don't think I care. I may come off like a prick cop, but I'm not afraid to admit when I've been wrong. Put 'er there, Dillon."

"It's ok, Joe. It can't be easy to run an investigation in a place where you're not allowed to know what is really happening."

"Listen, if I brought some stuff for you to look at, you think you could try to help me out?" Olah asked.

"What kind of stuff?" Hank asked his curiosity piqued.

"Oh, surveillance photos, that kinda' shit. You do get around this country in your work, maybe something'll ring a bell."

"Sure," Hank told him. "Though it's not the kind of pictures I would usually want to spend my day off looking at."

"I getcha," Olah grinned. "Sorry, but it's all I got."

"Okay, Joe, you bring your pictures over, and I'll treat you to some Scotch – just like they got at the Officer's Club."

Olah started laughing again as he started the Jeep back up and headed for the villa.

Chapter Seventeen

As Hank walked into the Elephant he had no idea if his summons to see Beebe was to get his ass-chewed over the incident with the MPs or some other unknown purpose.

"Hank, how do you feel?" It was Beebe's standard greeting.

"Fine, just fine, sir," Hank answered, waiting for an ax to fall on his neck.

"And your men?"

Oh no, here it comes. "Good, sir, just fine."

"That's good, glad to hear it. Have a seat. I need to bring you up to date on a few things."

Hank sat down. He was feeling slightly less uneasy than when he walked in the door. If Beebe was about to lower the hammer, he was certainly doing it in a round-about fashion.

"We've got some disturbing reports," Beebe began, "from our intelligence sources, of VC assassination squads moving into the area. Most agree that they are here already. Their only reason for being here is to kill Americans. Alert your men to take every precaution possible. Also, set up night watches around enlisted quarters. Your place at Li Loi, Hank, how is security?"

"We've got one of the Yards hanging around at night, sir. You can't tell he's there but he is. Nothing escapes notice."

"How much faith do you have in his loyalty?"

"One hundred percent, sir. With no reservations at all."

"I hope you are right. From what I've heard from these new sources confirms what we knew. Charlie is among us. No one could tell us who he is, but we have, at times, gotten information from a source as to operations of certain units around Danang. Before that, Vung Tau. We have people trying to work this story back to its source."

"It's not Y Bli, Commander; I'd stake my life on that."

"You already have," Beebe observed, "Now I have some instructions from the Consulate. They are expecting there will be some anti-American demonstrations soon. When your men are not at the base, make sure they stay off the streets. If there is an armed attack at your living quarters you will defend yourselves by any means necessary. If it's just mobs or students, call us and we'll have the Army clear them out. Do not take any violent action against them unless it's a clear case of self-defense. If they look like they are going to storm the place, just get out of there and come here at best possible speed. They may want to occupy the buildings for a while to prove a point that this is Vietnam. It says that they are Vietnamese and in control of their own country, and not bound to some Americans."

"What's going on Commander?" Hank asked, "Is there a coup in the wind?"

"No more than usual," Beebe allowed himself an ironic smile, "but demonstrations can get out of hand. That is especially true if they are Communist inspired with the goal of provoking a violent exchange for propaganda purposes. Most of them are going to be just students protesting the government, and it makes for better press coverage if they can involve the American military. Just treat them with caution. I realize that peaceful handling of opponents is not what you and your men trained for," Beebe paused, and then looked at Hank, "as was proved yesterday."

"Anyway, it won't be a problem for much longer. Quarters for your men are being constructed. Soon they'll be leaving behind the good life for Camp Tien Sha."

"They will be sorry to hear that sir," Hank grinned.

"A couple of them should be thankful that's the only change they are getting," Beebe grunted. "Now to another subject. I've been alerted by our people in the Philippines that the Norwegians you worked with in the Subic Bay before coming in-country are almost finished with the training we are putting them through. The CIA recruited these former Maritime Commandoes and mercenaries, and we've had joint exercises with them in the past. They are good men. They will take over the operation of the Nasties for missions north. This will eliminate the chance of our losing a boat crew, and at the same time, increase our deniability in case something goes wrong up there. They will bring two more Nasties and three Swift boats with them."

"What's a Swift boat, Commander?"

"They're light fifty footers used by civilian offshore oil rig crews. It's all we could get right now. They are tough and dependable. We need them for work in shallow waters. They have been stricken from the record books. Just like the boats we have now. When they go north they will be as clean as humanly possible. We also have a platoon of our people training LDNNs to replace us on missions north. Of course, a few of our people will always go along."

Hank nodded in agreement. The LDNNs, in Vietnamese, *Lien Doc Nguoi Nhia*, which meant literally, Soldiers Who Fight Under the Sea, were the Vietnamese version of the US SEALs. They were highly motivated, and went through a close parallel training to the SEALs.

"The plumbers are running a top secret resistance training center on Lao Cham Island, just north of Phoenix Island. The 'Weges and LDNNs will operate out of there as well as from our base."

"Looks like I'm losing my job, Commander."

"Not hardly," Beebe said dryly. "The tempo of activity around here, and for that matter the whole damn country, is really starting to increase. Don't worry; I'm going to have plenty of work for you and your people."

Beebe paused, and then picked up a folded slip of paper from his desk. "Now I've got a piece of bad news for you. This came in a few minutes before you got here." He handed Hank the paper. It was a cablegram from the Red Cross, "It's Slade's wife. She's dead."

For a moment, Hank was speechless, the wind knocked out of him. He remembered the very lively young women who flounced out of the C-130 at Ton Son Nhut only a short time before. She had not been his kind of person, but to die so young…

"What happened, Commander?"

"I don't know. That's all the information I have. Get him on a place for home ASAP. Hank, he's needed there."

"Yes sir," Hank said automatically, his thoughts were elsewhere. His mind was already searching for a way to break the news to Slade. Writing letters home for Bush and Ayotte had been bad enough. He was writing to strangers he would never have to face personally.

This was news he would have to deliver face to face to a man who was as close to him as his actual brother. He had no idea what he was going to say, or how he was going to say it.

For the first time since taking over the platoon, Hank felt completely unable to perform the task in front of him.

***

The following morning, at the airbase, Hank and Doc waited as Slade cleared his way with the people handling the flight manifest. He was going through the motions and doing the paperwork in a purely mechanical way. He still had shown none of the emotions that had to be tearing him up inside.

When he was finished, he returned to say goodbye. "I'll be back, sir," he told Hank.

"You don't have to, Dan," Hank assured him. "You know that. Maybe it'd be better if you stayed at the base in Coronado. Just until you get things sorted out. We're all going' back there in a couple'a months anyway. We'll see you in 'Dago, okay?"

Slade said nothing; he just stared at Hank, and then put his hand out. "You helped me a lot, Lieutenant. You know what I mean, sir."

Hank looked deep into his friend's face as he needed to him. Slade released his hand, gave Doc a clap on the shoulder, then walked stiffly out onto the tarmac.

Hank watched him go. Slade had shown no emotion since being told of his wife's death. Hank knew that Slade had been despondent since spending time with her in Saigon. He had kept everything bottled up inside. But he had always been a bit of a loner.

Now he was ticking like a satchel charge. Somewhere along the line it would all come out. God help anyone who might be close to him when it happened. One thing was for certain, Hank did not want Slade to be in the bush with his unit in this state of mind.

He reflected on what Shirl had written about Nancy Slade's condition on the airplane. If she had overdosed on drugs, that would mean he had now lost two men because of drugs. That was the same number as what he had lost to enemy action. What the hell was the matter with the world? Ordinary people put that kind of crap in their bodies and died? It made no sense.

Hank and Doc climbed into their Jeep just as Slade's C-130 could be heard roaring down the runway. The explosions of the JATO jet engines on the side of the prop driven transport plane echoed across the area. When they fired they caused the big plane to shoot forward and up into the air at an improbable angle and speed.

Doc turned the Jeep toward Danang. The two men were silent and glum, lost in their own thoughts.

Finally Hank asked, "Doc, do you think all of this is worth it?"

Padget seemed surprised at the question. He answered quickly as it was something he had been working on answering for himself. "I don't know, Lieutenant. Sometimes it seems like these people aren't worth defending. The only way they're gonna keep from going Red is if we nursemaid 'em forever. But you know, it seemed like that in Korea, at first. They didn't fight worth a shit. Their society was nothing to speak of. Now they are some of the toughest sonsabitches in the world. They are really building something over there. The problem with war is you usually don't know if it was worth it or not until it is over."

"Gee, that's a comforting thought," Hank responded sullenly.

"That's life, Lieutenant;" Doc said mildly, "Guarantees are for people in the life insurance business. Are you doing okay, Lieutenant?"

"Yeah, of course," Hank answered defensively, "Why do you ask?"

"I don't know. You just haven't seemed quite like yourself since Ayotte and Bush," Doc pointed out.

With a start, Hank realized he was right. Perhaps this had all been accumulating over almost two tours. It was the loss of two friends that had accelerated the process. Before that time they had operated successfully against Charlie with mostly minor wounds and scrapes to show for it. Then to lose two men in the same mission...it was too much death on his side of the fight. He wondered if men on the other side had the same thoughts.

"Is this what the men are saying?" Hank demanded.

"No sir, just what I've observed," Padget said cautiously.

"Well, I'm fine. I don't have to tell you to keep this shit to yourself, right?"

"Yes sir," Doc answered stiffly, as though he was a little insulted by the question.

Hank grunted in agreement. The two men sat in silence, lost

in their own thoughts. How could you live with the things they had done?

Doc was the first to break the silence. "Sir, I hate to bring this up now, but have you seen the binnacle list today?"

"No, not yet. Why?"

"Hardison and Bostic are on it. They got the clap."

"Damn, they know better," Hank said, clearly exasperated by the psychological weight he was already carrying.

"Those two have been jumping the bones of every woman they get near, sir. It was bound to happen. I'm giving them heavy doses of penicillin twice a day. They'll be okay in a couple of days."

"Be sure they stay put at the Alamo when they're not at the base, Doc. Tell those two that's an order. And no more boozin' until you give the okay."

"I'll take care of it, sir," Doc promised with a grin.

With that taken care of, Hank's thoughts returned to his conversation with Slade. It had been the first time he had voiced the fact that their tour had an end date.

Not talking about such things was more than a mere superstition. A man who was short acted differently. Thinking about the end of a tour could make a man overly cautious. He was less willing to take chances. In general, his efficiency in combat situation was lower. It was a dangerous mindset. Watching your ass too closely was just as bad as taking too many chances.

Leaving the platoon and the SEALs was not going to be easy, even at the end of the tour. Even to go back to his wife and daughter. How could he go back to that life, just like this life never happened? It was enough to drive you crazy. Hank had felt himself to be close to his men. He had not realized just how close until he had seen the naked despair on Dan Slade's eyes. He had been struck by the fact that he felt almost as badly about what happened as Slade did.

For the first time, going back to the rigid regimentation of the sea-going Navy did not seem like so attractive an option. In general, he would miss the close camaraderie of his unit. He felt they were different than other troops, a cut above. He would miss these men.

Hank shook his head to clear it. Like most sea-going men, he was a little superstitious. Thinking such thoughts was even worse than his doubts about the conduct of the war. Mentioning the end of a combat tour aloud was just tempting fate. He didn't do that sort of thing.

It was time to get back to the business at hand. Hank turned to Doc, and told him about the briefing he had received at the Elephant the day before. Then he outlined what he considered to be proper security arrangements.

All the while, in the back of his mind, he worried. He worried that he had jinxed every single man in his command with his short timer comment.

Chapter Eighteen

That night, Hank felt the need to unwind. He decided to take Ken Nanski up on his invitation to the new 'recreation area.' He pushed to the back of his mind the thought that for months now, unwinding meant as much alcohol as he could tolerate without vomiting. Hank set out alone in the Jeep he had managed to get out of Eli Kasman.

The spot of Ken's new hideaway was in the most isolated area of the peninsula that jutted out into Tourane Bay. It was about a half klick west of the Shark Pit, as the SEALs had dubbed the PT Boat Base.

There was no fence around the area. It wasn't needed. In the dusk, Hank could see Nungs on patrol around the perimeter. No one could possibly be blood thirsty enough to want to tangle with them. Besides, the plumbers had chosen the site well. It was remote and inaccessible enough that no unauthorized person was likely to come close unnoticed.

Hank parked his Jeep to the beat of loud music. It was being piped into the entire area through strategically placed loudspeakers. He walked up the sandy hill. He showed his blue plastic pass given to him by Nanski to a smiling Vietnamese soldier whose head was keeping time to the Beatles who were pleading to hold somebody's hand. The sentry took a good look at his pass. It left no doubt in Hank's mind that admittance was by invitation only.

Even by Vietnamese standards, it was a hot, muggy night. Hank's shirt was practically soaked by the time he got to the beach area.

There he saw people from the 'outfit' had already started the nightly party. Some sat in lounge chairs with a drink in hand under beach umbrellas. Others played volleyball under electric lights, while a few others were swimming in the surf.

Hank wandered around the compound. He wanted to check out their facilities. About thirty meters up from the beach, on a small rise, were five wooden buildings which were raised at least a foot off the ground on stilts.

Two of the buildings served drinks, hamburgers, cigarettes, and chips through large flap style windows. Hank accepted a Bud and a burger from a smiling Vietnamese man in civilian clothes. He guessed it was an enlisted soldier moonlighting for a few extra bucks.

In the next building, two Americans were sweating through an intense game of ping pong. There was a table in the center of a room. The remainder of the room was piled high with the kind of outdoor gear needed for a day at the beach.

The next shed-like structure served as a head. As Hank approached the next building, chewing on his burger, three attractive Vietnamese girls in brightly colored clothes, who were sitting in lawn chairs, were looking at him as though he were part of the menu. They were smoking and drinking. One of them made a comment in Vietnamese that started the other one giggling.

If Hank had any doubt about what the bungalow was used for, it vanished when he saw a VNMC come out the door. He was still adjusting his clothes. He was followed by a disheveled looking woman dressed just like those outside.

The plumpest of the three called out to Hank, "Hey, GI, you need boom-boom?"

Hank raised his beer can in a polite salute, and shook his head. As he moved on, the woman switched to Vietnamese. Her remark, whatever it was, elicited raucous laughter from the other women.

Hank felt his ears burn slightly as he walked away. Yes, the plumbers had supplied the best of everything.

About ten meters past the building, the picnic area ended abruptly. It was cut off by a scattering of huge dark colored boulders. Some were as large as ten feet high. Their incongruity was interesting to Hank. He had never seen anything like it. It was as though they had been dropped there from the sky. They ran from the scrub brush down to the white sand of the beach and into the water. Once in the water, the surf boiled through the openings between the rocks.

Hank wandered back to the beach area and looked over the forty or so people scattered around. He recognized a few of Nanski's Special Forces people, some of the VNMCs he had worked with, and two SEALs from Keith's squad. There were also a scattering of civilians dressed in cotton slacks and aloha shirts. Hank assumed they were plumbers.

He heard the familiar voice of Ken Nanski and turned

around. "Hi there, Lieutenant, how do you like the place?" Nanski approached with a long cigar in his mouth and a Budweiser in hand.

"It's got it all, Sarge, all the comforts of home," Hank answered jovially pointing towards the women.

"It's better they get it outta their system out here than uptown. At least these girls are inspected regularly. Uptown you can get anything from a cold to leprosy. Besides, this is all free."

"That makes it all better, Sarge. I know what you're talkin' about. I've got a couple of my guys on the binnacle list with the clap right now."

Nanski grinned, "Looks like we got set up just in time. They check the girls here." He gestured toward the people milling about, "There's not too many here now, but wait 'till later. This place really fills up. It can get pretty rip-roarin' Lieutenant."

"I believe you, Sarge. You got quite a mix of people here. Most of 'em are dangerous guys."

"What're you drinkin', sir, I'll get you one."

"A Scotch and water, if they got it."

"They got it, I guarantee you."

"How is your water, Sarge, is it okay?"

"It's okay," Nanski assured him. "They bring a full water buffalo out here every day from the base," he pointed toward a large black football shaped tank mounted on a trailer.

Hank and Nanski sat drinking and talking for about an hour in the dim light of the Coleman lanterns hanging around the area as the darkness set in.

Hank watched as the Americans and the Vietnamese mingled and talked with each other. With some, there was a comfortable respect. In many cases, the Vietnamese seemed to get more hostile towards the Americans the more they drank.

Scuttlebutt said the Vietnamese were singularly bad at handling liquor. Hank wasn't sure any race was better or worse than the others at it.

He did know that in any race it lowered the inhibition levels. In a situation where an uneasy alliance was the rule, that could be a dangerous catalyst.

Suddenly, the attention of everyone was captured by a Vietnamese soldier. He was all of five foot six on a good day. He was yelling and jabbing his finger into the chest of a Special Forces sergeant who towered over him.

Some other Vietnamese rushed over to try to calm their comrade. He was having none of that. He actively ignored their pleas. He struggled as much as he could in his drunken state to escape their grip, while, verbally abusing the American in Vietnamese the entire time.

Everyone on the beach watched uneasily. Whatever their other activity had been now forgotten. Hank saw the Vietnamese gather together nervously. The Americans placed their drinks in the sand to free their hands, just in case.

The Vietnamese soldier seemed oblivious to all this as he continued to yell as loud as he was able. They reminded Hank of a set of traps waiting to be sprung. He licked his dry lips in anticipation of the fight that now seem inevitable.

Around the edges of the light, Hank saw the civilians he assumed were plumbers slink away from the area. He could not help but grin. Once again, the CIA was leaving the fighting to the military. They always seemed to make sure their asses were safe, dry, and at a comfortable temperature.

The music stopped. The beach was abnormally quiet, with the exception of the pounding surf and, of course, the two men who were facing off in anger. The Vietnamese stayed right in the sergeant's face, and started shoving him.

Hank figured the man had reason to know he could get away with such actions. For some reason he was confident that he wouldn't get seriously hurt in this match-up. What the hell gave this little shit the right to treat an American soldier like this?

As Hank rose to his feet, the sergeant had finally had enough. He pushed back. He lifted the smaller man from his feet. The smaller man ended up planted on his ass in the sand.

The man looked surprised. He scrambled to his feet and came right back for more. This time the Green Beret was shouting back in Vietnamese.

Hank felt the whole place was just about to explode. He was not sure what was holding them all back. From either side. All it would take, he was certain, was for one person to make the wrong move. Then, all hell was sure to break loose.

Suddenly, the Green Beret turned his back on the little man.

He turned, and walked deliberately the other direction. The Vietnamese just stood there. His face was a mixture of embarrassment and confusion. Hank and everyone else on the beach waited to see what would happen next.

Before the man could react, a torrent of rain suddenly hit the beach. It came down in sheets. It drove everyone to shelter and served to diffuse the situation. The rain appeared without warning. One second nothing, the next they were soaked.

Hank and Nanski ran over to one of the refreshment stands. They stood under the overhang of the roof. Some of the rain still blew in on them. After living through the heat of the day it felt pretty good. Besides, they were already soaked during the time they sought shelter.

"Not a pretty sight, huh Lieutenant? Some of these little bastards got big egos. They get mad when they screw up in the field, so they blame it on us to save their pride. To make matters worse, tempers are running pretty high anyway; they got wind of what we think about their fighting skills. What we just witnessed is a classic example of how feelings are running around here. Damn, I never thought we'd have to put up with shit."

Even though the rain had cooled things off a bit, it was still an uneasy situation. Hank noted the groups that had formed in search of shelter were segregated between Americans and Vietnamese. It was obvious that a very serious 'incident' had been avoided by the sergeant's action and the superb timing of the surprise rainstorm.

"It may be over," Hank told Nanski, "but it's not forgotten. Not by the two of them, or by anyone else here."

"It was that close, Lieutenant," Nanski agreed. "That close. You know, sir, those bastards in Washington have us out on a limb here. I don't think they have the foggiest fucking idea what they're going to do about it. They're even bickering among themselves about how to fight this war. Bickering about how WE should fight this war. If that attitude catches on with the American people, it'll be just that much easier for Charlie to cut that limb off. Then we'll be the guys stuck with the dirty end of the stick."

"I couldn't agree more, Sarge, but we're committed. I don't see how we can turn back now."

As abruptly as it began, the rain stopped. One moment

there had been sheets of water lashing the beach, the next, not a drop was falling. Hank knew from now to November was typhoon season in Vietnam. He hoped they wouldn't be stuck out in the middle of the South China Sea in a PT boat when one hit.

"You want another drink, Lieutenant?"

"Lead on, Ken."

As the two headed toward the building, which was again open for business, Hank saw a familiar face coming out of the recreation building. Lieutenant Ngo caught his stare, and looked away as fast as he could.

"We'll be damned," Hank laughed, "Old Stoneface is dipping his wick. He has other things on his mind besides avoiding trouble after all."

"You know that one, Lieutenant?"

"Yeah, he's the CO of my VNMCs."

"That guy's been out here every night since we opened up. If I'm not mistaken, he's been in there every night with his favorite woman."

The rain seemed to have cleansed the air of trouble. The incident did seem to have dampened the spirits of most of the party, and many of them began drifting toward the road. After another drink and some small talk, Hank decided to follow their lead.

When he got back to Li Loi Street, he found a note waiting for him from Olah.

'Came by to show you those pictures, I'll get back to you later.'

"Oh, yeah," Hank muttered. He had completely forgotten Olah was stopping by. Dan Slade's situation had occupied his thoughts and driven most else out.

Suddenly, he was bone tired. Stress of combat was easier for him to cope with. "Well, shit, if it's so important, he'll come back," he said to no one in particular.

He went to the kitchen, grabbed a bottle of Johnny Walker, and headed for bed.

Chapter Nineteen

The following morning was Sunday. Hank decided to head over to the Alamo for a quick look. From time to time an informal inspection was in order. This was one of those times. He wanted to make sure the enlisted men were no longer leaving 'sensitive' material lying around.

It was just after 0900 when he drove up to the front gate. Hack and Brookwater were in the front yard getting a tan.

"Are you still working on that Kraut piece of crap?" Hank asked Hack. He had done the paperwork to have the old command car declared obsolete and removed from Navy inventory when it was obvious it couldn't be fixed quickly. Rather than junk it, Hack just kept working on it. As a Machinist's Mate he looked at is as a challenge. Besides, it gave him something to do between missions.

"Yessir. I managed to scrounge some stuff for it from the guys at the airfield. The Seabees are making some parts for it. I'll have it running before we leave this place, Lieutenant."

"Good," Hank encouraged him, not sure if he meant that or not but it seemed like the thing to say. "Stay with it." It was not as though Hank had any use in mind for the vehicle. It was also good to see a man doing something constructive with his free time – instead of developing the clap, like some of his buddies.

As Hank walked through the screen door, he saw Doc Padget. "Good morning sir. How 'bout a cuppa coffee?"

"No thanks, Doc, just had some," Hank declined politely.

"What brings you out this way so early in the day, Lieutenant?"

"Just wanted a quiet look around. By the way, what kind of security d'you have set up around the place?" he asked.

As Padget ran down the watch schedule, Hack and Brookwater burst through the screen door. "Sister Annie just drove up and she's got some kids with her, Lieutenant!" Brookwater had panic in his eyes, "Stall her as long as you can!" Then he followed Hack who was galloping up the stairs.

Hank got to the door in time to see Sister Annie unload the last of the dozen or so children from a public works truck they hitched a ride on.

"Good morning, Sister," Hank greeted her.

"Good morning, Hank," she called back, "How are you on this beautiful day?" The children with her were all dressed in clean, ironed clothes, and scrubbed to they almost shone in the bright sunlight.

"I'm fine, Sister. What's up? What can we do for you?" Hank asked, nervously wondering what his men were up to.

"It's not what you can do for me," the nun answered, "But what we are going to do for you, our favorite people. I heard Jasper and Henry are both sick. After all you have done for us, well, I thought I would have the children show their appreciation and cheer them up."

"Sick?" Hank echoed, "Who's sick?" Oh yeah, Hardison and Bostic. Yes," he answered slowly trying to cover the embarrassment, "they're inside, probably still in bed. Sister..."

Before Hank could go on, Sister Annie turned to the children. They were lined up in two rows and she raised her hand. When she brought it down, the lyrics of *Onward Christian Soldiers* emanated beautifully from the children's mouths.

The sound of singing filled the Alamo. It had to carry pretty far down Ly Thuong Trong Street. Hank could see people from adjoining houses and those on the street craning their necks to see what was going on.

Hank did not know what to do or say, so he just stood and smiled as the children sang their hearts and souls out. Some of the other SEALs who had jumped quickly into the clothes came out to show their appreciation.

From the corner of his eye, Hank saw two Vietnamese women sneaking out the side gate of the compound. One of them was still stuffing her blouse into her pants, while the other carried her shoes for her.

Please don't let her notice, Hank pleaded mentally. Just then he saw Annie's eyes following the women out of the yard. Hank would have given a year's pay to be somewhere else right at that moment.

As the children started on another hymn, more of the SEALs joined him. They were smiling and hoping to make the best of a completely embarrassing situation. Some of the others slipped inside to square away their appearance before rejoining the group.

As they sang, the words and music touched on something in

Hank that had long been dormant. It took him back to a time in life before all the killing and brutality. It took him to a time before the dreams. It took him to a time before he had to numb his senses with a bottle before he could get any sleep. He wondered if he could ever return to that time, or if it was gone forever.

He looked around at his men. He saw that the looks of embarrassment had been replaced by something else. They all had a faraway expression that told him many of them had been moved in the same fashion he had.

As the last words of 'Rock of Ages' faded away, there was a moment of silence. Finally the men, lost in their thoughts, realized the surprise concert was over.

On Hank's cue, the men gave the children a heavy round of applause. Doc and Vispo came out of the Alamo with a cooler filled with soda and some boxes of cookies.

Hack brought one of the beautifully crafted rattan chairs that had come with the place out to the yard for the Sister to sit in. The children broke out of their group and were playing with their 'Navy friends.'

Hank slowly walked to the Sister. He stammered out an apology for what she had seen.

She cut him off. She patted his arm and said, "My dear man, have you forgotten I'm an old China Hand? I am more than aware of the appetites of the American sailor. Not that I approve, but I understand." She patted his arm again, "Now don't let it bother you."

Hank started to say something. The Sister stood up smiling and waving. She looked up to the front of the Alamo. Hank followed her gaze. He saw Bostic and Hardison waving as they laughed and hammed it up for the children.

Hank looked at the ground and shook his head. Despite the beauty of the event, he could not escape the irony of the situation.

It was, he was absolutely certain, the first time in history that two men had been serenaded with hymns for having contracted a venereal disease.

Chapter Twenty

Hank was walking up the dark mahogany steps to the second floor of the Consulate and couldn't help but wonder what secrets these rooms had heard. What discussions had gone on here that the world, or more importantly the enemy, would like to know? Beebe had ordered him to show up for a briefing. Hank had been told about the "second deck" of the White Elephant, but had never climbed the stairs.

It was this floor where the plumbers hatched their bizarre plots. Hank knew from Nanski that the border jumping missions into Laos and Cambodia all came from discussions in these rooms.

Operationally speaking, things had been entirely too quiet. They'd had too much time between missions. Hank assumed that this down time was about to come to a full and immediate stop. He was certain they were about to be humping the boonies in the very near future.

He reached the top of the stairs and found a pair of armed Marines posted outside a door halfway down the hall.

"Could we see your ID card, sir?" the sentry asked politely, but firmly, as only a US Marine can.

Hank complied with the request. The sentry dutifully checked his name off the clipboard. It seemed a bit much, but what the hell, it was the nature of the business.

"Thank you, Lieutenant Dillon." The other guard opened the door. Hank found himself in a large, beautifully decorated room. It had a high, white, rounded ceiling trimmed in gold painted Vietnamese figures. The walls were filled with paintings of American scenes. It had several large couches and what looked to be comfortably upholstered chairs scattered around the room.

At the end of the room an oval table surrounded by a dozen high backed chairs, several men sat under a large portrait of President Johnson.

One of them was Commander Beebe, who motioned Hank to come over and sit. Beebe, as usual, was all business, "Lieutenant Dillon, this is Major Boertz, from the 5th Special Forces working for SOG, and this is 1st Lieutenant Dehart, also with SOG."

The men shook hands, and acknowledged they had met before. Another familiar face at the table was Eli "Trust Me"

Kasman, who nodded and grinned, "Lieutenant."

Hank knew for certain from Kasman's grin that fun and games were in the making. Eli could only be there to open his store to accommodate Hank's shopping list, whatever it turned out to contain.

The obligatory amenities and shop small talk were exchanged over coffee, until a civilian walked in. He was dressed in a short sleeve shirt and slacks. He carried his slim six foot two frame in a confident manner. He looked the room over with his dark eyes, which were the same coal black as his hair and moustache before introducing himself.

"Good morning, gentlemen, please, keep your seats," he said, motioning for them to not get up. Hank noticed that the back of his left hand looked like someone had worked it over with a machete some years before.

"I am Seth Thayer," he introduced himself, "A member of the Consulate staff." Those present immediately translated that to mean "high ranking plumber in need of a cover story."

For ten minutes, Mr. Thayer talked about the situation in Vietnam and what the American objectives were designed to achieve. Then he stopped beating around the bush, and came to the point of the meeting.

"Our intelligence warns us that regiments of the 325th division of the People's Army of North Vietnam have been training in the hills and forests of the Quang Binh Province, a few clicks north of the DMZ. We have every reason to believe that particular army will soon be joining the insurgents in the South. We also know that, for some time now, they have been moving ammunition and supplies into South Vietnam from the sea. They are also moving through Laos and Cambodia to support the Viet Cong. Just recently our sources located a cadre of the 325th PAVN in the Mekong Delta region. Major Boertz's people have placed others in the Kien Phong Province near the Cambodian border."

Thayer paused for dramatic effect, then announced, "Gentlemen, that is only seventy-five miles from Saigon. Do I make my point clear?"

He continued, "We have had reconnaissance teams working on the problem before, but now we need far more precise and detailed information."

It was the same old crap, just a different day, Hank decided. Even if they had the name, address, and the shoe size of every single North Vietnamese soldier in the area of interest, the CIA would be asking for "more precise and detailed information."

"We knew this situation was developing, but we did not know they could move this quickly. Not to mention, we don't know how they did it undetected," Thayer went on.

That was the comment, Hank observed, of someone who had never seen the jungle canopy for themselves. Charlie could move around under that stuff undetected even if the bastards had sent the CIA advanced notice by taking out a full-page ad in a Saigon newspaper.

"So, gentlemen, there you have it. They are here, and it won't be long until they are here in large numbers. I need not tell you how this development will affect the posture of the American military here in South Vietnam.

"Now, for the purpose for which I have asked you to be here today. Washington wants to know, and know now, how and what the North Vietnamese are moving into South Vietnam."

Dammit, Hank thought, as Thayer turned and took a dark felt cover off a large map of Vietnam, I knew we'd get roped into this border jumping crap sooner or later.

Apparently it was going to be sooner.

With a pointer, Thayer indicated a spot on the map. "Friendly Montagnards, near the village of Dox, located about a hundred klicks west of Danang, in the Thua Thieu Province, near the Laotian border, have told us of increased North Vietnamese activity moving south along a route about three klicks inside Laos. We have flight reconnaissance photographs showing strong evidence of staging areas in North Vietnam, just north of the DMZ. But, we have nothing to support the accuracy of suspected routes taken to move men and supplies into the south."

"We think, however, they are using these routes." He turned and traced lines on the map with his pointer. "We will place reconnaissance teams along these routes at various intervals to discover if this is, in fact, what is going on. We have to know for certain exactly what is happening and how much of it is going on. The information I have *must* be confirmed before any military or political action can be considered, much less taken. I must reiterate the importance of the accuracy of these reports. Our future plans will be based on the information they contain. Remember, you may not be able to trust anyone out there in any of the villages – or anywhere else, for that matter."

No shit, Sherlock, Hank wanted to say. Where did this guy think they had been spending their time? Honolulu?

"Now for another matter. You may find it necessary to enter Laos or Cambodia in order to obtain the level of accuracy we need in our data. I stress, we need accuracy above all else."

Hank was getting tired of the refrain. He was tempted to point out the grammatical redundancy. He and his men knew first hand, if a report was inaccurate, it was hardly informative or useful, now was it?

"You all know the political fallout that would be generated by the other side if our people are caught inside those borders." Thayer stopped talking abruptly. He looked at the men seated at the table before him. In an almost apologetic tone, he continued, "I'm sure you're aware we would have to disavow any knowledge of who you are and what you are doing if you are caught. Now, are there any questions?"

There were none.

"Good. I'll now turn you over to Commander Beebe who will give you the operational details of what this mission entails. It has been a pleasure seeing you gentlemen. Good morning."

With that, Thayer turned and walked from the room as quickly as he entered.

The pleasure's been all yours, Hank told the retreating man's back. You want us to risk our asses for your information. To top it off in the same breath you tell us you don't believe we exist.

It was not anything new. Hank had heard the spiel before. He knew the risks when he volunteered for this type of duty. He would just be a little happier if the REMF just didn't have such a goddam casual attitude about his neck being on a chopping block.

***

After Beebe's briefing, Hank headed back to his quarters. He hoped to catch up with Keith Blevins. Instead, he found Joe Olah hanging around the living room.

"Hi, Lieutenant, nice digs you have here."

"Hey, Joe, doesn't NIS take care of you like this?"

"Not hardly," Olah snorted.

"You should have picked a different branch of Uncle Sam's alphabet soup when you left the cape," Hank grinned.

"Any particular one?" Olah played along.

"I can't tell you that. Let's just say its initials are two thirds of the letters found in the word cat."

"Ah, so," Olah bowed comically. "Perhaps I should have taken up an honorable trade, like, say, plumbing?"

"So…what's up Joe?" Hank inquired, "I expected to see you here over the weekend."

"I went to Vung Tau for a couple of days."

"Hot lead?"

"Nice girl," Olah grinned sheepishly.

"So much the better. I'm relieved. The dedicated cop has other interests. Congratulations."

"I'm pretty lucky," Olah said, "But the congratulations may be a bit premature. Ask me again, later."

"You're lucky to catch me," Hank commented, "If you'd come by tomorrow, you'd have been out of luck for a couple of days, at least."

"What's goin' on?" Olah asked.

Hank just looked back at him wordlessly.

"Oh, yeah. Dumb question. Sorry I asked," Olah squirmed a little before getting to the point, "Listen, I've got some surveillance photos I need an expert to look at. You get around, and I think the guy I'm looking for might actually travel in your circles. We made a huge bust a few weeks ago. It led us to a large warehouse with a lot of activity. Instead of swooping down on it, we've been taking pictures of whoever goes in and out. If we can we follow them. We figure we can raid the place whenever we want, but then all these fish just swim away, and we never find the big one."

He brought out a large envelope. He handed Hank a stack of eight by ten black and white photographs. All of them had been taken from a distance. Some were much better quality than others.

Hank flipped through them slowly, deliberately. He was looking at each face carefully. He had never seen a single one of them.

Olah took the pictures back, and then picked one out for review, "Not even this guy?"

The picture was of a man with light hair and a darkened streak. His face was only two thirds in view. "Not a great shot, but that's some hairdo."

"This guy is good," Olah said bitterly. "He approaches the warehouse from a different route every single time. He always obscures his face without being obvious about it. Every time we put a tail on him, he slips it."

"He's had some training," Hank observed.

"Yeah, but by whom?"

"That's the sixty-four thousand dollar question," Hank said. "On the other hand, maybe he's just amazingly street smart."

"Yeah, maybe," Olah was not sold.

"Do drug dealers ever exercise this kind of tradecraft?" Hank asked.

"Not that I have ever seen," Olah said. "But then again, there's more money in drugs than ever before. So maybe they can afford more training than ever. Hell some of the bigger drug lords have security forces large enough and well trained enough to take on a small army and probably win."

"Well," Hank said thoughtfully, "there have been enough spooks and covert wars in this part of the world ever since the Japanese invaded China, that he could've been trained by just about anyone, including us."

"True enough," Olah said. "World War II seems like ancient history, but if this guy's in his forties, he's plenty old enough to have been in the Resistance."

"I guess, and you know who ran the Resistance to the Japanese in Vietnam, don't you…" Hank said.

Olah shook his head.

"Uncle Ho, himself."

"No kidding," Olah said staring at the picture.

"Not that it means anything," Hank told him. "Just wanted to let you know how things shift around this place. Now tell me, you said this was the one guy who was constantly slipping your tail. So who is fatso here?"

Olah looked at him for a moment, pondering his answer. It was not policy for someone from NIS to share information. They especially didn't share information with a member of the regular Navy.

"Listen," Hank prompted him. "You come clean with me, and I think I got an answer for tracking Mr. Black Streak to his lair. Deal?"

"Okay. I don't see the harm. At this point, I trust you," Olah said.

"Right," Hank began, "Now I'm sure your men are very good. That being said, we both know that it is next to impossible to tail someone who knows how to lose surveillance without a large team. You can't go the big team route. If there's an American on his tail every time he turns around, it won't matter if it is a different face. He'll know something is up just due to the racial rarity here. I've got a man who not only blends in with the scenery but as an added bonus, the Vietnamese are trained from birth to ignore them. Plus, he could track an ant over bedrock in a rainstorm."

"Okay, who is this miracle man?"

"His name is Y Bli, he's a Montagnard that works for us," Hank answered. "But you can't have him for a few days."

"A primitive tribesman?" Olah was surprised. "You think this is his kind of job?"

"Hey," Hank said sharply, "You look around this city. Then you go hang around with Y Bli for a while, and you tell me the definition of 'primitive.'"

"No offense meant, Lieutenant. If he's as good as you say, okay."

"He is that good," Hank said flatly. "You remember when you interrupted us down on the dock that night?"

Olah made a face, "Yeah, I think so," he said.

"Okay, that was a pretty tough looking bunch, right? I mean, you don't know specifically what we do, but you're starting to get the basics."

"I've picked up bits and pieces," Olah admitted.

"Then let me put it this way. Uncle Sam spent a lot of money training me to take care of myself. He spent a lot of money on all the people around me teaching them to take care of themselves, and each other, right?"

Olah nodded.

"Y Bli is my bodyguard," Hank closed his argument.

"Sold, Lieutenant. Enough said."

***

The pilot of the Bell UH-1A helicopter was cruising over the jungle at a mere seventy-five miles per hour to save fuel. He was still complaining about letting civilians mess around with his bird.

Hank grinned at the curses the SOG pilot hurled at the plumbers. They had insisted that some modifications to the helicopter be done by their guys, and not the regular crew.

Every helicopter engine vibrated with its own personal signature shake, rattle and roll. Pilots despised letting anyone new alter or, in any other way, intrude on the familiarity they had with their chopper. Hank was always sympathetic to their view. The more comfort a man felt with his equipment in wartime, the more likely he would be telling his grandchildren war stories some day in the distant future.

As Hank, Vispo, and Y Bli stared out the doors of the helicopter, the familiar scenery of jungle, broken up occasionally by rice paddies, villages and streams, blurred by.

Hank's mind kept going back to Beebe's final words to him. "Don't get into any trouble out there," the Commander had warned. "Get in, get the information, and get out. As far as the US Military and I are concerned, that is Charlie's territory. That is with the exception of what is currently held by the Civilian Irregular Defense Groups, and they don't know you will be operating in the area. Under no circumstances are you to engage the enemy, unless it is in self-defense. If you are detected, abort the mission right then and there. I don't want to hear about any heroics. You will be too far away for any kind of support from either the remainder of the platoon, or SOG. You will literally be on your own. This is what you were trained for. Remember your training, and in your case, your experience will serve you well. Remember, you can't trust anyone. Out there it is almost impossible to tell the white hats from the black hats. Besides, even if you could, neither side knows you are there so you will be essentially an enemy to anyone you see."

Even without the lecture, trusting people they came across in the bush was not high on Hank's to do list. Charlie was everywhere. SOG was taking over the reconnaissance of the border because the CIDG's had a tendency to act like renegades. On top of that the South Vietnamese 1st Observation Group had been disbanded after three out of four of their six man teams had been killed or captured. Those kinds of odds did not tend to make Hank trust the local populace in any fashion. He mistrusted them even though it was said the locals could be bought off for a few candy bars. Staying bought was a whole other question.

In addition to this team, one other was planned to come out of Danang. It was to be headed by Lieutenant Dehart who had also been at the CIA briefing.

Hank had decided the clear choice was for Vispo and Y Bli to come with him on this mission. Vispo was the best at patrolling of anyone on the SEALs, and Hank was confident in his ability to handle anything they came across. He could be a little wild at times, Hank thought, but he was all business when he was in harm's way.

Y Bli was a necessity. This was not just due to the language barrier, but also due to his unsurpassed knowledge of the land and the people. That was in addition to him being a good man to have next to you in a fight.

The chopper suddenly put its nose down and dove for lower altitude. It leveled out just above the trees. Hank grasped the D ring in the deck of the aircraft and leaned out the door. The jungle flashed by in an unbroken green blur.

He made his way behind the copilot who was occupied with French maps to keep track of their position. Hank had an identical copy rolled up in the waterproof packet strapped to his belt. He had requested maps of US origin, but was told they did not exist. 'Hell of a way to run an op,' he had muttered at the time looking at the date on the French map of 1950.

The flight was following the Tourane River, which ran to the west out of Danang. It had reduced down to about half the width of when they started and would reach almost exactly half its width as they neared the Laotian border. The co-pilot pulled a large photograph out of his folder, and then pointed to a large turn in the river. There was a rock filled shallow that extended half way across the water. "We're getting close," he shouted over the noise to Hank.

Hank acknowledged with a nod, which was easier than

shouting loud enough to be heard. He made his way back to Vispo and Y Bli. He would have felt better about this with the entire platoon along, but more men meant more noise, and more challenges hiding. Besides, it would be impossible to bring enough men to get them out of trouble out here. This mission was not about winning a fight, it was purely about avoiding one.

"Lock and load," he yelled over the rotor noise. Vispo and Y Bli armed their AK-47s provided for them by Eli Kasman. This was a sterile mission. Nothing the men wore, or carried, could link them to the United States in any way. In addition to the AKs, Hank and Vispo had their nine-millimeter Makarov hush puppies, Russian-made grenades, and Chinese knives. The only things they carried of American manufacture were Hank's Starlight, and two M-18 smoke grenades.

It was not enough firepower to sustain them in a firefight. But, it should be enough to help them evade capture long enough to escape.

Unless, of course, it was a washout or the spy amongst them had burned their arrival.

All of them wore the popular black peasant pajamas over Vietnamese underwear. Their faces, necks, and hands were smeared with cammo paint. They had cut some standard issue green t-shirts into strips and wrapped them around their heads as sweatbands, and then placed bamboo hats over that.

The part that bothered Hank the most was leaving behind his dog tags. It gave him the feeling of being a non-person. Since he'd joined the Navy, it had been ingrained in him that his dog tags were as much a part of him as his head. He felt naked without them. If he were killed out here, his family would never know what happened to him, nor would they ever see his body.

Given how they were dressed, Hank had absolutely no illusion about how he and Vispo would be treated if they were captured. He determined he would rather be dead than allow that to happen. No way they would take him alive.

With 'Sat Cong' tattooed on his chest, death would be the least of Y Bli's worries if he were taken.

The pilot pulled the nose back from the down position. The helicopter slowed quickly, then dropped to just above the surface of the water and hovered for five seconds.

The jungle on both sides was dark and ominous. The blast of air coming from the rotor blades whipped the water beneath them into a chaotic scene of white caps and mist. The nipa palms were being blown back and forth along the riverbanks on either side. The motion of the nipas seemed like it was a warning call to anyone who might want to do them harm.

This was the first false insertion. The idea was that if anyone were watching them they wouldn't know which "insertion"' the actual soldiers used. That was, unless they happened to be right on the spot when it happened.

The familiar feeling at the back of his neck and in the pit of his stomach was back. Hank had learned to handle this fear. He pushed it to the back of his mind the moment he hit the ground. From that point forward adrenaline would take over. It could be brought back out and drowned with alcohol once the mission was over-- if he made it back.

Controlling emotions was harder with each mission. In a couple of months he would be free of this fucked up war...Hank immediately cursed himself for that thought. That short timer shit was going to get him killed if he didn't stop it.

The front of the chopper nosed over, then it swept ahead, gaining speed and altitude as it traced the path of the river. A mere few moments later, they were, once again, skimming just above the jungle canopy.

After they made another three klicks, the copilot turned and shouted, "Get ready, you're out the next time we go down!"

Hank took his position sitting on the starboard door with his feet on the landing skid. Vispo and Y Bli, sitting on the metal framed canvass seat, checked their weapons once again.

The river was perfectly visible beneath them. Hank looked ahead, the chopper took a turn, and he saw the planned insertion point. It was a small spit of land jutting out into the river at a spot where the river made a large turn north before swinging back west again. He had spent so much time looking at the French maps and recon photos he felt he knew the area as well as he knew the dashboard of his first car.

As before, the pilot came in fast, pulled the nose up, slowed and the aircraft sank to within a few feet of the ground. In mere seconds all three men were knee deep in muddy, leach infested water. They wanted to avoid dirt for as long as they could to leave no tracks. The land formations in this area were merely reference points for pilots, not a way to keep their feet dry.

The men made the best possible speed for the cover of the jungle. They instinctively crouched to avoid the rotor blades, even though the skids of the chopper were now above their heads. When they reached the jungle, Hank turned and watched their only contact with civilization disappear behind the jungle canopy. They were alone. They were alone and one hell of a long way away from any help they would need should anything go wrong.

The men sat and waited for the jungle noises to return. Hank could hear the tempo of the helicopter's engine change in the distance as the crew made another false insertion. In his plan, they would make two more fakes on a line running north and south, then fly west to the Laotian border. From there, they would make a wide swing south, and return to Danang. That night, as the pilots drank at the club, or found a woman they could buy for the night; they might momentarily wonder how the men they had left in the jungle were doing. But those thoughts would leave them as quickly as they appeared. It was not their job to know, or care.

After the trip in the well-ventilated, wide-open chopper, the close heat and humidity of the jungle seemed worse than ever. But these men, for whom such weather had become second nature, only noticed it for a few minutes.

They sat and listened to the chopper's engine fade to nothing. The noise of the jungle gradually returned. The ever-present mosquitos quickly joined the noises. It had not taken long for the bloodthirsty insects to find them. But then, it never did take those damn bugs long. In seconds, they made the crouching SEALs their evening meal.

Hank hoped they had not been observed at the landing zone. He was not going to wait around to find out. They had about one hour of daylight left. That would give them plenty of time to distance themselves from the LZ. If anyone were looking for them, his team would have the benefit of darkness to help evade contact. With the limited manpower they had, evasion was their best friend.

It was doubtful they had been seen. The LZ had been chosen for its remoteness. There were no villages; roads or even trails anywhere near them. There was nothing but dark and dense jungle.

They moved in silence with Hank on point. They travelled a course twenty meters into the jungle and followed the river's path. In a few minutes they were soaked with sweat. After a few kilometers, the dense jungle gave way to bamboo. Because of the remote nature of the area, the men had to make only a cursory check for booby traps. As a result, they made good time as they put as much distance as they could between themselves and the LZ.

An hour later, they stopped and listened. Within a few minutes, the jungle sounds returned right on cue. There was no sign of anyone on their trail.

They were losing the light. Hank moved them closer to the river for better reference. Another few klicks and the light was all but gone. Hank moved into an area surrounded by willow bushes. They sat for a few minutes and listened. There was no noise except that of the jungle.

Hank opened his waterproof packet. He checked the map using his red flashlight. He found that, from their position, the river would angle north for one kilometer. Then it would split with one fork going north while the other angled back west for two klicks before passing along the southern edge of a village named Dox before turning north again. Recon photos showed that at the fork in the river, there was a rocky shallow. This was their primary extraction point.

They started to move again. They followed the river, moving slowly because of the lack of light. Even with the darkness, and the remoteness of the area, they continued to stop and listen to the jungle at random intervals. Hank knew the penalty for failure to follow good patrol procedures.

When they reached the point where the river turned north, they stopped. Hank checked his illuminated compass. They left the river and headed off at a course of 280 degrees. This took them well clear of the extraction point. It was an area they wanted to actively avoid so as to leave no signs of human activity anywhere near it. It would also keep them south of Dox.

It was an amazingly clear night, not that it mattered. The jungle blocked out most of the moonlight. The SEALs slowed to avoid running into trees. They also wanted to actively avoid being slapped in the face by low branches. Despite all of this they still made good time.

Suddenly the men heard a rustling in the bush off to the left. Everyone hit the ground and froze in place. Hank strained in the dark to see what might be making that noise. He had to know if their instant ass pucker was legitimate or not. His only problem was hearing over the pounding of his heart to determine what direction the noise was coming from. He expected muzzle flashes to appear at any moment. He expected to hear the popping and zipping of automatic weapons fire being poured into their location.

Before he could pull out his Starlight a low, deep growl rumbled from the shadows.

Hank could feel the hair stand up on the back of his neck, "Godallmighty," he breathed, "I think we just jumped a tiger."

"Sometimes tigers here," Y Bli confirmed in a whisper.

Vispo had been on rear security. Hank whispered to him, "Watch your ass back there, or it might get eaten."

"Hey, in Danang you have to pay good money for that kind of thing," came the answer.

"You're a sick man," Hank shook his head.

Beneath the crude banter, Hank detected a note of fear in Vispo's voice. He understood where it came from. He had never seen Vispo as much as flinch in the face of enemy fire. There was something different, something primal in the threat posed by the tiger that far surpassed that of an AK-47. Nothing in their training had prepared them to meet a quarter ton of claws and teeth in a dark jungle thousands of miles from home.

The men sat as still as they ever had in their entire lives for a good fifteen minutes. They heard no additional noise. Either the tiger was more patient than they were or it had gone away. Hank had to make a decision, "Let's move out."

It was two hours later when they smelled it. It was the familiar pungent aroma of *noc mam* fish sauce, along with smoke from cooking fires. It had to be the village of Dox.

They were almost inside the hamlet before the odors reached them. They were too close to these people for Hank's comfort. The last thing they needed was to get the village dogs barking, or worse, alert a sentry if the VC had taken the village.

Slowly, carefully, the SEALs worked their way around the edge of Dox. Then they concentrated on putting distance between themselves and the village.

They continued on for another hour before they came to a small clearing. Hank led them around the edge of it, and into another bamboo thicket.

"This is as far as we go tonight," he announced quietly. The men grouped close in together. "We're very near the Laos border or just inside it. No matter how you look at it, we are within a few klicks of what we are lookin' for. We'll stay here until it's light enough to see where we're goin' and what's goin' on around us. Then we'll move west until we make visual contact with Charlie. You two get some rest, you're gonna need it. I'll take the first watch."

"You sure, Lieutenant?" Y Bli asked. He was so used to watching over Hank at night that he was not comfortable with the role reversal.

"I'm okay," Hank assured him.

Hank did not tell his two companions that he had taken one of the yellow pills from his small plastic bottle. His normal sleep patterns had long since left him. The nightmares had gotten more and more frequent. Hank had taken the Dexedrine to make sure he would need none until they were back in Danang. The little helpers kept him on edge, and had an added bonus of making his senses, in particular, his hearing, more acute.

It was something that was not talked about. Many of the SEALs and Special Forces used the pills on missions, especially on those missions which kept them in the boonies for longer periods of time. For missions lasting only one night, most guys would just load up on caffeine. The pills were reserved for those missions lasting for two or more nights.

Vispo and Y Bli were soon asleep. Hank spent his time, as he always did while on watch, thinking of Shirl and Sue. All the while, the bugs, lizards, and ants crawled over his body, and scurried about the area while the mosquitoes feasted enthusiastically on his exposed skin.

As much as Hank hated and feared the jungle, he felt somehow part of it once he was on a mission. He felt like he was as at home in the jungle as the mosquitoes. He liked the protection it offered him. He also liked the knowledge that Charlie was here, but his inferior. He was confident, well trained, and in his element out here. He also knew the jungle was very non-forgiving to those who did not protect themselves properly.

It was well into what should have been Vispo's watch when Hank heard it, a subtle, almost indistinguishable movement on the other side of the clearing. He eased the safety off on the AK and strained to hear what it was.

The noise was gone.

A few moments later, it was back, only in a pattern of short rustling. This time it was off to his left. Hank used the Starlight, but the underbrush was so thick he couldn't make anything out.

It suddenly got quiet and stayed that way for fifteen minutes. Then, suddenly, he heard it again, only closer. This time, it was in the bamboo thicket directly behind where Vispo and Y Bli were sleeping.

Hank shoved Vispo with his boot. He wanted him to wake up. He moved right next to Vispo and pressed his finger against his lips and pointed to the threat. Vispo understood and checked his weapon. Y Bli was awake now, and silently moved to where the others crouched.

The rustling was louder and more frequent now. It was moving closer. It was deliberate in its movements, Hank thought. Some of the insect noises stopped as the rustling came closer. The closer to their position the noise came, the quieter the jungle noises were.

"I think it tiger," Y Bli whispered urgently.

"Holy shit," Hank breathed.

He had to fight down a rising tide of panic. What the hell was he supposed to do about a tiger?

We can't wait until it charges he decided. *Someone will get hurt – at least – even if we kill it. No, we can't wait.*

Hank took his Makarov from the holster. Vispo did the same. They waited and listened. They heard a low growl. It was startlingly close, and Hank's sphincter tightened involuntarily. He could swear that he could see a huge dark shadow in the brush, roughly the size of a house.

"Now," he said quietly. He and Vispo opened up together. The silenced pistols sent bullets in the direction of the growl. There was not much sound from the weapons themselves, only a cough, and the sound of the rounds tearing through the bamboo.

At least one bullet found its mark. The silence of the night was ripped apart by an ear-splitting roar that made the men cringe. They changed clips and prepared to fire again. They could hear the tiger thrashing as it loudly protested the pain that had been inflicted.

Not wanting to leave a wounded and angry tiger in the jungle they were going to inhabit for the next few days, they fired again. And again.

Just then, the enraged animal burst into the clearing and ran past them. It was moving with the speed and force of a runaway locomotive. Hank was firing as fast as his finger could pull the trigger. Vispo was doing the same. The cry of pain from the animal was so loud that he could not hear his own muffled shots. At the last second, the huge cat flinched from the pistol fire, and blew past their position. Hank could smell its breath as it roared past.

Then, as fast as it had appeared, the enraged animal disappeared into the jungle. Hank reloaded and kept firing. The tiger was moving too fast and away from them. They could not tell if they had any further effect.

"Let's get the hell out of here, now!" Hank commanded.

"Fuckin' A," Vispo agreed.

After Hank took a quick compass heading, the three men headed quickly into the night.

Chapter Twenty One

Hank, Vispo, and Y Bli moved as quickly as they could through what was left of the darkness. The roaring of the tiger had silenced every other jungle noise. The only sound they could hear was their own movements as they scrambled through the tangled undergrowth.

Hank felt speed was the only thing that mattered. The wounded beast was now even more dangerous than it had been before.

The jungle began to thin. The gray light of dawn made moving through the jungle easier. To their mutual relief, they could no longer hear the hungry jungle cat that had been stalking them throughout the early morning hours.

They stopped in brush reaching their shoulders as Hank checked his map. Ahead of them in the distance was a long tree line. Hank pointed to the forest on the map, then to the drawn-in border. He looked at the men, "We are now in Laos," he said simply. He paused to let that sink in. It meant their situation was now far more serious than it had been. This was the point of no return. Good patrolling procedures and staying alert at all times was all that stood between them and a long, painful death.

"There should be a river on the other side of those woods," Hank told the men. "If so, we're exactly where we need to be."

Hank saw Vispo's face was covered with welts from mosquitoes. It was also decorated with his own blood from when those annoying bugs had been smashed. There was so much blood; it had smeared the cammo paint on his face. Hank knew he must look pretty much the same way. The huge insects had been on all of them throughout the night.

Y Bli, however, was completely untouched. Some Vietnamese peoples were never bothered by these damn mosquitoes. He caught Hank's glance. He grinned, stroking the smooth brown skin of his cheek.

"It just goes to show even the bugs in this country have better taste than your wife," Hank growled in jest. Three Toes faked being offended.

The men moved toward the trees and into the forest. There, Hank called a break. It was great cover, and they were getting close to their objective. It might be their last chance for real rest for the foreseeable future.

He leaned against a tree whose trunk was almost four feet thick. He looked up into the tall trees around them. Netting-like vegetation hung from the branches. It served to block most of the direct sunlight, except for a few beams that streaked their way to the leaf-padded earth.

Small, white, butterfly-like insects fluttered their way through the light. They were in stark contrast to the prehistoric gloom. They hung in the sunbeams like small glowing lights. They gave the place an ominous, eerie, almost mystical feeling.

Hank sat back for a moment. The peacefulness of the spot washed over him as he reflected upon their situation.

Like the rest of the country they had traveled through, except for the village of Dox, there was not a sign of another human anywhere. There was not as much as a single footprint.

After an hour of rest, they were again moving west. They were headed into a forest of evergreen oak trees. Hank knew from the map that it extended a long way both north and south, but it was only about a kilometer wide. The terrain began to slope upwards. As they climbed, the forest thinned out.

When they reached the crest, they could see it. The water was six to seven meters wide and was more of a large creek than a river. It cut a distinct ribbon as it wound its way through the rugged terrain.

Hank brought the small French binoculars up to his eyes. He searched the other side of the water. They were a mere twenty five to thirty meters above the river. The dense jungle, which began around five meters past the water, was impenetrable to his eyes.

"No wonder Charlie can move around undetected whenever the hell he wants to," Hank said as he handed the glasses to Vispo.

"No shit," Vispo muttered as he examined the other side.

"Well, it's all downhill from here," Hank said cheerfully. They started to make their way down the slope. They moved slowly, carefully, knowing they were near their objective, and had very little in the way of thick cover to hide their presence.

Just before they reached the river the jungle thickened. They were able to get within a few meters of the water, before the cover vanished.

Hank signaled the others to wait as he crept forward alone. Between the jungle and the river, there were only scrub brushes and short nipa palms to hide behind. He picked his way forward slowly, and then stopped to listen.

At first he was not exactly sure what it was he heard. Gradually his ears adjusted to the noise of the area. Between the chattering and screeching of monkeys and the calling of birds, he heard what they came for - the sound of distant voices. They were speaking in rapid Vietnamese. It was a quiet, almost happy sound. They were not speaking boisterously in any way. Given the state of mind Hank was in, it was weirdly casual. Charlie was confident in the safety of his jungle lair.

Hank knew it had to be Charlie. There were no villages in the area. There was no reason for traffic through the jungle except for the infiltration of South Vietnam.

As he waited and listened, Hank determined that the voices were coming from about twenty meters into the bush on the other side of the river. He knew they needed to get closer. In broad daylight that would be foolish and of very little use to their mission. Any attempt to cross the river would be to invite disaster. They would have to wait until dark.

He worked his way back to Vispo and Y Bli.

"Did you smell it, Lieutenant?" Vispo asked.

"Yeah, I smelled it," Hank replied.

"Y Bli said it is a kind of charcoal they use for cooking fires. Says it doesn't smoke much, and that makes it hard to see from any kind of air recon. Little fuckers are pretty savvy," Vispo said.

"Let's move back under cover," they moved back into the jungle. Hank briefed them on what he had seen and heard, and what he planned once darkness fell.

Then the men had their C-rations and salt tablets as they settled in for a rest.

"I'll take the watch," Hank stated.

Vispo gave him a look, "You sure Lieutenant?" he knew Hank had gotten no sleep the night before.

"I'm sure," Hank said flatly. It was a voice that would not be argued with. He was still pumped on the pills, and knew there was no way he could sleep.

Vispo shrugged his shoulders, and the three men settled in

for the wait until nightfall.

***

At 2200, the three men made their way through the moonless night to the river. Hank swept the area with the Starlight. He was unable to see much of anything through the thick jungle.

Followed by Y Bli, Hank moved across the river. With every step they sank almost a foot into the thick, molasses-like bottom which gripped their feet with strong suction.

At the halfway point, Hank was up to his chest in water. Y Bli was up to almost his chin. Hank took the Montagnard's weapon, and held it above his head with his own. Y Bli grabbed Hank's waist, and the SEAL pulled him across to the far side of the water.

When they reached the riverbank, they stopped and listened. The sound of laughter and talk came floating through the inky blackness.

"What are they saying?" Hank asked.

"They want woman and drink," Y Bli whispered.

Hank laughed to himself. What else did men on a military mission talk about around a campfire?

The riverbank was a full arm's reach above them. The bank hung over the river for several feet. Vine-like vegetation hung from the edge of the water. The two men literally had to claw their way through it to the top. As they did, the earth, a thick goo held together by a rubbery sod, gave away to their pulling on the vines.

Hank choked as the rot and decay of centuries was released on their heads. It assaulted his nostrils. Breathing through his mouth was of little help. The odor was so thick he could taste it.

After getting to the top of the bank, the men quickly crawled to the thick brush and waited. They could hear the jabbering clearly. Hank could tell that the people speaking were moving around.

"We've got to get closer," Hank whispered.

He and Y Bli crept toward the sound of voices.

They moved forward a few paces and came across a trail that cut through the jungle. It was about two meters wide and was obviously well used as it was clear of overgrowth. They checked for booby traps and crossed quickly. They kept moving in the direction of the voices.

Hank could see nothing of the objective. He led them forward a little more then stopped abruptly. Tiny, glowing, yellow-green lights were bobbing up and down in the darkness. They were strung from Hank and Y Bli's right to their left. Hank watched, puzzled as these lights cut a path into the jungle and disappeared.

"Vee Cee," Y Bli whispered. "Smear firefly on back so man behind can follow in dark. Father do same while fight French."

Hank brought out the Starlight. He could see nothing but thick jungle. Charlie had evaporated into the night.

They waited quietly for a few minutes. Then voices could be heard coming from the right. A moment later, the strange bobbing lights appeared passing in front of them.

Hank put the Starlight on them. He could not believe his eyes. In the green light of the scope, Hank saw men and women. There were no old people. Everyone was strong and sturdy, moving in a column. They were making a good pace despite the darkness and the fifty to sixty pound packs on their backs. Each had a weapon slung over their shoulder.

The reconnaissance photos had been correct – for once. This was smack dab in the middle of one of Charlie's major supply routes. Hank had no doubt in his mind he was watching NVA regulars walk right in front of him.

Hank and Y Bli sat tight and monitored the traffic. A hundred or so of the human pack mules would pass by, and then there would be a ten to fifteen minute break before the next column of about a hundred people carrying supplies. Hank did the math. At this rate there were a hell of a lot of people and supplies moving into the South.

Hank wanted to get a look at where the smoke from the cooking fires was originating. He moved them parallel to the trail the NVA were using. They headed north for just a few minutes. The sound of voices drifted through the trees.

The jungle was very dense. Even the stars could not penetrate the canopy. Hank and Y Bli were able to move right up to the edge of a small clearing. The clearing was obviously used as a rest area for those moving south.

Hank swept the area with the Starlight. It was about the size of a softball diamond. There were a few good fires with food on spits or boiling in pans. There were a few square water containers scattered around. Even a few small hootches had been put up. These probably housed supplies and medical equipment instead of people.

Just then, another group entered the clearing. It was a smaller group. They were carrying heavy machine guns, tripods, and boxes of ammunition. The heavier loads were carried by two men, suspended from poles. Others in the group hauled Russian made RPG and light machine guns.

It appeared each group had a guide. The guide was greeted by someone, then taken to one of the huts, probably for a debriefing of some kind. The people he had brought with him were fed and had their canteens filled. If necessary they had their shoes and clothes repaired or replaced, and finally, any first aid necessary was applied by the several attendants who hovered around, ready to meet any needs that existed.

It was a highly efficient operation. Because these people were so good, and the volume of people moving through was so great, Hank was certain that he was looking at one of Charlie's main supply routes.

Hank and Y Bli settled in to observe the night's activities. Hank made mental notes of everything he saw. He instructed Y Bli to do the same. They were very close to the staging area. Despite their proximity, the two men were able to communicate in whispers by timing their conversations to coincide with the noise level of the North Vietnamese.

During the night, a familiar odor wafted toward them. Hank nudged Y Bli, "Pot?" he asked.

"Yes, they use much. Also heroin. Very bad. My people never use," Y Bli whispered.

Hank wished he could say the same. The American losses to drugs were tragic.

At 0400, Hank decided it was time for them to pull out. They began their careful withdrawal. They had to cross the river before it became light again. Hank wanted to give them plenty of time should something unforeseen happen.

They moved to the south and made their way slowly toward the river. They had gotten the information they came for. Hank resolved they were not going to fuck it up now by hurrying and making a careless mistake.

Hank and Y Bli reached the bank. They were just slipping into the water when they heard movement and clatter. It was different from anything they had heard before and was right behind them in the brush.

The two men froze. Hank had to make an instant decision. Had they been detected? Was this just a coincidence? If they were being pursued, getting across the river was their only priority. If not, remaining undetected was their best safety.

"Move ten meters down and hug the bank!" Hank whispered to Y Bli. Y Bli moved down the river, Hank stayed exactly where he was. He was trying to become one with the putrid riverbank without gagging and revealing his position.

The people behind them were making too much noise and were too casual about their conversations to be tracking them. No one in his right mind would act like that in the bush if he had any inkling that the enemy could be within earshot range much less rifle shot range.

After a minute or two, the noisy group reached the river. They were a dozen or so meters upstream. In the pre-dawn light, Hank could see what was going on. The banging noises had come from water cans. This was a party sent to refill the supplies from the rest area.

Hank suddenly had a strange feeling someone was watching him. He shook it off. He had learned to trust his instincts in the bush. If he was right it was probably Vispo, who would be ready to give covering fire if everything went to hell.

The rotting smell of the bank threatened to overwhelm Hank's senses. He tried breathing through his mouth, again, it did no good. He wanted to gag. He put his hand over his mouth to avoid inhaling a mosquito. Choking on one of Vietnam's most numerous inhabitants would be somewhat less than advantageous at this point.

He watched for about ten minutes as the group filled their watering cans. They were chattering and joking like college students at the beach. He was so absorbed in watching them, he didn't notice the sensation on his stomach until the leeches had a good hold.

Slowly he reached down to pull one off. It would not budge. He could not force it off without doing even more harm. He knew it was possible to remove a leech with a gentle yank. But ripping one off once it was good and set would probably leave the teeth in his belly. That would lead to an infection. Should pickup take longer than expected that could be deadly.

He could feel even more of the damned things attaching themselves to his legs. He caused him to shiver involuntarily. The thought of how they were steadily sucking him dry, growing fatter by the minute made his skin crawl.

He took the opportunity to relieve himself in the water. Take that leeches! He knew it was irrational, but he felt like it was a small strike back. It also made him smile to realize he was upstream from the VC who were filling the water cans. He just pissed in their drinking water!

The water party lingered for about ten more minutes. To Hank it seemed that for each of those minutes dawn was progressing at double the usual speed. He was sure that soon, he and Y Bli were going to be visible to the enemy.

Finally, he could no longer see people on the riverbank. He could hear them headed back into the jungle. He started to move downstream to Y Bli when he heard another group approaching. He cursed the damn luck. Hank moved back against the riverbank to hide.

Crouching in water up to his chin, Hank ran his hand over his stomach. He jerked it away in disgust after feeling the rubbery bodies of the leeches. They had swollen to twice the size of his finger from feeding on his blood.

He closed his eyes and prayed that Charlie would move away from the river.

His eyes were still closed. He lay motionless against the soft ooze of the riverbank. He felt the smooth, wet sliding movement against the back of his neck and again on the side of his face.

Hank froze. He knew what it was and tried not to move a muscle. He even slowed his breathing. He opened his eyes slowly not wanting to move a muscle no matter how small.

The snake had lifted its triangular brown head about six inches above the water. It was swaying back and forth, facing the watering party upriver. It moved a few inches. It stopped and slowly swiveled its head until the wicked looking yellow and black eyes were staring right into Hank's.

It began swaying, moving closer. A drop of water fell from its lower jaw. The drop seemed to fall in slow motion to the surface of the stagnant river. Gentle ripples spread from the point of impact. Hank knew his only defense was to remain perfectly still. He remembered what the instructor had told them in survival training. If a snake had elliptical pupils, it was probably venomous. In this case, the bite wouldn't have to kill him to be fatal. If he were to merely become sick from snakebite in this tenuous situation, he would probably be dead – maybe along with his two teammates.

It seemed like he and the viper were eyeball to eyeball for an eternity. Hank would not move a muscle on his body. He moved nothing except his eyes as the snake swayed back and forth. He could think of nothing except the deadly glare of the snake's eyes.

Suddenly, the snake hissed loudly. It reared its head back as thought it was going to strike. Its tongue flicked rapidly. Frantically, Hank considered trying to grab the reptile from under the water and hopefully throw off its aim.

Instead of striking, the snake slowly lowered its head down to the water, and slithered away. Its brown body gracefully glided over the surface of the river.

VC water party or no VC water party, Hank had had enough of this particular spot and slowly moved down to where Y Bli was silently hiding.

They hid together while the Viet Cong finished filling their water containers and headed back to their camp. They crossed as quickly as they dared, making the width before any more expeditions appeared. If they waited any longer, they would not be able to cross before sunlight destroyed their chances.

Hank started to boost Y Bli onto the other bank, when Vispo's hand reached down and yanked the Montagnard right out of the water. Hank dragged himself out of the river. The three waited for a moment, listening carefully.

When they were satisfied they had not been seen Hank hurriedly took a lighter out of his waterproof pouch and burned the leeches off his body. They fell writhing to the ground. He savagely stomped on them one by one. "Motherfuckers," he breathed in disgust.

When he was finished they began the trek to the primary extraction point.

Once they had scaled the rise and were back in the relative safety of the forest, Vispo felt safe enough to speak. "Holy shit, Lieutenant. I thought it was all over back there!"

"You're telling me," Hank answered, still fixated on the snake.

"That little bastard was right over your head. I thought he was going to pull out his little dick and piss all over ya'. For a second, I thought he had seen ya'. He backed away from somethin'. I was getting ready to drop him, but he got real casual, and didn't raise a holler," Vispo said.

"It was close," Hank agreed. He did not want to admit he had not seen or heard the North Vietnamese soldier. It was likely the man had seen the snake from the bank, and backed away from it. Hank wondered if the deadly reptile had saved his life while it was simultaneously threatening it.

He knew one thing for certain. It wouldn't be the strangest thing that had happened to him since arriving in Vietnam.

***

The three men travelled all day and part of the night, before stopping to rest a short distance from the extraction point. Hank took the watch. This time Vispo's eyes narrowed as he realized his Lieutenant needed so little sleep. He said nothing, but Hank knew that he knew. Vispo dozed off almost immediately.

At dawn, Hank and Y Bli crossed the Tourane River to the north side. They scouted the area. Vispo did the same thing on the south bank. It would not do to have the chopper fly into an ambush. With the exception of the natural inhabitants of the bush, they were totally alone.

At 1000 hours, right on schedule, they heard the familiar sound of the rotor blades. Y Bli pointed as the chopper made its slow orbit a thousand meters to the east. Vispo popped an M-18 smoke grenade. Yellow smoke billowed over the area.

Almost immediately, the helicopter swooped in from over the jungle and hovered a couple of feet above the fork in the river. The three men sprinted through the knee-deep water. They kicked up water, which added to the chop from the downdraft of the helicopter.

Hank and Vispo each grabbed one of Y Bli's arms. They threw him through the chopper's side door and jumped aboard themselves.

The helicopter immediately moved sideways and began climbing at full throttle as the men hung on for dear life.

After they gained altitude, a familiar face turned from the controls. "Here, Lieutenant," Jack Warden hollered. "Figure you could use a belt. That, and a shower." He grinned as he handed back a bottle of Johnny Walker.

Hank took the bottle. He looked at the other men in the cabin. He lifted the Scotch, "Bravo Zulu, men, Bravo Zulu," and took a long pull of the whiskey.

Chapter Twenty Two

It was late the next day before Hank finally rolled out of the sack. Even then he didn't think it was a good idea to do so. It had taken an inhuman amount of alcohol to overcome the effects of his little excursion into no man's land. The strains of the mission and his being awake for two solid days made his head feel like it was about to explode from the inside like a Claymore mine.

On top of everything that happened, he had to sit for the longest debriefing of his career when they returned from Laos. The plumbers had milked every detail the SEALs had in their brains. They even attempted to demand a few details that weren't in there. When Hank finally volunteered that the leader of the first group of supply mules had precisely seventeen pimples on his ass, Mr. Thayer had finally decided it was time to let them go about their business.

Hank waited for the initial flash of pain to subside, then made his way gingerly down to the kitchen. He winced at the bright rays of sunlight beaming in the windows from the west.

"Talk about late risers," Keith greeted Hank as he crossed to the refrigerator.

"Not so loud," Hank grumbled.

Keith gave a low whistle, "So where did you go to win hearts and minds the past few days?" he asked, noticing the large red mosquito bites covering Hank's face and arms.

"Laos," Hank said curtly. He grabbed some cold chicken and a beer.

"Holy shit, Hank. I swear if they sent you to Hell, you'd come back with a Martini on the rocks, and the ice wouldn't have melted yet!" Blevins said.

As much as he appreciated the admiration of his junior officer, Hank was not yet in the mood to brag about his exploits, "I wouldn't be so sure about that. Besides, who wants one of those pansy drinks?"

As Keith got up to put his dishes in the sink, Hank noticed he was moving a bit stiffly, "So where did the boats take you, hotshot?"

Blevins laughed, "We should both give up the Navy and become armchair detectives."

Keith's good mood finally began to lift Hank's. "What, and give up the big bucks we're haulin' down from Uncle Sam? You never know, one a' these days we might even start getting jump pay again."

"See what a great leader of men you are," Keith laughed, sitting back down, "Now I have something to look forward to, a reason to live again."

"So where did you take your little cruise?" Hank asked.

Blevins took a long pull at his beer, burped, and began. "We took out an oil storage facility about seventy-five miles north of the DMZ just south of Cape Vinh Son.

"It was me, Doc, and five LDNNs on one boat, and Brookwater, Bostic, and five more LDNNs on the other. They just finished their training so we were supposed to show 'em a good time."

"And did you?" Hank asked.

"It almost turned into a real party. We approached from the open sea, and shelled the hell out of the storage tanks and the other freestanding buildings. You know," he grinned, "a forty millimeter sure does a nice job on a tank filled with flammable materials. The LDNNs were understandably, impressed."

He took a drink of his beer before continuing, "Everything was four-oh 'til we came abreast of Quang Khe on the way back. Our radar picked up three bogies comin' from the mouth of the Giang River and headed our way, really fast. We put the throttles to full open and in no time, we opened the range between us. At the speed they were comin', Hank, they had to be Russian Swatow gunboats. I thought those babies had surface to surface missiles. If they had 'em, they didn't use 'em.

"We cut in the generators and made smoke, which have us an excellent screen. We kept opening the range. They stayed after us until I put Gio Island between us for cover. I was really sweatin' the missiles until we got there. After that, they were off our screens."

"Keith, that is a good bit of work," Hank said quietly, a faraway look in his eye.

"What is it, Hank, why so stiff?" Blevins asked.

Hank took a deep breath. "It's those damn Swatows. We knew about them and their base on the Giang as far back as '62; and we tried like hell to do something about it. Some of our people, along with Vietnamese UDTs, were to raid the place. It was a plumber operation. They used a motorized junk to get close. They were supposed to swim in and blow the boats up. They were operating with the submarine *Catfish*, and had constant communications with her. She was submerged off the coast and was to be used for extraction."

"What happened?" Blevins asked.

"I don't know," Hank answered. "No one knows for sure. At least nobody I know knows. We lost all hands on that operation. The *Catfish* never got the signal for extraction. We will probably never know why.

"A few things I do know, that base is still there, some next of kin got some official telegrams about loved ones lost at sea, or some bullshit, and I haven't been wild about joint operations with the Vietnamese ever since."

***

That evening when Hank stopped by the Alamo to check on his men, he was shocked to see Dan Slade sprawled on the couch, drink in hand.

He immediately went over to him, "Cutter, how are you?"

"Just fine, Lieutenant, all things considered. You look like you've been out in the jungle," Dan said.

"Yeah, that I have. I'm glad to see you back, Cutter. You sure you're ready for this shit?" Hank asked.

Slade looked him right in the eye, "Absolutely, Lieutenant. I've never been readier."

Later, it came to Hank why Slade's manner had made him so nervous. It wasn't that Slade was manic, or wild eyed, or out for revenge. In fact, he had been as cool as a cucumber.

Too calm.

***

Hank wore the darkest sunglasses he could find the next morning as he drove the Jeep to see Beebe. His hangover headache of the day before was still lingering. Every bump in the road reminded him of the abuse his system had taken.

He was getting too old for this shit. No way he should still have this fucking headache.

Once inside the White Elephant, he folded the glasses, put them in his pocket, and tried, like any good employee, to put his best face forward for his meeting with his boss.

Commander Beebe looked apologetic as he greeted Hank and offered him a seat. "First rate mission, Hank. Thayer himself couldn't say enough about the quality of information you brought back."

"Thank you, sir," Hank said.

Beebe snatched a paper up from his desk, looked at it disgustedly, and then threw it back down. "That just makes this all the harder. Hank, I've got bad news for you and your platoon."

Hank had never seen Beebe like this before. Fuck, he thought, they've cooked up some new crazy mission he doesn't think we can back down from.

"I put your people who've been wounded in for the Purple Heart. I also put you in for a Silver Star, and some others in your platoon for other awards." Beebe picked up the paper again, and shook it.

"Damn it, Hank, I'm sorry to have to tell you this. I've been informed by higher authority that as far as the United States and most of our misinformed government is concerned, 'this is not a war zone.'" He looked at Hank, "I'm sure this is news to you," he said angrily, his voice dripping with venom.

He read from the note with as much hatred as a human voice could carry, "'US military personnel do not operate in forbidden zones. They are advisors, and do not engage in combat operations. Their mission here is highly classified, and acknowledgement in any form, such as combat decorations, is out of the question.'"

Beebe let the paper fall from his fingers, "I disagree with them on this, Hank. I have been told not to take this any further. It seems as far as they are concerned, we're not here and you don't risk your ass."

"It's those goddamn politicians, Commander. They can't make up their minds about what to do over here. They are not even sure who we should do it to, if we were to do anything. In the meantime, they bounce us back and forth like tennis balls," Hank was a bit surprised at himself. He had never let his emotions take over in a conversation with Beebe before. He wondered if he had said a bit too much.

The stress of the moment left him when Beebe answered in kind, "That is about the size of it. Well, anyway, I wanted you to know what's going on. I also want you to know that I appreciated the work you and your men are doing. For your information, I am not letting this matter drop. Not without a fight. "Right now, I want you to rest up. You look like hell."

Hank knew exactly what Beebe was talking about. He felt like hell.

Beebe then turned the conversation back to his usual routine, "How's the wife, Hank?"

"Fine, sir. Thank you for asking."

"That's great, just great. A good Navy wife is very special. Consider yourself lucky," the Commander said.

"I know sir."

"Dillon," Beebe began casually. Hank braced himself for the hit. Whenever superiors started playing name games, troubles were ahead, "We will be going North again very soon."

"How soon, sir?"

"Very soon, Hank. Our ships on patrol have located plenty of prime targets. It's not going to be easy going up there this time. We've been kicking their ass in their own back yard. It has got to have them mad as hell. But we've got to go."

"I understand, sir."

"Good, now get some rest."

Sure, Hank thought. Sure, that news is really gonna help me rest.

***

That afternoon the mail came from home. Hank immediately headed back to the villa where he could shut everything else out and concentrate on his wife's every word.

He poured a Scotch and took it back out on the veranda. Damn, this headache was getting out of hand. Maybe a good slug of the hair of the dog...

By the time he was done with Shirl's letter, he had more than a headache. Something was starting to swirl in his gut.

The letter began in the usual way. It had all of the news from home he ached for. It was the news of others that bothered him. Shirl had included a clipping from the San Diego Union.

***

PARTNERS IN CRIME FOUND EXECUTED
By Gene Francis, Union City Desk

Three men, two of them brothers, were found murdered today, according to the San Diego Police Department. Juan Rivera, 30, his brother, Diego, 28, and Roberto Gallegos, 35, were killed sometime last night. Their bodies were left in various locations throughout the city.

Lt. Gary Day, of Homicide, told us that the brothers died after their throats were cut, and that Gallegos had his neck broken before his throat was slit. The right ear had been cut from each man's head. No effort was made to conceal the bodies. Each was left in a conspicuous place in a different part of the City. (See related story on Page A6)

"Someone wanted these men to be seen as an example," Lt. Day speculated. "This was a professional hit. There were no signs of a struggle, and their money and jewelry were not taken. All three men were still armed.

He further commented that even if the motives were revenge from another gang, he would have expected the killers to take the cash, jewelry and weapons. All three men had extensive police records. The latest arrest for one victim came just thirteen days ago when the police raided an alleged drug house on the city's east side. In that raid, police recovered heroin with an (please see "Execution" on page A6)

Along with the clipping, Shirl had written:

Hank, about a week before she died, I had to go bail Nancy out of jail. She had been caught shooting dope in a drug house. It was the same one that is mentioned in the story. I'm not sure what all of this means. Maybe it's a coincidence. I hope so. I just thought you ought to know.

On an only slightly different note, you'll like this. When Nancy died, the detectives came to question me, because I was listed as the person who had bailed her out. They asked me where her husband was and I said, "He's probably on his way back from Vietnam."

The older one looked at me and said, "Where or what the hell is

Vietnam?"

If I knew the complete answer to that, Hank decided, I could get a big paying Washington desk job.

***

Hank was sure he knew who had taken out the San Diego drug dealers. Dan Slade had put his expensive training to work in a place where the rules of engagement actually were clear cut. In that world such an action was called murder.

He tried to compose a letter to Shirl. His mind kept going back to Slade. What, if anything, should he do about this? Did anyone in the Navy know, or even suspect, Slade had taken matters into his own hands? If so, they had no qualms about returning him to duty.

Would he have acted any differently than Slade? It was hard to say. It was impossible to imagine Shirl in such a situation. Nancy Slade had killed herself. The dealers only made that possible. If someone murdered Shirl, Hank knew, no one could stop him from dealing out similar justice to what Slade had most likely done.

He took another sip of Scotch. He rubbed his temples, damn, this headache was murder...

He was interrupted from his reverie by a call from the door, "Hey, Hank, where've you been?"

"I could tell you..." Hank said with a smile.

"Yeah, I know. Don't bother. I have too much to live for," Olah grinned. "Obviously it was someplace with a whole lotta mosquitoes. Listen, I've been lookin' for ya for a couple'a days."

"What for?"

"You said I could borrow your bodyguard, try to have him tail the guy from the warehouse. I could have used him two days ago. The guy showed up. Now, who knows when he'll stop by again? Offer still good?"

"Yeah, yeah, I guess so," Hank raised his voice, "Y BLI!"

Olah was startled by Hank's yell, and look at him, puzzled, what the –

"Yes, Lieutenant?"

Olah thought he was going to jump out of his skin. He had

not heard the Montagnard approach, and suddenly this voice was coming just about from his elbow.

Hank saw Olah's astonishment. He smiled and almost laughed aloud, "Y Bli, meet Mr. Olah. He is a policeman for the United States Navy. He is looking for a very bad man who deals in drugs. He needs someone who is a very great tracker. He needs someone who can follow a man without being seen. I told him you are the best in all of Vietnam. I would consider it a great favor if you would accompany him for as long as he needs you, or until I send for you."

As he talked, Hank could see Y Bli's eyes reflect his pride at the great honor Hank was granting him in front of the important American.

"Drugs very bad, Lieutenant. My people never use," he explained to Olah. "I help Mr. Olah find drug man."

Hank pulled out a bottle and two glasses. "There you go, Mr. Olah. Your drug dealer is as good as caught. Pull up a chair and celebrate with me. You're going to be in line for a promotion."

Chapter Twenty Three

Hank did not like anything he heard in this briefing. It was all bad. It was another cross-the-beach operation. The plumbers were getting overconfident, and the planning was a giant cluster.

He shook his head in disgust. The pain nearly caused his head to fall off his shoulders. DAMN! What the hell was wrong with him?

The idea was to raid the North Vietnamese islands of Hon Me and Hon Ngu. They were approximately one hundred miles north of the DMZ. There was a radar station on Hon Me, and a patrol boat base on Hon Ngu. They would use the four PT boats with Vietnamese crews, there would be eight VNMCs in each and one SEAL along for supervision.

Hank was not in any way sold on the plan. For one thing, there would be too many people involved. Too many chances for a security leak; in other words, too many Vietnamese of unproven reliability.

The other, possibly larger problem was tactical. The plan was overly complex. It called for a large number of things to be going on at the same time in the same general area. Those in one area, if the timing is off, would be observed by the other target area. In light of what had almost happened to Blevins at Quang Khe, the whole enterprise was just too risky. But then those setting out the plan weren't taking the risk, as usual. They were tempting someone else's fate.

The whole thing seemed rushed. They were slated to go the following night. There would be no dry runs, no practice, and only one day to study the layout of the various facilities.

Hank couldn't help but wonder if the plumbers were so happy with the results of previous missions that they now just figured the SEALs just had the system down. Now, they think, we can just start running these missions off an assembly line. Just change the machine settings. Hank knew this was crap. Every mission had its own quirks to be worked out. The more people who were involved on the ground, the more complex the mission became.

He also knew there was no use voicing his concerns. During this briefing, the damn plumbers would never be swayed. He did not have the clout to change one comma in the mission plan. He would have to wait until this was done and go talk to the guy with the authority.

Hank followed Beebe to his office. He went over his arguments in his head on the way.

Beebe shut the door behind him, "Have a seat, Hank. What's up?"

"About this mission, Commander…" Hank stopped short as a violent chill suddenly came over his body. A flash of pain shot through his head. He could feel his pulse soar and felt as though he would lose consciousness.

With a confused look on his face, Hank sank to the floor before Beebe could get around the desk.

***

Hank lost all sense of time as he drifted in and out of consciousness. At times, his only awareness was of severe chills and sweat. He remembered a nurse commenting that his temperature was over a hundred and four. His heart was beating so hard it felt like someone was pounding on his chest with a rubber mallet.

At other times his head ached and he shook so badly that he yelled aloud and wished he would pass out again.

During one period of awareness, an Army doctor told him he had malaria. He said something like they would know how severe it was in another forty-eight hours. Hank vaguely remembered you could die of malaria. Then the chills hit him again, and dead didn't sound as bad as it used to.

***

Hank awoke to find Keith Blevins sitting next to his bed. He tried to speak but nothing came out. Keith saw his feeble attempt and leaned closer.

"You better get going," Hank finally managed, "You got a mission…" His voice was barely audible, and the effort left him exhausted.

Keith laughed, "You have been out of it, Skipper. I'm back

and cleaned up already."

Hank figured he would probably look surprised if he had been physically able to register any expression, "What...happened?" he asked faintly, struggling to raise his head.

Blevins spoke more somberly, "It was a first class SNAFU. The bastards knew we were comin', I swear to God."

Hank sank back into the pillow. His body and emotions were in such a state that he felt like he was going to cry in frustration. "Damn it, I knew it, I knew it."

Keith began his story. He was still leaning over the bed so he could hear if Hank had a question, "We separated from the other two boats about 2300 hours. We angled further north to Hon Me. At 2345, we closed with the island. We were right on schedule, time-wise, anyway.

"We loaded into the IBs. I had one, and Brookwater had the other. We headed toward the beach, and it wasn't a minute later we started taking enemy fire. If the stupid bastards had waited another couple'a minutes, I wouldn't be sitting here."

He ran his fingers through his close cropped hair, and let out a long breath, "As it was," he continued, "Brookwater's IB got hit, and started to sink. We were already starting back to the Nasty. We had to turn around and help them out of the water.

"It was a fuckin' nightmare, I'm tellin' you. The goddam Vietnamese panicked. They let their weapons sink, and started throwing all their gear out of the boat. They even tossed the fuckin' radio! Brookwater's chewin' 'em out, but they aren't paying any attention. I thought he was gonna shoot the whole damn boatload.

"The income fire was getting accurate. Some of 'em got hit. They just lost control. They were screaming so loud the gunners on the damn island could probably hear 'em. I swear I could hear the echo bouncing off the beach. Even over all the shooting.

"Anyway, we came alongside. They were still in a damn panic. They were grabbin' at us, and screaming. All of them were trying to crawl over each other onto our boat. I got Shelly over, and I damn near left the rest of the bastards. Man, it was a cluster fuck if I have ever seen one.

"With all the extra weight, we were taking on water, and still takin' hits from the gunners on the shore. Finally, the PT boat captains figured out what the hell was goin' on, and came after us.

They started raking the shoreline with the twenties and forties. That took some of the pressure off us, and the little fuckers calmed down.

"Hank, I was really pissed. Those assholes really took their time getting to us. When they came alongside, the Vietnamese in our boat scrambled aboard. It was every man for himself. No discipline at all.

"I was the last to board. We didn't have time to load the IB. It was time to get the fuck outta there. I shot the IB up pretty good, no sense in leaving anything worthwhile for Charlie to use against us.

"Just then, the aluminum mast took a hit from a short battery. It sprayed shrapnel all over the damn place." He grinned, "That's why I'm here with ya. I caught a few pieces in my shoulder and ass. Guess I don't' need to put in for a Purple Heart, huh?" he asked sarcastically.

"Anyway, I went to the bridge, partly to assess the situation, partly to chew out the captain. I wanted to tell him to put on all possible speed. I take a look at the radar, and this asshole had put us in on the wrong side of the fuckin' island! I'm not wrong about this either. You know those British Deccas paint an amazing picture. I'm looking at sheer cliffs on the shoreline! I didn't say a thing. I was so pissed off I was afraid I might pull out my K-bar.

"They knew we were comin' Hank. It's the only explanation. We must have run into the lightest part of their security. They probably had twice the reception waiting on the beach side. They just ringed the island with troops, and waited for us to show up. Actually, if our captain hadn't messed up, we'd have all been dead. What a screwed up mess.

"Sorry, Skipper, but for what it's worth, the other guys shelled the hell out of the patrol boat base, so it wasn't a total loss."

Hank opened his mouth. On his second attempt to speak he asked, "Were any of our people hurt bad?"

"No, we're okay. Brookwater didn't get a scratch. I just caught a few splinters in my butt. Smartass Army doctor said a few more inches and it would've hit my brain.

"Hank, seriously, we got a real security problem. What the hell are we gonna do?"

Hank had no answer. He was out cold once again.

***

It was almost 1800 hours the next evening when Keith Blevins approached the White Elephant. He was a little nervous. He had been summoned by Commander Beebe. This was unusual. He wondered what could be so important it couldn't wait until Hank got out of sick bay.

"Hello there, Blevins," Beebe greeted him jovially. "Grab a chair, you want something to drink?"

At least it appeared he wasn't in trouble, "No thank you, sir."

"Have you seen Dillon today?"

"No sir. I was heading over there next thing. It's been kind of a busy day."

Beebe got right down to business. He looked Blevins square in the eye and said, "Three Soviet built North Vietnamese PT boats attacked the destroyer *Maddox* southeast of Hon Me a couple of hours ago."

Blevins was so surprised, he had no reply. He just waited for Beebe to continue.

"They didn't do any damage to her, and Maddox managed to disable two of them before the planes from the *Ticonderoga* got there to assist. I want your men living uptown in civilian housing to stay off the streets for a while. We don't know what the civilian reaction is going to be. Keep a low profile; we do expect Charlie to be active around Danang. I've given the same orders to all our units in the area. The last thing we want is to be put in a situation where we end up killing some civilians."

"What about the mission tomorrow, sir? Is it still on?" Blevins asked. Surely it had been scrubbed.

Beebe startled him by answering in the affirmative, "Yes, we're still going. Just keep your men off the streets, okay?"

"Yes, sir."

"Good, now go over and fill Lieutenant Dillon in."

"Yes sir." That was one order Beebe need not have given. Wild horses could not have kept him away with this news.

***

"Yeah, I know," Hank answered wearily when Keith reported Beebe's news.

"What do you mean, you know?"

"Haven't had the radio on today, have you?" Hank grinned weakly.

"Hey, I've been doing both our jobs all week," Keith retorted. "Who has the time?"

"You should try it sometime. You get better intelligence reports than we get from the plumbers. I swear this country is one big grapevine. Maybe I should be surprised when a mission *doesn't* get blown, not when one does.

"But that's nothing," Hank continued bitterly. "You should hear what those bastards in Washington are saying. You and I both know what is happening. The *Maddox* caught flak because of our little escapades in the north. The Reds think we were working with her, and she was our support. But in Washington, they're saying that it was an unprovoked attack. They are carrying on like it was the sinking of the *Lusitania*. Can you believe the propaganda?"

"What a bunch of hypocrites – someone jumped all over poor old Uncle Sam for no reason at all. Hell, the North Vietnamese know what we've been doing. The Russians know what we've been doing. The Chinese probably know. Who the hell are they trying to bullshit? The American people, that's who," Hank punctuated his point by gesturing with his index finger, but the effort cost him. He quickly dropped his hand back to his side.

"We've been kickin' their ass all over the place. I'm surprised they haven't tried something like this sooner to save face. You can bet your next paycheck on one thing, Keith..."

"What's that, Skipper?"

"Our friends here in the South are jumpin' for joy over what's happened. The *Maddox* thing is gonna draw us in even deeper. There's no getting' around it. Some bigger guns are gonna start poppin' around here, sooner or later."

"Gee, Hank, maybe you better give it some thought. Get back to me later when you have an opinion," Blevins laughed.

"Shit," Hank snorted. "Wait 'til you come down with this. Thinking is all you got the energy for."

"I'll pass. By the way, you know we're going back up

tomorrow night, right?" Blevins asked.

"You're shitting me! Damn, sometimes I think they're trying to get us all snuffed!" Hank exclaimed.

"Well," Keith said, "As the saying goes around here, I don't' have to like it, I just have to do it."

"One thing's for sure," Hank said, "Now that they got things stirred up, they aren't gonna let it die down. You know, my old man maintains no President ever tried as hard to get into a war as FDR did. I'd say old LBJ is goin' for the record."

Blevins snorted, "I think you need to credit his pal McNamara with an assist, at minimum."

"You got a point there. Listen, you watch your ass up there. You tell Vispo, Brookwater, and Hack to keep their eyes on the radar 'til you know you are where you're supposed to be. Don't have any Swatows poppin' up around ya'. If you see any of them, or the Russian Kormars around, abort and get the hell outta there. Got it?"

"Got it, boss. We shouldn't have any navigational problems this time. Wegees are taking over as boat crews."

Hank nodded. Keith was right. The Norwegian mercenaries had pleased him with their performance so far. Suddenly he felt very tired. Talking to Blevins had been the most energy he had expended since he found himself in this bed. Hank closed his eyes.

"I was starting to think we'd left this security problem behind us in Vung Tau. But the bastard's doggin' us again. What're we gonna do?" he muttered sleepily.

"We got back to keeping everything buttoned up tight for now." Keith stood up. "Why don't you put away the soapbox and get some rest. I'll check in on your tomorrow."

"Smart ass," Hank mumbled, and slipped into a deep sleep.

***

Across town, Joseph Olah rubbed his eyes and yawned, "Your turn," he said to Waller and handed him the binoculars.

Waller put down his Playboy magazine. He took the seat by the window next to the camera, complete with telephoto lens, aimed at the entrance to the warehouse. He settled in for a long wait.

Olah stretched, and marveled at the patience of the three-toed Montagnard who sat in the corner. The sweltering heat in the cramped bare room seemed not to bother him. At least not like it bothered the two Americans, who spent their time wiping the sweat out of their eyes and trying with desperation to get some benefit from the tepid breeze provided by the small electric fan. For four days Y Bli had sat and kept to himself, or slept silently in the corner. He showed no restlessness or even so much as a passing interest in Waller's girlie magazines.

Of course, he may have been nervous about the response the two white men would have when a brown tribesman was seen ogling American women. The thought made Olah smile when he considered his own situation. His girlfriend's skin was closer to the color of Y Bli's than it was his own.

This weekend he simply had to get down to Vung Tau to see Monique. The surveillance on the warehouse had been a daily assignment. Because of this damn assignment they had not been together in two weeks. She had not complained, and he was not insecure or jealous; he simply had to see her.

Joseph Olah was head over heels in love. He was happy to admit it.

He was starting to wonder about the consequences of his situation. A major bust could lead to a promotion. It could launch his new career in fine style. He knew enough about bureaucracies to know that, much like with military officers, the right wife could make a big difference in how far a man could climb.

As long as he was in Vietnam there would be no problem. If he were transferred back to the States, God only knew what would happen.

That did not matter. What would happen would happen. What he did know what the he could not live without Monique by his side.

Now if this silver haired asshole would just show his face, Joseph Olah could get on with his life.

Chapter Twenty Four

As he listened to the conversation in the Alamo, Doc Padget became worried about discipline in the platoon for the first time. Without Hank's stabilizing influence, the drunken ramblings among the enlisted men had become cynical and wild.

The problem was made worse by the orders to stay home and off the streets. After a daily routine at the Shark Pit, the men had very little to do but sit around and drink...then discuss the daily scuttlebutt.

The men had been listening in shock to the propaganda pouring out of Washington. The one and only topic was the "unprovoked" attack on the Maddox.

The night after the daylight attack, four Nasties with a SEAL in each, and Norwegian boat crews had shelled radar sites at Cape Vinh Son and at Ron. They shelled the sites for thirty minutes, and as they started south after the raid, North Vietnamese patrol boats gave chase. But they were quickly outdistanced by the faster Nasties.

The following night, August 4th, the Destroyer *Maddox* was attacked again. This time, so was the *Turner Joy*. The attack came in the middle of a blowing rain storm at approximately 2100 hours. They had been on Yankee Station in the Gulf of Tonkin, southeast of Hon Me. *Maddox* had called for help from planes from the Ticonderoga and the Constellation. The air cover was of no use because of the storm. Finally, at 0100 on the 5th, the destroyer lost contact with the attackers in the rough seas, and steamed south at full power.

The only topics consuming the Alamo for a three day time period were the attacks on the *Maddox*, the response from Washington and the response on the streets of Danang.

Padget cursed the malaria which had Hank out of commission at just the wrong time. First the SNAFU at Hon Me, and now his calming effect on these men, who trusted him implicitly, was missing just when it was needed the most.

There was no danger of things breaking down completely – even the enlisted SEALs were trained so well that they could function independently down to the last man.

In Padget's opinion, Hank was the finest officer he had ever served with. He was not only a skilled warrior, and the best of any of them in the bush, he always seemed to know just what to say to keep the men in line.

Dillon was an officer, and he always conducted himself as such. But he was also a SEAL. He communicated the party line, he stuck to the book, and he also had little ways of telling the men just how much of it he believed. This meant that the men took what he said when he was emphatic as though it were gospel. They did not take it with the grain of salt that accompanied most pronouncements from the brass.

That quality of Hank's had helped keep morale high among the young men through all of the bullshit they worked with. The strangest of those was the denial of their very existence. That didn't include the extremely annoying denying of deserved medals and the constantly shifting rules of engagement.

As a veteran of Korea, Padget was used to fighting a war with ludicrous restrictions. He was accustomed to the gap between propaganda and reality. But the shameless, self-promoting posturing in Washington across the past few days had made even him cringe. He knew it had to be bad for the younger men's morale.

These men were idealists. They were volunteers and dedicated. Yes, they were adrenaline junkies. True, they were highly trained killers. Some might even call them assassins. They had been handed a dirty job. They had accomplished everything assigned to them with brutal efficiency.

Deep down, what they believed in was America, and the rightness of their cause. The blatant lying and hypocrisy of their government the past few days had deeply disturbed them. It had served to cheapen their mission. These men had been used to escalate a war. Now the government would not even own up to the nature of their mission.

As Lanny Vispo said, "It makes me feel like a two dollar whore."

"Hell," Hank had shot back, "You'd be overchargin', big time."

The laughter that followed did not put a damper on the discussion. The upshot of all of this was that the SEALs thought the American people, or at least the Congress, ought to know about

SOG's 34 Alpha Missions, as the SEALs operations were called. They needed to know these things before they came to a conclusion based on what had happened at the Gulf of Tonkin.

Hardison was all worked up over the reaction in Danang. "It's like they're all havin' a fuckin' party because the Commies took a shot at our ships," he complained.

It was true, Padget reflected, the South Vietnamese had every reason to be happy about the events of the past few days. That was especially true in light of the twist Washington was putting on what had happened. An unprovoked attack by the regular military of North Vietnam on the United States Navy was sure to provoke reaction. American involvement in the Spanish American War, and World War Two had begun with attacks on American naval vessels.

It was getting late. Padget set his Scotch aside, and headed to his bunk.

Two hours later, he was roused by a pounding at his door. He sat up and growled, "Come in."

It was Vispo.

"What the hell is it?" Padget said groggy from the booze and small amount of sleep.

"It's Slade," Vispo reported. "He's passed out on the lawn, and he's covered in blood."

"Fuck!" Padget jumped up. Still in his underwear, he grabbed his medical bag and dashed after the already sprinting Vispo.

Each of the past two nights, Slade had disappeared from the Alamo after everyone else had fallen asleep. This flew in direct contrast to the standing orders. He had come in early in the morning with no acknowledgement he had been gone.

Cutter had been moody in the extreme since returning from his wife's funeral. Doc had been meaning to discuss Slade's behavior with Hank, but had figured it could wait until Hank had recovered more fully from malaria.

The other enlisted SEALs in various states of drunkenness were already gathered around Slade. Brookwater, who seemed pretty sober, looked up as they approached. "I can't find where the blood's coming from," he reported. "I don't think it's his."

Padget knelt beside the unconscious SEAL and worked

quickly. He swabbed at the places where the blood was thickest and found no bodily damage or torn tissue. He quickly felt along Slade's head, and found no bumps or cuts.

"I think you're right," he said to Brookwater. "He's not hurt, he's just drunk."

"I'd hate to see the other guy," Hack slurred, and Hardison laughed.

"Very fucking funny," Padget snapped back. "We might have a dead civilian on our hands. What a scream. You guys need a new sense of humor. Now help me get him inside."

Shit, what a mess.

***

That afternoon, Hank was released from the hospital. He left with the stipulation that he spend most of his time in bed, or at least not leave his quarters. The Army doctor forbade all other activity for the next seventy-two hours. At that time, Hank was to report back to him before he could be authorized to return to duty.

Hank was drinking a *Ba Muoi Ba*, a Vietnamese beer those name meant thirty-three, when Keith arrived.

"Welcome back," the ensign greeted him. "Hey, I thought drinking was strictly *verboten* for recovering malaria patients."

Hank pulled a face. "This is not drinking, this is beer. Scotch is drinking."

"Hank, we got a problem."

"This?" Hank feigned surprise and waved the beer, "I can quit any time," he slurred, doing a very bad impression of a drunken W.C. Fields.

"No, a real problem."

"Spit it out, Keith."

"It's Slade. The guys found him out in front the Alamo last night, unconscious and covered in blood."

"Is he hurt bad? How did it happen?"

"It wasn't his blood."

"Whose was it?"

"I don't know. I don't know how to find out without opening a can of worms that we may want to have stay closed."

Hank briefly thought about Olah. He vetoed that idea. He

was not ready to trust the man from the NIS that far just yet.

"Hank, it's not just last night. He's changed somehow. Ever since he came back, he's been…moody. I gather he's been slipping out every night, even since the *Maddox* thing and the new orders. He knows it's against orders. When I broached the subject with him, he didn't even bother to deny it. He made no excuses. What the hell are we going to do with him?"

"Slade's a good man. We don't want to lose him. He's been through a lot, and he's just gonna have to work it out for himself. But…we can't put up with this crap. Tell him no more trips to town until you give the word," Hank paused, "And tell him I want to talk to him, okay?"

***

That afternoon the mail came. Hank was glad to see a letter from Shirl. This time there were no startling revelations or strange goings on. It was just domestic news. Shirl was planning a fourth birthday party for Sue on July 30th. She was excited, and had helped write the invitations herself. One was included in the letter. It had "I love my Daddy" written in crayon and a childish handwriting.

"My God, she's growing up," Hank murmured aloud. He leaned back against his pillow, tears in his eyes. He felt the deep, familiar guilt at being away from his family on this milestone. He would never be able to recapture these moments in time with his daughter. What the fuck was he doing in this damn country, anyway?

Thank God for Shirl. She had been the stabilizing factor in his hell-bent life. He had screwed his way around the world, had some wild times, but that was not really the life he had been looking for. When Shirl had come his way, he had known that he had found the woman he wanted to spend the rest of his life with. He didn't miss the other life in any way.

Originally, he had been attracted to her by her looks. He thought she was the sexiest woman he had ever met. That was not why he had stayed with her. That was not why their marriage had lasted through six years of prolonged absences. If ever there was a decent, caring woman, it was Shirl. She was true to him. She had raised their daughter, essentially, by herself.

Yes, he thought bitterly, she was raising their daughter in a Christian manner. She was doing this while her husband traveled half way around the world to slaughter people and help drag the United States into a war. In order to do that, he was willing to miss out on the most important years of his daughter's life. For a moment, he allowed himself to wonder if Shirl would be so supportive if she knew what he was up to. He quickly brushed the thought aside. Shirl loved him. She was a good Navy wife. She had known the down side going in.

A good Navy wife was hard to come by, and when you found one, they were something special. She had to be able to handle long separations from her husband, and run a household without his help. She had to care for children, while resisting and avoiding the temptations which had torn so many Navy families apart – like Dan Slade's.

Hank shook his head. He was not going to think about Dan Slade right now.

He put his hands behind his head. His thoughts returned to home. His thoughts fixated on Shirl and his daughter. While the world fell apart around him, Hank Dillon found comfort in these thoughts.

***

Hank heard a Jeep skid to a halt in front of the villa. Keith Blevins burst through the door.

"Hank, remember what you said about bigger guns poppin' soon? Turn on the radio!"

Before Hank could gather the energy, Keith had the radio on.

The familiar Texas drawl filled the room. The President was addressing the nation, and the world on a static filled radio.

"…action against the United States ships on the high seas…take action in reply…air action is in execution against gunboats and support facilities in North Vietnam…our response, for the present will be limited and fitting…we seek no wider war…"

"Bullshit!" Keith yelled at the latter statement.

"Hell," Hank breathed, knowing a 'wider war' had just been made inevitable.

Chapter Twenty Five

Hank put his feet up and reclined the lawn chair as far back as it could go. He wanted to soak up some sun at Black Beach, as the plumbers' R&R area had been nicknamed. It was good to be out of the villa finally. He was so bored; it would even be good to be back on full duty. But that was tomorrow. Today was a day for sun.

Beside him, the portable radio pushed out the news. The broadcast even included the description of the targets hit by the Navy bombers – the patrol boat bases at Quang Khe and Phue Loi, the oil storage depot at Vinh, and even the patrol boats at Hon Gai, way up north of Haiphong. It struck him that one Navy bomber could do more damage than a platoon of SEALs, and at far less risk to the Americans involved.

"I bet the American people know where Vietnam is now," he muttered, recalling Shirl's letter.

General Khanh was publicly ecstatic over the escalation of hostilities. Hank figured he probably felt vindicated after the scornful reaction by the media to his earlier "march to the North" speech.

Yesterday, Khanh had declared a state of emergency, re-imposing press censorship, and had made a speech telling the South Vietnamese people to, 'Keep calm so as to clearly see your responsibilities in the face of events. Commit yourself to the national discipline.'

Student groups and Buddhist factions were not impressed by his argument. They took to the streets in great numbers in violent demonstrations.

The SEALs stayed off the streets and out of sight. Operations north, except those by a SEAL unit operating further down the coast, had been called off for the time being. Hank's platoon put their time in at the Shark Pit, and then headed back to the Alamo.

Blevins returned, followed by Jack Warden, and handed Hank an ice cold beer, "Look who I found."

"Mr. Warden."

Jack nodded, "Lieutenant. Not drinking any of the hard stuff, eh?"

"No, that malaria laid my ass out for awhile."

"Yeah, I heard you was in the hospital, you doin' okay?"

"Sure, I'll be back in battery by tomorrow. So what news do you have that I can't get on Mr. Marconi's magic little box here?" Hank gestured toward the radio.

"Well, there's a lot of recon flights north because of rumors of troop activity below the DMZ. So far, no one has seen evidence of it." Warden stretched and picked up his bottle of Jack Daniels.

"Guess who I saw over at the hootches?" Blevins cut in.

"Who's dippin' their wick now?" Hank asked.

"Old Stoneface…Ngo. I saw him headin' in with a girl," Blevins grinned.

"He talking about the VNMC lieutenant of yours?" Warden asked.

"The very same," Hank replied. He remembered the poignant story behind Ngo's seeking out of whores. He didn't feel like giving a sermon on tolerance today. Besides, he wasn't sure Warden would give a damn if he knew the whole story.

"Sheeit," Warden said, "The guy's up here every day. He is kind of a permanent fixture, must be takin' Spanish fly or somethin' to be able to get it up the way he does."

"The dollies uptown are losing a lot of money off him because of this place," Blevins laughed.

"Hell," Warden drawled, "He probably thinks it's not safe to go up there anymore. Those candy-ass bastards are startin' to kill each other. They found another one this morning, killed last night. Brand new big smile cut under his chin, but you know what makes it weird?"

"What's that?" Hank asked, only half interested.

"The bastard took his ears," Warden answered.

Despite the hot afternoon sun beating down on them, Hank felt a sudden chill.

***

"Quick, Y Bli, come here!"

Y Bli was startled awake by Joseph Olah's excited summons. He quickly got to his feet. He joined Olah by the window.

"That's our man – with the silver hair, you see?" Olah

pointed down to the street below and handed Y Bli the binoculars.

Y Bli focused on the man lighting a cigarette. He was standing outside the door at the east end of the warehouse. He was scanning the street in both directions without appearing to do so.

"Stay with him until he goes to bed. Once he does report back to me, got it?" Olah ordered.

Y Bli nodded, and then quickly left the room.

He followed the silver haired man as he headed down Quy Cap Street. The waterfront district was crowded with people. There were workers unloading ships, stevedores, forklifts running up and down the street as well as the sidewalk, and peasants loading their own supplies onto boats in the harbor. In all of the confusion, it was easy for the Montagnard to keep people between him and his quarry.

On two different occasions, Y Bli got close enough to the man to get a good look at him. He had hard features and always remained expressionless as he looked ahead. The silver hair was marked only by a black streak running the length of his head over his right ear. Perhaps it was the result of some wound? Y Bli had once known a man whose hair had turned gray over the wound after a machete had glanced off his skull, causing a deep cut in the scalp.

The man turned north at the next intersection and kept walking. A cab or a pedicab would have been totally useless in the crowd of bodies. The street was stuffed, not only with the people who usually did business in the area, but there was also a demonstration against Khahn. There were also those with the opposite point of view who were celebrating the strikes against the North.

Because of the civilian attire Y Bli moved easily among the people. They might have made things difficult for him had they realized his tribal roots. He was also impressed by the pace and the strong gait of the man. He moved with a grace and economy of movement that reminded Y Bli of a wild tiger. It was the same efficient way in which Lieutenant Dillon moved around.

Y Bli swelled with pride at the thought of the Lieutenant entrusting him with this important mission. That this great warrior from another land would have such great confidence in him was an unending source of honor for the tribesman-- for him and his tribe.

It amazed him that these white people would come so far to help his people. If most Americans were like the men with green faces, and especially if they were like Lieutenant Dillon, then America must be a wonderful country.

He was confident he had done his job as a warrior in a way that pleased the Lieutenant. There were not many overt expressions of approval. He knew by the tone of his voice and the look in his eye that the Lieutenant was satisfied with him.

He wanted to keep that approval by performing this new task with which he had been entrusted.

Suddenly, the quarry turned into a small shop. Y Bli resisted his natural instinct to sprint ahead. Immediately, the man stuck his head back out of the doorway. He looked back along the path he had walked hoping to catch any surveillance running to catch up with him.

Seeing no one, the man doubled back the way he came just to add to the confusion. He crossed the street, stood for a moment as if waiting for someone. He was making a great show of checking his watch, then he continued on north. He stopped several times, always pretending to look at a street vendor's wares, but in reality he was scanning the street.

Finally, he walked into the Hotel Dang Do, a four story French colonial. For fifteen minutes, Y Bli positioned himself so he could see the other two of the three directions man might go if this should be another trick.

When the man did not emerge, Y Bli moved to include the main entrance as part of his surveillance.

For the next two hours, Y Bli wandered among the street vendors. In no way did he appear to be watching the hotel. Whatever he was hunting, Y Bli knew the secret to success was in becoming one with the surroundings. It would not do to appear out of place, or be doing anything that someone would not normally do in this part of town.

Several Vietnamese approached him to try to sell him drugs. He rebuffed them sharply. What a disgusting people these are. No sense of the tribe. No sense of what is good for their own bodies.

Several old women were sitting by their wares. Their mouths, numb from years of chewing the slightly narcotic betel nut, were blackened and repulsive. He longed for his village. There, the old women took care of the children, instead of sitting around high on the nut with flies crawling in and out of their senseless mouths.

Finally, the silver haired man came out of the hotel. The hunt resumed.

***

Joseph Olah could not keep from pacing the floor as night fell. Y Bli had still not returned and time seemed to crawl. He had told the small man to stay with the suspect until he went to bed. So Y Bli was not really late. But, it had been seven hours with no word, and Olah was worried.

He sat back in the chair by the window. He tipped it back on two legs and stretched his body. He needed some exercise. Staying in this damn room and sitting by this window was driving him crazy. He needed to do something. He could feel his muscles atrophying from the inactivity. As soon as he got out of here, he was going to find a gym, and get the best workout...

"Mr. Olah."

Olah was so startled that he almost lost his balance. He had to steady himself against the wall so he wouldn't fall on his ass.

Face red from embarrassment, he brought the chair down successfully and stood up, "Y Bli, I didn't hear you come in –" he saw the smile on the dark face. He realized the Montagnard already knew that.

"Did you do what I asked?" Olah asked quickly.

"Y Bli do," the warrior said.

"Where did he go?" Olah demanded.

"He go to hotel that way," Y Bli pointed, "Then to American building with eagle on it, then to market, then to home."

Olah got out his note pad, "Okay, give me the addresses."

Y Bli looked confused.

"You know, the locations. The streets and numbers."

Y Bli still didn't understand.

Olah could not believe the damn luck. Two weeks of waiting for this asshole to show, send someone to follow him and now they can't communicate about where he went. What the hell was Dillon thinking? "How the hell am I supposed to know where he went?" he asked, visibly frustrated by the situation.

"I show," Y Bli said calmly. His face broke into a wide, proud smile.

***

The streets were still busy after dark. But they could be navigated. Olah led Y Bli to his car.

"Okay, show me," he said simply. Y Bli pointed the way.

They retraced the silver haired man's steps, until they came to the Hotel Dang Do. "He stayed long time," Y Bli told Olah. "Maybe two hours. Before hotel, he act like he know I follow, but he did not know. He try to lose, but I stick like glue," Y Bli smiled proudly at the correct use of American slang. It made Olah smile as well. "After hotel, he act like he not worry. Go straight to places."

Olah made a note. He would get the Danang police over to the Dang Do in the morning to question the staff. "Got it, now where?"

"To American buildings, white building with eagle."

This was going nowhere. "What way?" Olah sighed. Y Bli pointed back toward the waterfront.

They traveled back through the docks area, Y Bli giving directions as they went. Finally, he said, "Here," and Olah stopped the car.

They were in front of a white, two story building. A Marine guard stood sentry outside. There was a bronze plaque with a large eagle over it, announcing to the world this building was the 'Consulate of the United States of America.'

"Holy shit," was all Olah could say.

Olah sat there for a moment. He digested the information he had just learned. He was more convinced than ever this Vietnamese Y Bli had followed was a big fish. The thought crossed his mind, but he did not even allow himself to hope he was the Fixer. If he thought it he might be jinxing himself.

"How long was he here?" Olah demanded.

"Long time, not as long as hotel," Y Bli reported.

"An hour, less, more?" Olah prompted.

"Maybe hour," Y Bli said with a smile.

Olah realized he had prompted his witness too far. He didn't ask anything further. How ever long the man had been there, it was long enough to be significant. Just then he noticed the Marine guard eyeing him curiously, and he put the car in drive.

"Where to now, Y Bli?"

The small man pointed. "Turn next street."

The silver haired man's next stop had been a large ornate bank building with granite columns. "Figures," Olah said as he wrote down the address.

Next, Y Bli led him to the open market on Hong Dieu Street. "He talk to two people here. One he give something to, here." Y Bli pointed to an empty stall, "And one give him bag, here," he finished, pointing to another.

Olah sketched a diagram, so he would remember exactly which stalls. This would be another job for the Danang police. He had no idea if the same merchants came to the same stands every day, or not. Besides, the people would not communicate with him, even if they could. The Danang police could find out if those merchants could be identified.

"Now what?"

"Now he go home."

"Let's see," Olah said, and restarted the car.

Home for their target was a large villa in an upscale neighborhood on Tran Quoc Toan Street. Olah whistled when he saw it. He felt his pulse quicken. This was not the home of a small time dealer. If this was not the big dog, he would certainly know who was.

"You did a great job. I'll tell Lieutenant Wainwright you deserve a real pat on the back," Olah told the smiling Montagnard sincerely.

Y Bli jerked his thumb toward the house, "Man sleep with two women," he told Olah.

"Yeah? How do you know?"

"I see them."

"But how do you know he sleeps with both?"

Y Bli pointed toward a tree by the east side of the Villa. "I climb up and see them," he answered with a larger smile than before, if that was possible.

Olah laughed. He quickly drove away from the villa. There was no point in sitting around. Alerting the suspect would not be funny, or helpful.

He clapped Y Bli on the shoulder. "You are a real piece of work. A real piece of work."

Y Bli smiled, knowing it was a compliment. He filed the expression away for future use.

Chapter Twenty Six

Olah rubbed his eyes as the early morning twilight gave away to dawn. They were looking at the suspect's villa. He opened the door to get out, and at the same time, so did the other three men.

Of the men Olah had brought with him, none – except for Waller – were paper pushers. He had asked for the best of the best. There was no room for a screw-up. This would be their best shot to get this guy.

He had no choice but to bring Waller along. He had been part of the investigation all along. The other three team members were entirely of his choosing.

Douglas Seymour and Gerald Terman had transferred from the FBI, bored with the stateside routine. Both were still sore from Hoover trying to squeeze all FBI agents into the same mold. They were tough, competent and very well trained.

Next to the four beefy Americans, there was Detective Tran Quo of the Danang Police. He looked like the waterboy on the football team by comparison. Olah knew if things went badly, we would much prefer Quo at his back than Waller. Quo also served as a CYA measure, in case of a Vietnamese protest.

After hearing their suspect had been a guest of the Consulate for an extended time, Olah would have preferred it to be an all American team. But, they were required to cooperate fully with the Vietnamese authorities. Quo was reliable and respected. He had figured out the future of this country, and it was bathed in red, white and blue. Quo knew the best ticket up in his career was with the Americans.

It was decided that Quo would breach the door. He would also be the first to enter the villa. That way, in the reporting afterwards, they could claim this was a Vietnamese raid. The NIS would be along as a "courtesy." That would keep the paperwork neat and tidy. Olah knew he was taking a chance by going after a Vietnamese civilian. He was not willing to cut his chances of getting this bad guy by bringing a large part of the Danang police force along with him. This bust could involve American classified information or operations, and that could not fall into their possession.

"Okay," Olah said in the quick huddle before the breach. "Just like we planned. Quo and I will take the front, Seymour and Terman the back. Waller, you stay outside and make sure no one comes out any windows. Doug and Gerry make sure you don't enter until you hear us."

The two ex-FBI men nodded and trotted away. Waller hung back in the middle of the lawn as Quo and Olah approached the house.

Olah's heart was pounding. He could feel beads of sweat forming on his forehead. This was the big bust he had been chasing. This would make his career.

Quo tried the doorknob and found it locked. You never know and have to try. He drew his American forty-five pistol. He put the muzzle an inch away from the door. He aimed just above the door knob. There was no evidence of a dead bolt. This should destroy the only lock on the door.

The forty-five was deafening. Splinters flew from the door as the knob clattered to the flagstone porch. Olah and Quo put their shoulders to the door. It gave away so easily they almost tripped as they entered the foyer.

Olah noticed the luxury of the building--white carpet, brass fixtures-- as he and Quo raced up the stairs, weapons drawn. They ran toward the room where Y Bli said the suspect slept with the two women.

Quo screamed out the Vietnamese word for police as they pounded up the stairs. Then he screamed surrender in the same fashion.

The only answer was a woman's screech.

Olah and Quo set up outside the door where they heard the noise. It was the same room they had already decided was the primary target. A few seconds later, Terman and Seymour came up behind them.

"Downstairs is clear," Terman reported, panting.

"Okay. We're goin' in. You two cover and make sure he doesn't come poppin' outta one a' these doors," Olah said quickly.

Terman and Seymour nodded, and Olah turned to Quo, "One, two...THREE!"

Quo kicked open the door and sprang into the room. Olah covered him in a crouch.

In a king sized bed, between two amazingly attractive Vietnamese girls barely covered by lingerie, their man sat with a smile on his hard, weathered face. He was naked to the waist. His wiry muscles rippled as he started to shift in bed.

"Don't move!" Olah ordered breathlessly, as Seymour and Terman came in at the ready.

"At ease, gentlemen," the man said smoothly. He had no trace of an accent. "Who is in charge of this mistake?"

"I am," Olah said, "And you're the one who's made the mistake."

"Touché," the man said sarcastically.

Olah was amazed at the man's control. He acted more like a school principal dressing down misbehaving grade- schoolers than a drug kingpin caught red handed.

"I thought," the man continued, "That someone yelled 'Police.' I know of no Americans on the police force here."

"I am Joseph Olah with the Naval Investigative Service," Olah informed him. "We are acting in cooperation with the Danang Police, represented by Detective Quo."

The man's lips curled as Olah gave the official explanation. "He appears very cooperative."

Quo surprised everyone by slapping the suspect across the face with a rocking blow from an open hand. It made a loud cracking noise as the blow connected. Both women screamed in protest.

For the first time, fury filled the man's features, "Uh, uh, uh," Olah grinned and motioned with his pistol before the man could react.

"Now you know who we are. It seems only fitting that you introduce yourself. After all, this is hardly a formal setting. We should all be on a first name basis."

"I am Duong Van Duc, which is what you should tell Mr. Seth Thayer at your consulate when you call him. I suggest you make that call immediately, if you value your career," the mask of superiority was back.

"All in good time my boy," Olah grinned.

The 'I'll have your job' tactic had been tried on him before. After working in Washington DC for years he was immune to it. The only person who had ever made it stick was Dillon and even then, the warning had only made him more careful. He was not about to completely back off.

"First, we're gonna take you somewhere so we can have a nice chat. Terman, Seymour, toss the place. See what you can find." With their experience, those two could conduct a search in minutes that would take him hours to do.

As the two agents left the room, the fury returned, "You have no authorization!" Duc protested.

"That's where you're wrong," Olah smiled. "Mr. Quo, may we search the premises as long as we're here?"

"Of course, Mr. Olah," Quo answered with mock formality.

"See?" Olah spread his hands, "I told you so. Now, if you want to get a shirt on before I handcuff you, feel free."

Duc glowered, climbed out of bed, and slipped on a khaki safari shirt, and a pair of American Levi's jeans, then held his hands out in front of him.

"It's not quite that easy," Olah told him. He grasped one wrist, pulled it around his back in a motion that he had done a hundred times before. "There, that's better."

For a moment, Duc had considered resisting; Olah knew this from the tenseness in his muscles as he was being handcuffed. Feeling the man's power, he knew in that moment that the cuffs had been the right decision.

"Mr. Quo, you might want to secure the women. They may or may not need more clothes. I'll leave that up to you."

Quo grinned, "I think they are just fine the way they are. It gets very hot in our cells."

For a moment, Olah had qualms about sending the frightened women with the Vietnamese detective. Then he realized there was nothing else to be done with those women. It was not his problem.

"Ta dah!" Seymour provided his own fanfare as he and Terman entered the bedroom. Seymour was holding several cellophane bags with light brown powder. Terman had a loose leaf notebook. "Found these in the kitchen," he reported.

"Baking supplies and a cookbook?" Olah taunted a glowering Duc. For an instant it crossed his mind that Duc must have been very confident to have left incriminating evidence lying around in such a manner. He was looking forward to finding out just who this Seth Thayer character was.

Terman was looking through the notebook, "Shit, this is more than drug deliveries, there's troop movements in here and all kinds of shit." He looked up, "Hey Joe, what's a SEAL?"

Olah looked back at Duc thoughtfully. He had sagged a little at the sight of the notebook. This was big. It was very big.

"I could tell you..." he mused, then finished aloud, "It's something that's going to put this guy in very deep. We may have just found the Fixer."

***

Olah came out of the interrogation room and kicked the water cooler in frustration. "Shit!" he exclaimed. "Shit, shit shit."

He leaned over and took a drink. He let the cool wetness refresh him as he regained his composure.

It was now nearly noon. He, Seymour, and Terman had questioned Duc for over seven hours and gotten nowhere. Once, a little over an hour before, Olah had slapped Duc across the face hard enough to knock him out of the chair. He had merely glared at the NIS agents, got to his feet, and sat back down in the chair.

Terman, at that point, had suggested the old telephone book trick. The concept was simple. You batter the subject's head with a thick book until he was disoriented enough to answer questions. The book left no marks and no injuries that could be proved without an autopsy. But, over time, it had proved to be painful and effective.

Olah vetoed the suggestion. He was starting to realize that even if Duc was the Fixer, he was much more than just a drug dealer. The notebook proved that. It was odd. Duc had kept the notebook in English. Probably because it would be less likely to be read by servants, whores, other dealers, his women, or whoever else came in and out of that villa.

The actual result was to make it easier for Olah to interpret. He now knew more about the SEALs than Hank would ever reveal. He had a whole new slant on recent events in the news.

He also knew Duc was some kind of enemy agent-- a well-trained one. He might eventually give in to some of the more brutal interrogation methods, as anyone would, but it would take more than Olah was willing to do.

It was time to call the Consulate. Perhaps Mr. Seth Thayer could clear some of this up.

***

It was Hank's second day back on full duty. He was at the Shark Pit inspecting the boats when the call came in, "Commander Beebe wants you up to the Elephant ASAP," the MST crewman reported.

Hank knew with the crowded streets due to all the demonstrations, he would have a hell of a time getting there.

He hopped aboard the nearest Swift boat. He looked at the crew and said, "Crank it up."

As the boat roared across the bay, Hank stood in the stern and enjoyed the power of the engines as he felt the salt spray. All things considered, it was good to be back in the saddle. Sure beat malaria.

Even Y Bli was back. He had seen the Montagnard back in his ever watchful position that morning.

"Did you get the job done?" he had greeted him.

"Yes, Lieutenant. I find for Mr. Olah," Y Bli had answered proudly.

"Good man," Hank replied. He was rewarded by seeing Y Bli's happy smile.

As he had gotten out of bed that morning, Hank realized, to his surprise, that he'd had no nightmares since the malaria kicked his ass. Of course, the sickness had been nightmarish enough, and hardly a beneficial tradeoff. However, the night before he had gone to bed without the help of hard liquor. Not only had he managed to go to sleep, but he woke up this morning feeling refreshed.

Perhaps the tonic he had been drinking actually fueled the dreams.

Whatever the reason, right now he felt better than he had in ages. He wanted to keep it that way. Hopefully Commander Beebe wasn't going to screw it up for him.

The Swift captain roared up to the pier then, throttled back and came to a textbook landing. Hank waved his appreciation as he jumped to the pier. The Lieutenant let him know he was indeed impressed.

He quickly moved up the pier, crossed Bach Dang Street, and hurried into the Consulate.

Beebe wasted no time as Hank entered the office.

"We have a sensitive situation here," he informed Hank brusquely.

What other kind is there Hank wondered silently.

There was a map on the wall of the office. With a pointer in hand, Beebe said, "We've got a recon plane down somewhere, here, just north of Hoa Phong. It's about sixty klicks almost due north of here. It is near the coast of the South China Sea. The pilot was on a photo recon mission near the DMZ and reported being hit by ground fire. He turned south and tried to make it to the airfield here at Danang. They had to bail out somewhere around here in the Thua Thien Province. It looks like he was trying to make it to the drink at the last moment."

"Who is he, Commander, one of our guys?"

"No, one of the Air Force people flying out of Bian Hoa at an old beat up French airbase north of Saigon. It's a hush-hush operation, Hank. That bunch of pilots has been trying to teach the Vietnamese to fly the AD-6. At the same time they are flying psy-ops missions dropping leaflets over enemy controlled territory. They also engage in a little bombing and strafing on the side," Beebe explained.

"I thought those were all Vietnamese pilots flying those missions," Hank commented with a smile.

Beebe snorted, "Yes, and the PT boat raids along the coastline have all been South Vietnamese operations, right? The Vietnamese were supposed to fly the missions, but couldn't hack it. So, the Air Force just took over. Their concession to the rules of engagement is to have a Vietnamese in the second seat. The pilots call them sandbags.

"Anyway, Hank, this guy's head is loaded with high powered information the people up north would just love to get their hands on-- and could really use. If they get him, Hank, you know they know how to get it out of him."

"Yes sir, I understand," Hank answered grimly. He did not bother to point out that those were the same people who would want to get their mitts on him, if things went wrong.

"Are you up to it after your stay in sickbay?" Beebe asked.

"I can handle it," Hank said, "I feel fine, sir."

"Good, I've called the chopper boys. They are ready to go when you are. They were in communications with the pilot just before he left the aircraft. Get in and get out fast."

"Yes, sir."

Chapter Twenty Seven

At the helicopter pad, Hank was shown on a map the coordinates that the downed pilot had given them before bailing out. This particular grid map showed all of South and North Vietnam divided into one kilometer numbered and lettered squares.

"Girard said he was headed for the coast. He said he could see it from the air," the chopper pilot explained. "Of course it's a lot further through the jungle than it looks from the air."

"You can say that again," Hank replied.

"Yeah, I guess you would know more about that than me. Anyway, Lieutenant, there are active VC units in this area. So I have very little doubt they will see, or at least hear, you coming. They'll probably know exactly why you are there as well. There's not too many airplanes falling out of the sky that far out in the boondocks. They'll have seen his chute, and are without a doubt already looking for him-- if they don't already have him. Let's hope he doesn't try to contact any locals for help. They will sell his ass out to Charlie in a minute. That is real Indian country up there.

"Here's the picture of the guy, though I think up there you can tell the American from everyone else. So just pickup any of them you see wondering around," the CO grinned. "It'll either be another one of our lost souls, or somebody who'd make a valuable prisoner."

"You got people falling out of the sky too fast to keep track?" Hank jabbed. He was committing the man's face to memory. Captain William Girard was about his age, but looked much younger. Of course, Girard's combat had been conducted in a little more detached fashion than Hank's. The cocky, brash attitude most combat pilots have came through even in an official photo.

Padget and Vispo were checking their gear as Hank left the operations hootch. Y Bli and a VNMC named Than Quat stood off to the side. Hank did not like taking so many with him. He would have preferred to take only Vispo or Y Bli. However, they were going into a hostile area and would be announcing their arrival by the ludicrous noise level of the chopper. In this case the extra firepower was absolutely necessary. Quat was along because of his familiarity with the area.

Everyone took a second to admire Hank's Ithaca automatic

shotgun. It was the first time he would be taking it into the bush.

Everyone, that is, except for Y Bli. He only had eyes for the M-16 Hank had finally given him. He was now proudly carrying it in his right hand.

Hank checked his watch. Blevins should be at the Shark Pit. He was warming up the two PTs for secondary extractions, and potentially for fire support, should it be needed and possible.

Flight crews were bustling around the UH-1A helicopter working on the standard pre-flight checks. There was a sense of urgency in the air. Everyone was hustling around. Even though the movement was so rapid, the checks were very deliberate. Careless haste now could mean someone died later.

The pilot, whose name tag identified him as Warrant Officer Larry Block, fired his bird up, and the rescue team climbed aboard. They arranged themselves with the SEALs and Y Bli sitting at the open doors with Than Quat in the center.

As they lifted off, Hank reflected that, whether or not the poor bastard they were after lived or died, depended on who got to him first.

***

"I'm looking for Mr. Joseph Olah," the tall, dark haired man in the civilian sport shirt and light trousers said.

Olah came forward, "I'm Joe Olah."

"My name is Seth Thayer; I'm with the Consulate staff."

As they shook hands, Olah noticed the man's left hand had been horribly scarred. He wondered if it had been an accident. If it was, it was probably a plumbing accident.

Olah got down to business, "We have a prisoner named Duong A Van Duc who is using you as a character reference."

Thayer smiled thinly, "Well, I can't vouch for his character, but Mr. Duc is a highly valuable asset to the United States Government."

"Well," Olah said, handing over the notebook. "He's a valuable asset of somebody's government. I'm just not sure it's ours."

For a quick second, Thayer's mask of control slipped slightly. He snatched the book from Olah's hand with a rude, "Let me see that."

Thayer scanned the pages. His lips compressed so tightly Olah thought he must be about to get a cramp. After a few minutes he looked up from the pages, "Where is Duc?" he asked. His voice took on a menacing tone that took Olah by surprise. He put the notebook under his arm.

"Right this way," Olah told him. He was enjoying this after Duc's arrogance. The prisoner's fire escape from trouble was looking like it just fell off the building.

Olah led him to the interrogation room where Terman still stood guard. Thayer turned to him, "If I ever get any indication you have eavesdropped on this conversation, your career will be done. That is not an idle threat. Don't test me."

Olah raised his hands, "He is all yours, Mr. Thayer."

Thayer shut the door behind him. Terman looked at Olah, who merely shrugged his shoulders.

After ten minutes, during which Olah could occasionally hear shouting from behind the door, Thayer came back into the hallway.

"Keep him here," he ordered. "No one is to speak with him. I will be back to take possession of him shortly."

"Just one minute," Olah protested, "He is my prisoner..."

"Who happens to be a Vietnamese citizen whom you have zero authority to hold," Thayer cut him off.

His tone softened slightly, "Listen, Joe, I'm sure you have done a great job here. This had to be some top notch police work, if a bit on the unorthodox side. I am confident," he said meaningfully, "that you will receive the commendation you deserve. But this is no longer your concern. Do you read me?"

"Yeah," Olah answered. "Loud and clear."

"Oh, yes. I'll be taking this notebook with me also," Thayer waved the binder they had recovered from Duc's villa. "You will conduct no more searches of Duc's home. You will leave that up to us. Is that clear?"

"Crystal," Olah, said annoyed.

Terman looked startled by Olah's uncharacteristically rapid capitulation as Thayer strode out of the room. "Hey," Olah said, "unless you got some bright idea, we got no other choice."

***

Twenty minutes later, the rescue team's chopper was in the area of the grid coordinates the downed pilot had radioed in. The pilot banked and turned toward the coast and slowed. He made the sweep of the area at an altitude of about five hundred feet until they got close to the sea.

Nothing.

The jungle canopy was the thickest Hank had ever seen. It swallowed up not only the pilot and his parachute, but the aircraft that crashed as well. Apparently, the aircraft had crashed without burning or it would have been easily located. There was a silver lining to that dilemma. Flaming wreckage would also be a beacon to every Viet Cong unit in the area.

The pilot gained some altitude, turned west, and made another sweep.

Still nothing.

As the pilot banked to the east they headed back toward the sea. They were about two kilometers from the coast when suddenly, Padget, who was leaning out the portside door yelled, "Smoke! I got smoke!"

Hank climbed over and followed Padget's finger. "There, over there!" Padget yelled in his ear.

Through the canopy came a faint trail of yellow smoke being dissipated quickly by the wind.

"BINGO!" Hank exclaimed. He recognized the distinct color of the markers provided for pilots in case of a forced landing.

He tapped Block on the shoulder and yelled, "We got smoke at four o'clock!"

Block gave thumbs up and headed down to the deck. He picked up the trail, followed it back to the origin, and circled.

Hank peered into the green darkness. He could see absolutely nothing. The cover was just too thick. The only thing that made this patch of jungle stick out was the yellow smoke coming from below.

Hank scanned the area. He tapped the pilot on the shoulder again, "Set down over there," he yelled. He had spotted a small clearing about a hundred meters away.

Block slipped over to the spot and hovered the helicopter,

"It's not big enough. I can't get all the way down," he shouted back.

"That's okay," Hank yelled. "Get down as low as you can."

Block eased the aircraft slowly over the clearing and started to descend. The foliage swayed back and forth in the heavy wash from the rotors. To Hank the foliage seemed to be beckoning to them like the sirens in Greek mythology. Well, these sailors were warned and ready for trouble.

Block stopped when the rotors were a mere few feet away from the swaying foliage.

Hank and the men made the six foot jump to the soft, overgrown jungle floor. The chipper climbed away to await their signal.

They quickly set patrols. Vispo was on point; he was followed by Y Bli and Than Quat. Hank pushed the pace, knowing speed was much more important than stealth at this point. They had come in straight, they had no false insertions, and even though the chopper was now off somewhere else, they had spent a long time in the air above this location.

He hoped Girard would not be wounded or injured. Time was of the essence, and if Charlie was not yet here in the area he would be any minute.

They had moved about a hundred yards, when they heard a crashing in the bush in front of them.

Hank held up his hand. Everyone came to an immediately halt, waited and listened.

The noise was getting louder. Whoever was making it was in a huge hurry. They seemed to care less than the SEALs about remaining quiet.

A minute later, a man in a brown flight suit stumbled into their line of fire. He came to a halt, wide eyed and frozen with fear as Vispo and his six foot two frame came out of the bush a mere two feet in front of him.

Girard recovered quickly, and grabbed for his sidearm out of instinct. He found his wrist gripped in Vispo's vice-like hold as the SEAL was just too fast for him.

"Easy there, big fella," Vispo drawled, as he sheathed his K-Bar just in case this was a trick by the VC.

The rest of the men stood from their cover. Girard almost

wept from relief.

"Holy shit, am I glad to see you people. I thought you were Charlie for a second." He stuck his hand out to Hank, who had stepped forward, "Captain Bill Girard. Who are you guys anyway?"

As he took the hand, Hank decided Girard no longer looked as young and cocky as he did in his picture. The blond wavy hair was slick with sweat and disheveled. His eyes were frightened and exhausted.

"Navy," Vispo offered, "Come to pull some Air Force chestnuts out of the fire."

"We're Navy, working out of Danang," Hank answered the question.

"Yeah," Girard smiled. "We've heard of you spooky bastards. Man, I'll never bad mouth the Navy again."

"Have you seen any other humans since you hit the deck?" Hank asked. Small talk was over and, identities established, it was time to get the show on the road.

"Not a damn thing. This crap is so thick, you can't see anything. I thought I heard something a ways back before you guys hovered over my smoke, but it could have been anything."

"Okay," Hank said. "Our primary extraction point is due east of here. It is about a klick away, half way to the coast. Let's move fast, they must know we're here by now."

Hank took point, leaving Vispo as rear security. Then Quat and Y Bli were next, with Padget and Girard in the middle of the group.

They moved as quickly as they could. Hank felt their best bet was to reach the extraction point as soon as possible before any kind of ambush could be set. Besides, with the pilot who was inexperienced in the bush, they would not be able to move silently enough to justify the lost time.

They had only been moving a short time, and were just entering a wooded area, when Y Bli reported from the rear, "Vispo say we got company."

Chapter Twenty Eight

Forty-five minutes later, Seth Thayer was back to meet Olah. This time he was accompanied by two Asian men in fatigues. Olah gave them a hard look. They were good sized men. He had never seen anyone of their stature from this part of the world. That much he knew for certain.

Thayer did not explain their presence. He just said cryptically, "I am back to collect Duong Van Duc."

"He is all yours," Olah said flatly.

Word had come down from his superiors that Mr. Thayer was to get his way in all manners concerning this prisoner.

Without a word, he led the three men down to where Terman still guarded the interrogation room. Terman eyed Thayer's companions thoughtfully. He did not offer any opinion or objection to their action.

Olah unlocked the door and walked in. "Your friends are here to get you," he sarcastically informed Duc, who was slowly getting to his feet.

Duc looked up, color drained from his face as he saw who had come for him. For the first time since he had called Thayer, Olah felt a small twinge of satisfaction. Then Duc composed himself and came forward.

Thayer merely said, "Let's go," and turned his back. Duc fell in behind him. The hard looking large Asian guards closed ranks behind him.

Olah saw Duc's shoulders shudder as the two escorts took up their position. Whoever these guys were, they were enough to make a man nervous who, up until now, had been nothing but cool.

They led the way down the hall. Olah did not bother to follow them. He hung back with Terman, and watched the procession leave.

"What the hell was that?" Terman asked.

Olah shrugged, "You got me. All I know is those are the meanest looking bastards I've seen since I got to this country. One thing I know, I wouldn't want to be in Duc's place right now."

He paused, then grinned, "So, Jerry, my boy, you got the photos of that notebook handy?"

"Absolutely," came the reply.

"Then let's get to work."

***

Hank was moving back toward Vispo when he heard the familiar sound of an AK-47 cutting loose. He hit the dirt as rounds cut the air above him and hit trees all around the area.

He crawled over to where Vispo had taken up position, "How many are there?" he asked.

"Three or four at least," Vispo answered. "Not any more than that. We can't stay here, Lieutenant."

Hank agreed, ""We'll head for those logs about twenty meters ahead. You cover us, then we'll cover you."

"Roger," Vispo replied as he began methodically cranking grenades out of his M-79 launcher.

Hank took off, staying as low to the ground as possible. As the first grenade exploded, the others fell in behind him.

The VC fire, which had been picking up frequency, tapered off as the grenades started to explode.

The second everyone made it to cover, Hank yelled, "VISPO NOW!" and he began pumping rounds from his Ithaca shotgun into the woods over Vispo's head.

Padget and Y Bli opened for with their fully automatic M-16s, following Hank's lead. Vispo made good time coming their way.

"I was a hell of a lot safer before," Hank heard Girard mutter. He chose to ignore the comment.

"We gotta keep movin'," Hank told them. "This is probably just a point squad we ran into somehow. There's gonna be more not far behind them. Doc, you take off with Girard..."

"GRENADE!" Vispo yelled.

Hank felt something give him a hard shove. Instantly the world was shut out by a blinding flash and deafening noise. The sounds of the firefight were instantly gone. They had been replaced by an all-encompassing ringing in his ears.

He rolled over and bumped against Y Bli's leg. The Montagnard made no effort to move. He rolled the other way. He saw Padget crouching while returning fire. Vispo was on his stomach, sending grenade rounds with his M-79 in the direction of enemy gun flashes. He could still not hear the gunshots.

Everything seemed to be moving in slow motion and silence. Most of Vispo's pant leg had been blown away. He was bleeding from his ass.

Hank turned back to Y Bli. His heart sank from his chest. The man was slumped against a decaying log. His body was opened from his chest to his crotch. Jagged pieces of rib protruded from his chest.

"NO," Hank yelled as he crawled over to the fallen man. Bluish intestines oozed between Y Bli's fingers as he tried to keep his stomach from falling out onto the dirt below.

Next to him was Than Quat. He was not moving and very clearly dead. Hank realized Y Bli had to be the one who shoved him out of the way of the grenade's blast.

"Get out of here!" Hank yelled to Vispo and Padget. "I'll cover you. Vispo, can you move?"

"Roger, Lieutenant." Hank could barely hear Vispo's reply, but his hearing was coming back little by little. He realized he could now hear the sounds of the fighting again.

Hank fired a long burst as the two SEALs disappeared into the thicket with the pilot.

Hank turned to Y Bli. There was nothing he could do to save his life. He saw the 'Sat Cong' tattooed high on his bony chest. He knew what the communists would do to the little man—his friend-- if they captured him alive. There was no way he could survive his injuries.

"Don't let them have me, Lieutenant. You know what they do," Y Bli gasped. His bloody hand gripped Hank's arm.

Hank took Y Bli's hand and squeezed it hard. "Don't let them have my weapon," the tribesman said.

"I won't," Hank promised.

Y Bli tried to smile, but only managed to grimace, "You real piece of work, Lieutenant."

Hank's eyes glazed over with tears at the Americanism. It was his friend's final attempt to please him. He was too choked up to answer at all. He just squeezed Y Bli's hand.

"Come on, Lieutenant!" Vispo hollered. There was a frantic tone starting to creep into his voice, "Are you okay?"

"On my way," Hank hollered back.

Y Bli turned his head away, "Please, my friend, do it now."

***

Padget had just started back toward Hank when the roar of the shotgun filled the jungle, and Hank came sprinting towards him.

He rolled in beside them. When he lifted his head to tell them to move out, no one could miss the wetness of his eyes.

No one asked a question. Each man moved quickly, silently into the bush.

***

For the next hour, the SEALs and their charge moved as quickly as possible through the jungle. The only time they stopped was to listen. Hank wondered just how many VC were on their trail, and just how good they really were. They seemed to have lost the bastards with ease. He knew that would not last forever.

"Okay, Doc," he said as he moved in behind Padget, "Let's see if we can get them."

He worked the switches on the PRC-77 strapped to Padget's back. "Let's keep moving," he told everyone, "Okay, Doc, try it."

"Whitehorse, Whitehorse, this is Jockey One, do you copy, over," Doc transmitted.

There was no reply. There was only the faint static that told them the equipment was, indeed, turned on.

"Try again," Hank prompted.

"Whitehorse, Whitehorse, this is Jockey One, do you read, over," Doc tried again, uselessly. "Nothing, Lieutenant."

"Damn!" Hank exclaimed, "He should be copying us. Keep trying."

They moved east for another thirty minutes before they heard it.

"Listen," Vispo pointed ahead. They could hear the beating of helicopter blades in the distance.

"Doc, try now," Hank ordered.

"Whitehorse, this is Jockey One, do you copy, over."

"Roger, Jockey One, how me? Over," came the long awaited

reply.

"Five by, Whitehorse. What's your posit?" Padget radioed back.

"I'm at the primary extraction point Jockey One, and waiting, over."

Shit, Hank thought, he stopped short of asking how long they had been hanging around there. "Come on," he urged the others, "Double time."

They couldn't see the chopper because of the jungle canopy. Hank could tell they were getting closer because of the increased noise of the chopper blades. They were right on course. Once again, their compass and survival training had served them well.

Suddenly a burst of automatic weapons fire cut through the trees above them. Vispo returned fire with a few of his dwindling number of grenades.

"Whitehorse," Padget called, "We are taking ground fire from an area just south of the extraction point. We got a hot zone, here."

Just then, Hank caught sight of the Huey. It passed just above them in one of its circles over the extraction point. The primary extraction was a clearing in the middle of the jungle. It was for some unknown reason devoid of heavy vegetation. Hank and the CO at the chopper pad had chosen it from the picto map during mission planning.

The SEALs reached the edge of the clearing. Smoke suddenly erupted from the side of the chopper.

"Jockey!" came the call from the Huey pilot. "I got big trouble here, am aborting, am aborting. Use secondary, use secondary...oh SHIT!"

The men watched in horror as the Huey went into an impossibly steep bank. It was headed right for the deck. Just before it got to the tree line, Hank thought he saw it start to level out. He realized he was just trying to help it along with his own body language.

The Huey exploded in a huge ball of fire and smoke. It scattered flaming debris all over the area.

"Omigod," Girard breathed softly.

The men could not take their eyes off the space the Huey once occupied. Mere seconds before they had been watching their ride home circling in to pick them up.

Hank was the first to snap out of the trance, "Come on," he urged. "Move it, go, GO!"

He knew the people chasing them could not have been the ones to shoot down the chopper. The fire had come from the other direction. They had to be stuck in between two different units. Charlie had to be all over the place. They had probably been drawn in by the helicopter whose pilot made the fatal mistake of being in one place for too long. He would not repeat that mistake.

"I hope those boats are there, Lieutenant. This is going to be close," Vispo said.

"Me too, Gunner," Hank answered, "Or we're gonna have one hell of a long swim, and that wound in your ass is gonna hurt like hell in the salt."

"Don't worry about me, Lieutenant," Vispo answered Hank's unspoken concern about his wound, "I can carry my weight."

Hank did not answer, but he knew if there was one thing he had never worried about, it was whether Lanny Vispo could be counted on in a tight spot.

They started off again, Hank at point, and Vispo taking rear security.

***

Keith Blevins saw the chopper blow up, and prayed Hank and the other SEALs were not aboard when it happened.

He had taken two PT boats up the coast at full throttle from Danang. They were ready in case the rescue team needed to use the secondary extraction point.

They were waiting close to the shore. The call came in, filling them with relief, "Greyhound One, this is Jockey One, how copy, over."

He grabbed the mike, "Loud and clear, Jockey One."

"Greyhound, we might need some help. We got Charlie breathing down our neck. We lost Whitehorse," Hank said.

Keith had positioned the Nasties several hundred yards apart, parallel to the beach, and was scanning the jungle with binoculars. Every set of eyeballs on the boat was trained on the beach. They were waiting anxiously for their comrades to emerge from the bush.

At Blevins' signal, the boats closed with the beach. The water began to shallow quickly. Hardison hollered from the bow, "Mt. Blevins, I can see the bottom. Nothing but rocks down there."

Blevins signaled again, and the boats hove to. He wanted to be as close as possible when Hank and the others made the water's edge.

In each boat, SEALs were at the ready to provide fire support. Brookwater and Hack readied the IB. Blevins had split the whole platoon between the two Nasties. He did not want the Vietnamese screwing up when it was his friends' lives on the line.

They were ready, now all they could do was wait.

***

Hank could smell the salt air. They were close to their escape. They were also close to Charlie. He hoped the boats would be ready when they arrived. He immediately dismissed the thought. Blevins would be ready.

He saw the light ahead. The jungle thinned. He felt like shouting in excitement. They were going to make it home!

Just then, four black pajama clad figures came into view. The Vietnamese had shocked looks that said they were as surprised as the SEALs.

The VC were too slow bringing up their weapons. Hank's shotgun fired three times so quickly that the amazed Girard thought it sounded like a single shot.

Hank shifted to fire at the remaining VC. Vispo had already taken care of him with a quick pistol shot.

Scattered fire came form the brush. Hank fired his remaining two shotgun shells, then turned to Y Bli's M-16.

The blood lust was welling in him. He yelled to the others, "Head for the beach, I'll cover you."

The sight of Y Bli lying broken and bloody in the forest came flooding back in his mind. Hank let out a primal scream. He emptied the weapon's magazine at the unseen enemy in the brush.

He reloaded quickly. He backed his way to the beach, firing with every step.

Suddenly, there was sand under hid feet. Hank could hear the IB's outboard engine as it approached the shore.

He joined the others. They were wading out into the surf. "Let's go," he shouted.

"I don't swim so good, Lieutenant," Girard confessed.

"Time to learn," Hank snapped. He was still watching the shore for gun flashes. He gave Girard a stuff shove into the deeper water.

He slung his weapon and plunged in beside the pilot. They had not gone more than a few before the IB was on them. Hack hauled Girard out of the water and over the side. Hank, Vispo, and Padget rolled in beside him.

The second they were in, Brookwater gunned the engine. The IB turned sharply and headed for the nearest Nasty.

"Hey, Lieutenant, do you see what I see?" Vispo asked.

Hank had to look twice to make sure he was not seeing things. He broke into a smile, "I sure do Vispo, I sure do," and laughed aloud.

Flying from the masts in the dazzling sunlight, was the bright red white and blue of the US Flag. Hank had never been so glad to see a violation of orders in his whole career.

"When Mr. Blevins breaks the rules, he does it right," Vispo commented, a note of awe in his voice.

Just then, every gun on each Nasty cut loose, raking the jungle. The PT boats weaponry was effective as a giant scythe. It cut a swath through the thick brush and even felled trees. The deadly fire chewed up the trees, the foliage, and, Hank noted with satisfaction, anyone who was concealed by them.

"Take that you motherfuckers," he said softly. He thought of how Y Bli would have taken great joy at the sight. He felt the tears return to his eyes as he fingered his copper bracelet.

Minutes later, the Nasties were racing back toward Danang at full power, flags flapping in the wind and salt spray.

Chapter Twenty Nine

No matter how much he drank, Hank could not erase the picture of Y Bli's head disintegrating in the shotgun blast. The longer he drank, the more he visualized the grisly scene.

Hank had never killed anyone he had known before, and certainly not a friend. He'd had two friends die near him in combat. Two more had died in training accidents. None of those were by his own hand.

Sure, some of the targets he had been given to capture or eliminate had been known to him by name. He had never interacted with any of them, other than his brief unpleasant encounter with Tuk Ba. They had been nothing to him but names on a blackboard or captions below pictures.

None of them had ever made him a brother.

He had been an idiot to think he could give it up, he thought as he took a long swig from the Johnny Walker bottle. This was the only tonic he had out there. It was his only escape until his tour was up--thank God that was soon.

The villa was quiet. That suited Hank just fine. All of the rest of the men, including Blevins, were drinking at the Alamo. Hank had chosen to drink alone. The rest of the SEALs knew why, and respected his wishes.

The front door opened. Hank put his hand on the Ithaca. It was still caked with Y Bli's blood. He no longer had anyone watching his back. He would have to take even greater care than he had before.

"Lieutenant Dillon," came a call. Hank recognized Joe Olah's voice.

Shit, he did not feel like coping with the NIS today. He decided not to respond.

"Hello, Lieutenant Dillon," came the call again.

What the hell, Hank decided. The cop could hardly make his day any worse. "Back here," he called to Olah from the kitchen. He took another long pull from his bottle of Scotch.

Olah came into the room, peering into the shadows in the near twilight. He caught sight of Hank and the shotgun, "Oh, sorry to bother you, but it's very important."

Hank waved him to a seat.

"By the way," Olah said, trying to start things out on a nice note, "Your man Y Bli did a great job for me. Give him my regards."

"Y Bli is dead," Hank informed him emotionlessly. He neither had the energy--nor was he in any mood--to sugar coat facts.

Olah was startled by this news, "I'm sorry to hear that," he said. "He was a very good man..."

"For a gook?" Hank snarled.

"No," Olah did not rise to Hank's level of temper, "Just a good man."

He picked up the glass Hank had started with before he decided it was more efficient to drink straight from the bottle and held it out, "Do you mind?"

"Why not?" Hank poured a large amount of Scotch.

Olah raised his glass, "To Y Bli."

Hank raised the bottle, and they both drank, then the villa was silent for a full minute.

"I've got something important to tell you," Olah began. "It really shouldn't wait. Your Lieutenant Ngo is a plant. We've got a witness and documents to back it up. He's been selling you people out."

Hank just stared him. He was not nearly as surprised as he should have been. It made perfect sense, now that he thought about it. The only missions that had been burned involved the VNMCs. Ngo had always been hanging around, trying to find out what was going on. He was always offended that he was not more involved. Not, it turned out, it wasn't just out of ego, as he assumed.

"Joe...are you sure?"

"There is no doubt. Remember Gill, the fat guy I showed you the surveillance photo of? He rolled over like we offered him some kind of deal, which we didn't. He thought Ngo was just a drug dealer, just like him. But, when we picked up their boss, he had it all down on paper," Olah explained.

"Good God!" Hank exclaimed. "The VC killed his wife! Why the hell would he go over to them?"

"That's his story," Olah said. "Now we're not so sure. His wife was killed; we know that much for certain. But...she also had made an appointment with a member of the South Vietnamese military secret police for the day after she was killed. We also found out that Ngo's station in life improved considerably by marrying her. They were pretty much in the same social class, but he was at the low end, and her family was at the very top."

"So, maybe she found out that she was really married to a VC informant. Somehow he figured out that she knew?" Hank shook his head. "What a fucked up mess."

"That is one theory. It's gonna be hard to prove after a couple of years. Besides, it's just one more thing the Vietnamese don't really want to believe. Listen," Olah leaned forward a bit, "I probably shouldn't do this, but if it wasn't for you, and Y Bli of course, we wouldn't have cracked this thing. They're gonna pick up Ngo tomorrow, and they might be setting the wheels in motion for a big investigation. I didn't want it coming down on you with no warning. If you have any ass covering to do, do it now, okay?"

"Who's pickin' up Ngo, us or the Vietnamese?"

"Both. You know how it goes. Who knows if anything real is even gonna happen to the bastard."

"What the fuck does that mean?" Hank demanded.

"The miserable shit's pretty well connected," Olah told him. "That's how he got his commission in the first place. Her family may not buy our theory on him. They have a vested interest in the current martyrdom of their daughter's story. Besides, this is real bad timing for the Vietnamese to have a scandal in their military."

Hank knew Joe was absolutely correct. The South Vietnamese had been taking a lot of crap from the American military because their people, in general, were just not cutting it. They were on the defensive already. It would be in everyone's best interest if this whole situation just went away.

"Who knows," Olah opined, "they might just decide to ship the guy out someplace and put a lid on the whole thing. It has been done in the past, in both militaries. They certainly aren't making a huge deal out of Ngo's boss, and he's not even in the military. I don't know why they'd do anything different with Ngo. At least you guys have your leak plugged finally," he said, trying to put a silver lining on the situation.

"You really think he might get off?" Hank asked. "I can't think of anybody getting away with anything this big before. I would think Ngo would die slowly in some secret Vietnamese Police basement for this."

"He just might. I'm only saying that I wouldn't bet anything I couldn't afford to lose on it," Olah said bitterly. "One thing I do know, they don't want the press to get a hold of it. It would probably ruin whatever relationship the military and the Vietnamese have left."

As Olah spoke, Hank had to physically control himself. Rage was building inside him, yet outwardly, it could not be allowed to show. Considering the amount of Scotch in his system, it was no easy feat.

The news of Ngo's treachery had sobered him considerably. In place of the warm glow of Scotch, there was now the fire of rage warming his stomach.

"Thanks, Joe. I really appreciate you coming by. I know this is a little out of line, and I like the way you take risks for what you believe in." The sentiments were sincere, but Hank had another agenda for them. He wanted to sound like he was dismissing Olah so he would leave.

Olah got the hint. He stood, and put out his hand, "You take care, Dillon."

Hank took the hand, then made a show of taking a swig from his bottle. "I'll see you around, Joe."

A suspicious expression fleetingly crossed Olah's face. It passed like a wispy cirrus cloud passing in front of the moon, and then it was gone. With a wave of his hand, he turned and walked out of the room.

Hank waited until he heard Olah's car crunch its way past the gravel at the end of the driveway before getting to his feet.

He had work to do.

**

Hank sat among the large rocks at the end of Black Beach and thought of Ayotte and Bush. They had been on his mind ever since Olah told him of Ngo's betrayal. He remembered the way their bodies had been torn apart in the crossfire. He remembered his anguish at having to leave their bodies behind. Perhaps, while he ran, they were still clinging to a small spark of life which Charlie would end in merciless fashion.

Hank knew from experience what the Viet Cong would have

done to the bodies. He had seen it before. He had seen bodies with their genitals hacked off and stuff in their mouths. The bastards would leave horribly mutilated corpses in mock sexual positions.

The door to the hootch opened. Ngo stepped out and stretched as though he was content with the world. The light from inside shone faintly on Hank's face. Ngo stopped suddenly, startled at the sight of the SEAL Lieutenant sitting among the rocks.

Ngo knew something was very wrong. He smiled nervously. "What are you doing here, Lieutenant?" he asked. His voice was an octave higher than normal.

"I've been waiting for you, you murdering son of a bitch." There was no turning back now. Hank started forward, and felt the familiar, welcomed, rush of adrenalin. He knew what he was about to do was wrong. He didn't care. Morally he was justified. His anger would not let him stop, nor did he want to.

Ngo stepped back and turned to run. He was not fast enough. In an instant, Hank was on him. He smashed the Vietnamese Lieutenant in the face. His nose broke badly. Blood spattered on Hank as Ngo cried through his battered face, "What are you doing?"

Hank reached down and dragged Ngo to his feet. He kept pummeling his face with his fist. He found to his surprise he was amazingly calm-- even detached.

"Why?" Ngo screamed.

"You know why, you little fucker," Hank said. He never let up his assault.

He started dragging Ngo through the rocks, into the ankle deep water of the surf.

"Duong Van Duc," Ngo cried. Hank turned the man and put a chokehold on him. He cut off the air before he could cry for help again.

Ngo tried to kick Hank in the groin. The SEAL saw it coming and easily turned it away. He took the hit on his thigh and barely noticed the impact. Ngo was frantic. He succeeded in momentarily breaking Hank's grip as he was countering Ngo's kicking.

Before he could get away, Hank grabbed him by the wrist. He whipped it around behind Ngo's back. He brought it up with such force that the bone gave away with a sickening crack.

As Ngo gasped to fill his lungs for a scream of agony, Hank took him down with a sweep of his legs. He forced his mouth open on the wet beach. The sand choked off the scream. Ngo managed only a sputtering squeal.

Hank put a knee in the man's back. He wanted to get this over with quickly. He didn't want to back out and let the bastard live. Ngo spit the sand out and cried out again, "Duong Van Duc!" before Hank pushed his face back down into the sand.

If it was some kind of prayer Ngo was screaming, it would not going to do him any good. As Hank held Ngo's struggling form pinned to the beach, it seemed as though he was outside himself. It was as if he was looking down at the scene from a distance. He was not doing this. It was someone else, and Hank was merely a spectator.

The surf lapped around their bodies, then ebbed away. Ngo's face sank deeper into the sand as the hole filled with water. Ngo was squirming underneath him. His efforts to free himself were getting weaker by the second.

Suddenly the man's body went rigid. It quivered for a moment, then was still. Hank kept up the pressure for another couple of minutes that seemed like an eternity as he knelt over Ngo's corpse.

Hank rolled off the body. He sat in the sand looking at it. For the second time in less than twenty-four hours he had killed someone he knew. For the first time, he had no regrets.

It bothered him that he could feel no guilt or sense of remorse for his actions. He just had an overwhelming sense of being numb.

Hank got to his feet. He stumbled into the gentle surf. He was dragging Ngo's body with him. Then he let it go and began swimming along out into the warm water. It was a moonless night. He swam aimlessly out into the darkness. Hank stopped, and let the soothing surge of the sea swing his body back and forth.

Looking back at the beach, he saw the lights in the buildings. He saw people moving around and making merriment to the constant beat of rock and roll.

To escape even that, he dove under and swam for the bottom. He opened his eyes to the dark. Here was the peace he wanted. Total and complete silence in the primal peacefulness of the sea. After the horror of the past few days, it was like the innocence of the womb. Here he was safe. Here it was peaceful.

The pain in his chest snapped him back to reality. He was drowning. For a moment he thought that might not be so terrible. Then he found he was clawing his way, almost involuntarily towards the top, and air.

For a moment, Hank treaded water, gasping for breath. Then he swam parallel to the shore until he was past the lit area. Then he went for the beach.

Hank knelt in the surf until he regained his strength. He moved quietly in the darkness to the place where he had parked the Jeep.

Back at the villa, the insanity of what he had done set in. He grabbed a bottle; drank an amazing amount of Scotch, and finally passed out.

He escaped the anguish that gripped his soul...for a few hours anyway.

Chapter Thirty

Olah had Hank meet him at the officer's club the Air Force maintained near their corner of the Danang airport. The airport was currently serving as a temporary air base.

Monique had joined him for the weekend. He did not want to take her into town, or leave her alone. All of the unrest made him worry for her safety.

His investigation had hit a snag, which was keeping him preoccupied, to say the least. He had gotten word this morning that Lieutenant Ngo had apparently gotten drunk and drowned himself at a restricted R&R facility the night before.

Joe wondered if Ngo was assisted on his way out of this world. He also wondered if he had played a part in giving someone information who had helped Ngo on his way.

The thought bothered him a little. He had to admit more justice had probably been done this way more than would have happened had things run through the official channels.

The other thing stuck in his mind was the diamond ring he had not found the courage to bring out of his pocket. He failed to ask Monique to marry him the night before.

It wasn't as if he had not had several opportunities to pop the question. It was just that the words wouldn't form around his lips. However, he thought, on a happier note, something else had formed around his lips.

"What are you grinning about," Monique smiled, "You look like the cat that swallowed the canary."

Before he could answer, Dillon came through the door and scanned the room looking for him. Olah waved him over to the table. As the Navy SEAL came closer, Olah decided the man looked like hell. He had seen Dillon tired and stressed out before, but this was far worse. It made him think again about what really happened to Ngo.

Introductions were made…Monique excused herself, as they had pre-arranged, and went to the bar.

"What's on your mind?" Hank asked.

Olah grinned, "Right now I'm trying to come up with the words to ask Monique to marry me."

"She your girl? She's…" Hank tailed off.

"Yeah," Olah snapped, "she's black, all right."

Hank looked shamed, "I meant to say she's positively stunning, not to mention a whole lot of woman."

Olah looked at him for a moment. He found to his surprise that he believed him. Then he laughed at himself, not only for being defensive, but also because he could talk to Hank about what he could not talk to Monique about. At the same time he was having a very hard time bringing up the subject that applied to Hank.

"Yes, she is," Olah replied proudly. "I still can't believe she has anything to do with me. I guess I'll want to stay here for a while if we get married. People back in Washington sure aren't ready for us. That won't break her heart. She actually believes everything she hears about the United States on TV. That is especially true when the subject is black people and politics," he shook his head. "No way am I telling her I'm voting for Goldwater, ya know?"

Hank laughed, "If she believes what she sees on TV, that would break you two up for sure. But I doubt that's why you called me down here."

Okay, Olah decided, let's get down to it. "Ngo died last night."

"Yeah, I know," Hank answered.

"How do you know?" Olah was shocked at the admission.

"I had an early meeting with Commander Beebe, you remember him," Hank said dryly.

Olah blushed at the hint of his earlier encounter with Beebe.

Hank did not notice and continued, "He called me in to say my platoon is standing down. He also told me Ngo died last night and that he had been the leak in our camp. Of course, I already knew that, didn't I?"

"Knew what?" Olah demanded.

"Why that Ngo was the leak, of course," Hank said innocently. "They think it may have been suicide. Maybe he didn't know the fix was in and was afraid of what the ARVN would do if they got their hands on him. By the way, do you have any idea what *duong van duc* means?"

Olah was startled by the abrupt change of subject. Where the hell had Dillon come up with that name? Of course, he hung around with a lot of spooky people. If he'd gotten the name from them...would they have told him who Duc was?

He took a photo they had taken of Duc sitting in the interrogation room without Thayer knowing. "That is the guy, the Fixer. He is the guy I had Y Bli follow," Olah answered, watching intently for Hank's reaction.

"He was Ngo's contact. We picked him up a few days ago. He is the one that had the documents with Ngo's name on them. A guy named Thayer from the embassy came over with two guys that looked sort of like they were Chinese, but not quite, and took him away. What happened to him after that, I don't know. I've just been told 'It's none of my concern.' I've got to admit, I'm not inclined to look into it.

"I've gotten a lot of attaboys for shutting the guy down, and I'm enjoying it. Hey, a bump in pay will be nice. I am hopefully going to be married soon, so that would help. That's the other reason to stay here. As the situation gets bigger, there's going to be more of this kind of shit, not less. I think there's a lot of opportunity here for a guy like me," Olah said.

Hank clapped him on the shoulder. His face had gotten a grim look as Joe spoke, but now he was jovial again. "You're right not to worry about it. You did a damn good job, and you deserve to enjoy it. I'm sure you're gonna have to worry about larger quarters soon. I'm never wrong about these things. It's great to see one of the good guys getting something out of being in this shithole of a situation." He stuck out his hand, "You take care Joe, and watch your back."

Olah concluded he was not going to get anywhere on the subject of Ngo. He decided he really didn't care. He thought he knew what had happened, and that was that. He had the feeling that no one really believed Ngo's death was accidental or suicide, and nobody was going to look too closely at it. Most people were just glad to have the situation over with. Ngo deserved what he got.

He took Hank's hand and shook it firmly, "You take care, Lieutenant. It's been a real pleasure."

"I guess it's time to let things go when we can't do anything about them," Hank opined. "Like the man said, 'If there's no solution, there's no problem.' Besides, the Air Force guys gave me a saying, I'm in my FYIGMO mode."

"What's that?" Olah grinned.

"It means, Fuck You, I Got My Orders," Hank laughed. Olah joined him. "Listen," Hank said, "One last favor."

"Yeah?"

"Look in on Sister Annie at the Orphanage once in a while, okay? Just to see if they need anything."

"You got it, Hank."

"See ya', Joe."

As Hank walked out, Monique rejoined Joe at the table. "Your friend is very handsome," she said speculatively. "But I think he is also a very dangerous man, yes?"

"Yes," Joe answered thoughtfully. "But I think a damned good man as well."

***

"That is none of your concern, Lieutenant."

It was the answer Hank had expected to come from Commander Beebe, but he had to ask the question.

"Commander, this man is responsible for at least two of our people being killed, not to mention four Vietnamese Marines under our supervision," Hank argued.

"Listen to me carefully, Dillon. I'm not saying this is the way I would handle it. As far as I'm concerned, he should be as dead as Ngo." Beebe paused long enough on that point to make Hank feel uncomfortable before going on.

"However, the plumbers say they can use him. We could get our revenge, our pound of flesh, and nothing else. On the other hand we can make things very unpleasant on this tiny little man and at the same time, we can feed bogus intelligence to the enemy. If you think about it, the choice is pretty easy."

"If it works," Hank said. "The plumbers thought they had this guy under their thumb once before and look where that got us. They think they can control everything. I'm not too impressed with their batting average."

"Fair point, but Duc was not under direct supervision. Look, he has had all of his toys taken away. He's not laying two women at the same time, nor is he living in a luxurious villa anymore. He's living a really Spartan life. His constant companion is a Nung. He might be alive, but he really isn't happy," Beebe explained.

"I guess that's gonna have to be enough," Hank replied.

"That's right. Now listen, you're out of it now. You have done a damn fine job here. You have a lot to be proud of. Your platoon's success is going to have a lasting impact on the role that SEAL teams will be given in the future. The experiment was a success, and you deserve a great deal of the credit. We also would not have broken this man's operation without you. For the next few days, observe rope yarn Sunday. Get your shit squared away and do some celebrating. You're going back to Dago', and will get to spend time with your family, while the rest of us are sweating our asses off over here. You have a promising career, Dillon. I am confident you are going to go far. Don't jeopardize all that by taking this any further. Am I clear?"

"Very clear, sir."

As Hank left Beebe's office, he knew the Commander was right. They should get whatever they could out of Duc. He would be a fool to pursue the matter further.

But he could not shake the nagging feeling that he was leaving Vietnam with unfinished business.

***

When Hank returned to the villa, Giai Vu handed him a note from Doc Padget inviting him and Blevins to an end of tour party at the Alamo that night. "Come hungry and thirsty," the note read. "It will be a long night."

Hank wondered what the old man was going to do after they left. The plumbers would probably have someone else move in...maybe even Duc. That would be ironic, he thought. He always had a creepy feeling about the way Vu had hovered around and wondered if he might not be a VC plant.

When Hank and Keith arrived at the Alamo, the party was in full swing. There were about ten military vehicles parked in the street. Loud music reverberated across the lawn. The sound of men yelling and the sound of *hoo-yah* could be heard in the building and on the roof.

"Hallzapoppin'" Hank grinned.

"Like you say," Blevins agreed.

Inside the compound, the common area was stacked high with boxes of canned food, soda, and first aid equipment. There was even some motor oil. There was also a large stack of pillows, sheets and blankets. It was like many other parties at the Alamo, only on a much larger scale. There was one difference this time; there were no women at this party. This night was just for the men.

Doc came over to greet Hank and Keith, "The Air Force guys brought this stuff over, as a favor, to give the orphanage before we leave. It was kind of the price of admission to the party. They seemed glad to do it. Now you'd better get some food before these fly boys and mechanics eat us out of house and home."

Hank and Keith separated and made their way around the room. They grabbed plates at the huge buffet. They worked the room, talking to each SEAL they had served with.

"Hey Bostic, where's Penelope?" Hank asked curiously. It was the first time he had seen the young man in the Alamo without the bird.

"I gave her to Sister Annie," Bostic replied.

"You gotta be kiddin'," Hank smiled. "You gave that foulmouthed bird to a Catholic orphanage?"

"I warned her, Lieutenant. I told her the bird used swear words, but she said she would take care of the situation. You know, Lieutenant, I'm not gonna tell that Nun there is something she can't handle."

Hardison chimed in, "You know what he told her, Lieutenant?" he laughed. "He said he was gonna eat the thing if she didn't take it."

"Hey," Bostic tried to defend himself, "I was only kiddin'. I just wanted to give her to someone that I could trust. If anyone can straighten Penelope out, Sister Annie can."

Hank just shook his head and smiled.

Lanny Vispo joined them, "That glass is lookin' pretty empty, Lieutenant. Let me fix you up." Hank held out his glass. Vispo filled it back up with Johnny Walker. "That better?"

"Much. Thanks Gunner."

"No problem, Lieutenant. Listen, I didn't get a chance to say it the other day, but I'm sorry about Y Bli. He was a damn good man in the bush. I guess that bracelet proves you thought a lot of each other. After our little trip to Laos, I can understand why."

It was possibly the longest, most serious comment Vispo had ever made. Hank looked at him, a little surprised. Vispo had always been the best man on point, but when they weren't in the bush he was always, without fail, the platoon clown. Now as he appraised the man, Hank wondered if Vispo had been fulfilling a role he thought the platoon needed to keep morale high.

"Thanks, Guns, I appreciate it. He was a good man, and you are not bad for a surf bum, yourself," Hank said.

Before things could get too serious, Vispo turned and made his way across the room with his arms spread, as though riding an invisible wave. To add to the clownish move, he started humming a surf rock and roll tune.

Hank laughed out loud with the rest of the room. He suddenly realized Vispo had the potential to be a real leader. He would be good for this platoon long after Hank was gone. He would have to talk with Keith about giving the goofball more responsibility. If Lanny handled it well, he would have a bright future.

Just then, a large truck pulled up. Doc yelled, "Everybody pitch in and give us a hand, here."

The supplies for the orphanage were quickly loaded on the truck. Once complete, the truck departed for its one and only delivery. Hank noted that almost everyone was grinning ear to ear. The only exception was Dan Slade. He was sitting alone staring at his drink.

For these men who, one way or another, dealt with death as a profession, it was a good feeling to be involved with something as life affirming as Sister Annie's work. Every man here had to feel it, even if he couldn't put it into words.

After an hour or so, everyone had gone except the SEALs. . Gradually, the men gathered in a large circle in the main room. Doc started things off with a toast, "Bush and Ayotte, the two men who aren't going with us, but will always be by our sides, no matter where we go."

Things degenerated after that. They toasted the REMFs who made the rules of engagement. They lifted their glasses to particular VC cadres they had assisted into the afterlife.

"It's been a hell of a little war," Blevins said, raising his glass unsteadily. "At least while it stayed little."

That turned things serious again. The talk turned to one of war, in general, and whether the Vietnamese would ever get serious about the conflict and fight it on their own.

"Maybe there is no need for that now," Brookwater said. "Now it looks like Uncle Sam is going to come in with both feet and fight for 'em. Why work when you can be on the dole? I don't know about that concept, though. Infantry and jet bombers against guerillas? It doesn't seem like the right way to do anything. Lieutenant, what do you think? Did we make any difference here? Did we show them how to do their job, and will they pay attention to the lessons?"

The men turned to Hank eagerly. He chose his words carefully. His immediate cynical thought after what Brookwater said was maybe heavy involvement from the Soviet Bloc was exactly what the US was after. They could send over a ton of AK-47s and a few more radar stations. Maybe they would even send some jet fighters along with some surface to air missiles. It would be pennies next to what America would invest, not to mention the cost in American lives yet to come with a deeper dive into this conflict.

"I don't know Brookwater. We'll just have to see how the war is conducted to get the answer to that. I guess no one will ever know for sure, or maybe even give a damn what we did here. I will tell you one thing for certain. Charlie sure as hell knows we were here!"

"I'll drink to that!" Vispo exclaimed. He was followed by the cheers and raised glasses of every man in the room.

"Tactics are not the only problem," Doc said soberly. "Those politicians had better get squared away back in the States. If they keep dictating rules of engagement from ten thousand miles away, we will lose our asses over here. You know what they say, 'Never get involved in a ground war in Asia.' I've been in one, and we didn't win the way we could have. They don't seem to have learned a damn thing from Korea. They seem to think we need more of exactly the same methods, only this time it will work. I don't understand that thinking."

Hank was surprised by Doc's candor. He was usually the

driver behind keeping morale up. Perhaps he was just voicing what he knew everyone was thinking, and wanted Hank to address it on their last night in country together. "You hit the nail on the head, Doc. They just don't know what it is like on the ground over here. I know most of you were as pissed as I was about how the *Maddox* incident was handled. We have to keep in mind that the North *did* start this war. They are the aggressors. They have been supplying arms and sending guerrillas down here for a long time.

"We've all seen the kind of atrocities they commit in the villages. You can magnify that to a national level if they do take over. Every place the Communists have conquered it's the same – repression, concentration camps, and wholesale slaughter of people who disagree with them. The fact that a trumped up incident is being used to sell this to the American public doesn't change that.

"The problem isn't what are we fighting against, but what the hell are we fighting for? The Communists always pick a spot where the government is pretty bad. There has got to be a problem for people to rebel against. Doc mentioned Korea. Well, they had the same problem then with the South not fighting. But now, they're some of the toughest sons a' bitches around.

"Can that happen here? I don't know. In Korea, you didn't have Charlie in your own back yard. The government may have been a lot more determined than they are here."

Hank stopped to think about his words before continuing, "But we can't get caught up in all of that. Think what it's gonna be like for some grunt straight from boot camp to try to fight under these fucked up rules. We have the training, and we have the men to accomplish any mission they choose to give us--not just because of our training, but because of who we are. We just have to roll together, and trust our man on point. The politicians may let us down, but we know we can rely on each other. That's what we have to hang on to."

"Hear hear!" Vispo hollered, and another round of toasting began.

Hank hoped he had left them with the right message. He could not lie to them and give them some line of gung ho bullshit. They deserved better. He also couldn't tell them exactly how he felt.

He knew many more men would follow into the dark places

they had fought. To what end?

He could not see that they had accomplished much, except to test out a new type of unit and show how war could be fought. These lessons were likely to be largely ignored by a bureaucracy, which still loved the tactics of twenty years ago.

Perhaps they also helped drag the United States into a more wide scale conflict.

Hank decided to take his own advice. Forget about the rest of the world and concentrate on his men. Lord only knew how much more time he would have with them.

***

A shadowy figure dangled from the second floor window of the Alamo. He dropped silently to the ground and made directly for the edge of the compound.

Hank moved stealthily to intercept it. He was within ten feet of the man and said quietly, "Hold it, Cutter."

After the party wound down, Hank had sent Keith ahead to the villa. He said he had forgotten something, and needed the walk anyway. Blevins shrugged, and drove away.

Slade stopped dead in his tracks, "Is that you, Lieutenant?"

"Yeah, Dan, it's me."

Even in the darkness, Hank could see Slade's shoulders drop like heavy weights were suddenly attached to his hands.

"How'd you know I was comin' out?" Cutter asked.

"I didn't," Hank told him, "But you've been edgy all night. I've been needing to talk to you, anyway"

"What about?" Slade asked wearily.

"Breaking curfew for one. But I think you know it's more than that. This shit has got to stop. You know that, don't you?" Hank asked gently.

"Slade was quiet for a moment then, with a catch in his voice said, "But they are spreading death, Lieutenant, they deserve it."

"Listen Dan, do you think one less person in Danang has been able to get their hands on any kind of dope they want because of you?" Hank asked.

"Not really," Slade said reluctantly.

"It's not worth it, Dan. You're a good man; don't throw it

away on this shit. What happened in Dago is one thing. Maybe those people were responsible for Cathy's death, but these dealers over here, are just another segment of the merchant class in this country. This damn place is so full of the stuff."

"You know about Dago?" Slade asked numbly.

Hank smiled in the darkness, "Don't become a criminal, Dan. You are not cut out for it at all. Hey, it's one thing to go after someone who is responsible for the death of someone you loved. I can respect that. But it's a little over the edge to randomly hunt down small time dealers ten thousand miles away."

"What about Sasser? He was right here," Slade said belligerently. "What about Ngo? That was pretty convenient."

Hank felt a small chill run down his spine. It seemed like everyone who mentioned Ngo had a good idea of what really happened. If Slade even suspected, how many other people had ideas about the story of Ngo's death. He could feel the noose tightening around his neck.

"Yeah," Hank said nonchalantly, "But that is a different subject. Listen, Sasser killed himself. Somebody sold him the shit, but he pumped it into his own veins. That is hard to accept, but that is reality. The Rivera brothers didn't kill Cathy; she killed herself. She made some bad decisions. She bought the dope, she cooked the needle, and it was her thumb on the plunger. It was her fault, not anyone else's. And," Hank paused significantly, "it wasn't your fault, either."

Slade had no answer. Hank could see his shoulders shaking. The man was weeping silently. Finally, he said, "But she was so beautiful, Lieutenant. She needed attention, and I was over here…"

"Dan, she knew what she was getting when she married you. A lot of people have problems without putting poison in their veins. I don't expect you not to grieve for her. Hell, I feel bad about her. She was so full of life. But you've got to go on, and you've got to get your head squared away. I want you to promise me this shit will stop, and I want you to swear you'll get some help when we get back stateside. I trust you Dan, and if you give me your word, nothing will go any farther than this conversation."

"I'll be okay, Lieutenant…"

"Your word, Dan."

There was a pause. Hank's body tensed; maybe he had

pushed the man too far. Maybe Slade was farther gone that he thought.

"Okay, Lieutenant, you have my word."

Hank breathed a sigh of relief, surprised to find he had been holding his breath waiting for the man's response.

"Go get some rest; we got a long plane ride day after tomorrow. You still need to pack all your stuff."

"Yes sir."

Slade turned away, and then stopped. "Thanks, Lieutenant."

"Get out of here." Hank put a smile into his voice he wasn't sure he fully felt. He watched as Slade walked back into the Alamo and wondered if he had done the right thing.

By all rights, Slade should be discharged under a Section 8 for mental distress. But that was a tricky thing.

Would the killings be ignored because of his mental state?

What kind of treatment would be required?

He was not ready to condemn Dan Slade to a long stretch in a mental hospital without first trying to save him not when the difference between what Slade had done, and what he had done was a matter of a very small degree.

Hank turned and started toward the villa. He still wondered if he had done the right thing. He was getting used to that feeling. It seemed like he had been wondering that for most of his time in Vietnam.

Chapter Thirty One

There was no missing the tension in the White Elephant. Hank was making his way to Beebe's office after an urgent summons. It was nothing an outsider would notice...the worried expression on a man's face, the slightly quicker pace everyone walked, the look on the secretary's face like she had been crying recently. To Hank, it was as noticeable as the heightened atmosphere at a SEAL camp just before a mission launch.

Beebe was just as preoccupied as everyone else when Hank opened the door. "What is it, Commander? What's goin' on around here?" Hank gestured broadly to the Consulate.

"Duc killed his Nung guard last night. He then went and found Mr. Thayer at his quarters and murdered him while he slept," Beebe reported wearily. "Mr. Olah is in protective custody, and it wouldn't be bad if you watched yourself. He knows a lot about you, and who knows how far he wants to carry his revenge. He may also be trying to regain some stature with his employers in the North, and you would be a good way to do that."

Hank sank into his chair. So, after all of this, the real culprit in the deaths of Ayotte and Bush was going to get away after all. "If he's that good, there's no chance we're going to catch up with him. He's probably already with a VC unit and on his way north."

"Maybe not," Beebe said while rubbing his chin. "But he is good. You should not underestimate him. Duc was trained by the Legion, and he even fought with them in Algeria. He was in a special counter terror brigade at the time. Nasty people, but good anti-Communist credentials, which was why the CIA trusted him. They thought his only sideline was the drugs. Who knows? Maybe Duc's commercial operations were part of his cover. A way to explain what might otherwise be suspicious behavior.

"Anyway, the hold Thayer thought he had over Duc was a widowed sister with two children near the village of Quang Tri, here," Beebe pointed to the map on the wall. "Thayer had two Nungs get their picture taken at the doorway to Duc's sister's home. He figured that would keep Duc in line."

"Ve haff your relatives in ze homeland, so you better do vat ve say," Hank cracked.

"Something like that," Beebe said. "The Nungs are still

there, watching the house. But we have no regular communication with them."

"Commander, were they really ordered to kill the family if Duc escaped?" Hank asked.

Beebe have him a hard look, "Of course not. They were to watch in case the family made a sudden move. That would mean Duc was about to, or-- and this now becomes a real situation-- they would be there should Duc attempt to rescue them."

"Yeah, but Duc knows they are there because of the threat, and they have no idea he's coming. Someone should warn them." A realization suddenly came to Hank. "What are my orders, Commander?"

"Hank, this is more of a request, if you want to do this."

"That depends on the rules of engagement, Commander."

"Whatever you decide is appropriate."

"Just where, exactly, is this house?" Hank asked quickly.

***

As he sat in the copilot's seat next to Jack Warden he saw the jungle flash by. Somehow, Hank felt better than he had in months.

This was it. The last mission, if anything came of it. The best part to him; it was something he could really sink his teeth into. He was going into battle against the bad guys with the full support of his superiors. He was being given a chance to avenge the deaths of Ayotte and Bush. That night they died represented the bleakest point of his career.

"I hear you guys are standing down," Warden hollered.

"Yeah, we ship out tomorrow," Hank yelled back.

"Well, Lieutenant, in case I don't get another chance to tell ya', it's been a real pleasure."

"Same here, Warden, same here."

Hank thought of Duong Van Duc's decision to make a break for it. The threat didn't seem to matter. It was a choice he could understand. It was the choice of a warrior. Duc would rather fight it out than live his life under the thumb of someone else. Judging by the fact that he had dispatched his Nung with relative ease, fighting it out was apparently something he was good at.

They approached the village from downwind so the noise of

the chopper would not carry as far. Warden found a clearing about a klick west of Duc's sister's house, and Hank got out as fast as he could.

The helicopter lifted off quickly. It moved to the west, where Warden would make two false insertions. There was no sense in alerting the VC that something was up. The thought was this would help, whether Duc had communications with them, or not.

Hank stashed the radio as well as he could. The Nungs should have one, but he was not going to take a chance. Without coms he would have real problems.

Hank made the run to the house in about three minutes. He was careful, but moving fast.

When he thought he was within two hundred meters of the house, he slowed. He made his way very carefully, and moved as silently as he could. The Nungs might be more apt to shoot first and ask questions later. All of this would be in spite of his American uniform.

Everything was quiet. Hank sat still and listened. The jungle noise did not return. Was he being stalked?

He moved a short distance, and then stopped again. Still nothing. There were also no telltale sounds of pursuit, being caught off guard, and stopping too late.

The house was in sight now. It was small and made of stone. It was much better than the average Vietnamese house. It was obvious the Fixer had at least some measure of attachment to his sister and her children.

Hank's eyes caught an out of place lump at the edge of the yard. He cautiously made his way over.

It was a Nung tribesman. He throat was cut ear to ear. Hank felt a chill go up his spine. Duc was very good; there was no way to deny that. There was little doubt that the Nung never knew what hit him. Duc must have killed both of the sentries. There was no way he would have killed just one.

A child's cry came from the house, and Hank whirled around.

Duc was still here!

Hank carefully made his way around to the east side of the house. There was jungle closer to the front door on that side. He would have good cover until he was about fifty feet from the porch.

He was about half way there when he found the other Nung. He was lying in a heap, weapon unslung. His neck was twisted at a very strange angle.

Hank continued through the brush. When he was at the nearest point, he sprinted for the door. He ducked under the window, with his back up against the wall of the house. His Ithaca was pointed toward the door.

Sooner or later, they would have to come out. Duc would be in a hurry. He would be rushing them along. By the time he knew Hank was there, Duc would have a shotgun pointed at his back, hopefully at point blank range. It was not only his best chance at surprise, it was his best chance to do something without endangering the children. He was not shooting any kids on his next to last day in Vietnam.

The minutes dragged by. What the hell was taking so long? Hank could hear people moving around in the house. He could hear the occasional sharp word between brother and sister. Hers were angry with a bit of a whine. His were curt and demanding.

Maybe Duc had seen him and was even now coming up on his flank after coming out a window. Sweat trickled into Hank's eye. He had to wipe it away, he had no choice.

Just then a small boy of about three barreled out the door. He was followed by a girl of about five, being pushed by a slim woman. They were being herded along by a silver haired Vietnamese man in a cammo uniform.

"Hold it, Duc," Hank ordered. He had leveled the Ithaca at the man's head.

Duc tensed as if to make a move. He was brought up short by the business end of a shotgun as his sister screamed in fright. The children began to cry.

"Who are you?" he asked calmly. He was the man Hank had seen in Olah's photos. Up close he was even harder looking than Hank remembered. His chiseled features betrayed no fear as he looked Hank directly in the eye.

"I could tell you, but then I'd have to kill you," Hank taunted.

"You are a SEAL," Duc decided. "Are you Lieutenant Dillon or Mr. Blevins?"

Hank was a little unnerved to hear his name come from the lips of an enemy agent. This man had completely penetrated their unit!

His finger tightened on the trigger, and Duc challenged him, "Why don't you shoot?"

Hank relaxed, "I think I'll let the Nungs on Phoenix Island have you after I tell them what you did to your sister's two minders, as well as your escort back in Danang," he smiled.

Before Duc could form a response, Hank was driven back. Stone splinters stung his check. A burst of automatic gunfire had missed its mark.

A blow from Duc knocked the shotgun out of line. It roared as Hank's finger tightened on the trigger. The kick from the gun combined with the impact served to knock the Ithaca from his hand. With an impossibly quick sweep of his legs, Duc knocked Hank to the ground.

He was dead. Not only was Duc grappling with him, but he had reinforcements. How could he have missed them as he reconned the house? Damn! He would never see his wife and daughter again. All because he wanted to play hero one last time.

Duc aimed a front snap kick at Hank's head to finish him off. Hank reacted quickly. He moved his head just in time. As Duc's foot flashed past his ear, Hank threw his arm up in a block that caught the back of Duc's calf and pushed his leg up and over. This unbalanced the Vietnamese double agent who fell backwards. This allowed Hank to scramble to his feet.

The two men closed on each other. Hank saw that Duc had a huge purple bruise on his right cheek. One of the Nungs had put up a fight, probably the one with the broken neck.

Duc landed a stunning jab to Hank's cheek. He grinned as he followed it with a kick at Hank's head. Hank ducked and landed a blow to Duc's sternum, driving him back, gasping for air.

Hank thought about the scorn his hand-to-hand combat instructor had for sport karate with its emphasis on high kicks. 'Kicking is for the groin and below. Punching is for the stomach and above,' Giordello had lectured them endlessly.

Balance, he reminded himself. Keep your balance. Balance is life.

Behind them, Hank could hear the sister shrieking in horror.

The little girl was crying. He was suddenly struck by the fact that she was about his daughter's size. However, he did not want his back to them. He had seen too many dead men who had turned their backs on Vietnamese women or children.

Hank did his best to keep the house at his back. He wanted Duc between him and the direction the shots had come from. It must be working, he thought, there were no more rounds flying his direction.

But why? Why would Duc's helpers be content to fire from cover? Why not just come running and help Duc put him away?

He moved around, dodging Duc's blows. He was failing to land any of his own. His right hand was numb, but not useless. His eye was puffing up from a jab Duc had landed. His cheek was bleeding and stinging from where the stone splinters had struck him. Luckily they had missed his eyes. He could see the woman now, but she was paying no real attention to them. She was kneeling over the boy and wailing.

Hank realized that Duc was fighting in the French Legionnaire style of manual combat. He was relying on his punches to set up powerful kicks. Hank thought that gave him an advantage of some type. Hwarang Do was equally lethal with hands or feet.

However, his opponent had just succeeded in killing two deadly adversaries. He was damned good.

Hank eyed the shotgun. Duc would be on him before he could get to it. He knew the man had a knife. Duc's eyes were also darting around the yard when he could. Hank realized with a start that his opponent also had no idea who had taken the shots. He began scanning the area more diligently than before.

Hank blocked a jab with his right arm. He used a swan motion, then tried to slide down Duc's arm for a fingertip thrust to Duc's throat. At the last instant, Duc was able to deflect the motion and twist away. The man was amazingly fast. He was able to recover almost instantly from mistakes that left him open for an attack. If not for Hank's superior strength and training, he knew that Duc's quickness would have already won the fight.

Hank saw an opening. He landed a solid driving backfist to Duc's cheek. It landed just below his left eye. He had been aiming to crush the nose, but Duc had moved his head just in time to avoid a more debilitating blow. Hank tried to follow with another punch to the sternum, as he knew Duc must be in pain. The Vietnamese was able to deflect it and counter attack with a punch of his own. Hank was barely able to block in time.

Hank saw the movement out of the corner of his eye. An M-16 was rising from the grass. It belonged to the Nung with the broken neck. The man must still be clinging to life. The gun wavered as the man struggled to bring it to bear, but the rounds went harmlessly into the air.

It was enough to make Duc flinch. It gave Hank the opportunity he needed. He broke two of the man's ribs with one punch that landed perfectly. It went just like he had been trained. He followed it with a chop that sent Duc reeling back stunned by the blow that just missed crushing his larynx. Amazingly, Duc was able to defend himself with a kick that kept Hank from finishing him off, but Duc was driven back and stunned slightly. That gave Hank a chance.

As Duc gathered himself, Hank went for the Ithaca. In one sweeping motion it was aimed at Duc's head.

Before the man had a chance to make the decision to go down fighting, Hank pulled the trigger, and splattered Duc's brains all over his sister's front yard.

Hank sat back on the grass. He was exhausted. Duc's sister had stopped wailing. She was just staring at him in shock. Her little girl's head was buried in her shoulder. She was protecting the girl from the view.

Hank motioned for her to be calm. He slowly approached the still form of the boy. A machine gun round had caught him high in the body. His eyes were closed. The little chest was not moving. His shirt was soaked in blood, as were his mother's hands and much of her dress.

Hank felt for a pulse in the boy's neck and felt a faint flicker. He knew there was no hope. His radio was minutes away, the chopper several more. If the boy were not dead by then, he would be before they could get him to help.

He cursed aloud. Nothing ever went as it was supposed to in this damned country. It was always the innocent who paid the dearest price.

Then a thought hit him. Just a minute, he sprinted to the Nung minder who had fired the shot. They had to have radios.

They had to report in if the family started acting suspiciously or tried to flee.

There was no pulse in the man's broken neck. The harmless burst into the air that had given Hank his opening must have been his final effort in life. Hank turned him over.

Bingo!

Hank hit the switches on the radio, and found the designated frequency, "Hunter this is Hound, do you copy, over."

Warden's voice came back immediately, "Five by, Hound. What's your position? Over."

"The house, Hunter. Hurry, we need a medic, and fast, over."

Hank returned to the fallen child, and applied pressure to the wound.

Lieutenant Hank Dillon of the United States Navy SEAL Team One, under the accusing eyes of a grieving mother, prayed and worked desperately over the still body of the nephew of a communist double agent whom he had just killed. Please God, just this one thing before I get out of this country you've forsaken.

Chapter Thirty Two

Hank awoke to the sound of his alarm. He had a full bottle of whiskey in his hand. The cap was off, but not a single drink had been taken from the bottle.

He tried to remember how this had come to be. He spent the rest of the day at the Army hospital. He wanted to see if Duc's nephew would pull through. The plumbers who had wanted to debrief him had done so. It truly annoyed them that they were forced to come to the hospital to see him.

The doctors and nurses, who saw him racing anxiously in the waiting room, gave him pitiful looks. They almost assuredly thought he had shot the young boy. Hank did not bother to explain.

Even Ken Nanski had come by. It served two purposes, to check on him, and say goodbye.

By the time he found out the boy would live, the day had passed. In fact, it was late into the evening. He had come back to the villa, grabbed a bottle, and headed to bed. Obviously, he had been too tired to need the liquor.

Then it hit him. This was his last day in Vietnam.

His feet hit the floor. This would be his last day to wake up in these quarters. It would be his last night in this bed. Tomorrow he would see his daughter. The next morning he would wake up with Shirl. The thought seemed so distant somehow.

He looked at the bottle in his hand. Yesterday had not followed the usual after mission routine. He had not come in with his adrenaline pumping. He did not need to anesthetize his nerves. Instead, he had been forced to sit around all day, waiting for good news. That news had finally come. Instead of coming to bed with death and destruction on his mind, he had come here focused on life.

He tried and failed to remember any nightmares from last night. There were none.

Hank looked at the bottle in his hand like it was an old friend who had betrayed him somehow. Then he got to his feet, walked to the bathroom, and poured the entire contents down the drain.

He watched the whiskey swirl in a caramel colored whirlpool down the sink. Hank knew this wasn't going to be easy.

Not all of his demons were heading for the sewer of Danang with the Scotch. He would still have nightmares. He would still have to come to grips with some of the things he had done in Vietnam. This was not the end.

But it was a start.

***

Bravo Platoon gathered at the airfield to leave Vietnam. The skies were gray and there was a light rain.

As the SEALs waited to board the C-130, Hank reflected that it seemed strange to see them all ship shape and in clean, pressed uniforms. It had been a long time.

Keith Blevins had cocked an eyebrow at Hank's beaten and bruised appearance. Hank had offered no explanation, and Blevins did not press the matter.

As they waited, an Air Force jeep pulled up and skidded to a stop. The driver asked, "One a' you guys named Hack?"

"Yeah, what's up?"

"You got a visitor at the gate. Get in, I'll take you over."

As Hack climbed into the jeep, Hardison called out, "Tell her she's gonna have to earn her money somewhere else!"

His only answer was a one finger salute by the departing SEAL.

"Hurry up," Hank called, "We're boarding in a few minutes."

Hack was back almost immediately, this time he was riding shotgun in their old German command car, driven by Sister Annie. The car had been painted bright yellow, and the words, 'Annie's Wheels' had been painted on the side in script.

Hank couldn't help but notice how small she looked in the huge car, even sitting in the rigged up seat Hack had made for her so she could see to drive.

The SEALs all gathered around to see her for one last time. "I had to talk her through the gate," Hack explained. "They didn't want to let her in."

He gestured toward the car, "How do you like it, Lieutenant? It took a long time, but I'd say she's runnin' better than she ever did for us. The paint job was the kids' idea."

"It's just fine, Hack," Hank smiled.

Everyone took a minute to say goodbye to the Sister. She dispersed bags of sandwiches she had brought for her "Navy boys."

Hank was the last to take his turn. Annie squeezed his hand very hard in both of hers. There were tears running down her face as she said, "You've been a blessing to us, and I know God will bless all of you."

Hank could not help but feel a lump forming in his throat, "Thank you Sister."

Before he could pull away, Annie tightened her grip on his hand, "Hank, I have only known you for a few months, but even in that time, you have aged before my eyes."

Hank was surprised by the observation. It seemed his inner life was an open book these days.

"You are a good man, Hank Dillon. That is why things have weighed heavily on you. I want to leave you with one thought. Mistakes made in war while fighting evil are not mortal sins. Make no mistake; the Communists in this place are evil. I have seen what happens to a country when they take over. South Vietnam is a bad place and many of the men who run it are corrupt or even evil, but not all. Not like in the North where evil is a job requirement. It is because you care that a toll has been taken on your spirit and shows in your face. You care because you are a good man. Right and wrong mean something to you. You will find the forgiveness you seek, Hank. But you should not come back to this war. You have had enough."

A crewman hollered from the C-130, "Come on, let's go. Get aboard!"

Hank shook the Sister's hand one last time, "Thank you Sister." Then he stepped back and snapped her a sharp salute as tears ran down her face.

Hank watched as his men filed into the airplane. Damn, he was proud of them! These very young men knew more about killing and death than they'd had time to learn about life and living.

What was it about these men that made them able to do the things they did and endure what they had endured? Maybe it was the training that paved the way and made it easier to step into the role of predator. Maybe, but Hank knew much of the training had to do with finding out which one of them was already capable of these things. Then it was just a matter of fostering the capability.

Many of them would be back for more tours in this damned place. Some would never be able to change what they had become. That rush they experienced in violent situations would follow them into all walks of life. Maybe they would channel it into positive directions. Maybe not. Most would, he was confident. For others, in time, it would fade from their minds. It would only be awakened in dreams.

The thought of those dreams made Hank look at his hands. He thought of what happened that night in the Victoria in Saigon. He shuddered to think it might happen again. He tried to find comfort in Annie's well spoken words. He hoped she was right.

Through thousands of years of experience, countries had come to understand that the only way to blunt the after effects of war on soldiers was to heap them with praise, parades and veneration. For these men, there would be no parades upon their return. This was a secret war. There would be no place of honor among the citizens, only indifference. If the war did gear up, he hoped that would change for the thousands who would follow them. If not, the men who were suffering from the mental ravages of war would not be the only ones who paid the price.

He wondered again what made men willing to risk death for their comrades. Surely such sacrifice did not come through instinct alone. It was not just ingrained in training, although that was where their bond found its foundation. It was more than courage. It was more than commitment to the mission. Those things were important, but not worth giving your life.

As he looked back at Sister Annie, and the look in her eyes as each SEAL took her hand and said goodbye, a verse suddenly came to him. It was something he had learned long ago, "Greater love hath no man than this to lay down his life for his friend." Of course, the one who had said it had taken it one step further, by giving His life for His enemies as well.

Though they would never say the words, that was it, the ingredient he was searching for. These men had spent more time together, shared more intimate conversations, been through more crisis, than most married couples did in a lifetime. That unique bond could not be described in any other way.

There was certainly no other way to describe what Y Bli had

done for him.

They might have joined the Navy out of patriotism, or even for adventure, but when they died, they did it for each other.

It came to him that even Dan Slade's actions, misguided and twisted though they may have been, were the result of love; however odd that may sound.

Before he stepped into the airplane, Hank took one last look around the area. He would not miss this place. What he would miss was the men. He would miss the bond that held them closer than brothers. Eventually, each would go his own way. In time the memories would dim. Each would know, however, when the chips were down, there was someone, somewhere, he could call and count on.

The cargo door closed behind him. Hank strapped himself into his seat. The huge airplane thundered down the runway. Hank looked out the window and saw the small figure in the yellow vehicle standing and waving.

As the JATOs fired, and kicked the plane up into the gray clouds, Hank thought she was the best thing that happened to them in this place.

Epilogue

Washington D.C. August 4, 1992

Hank had been sitting under a tree in the wooded area since about four o'clock that morning. He was lost in the quietness, and watching fireflies dance across the lawn.

It was almost dawn. He had been staring at the long, chevron shaped black granite tombstone, which lay on the grassy knoll in the distance between the Lincoln Memorial and the Washington Monument.

He had read everything about it and for the past two hours, studied it. He had become intimately acquainted with its shape and dimensions. He knew from the pamphlet that the wall was five hundred feet long. It consisted of one hundred and forty panels, and contained the names of over fifty-eight thousand KIAs and MIAs. These names were listed in chronological order as to when they were lost. He knew from observation how it rose on an angle from a short start to the west. It grew taller until the apex in the center, and then tapered off again at a one hundred and twenty five degree angle to the east.

This was the country's attempt to right the terrible wrong that had been done to thousands of returning veterans. Not only had there been no parades for them, many were spat upon and countless others treated with general contempt. The media concentrated on their failures. They concentrated on the brutal actions of a few. It had only served to deepen the spiritual wounds that war inflicts upon the participants. This war had done that to an even greater extent than most others.

Thankfully those mistakes had not been repeated in the more recent Gulf War--despite a few critics. There had been an attempt to include Vietnam vets in the celebrations. However, for many it had been too little, too late. Many Vietnam Veterans focused on the contrast, rather than the implied apology. Hank's own feelings had even been somewhat ambiguous on the matter. He thought his opinions on the subject were pretty moderate compared to some.

Maybe the celebrations had been overdone. But it was one

hell of a lot better to err in that direction than to go the way America had two decades prior.

There were also some Vietnam veterans who had marched in the parades because they were still in the military. They had done as much to rebuild the institution as any politician who had pushed for bigger budgets. Like most problems, to rebuild an institution took more than just money. These men had taken the lessons from Vietnam and applied them well. Could it be that the dead represented here had some legacy after all?

He had dreaded coming to the Vietnam Veterans' Memorial. He had been trying to talk himself into it for years. Many times he had talked with Shirl about coming here. She had even urged him to go. But, until today, he could never bring himself to do it.

He didn't know why. He had certainly been to enough gatherings and meetings concerning Vietnam veterans. He just had a dread of coming to this place.

There was something missing from his feelings and memories of Vietnam. It was something that had eluded him for all of these years. He could not put his finger on it, but it was always there. It never let him be completely at peace with the past.

He had yet to approach the wall. He merely sat with his back to a tree. He watched them come and go. Some appeared out of the darkness beyond the well-lit wall. Some appeared out of the darkness beyond the wall. Some came from the trees surrounding the illuminated area. Like him, many had probably stopped to gather their nerve, or to reflect on the past. They came in all manners of clothing. Some in faded cammos, field jackets, bush hats, or berets. Many had service ribbons on their hats or chests. Some approached the wall slowly, awkwardly, as if lost in why they were there.

Some would find the name or names they were looking for, then immediately vanish back into the darkness. Others, Hank could see, were visibly shaken by the experience. They stood as if rooted to their spot.

Hank was up and walking toward the wall before he realized it. He had no recollection of making the decision, or of getting to his feet.

The past seemed closer now than ever before. As he approached, what had happened so very long ago and far away all came flooding back to his conscious mind.

For a moment he sensed danger. It passed as he saw the mementos and personal offerings people had left at the base of the wall. There were the expected photographs, uniform patches, medals and even some personal letters. These were joined by stuffed animals and children's toys. These were probably left by a grieving parent who preferred to remember the innocence of their lost loved child's youth.

As Hank moved along the wall, he knew what he was looking for. He found the short panel with the names from 1964.

Then he saw them.

He quickly stepped back and stood shaking as he saw Ayotte and Bush's names engraved in the cold black granite. He pushed from his mind the flood of thoughts that threatened to overwhelm him.

Still denying, he moved along the wall, until he stopped at another numbered panel.

Jasper Hardison's name jumped out at him. Hank was shaking as he reached out and touched it. He ran his fingers over the sharp, crisp edges of the engraved letters. Memories of Hardison filled his mind. He saw him the last night at the Alamo, laughing and carrying on about his bird.

His gaze wandered down a few lines until he found Henry Bostic. He felt the same rush of emotions. He wondered if anyone else had been here to grieve for the man who had grown up in an orphanage. He had taken the orphans of Sister Annie so completely into his heart.

Both Hardison and Bostic had been cut down in a VC ambush on their third tour. That was long after Hank had left the SEALs. Like one might say about an old married couple, Hank could not help but think it was a blessing they had gone together.

He realized that of the couple dozen or so SEALs lost in Vietnam, he had commanded four of them. There was one other that was not acknowledged on the wall, besides.

He could not keep his emotions in check any longer. He did not know it was going to happen, and he could not have stopped it if he had. Standing in front of the names of his friends, Hank began to weep uncontrollably. Years of anguish poured out of him. It came along with the feeling of guilt for having survived when they did not.

He knew now why he had avoided coming here. Somewhere in his mind, he had not been able to fully accept their deaths. After seeing their names etched in the black granite slab…it was final. They were gone.

And they were not the only ones.

Hank knew there was another name that could not appear on the wall. He knelt, and took from his pocket the bracelet he had removed from Y Bli's limp body. He placed it at the base of the memorial. He wished he could engrave his name into the wall. He wished he could take him into his tribe as surely as Y Bli had taken him into his. This wasn't enough, but it was the best he could do.

After a moment, Hank stood. He looked up and down the length of the wall. He was trying to fathom the enormity of the fifty-eight thousand names carved into the black stone.

For the first time in nearly thirty years, he felt like he had made peace with the past. He felt that he had put the past to rest.

As he turned to walk away, he knew with a start, he finally felt something else that had been dormant in his feelings of the war he fought so long ago.

It was pride.

Without so much as a backward glance, Hank Dillon turned and walked into the new dawn.

22162365R00182

Made in the USA
San Bernardino, CA
22 June 2015